❧ GRAYSTONE ☙

MARTA K. STAHLFELD

BOOK PUBLISHERS NETWORK

Book Publishers Network
P.O. Box 2256
Bothell • WA • 98041
PH • 425-483-3040
www.bookpublishersnetwork.com

10 9 8 7 6 5 4 3 2 1

Printed in the United States of America

LCCN   2014954047
ISBN   978-1-940598-52-9

Cover designer: Laura Zugzda
Typographer: Melissa Vail Coffman

DEDICATION

In loving memory of Faye,
a role model always filled with God's grace;
she will always hold a place in the hearts of those who love her.

To Talon—

A book puts a great adventure into your hands.

Martha Stehlfeld

November 14, 2017

CONTENTS

ACKNOWLEDGEMENTS

First and foremost, my mother gets my thanks. She was always there to give me a good kick when I needed to move a little faster, and as usual, I could not have published this without her. Love you, Mom!

Thanks to Julie, my editor, for her fantastic patience and eagle-eyed editing. Thanks also to Laura, for the beautiful cover design.

I'd like to thank Selah and Caleb, fellow literature lovers, who offered me literary help, constructive criticism, and priceless encouragement. Thanks also to Haleigh, for all your insights. You are all fantastic!

Thanks to all my college literature professors who nurtured my appreciation for enriching writing and constantly reminded me that there is no such thing as a fully-matured love of books.

Thank you to Mrs. Suggs, for always believing in me.

Special thanks to everyone who told me how much they liked *Darkwoods* and *Pasadagavra*, especially my friend Erin. You all constantly reminded me what I was writing for – to make a reader's day a little brighter.

And last but most certainly not least, all glory and thanks go to God. May He bless everyone who reads the latest adventure in Princess Zuryzel's world!

Without further ado … welcome to *Graystone*.

CAST OF CHARACTERS

Miamuran Mice

Asherad	first prince of Miamur; younger brother of Galledor
Beshinor	third prince of Miamur; younger brother of Galledor
Elvinene	queen of Miamur and now Galledor's co-ruler
Galledor	king of Miamur; known for wisdom and courage
Kiarna	first princess of Miamur and Galledor's former co-ruler
Lacritta	second princess of Miamur; blind
Lochuran	fifth and youngest princess of Miamur; very secretive and wily
Nurida	fourth princess of Miamur; a timid creature
Orlian	second prince of Miamur; younger brother of Galledor
Ressora	third princess of Miamur; very confident and a bit of a bully
Vindorra	mother of the royal Miamuran mice, formerly the queen of Miamur

Cliff Mice and Graystone Mice

Annor'a	a young mouse living in Graystone
Fal'ne	daughter of Ol'ver
Feldspar	father of Annor'a
Glor'a	mate of Feldspar; mother of Annor'a
Nathan'el	adopted son of Ol'ver; young but skilled
Ol'ver	a cliff mouse trying to take care of his children alone
Opal	Graystone's primary leader
Ran'ta	mate of Ol'ver; mother of Fal'ne and Nathan'el; has gone missing

Sea Otters

Abalone	friend of Conch
Brine	sister of Mollusk; the tribe's healer
Conch (Wren)	young sea otter warrior; son of Anamay and Mollusk
Current	chief of one of the sea otter clans; universally mistrusted
Eagle	chief of Conch's tribe
Limpet	brother of Oyster, friend of Conch

Mollusk   father of Conch and Starfish
Oyster   sister of Limpet, friend of Starfish
Pearl   one of Conch's friends
Saline   sister of Eagle
Starfish
(Warbler)   older sister of Conch; daughter of Anamay and Mollusk
Warbler   river otter name for Starfish
Wren   river otter name for Conch

River Otters

Audayin Creeksand   aide to Danaray Mudriver
Baklenne   a female merchant with another name
Danaray
Mudriver   aunt of Conch and Starfish; an ally of the sea otters
Doomspear   a chieftain fighting on his own terms
Greeneddy   senior captain to Chieftainess Danaray Mudriver
Kermunda
Bluebrook   healer and confidante for Danaray Mudriver
Kyka   a loner who builds and loans out boats
Moonpath   a half-crazed chief who will stop at nothing to destroy the
                 sea otters
Orionyap   ally of Danaray Mudriver
Rain   ally of Danaray Mudriver
Redfin   a young warrior in Shorefish's tribe
Shinar   chieftainess who rules a tribe near the Wraith Mouse
                 capital
Shorefish   chief of the smallest tribe, determined to regain her
                 ancestors' land
Streamcourse a tentative ally of Danaray and confirmed enemy of
                 Moonpath; aunt of Shorefish
Treefrost   a warrior in Moonpath's tribe
Wave   ally of Danaray Mudriver, sister of Rain

Keron Mice

Al'ce   Keron Mouse deputy
Coll'n   Keron Mouse leader
Jul'an   Keron Mouse scout; male
Nad'ne   Keron Mouse scout; female

Squirrels

Rhonndan	tribeking of the Stone Tribe, brother of Shaynnah
Shaynnah	sister of Rhonndan, first friend of Nathan'el

Wraith Mice

Dejuday	a Wraith Mouse who visits Miamur from time to time
Demeda	mother of Zuryzel, Mokimshim, and Johajar
Dikiner	commander-in-chief of the armies at Arashna
Eyixid	an insane Wraith Mouse hiding from mysterious enemies
Johajar	the youngest Wraith Mouse prince
Karena	queen of the Wraith Mice, Mokimshim's mate
Mokimshim	the oldest Wraith Mouse prince; now king of the Wraith Mice
Zuryzel	renowned princess who has vanished from the face of the earth

Others

Arasam	a fox; former ally of Zuryzel; his allegiances are shifting
Eneng	a ferret; brother of Winterblade; pirate and ally of Zuryzel
Korep	a ferret; pirate ally of Zuryzel
Ksheygha	a ferret; pirate ally of Zuryzel
Norya	a crow; ally to Rainbow
Oracle	
Hemlock	a fox; old leader of Darkwoods
Rainbow	a female Ranger Orlysk mouse
Sh'vendi	a mouse merchant with another name
Shartalla	a pine marten; best friend of Zuryzel; a pirate who loves adventure and the sea
Snowhawk	a ferret; pirate ally of Zuryzel
Una	a raccoon who owns the Hidden Glade Inn
Winterblade	a ferret; sister of Eneng; pirate and ally of Zuryzel

PROLOGUE

Two Wraith Mice slid northward just out of sight of the coast, keeping watch for both pirates and their own kind. Dejuday had grown in stature and cunning; his black eyes darted to and fro with startling speed. Zuryzel was lither and not so plain anymore but with a finely shaped face and twinkling eyes.

Lady Raven had once had ferret pirate friends. So did Zuryzel and Dejuday, though not the older, more experienced ones Raven had known. Showing through the trees was the nearest tavern where their friends normally gathered on a day like this with little wind. They approached the building not so much for socializing; they were searching for Shartalla, an old friend of theirs, a captain of an adventurer's ship. They had not seen her for a long time.

Making sure their weapons were close to paw, the two Wraith Mice pushed open the doors. The musician in the corner stopped playing momentarily to hail them, and then resumed his rowdy shanty. The princess smiled at the raucous scene.

"Dejuday! Zuryzel!" Captain Eneng of the frigate *Searaider* called. He gestured both Wraith Mice over with a wave of his paw. Sitting around his same table were other friends of the Wraith Mice. Snowhawk leaned half her weight against the table, watching the two Wraith Mice carefully. Beside her, to Zuryzel's dismay, lounged Eneng's sister Winterblade. Every time Winterblade and Snowhawk came within shouting distance, there was trouble. Next to Winterblade and sipping at a mug of grog, Ksheygha completely ignored the Wraith Mice, her amber eyes darting around the tavern. In the next seat, Korep sat up straight and alert.

"Bad sailin' day, ain't it," commented Snowhawk. Her smiling black eyes and short white fur hid a ruthless foe and a capable captain. Beside her, Winterblade slammed her mug of grog down, looking eager.

"S'pose it is," Dejuday replied.

"What news from Arashna?" queried Eneng.

"Not much," Zuryzel replied. "A couple more trainees were made into warriors."

"Have you heard what happened to Korep?" smirked Ksheygha. She was a ferret with a mouthful of gossip, and Korep always seemed to be the object of her teasing.

"Really?" Korep muttered through clenched teeth. "I don't get this enough from my crew?"

"Now we all know what 'tis about," Winterblade smirked.

"Someone opened a water cask," Ksheygha grinned, "and found a rosy pink jellyfish floating in it."

A jellyfish found in a water cask was taken by pirates to be a sign that the captain was in love. It was never true in Korep's case, as Ksheygha well knew, but Korep's crew regarded it with utmost seriousness.

"So who does yer crew suspect *this* time?" Eneng demanded gleefully.

Korep took a dignified drink from his mug of ale. "I ain't asked."

"I saw it, Ksheygha," Zuryzel said, holding up her paws where scores of stingers had irritated the pads. "I *felt* it, even, when I opened the cask. And I had a job explaining it to my brother, too!"

The table fell silent at that. Then Winterblade spoke her thoughts. "What's the prince regent been up to?"

Dejuday took a deep breath. "Nothing in particular. He has made some interesting decrees, but nothing to worry about. Nothing concerning the army or the seas."

Winterblade looked almost disappointed; she relished adventure and danger as much as Shartalla did. Snowhawk met Zuryzel's eyes over her beaker. Zuryzel blinked in reply.

Eneng waved his dagger airily. "Not much fer us t' worry about, then, eh?"

Both Wraith Mice shook their heads soundly.

Korep glanced at Zuryzel's paw. "Well, you'd better git somethin' for those stingers at any rate, or Mokimshim'll know it ain't from a nettle. I don't think he'll take kindly to you chattin' with pirates."

"He doesn't take kindly to me doing anything anymore," Zuryzel shrugged. "But he can't do anything about me until Queen Demeda dies and he is made true king—which, Bear King willing, will not be for some time."

Snowhawk called to one of her crew ferrets. "Have Tine come up 'ere wi' 'er case o' cures."

Winterblade watched the ferret scrambling out. "I dunno why y' bother with Tine, Snowhawk. Outta all the creatures on the seas, she's the softest!"

Ksheygha rolled her eyes as Snowhawk turned her dangerous glare on Winterblade. "Simple. I ain't short o' brain an' long o' mouth, unlike some."

Before Eneng could intervene as he normally did, Winterblade stood up, whipping a saber from her belt. "A swift blade c'n sometime make up fer that, though," she snarled.

Snowhawk jumped up, tugging a hidden knife from her sleeve.

"Sunny sails!" exclaimed Eneng, thrusting his way between them. "Will y' two give it a rest?"

"There's no point being at each other's throats all day!" Korep added irritably.

Snowhawk and Winterblade surveyed each other a moment before they both sat down and glared pointedly in opposite directions. The two often engaged in verbal altercations—and some that progressed further—although Snowhawk was usually the aggressor, not Winterblade.

But that day's incident was snuffed out before it enflamed, and the two Wraith Mice left the tavern nearly an hour later, relaxed and cheerful.

"I can't believe there's been no sign of Shartalla for two months!" Zuryzel commented.

"I guess in her case, no news is good news," Dejuday commented thoughtfully. "She's an adventurer."

Zuryzel shrugged. "She can take care of herself, but it's not like her to be away from Arashna so long—couldn't something have happened?"

Dejuday shook his head. "Nah, she's just off somewhere, trying to enhance her reputation. But you can bet if trouble shows here—"

"What kind o' trouble?"

Dejuday jumped and turned around. Zuryzel looked up.

Merely a few branches above their heads, the fire-colored pine marten sat perched lightly in the pine tree.

"Y' know, pines are a lot like masts, save masts're harder t' climb. Ye were right, by the way; I *was* off trying to 'enhance my reputation' as you so quaintly put it."

"What are you doing here? Why aren't you at the tavern?"

Shartalla winked. "Just got 'ere."

She dropped from her perch to face the two Wraith Mice. "How're the others?" she asked, changing the subject. "Winterblade an' Snowhawk still at each other's throats?"

"Go into the tavern and ask them," suggested Zuryzel.

Shartalla shook her head. "I'd better not. A rumor says Demeda's indisposed, an' I'll need t' sail away soon if that's true. That could mean trouble for me—and the two of you," she added seriously.

Dejuday frowned at her. "What makes you think trouble is coming?" he inquired.

"'Cause Mokimshim's been watching Zuryzel an' he just practically became king. I dunno how it's done on land, but on a ship, if a captain dies prematurely, there's an assassin aboard, and that means trouble. The killer 'imself ain't the trouble; he's an omen."

"So you think my mother's illness is an omen?" Zuryzel queried.

"I dunno," shrugged Shartalla helplessly. "I don't buy into omens, but at the same time, I feel in me fur that somethin's about t' happen. Mokimshim's gonna make a move soon, Zuryzel. Just you wait 'n' see."

Many seasons passed, and lands previously well cultured became desolate.

For Chieftainess Danaray Mudriver, the ailing lands were a clear prelude to war. What truly concerned her was that she had no idea where her enemy would strike first. There was a possibility of a strike into her territory from the north, but it could also come from the west. Of course, if it was a strike from the west, it would go straight through sea otter territory.

Where Conch and Starfish were. Her sister's children. *Bear King, please, grant that the first attack won't be at them.* Danaray was ready for a fight; she doubted the sea otters were.

She sat on a mound of autumn leaves, watching as the Othyrn River murmured its way south. It was rare for the rivers in this part of the world to freeze, even in the dead of winter, but it would not be long before the golden branches above her were bare and ice-coated. Any day now, the sea otters would commence their annual migration from Zurez to inland camps on the other side of that river, so they could give the food they found in the sea time to replenish itself. Danaray used to think that was a ridiculous practice, given how large the sea was, but Conch and Starfish had explained it to her once, and she understood it better now.

There was a rustling in the autumn leaves behind Danaray, and she twisted, her knife ready; but it was only Kermunda Bluebrook, the healer in her service. He disregarded her drawn knife—she had drawn it on him by mistake before—and sat down on a tree root beside her.

"Are you waiting for them to come back?" he asked her. The tone he used was not the tone of a healer speaking to his chieftainess but that of an old friend and confidante. "Do you plan to greet them? Renew our alliance?"

Danaray sighed and laid her knife across her knees. "I don't know yet. I think it might be better to wait for them to come to me, at least until we know how the other sea otters are adjusting to a new chief."

Kermunda smiled gently at her. "They didn't mind when their last chief accepted your alliance. I can't see how they'd mind an alliance with you under a new chief. But, on the other paw, it can't hurt to be careful."

"At the very least, I hope the other sea otters tolerate my sister's children visiting me," Danaray said, smiling back.

The two otters were silent for a bit; then Kermunda murmured, "Greeneddy needs you back at the camp. He sent me to fetch you."

Danaray frowned at her friend. "He should know better than to treat you like an aide. That's what I have Audayin Creeksand for."

Kermunda tried to smile, but it resulted in a grimace. "He does know. It's just ... he deemed it wiser that I should find you rather than Audayin."

Danaray's blood chilled at his solemn voice. "Bad news?"

Kermunda rocked his head from side to side. "Well ... an envoy from Miamur. We don't know if it's good or bad yet."

Danaray was on her paws in a swift, fluid motion. "Let's find out."

Kermunda followed her, slightly relieved that his dauntless chieftainess was more given to action than to worrying.

As they reached their cluster of wood-and-canvas buildings that marked their main base, Danaray straightened to a more regal bearing. Greeneddy, her senior captain, met her at the entrance. "Chieftainess," he saluted her. "I take it Kermunda already told you of the Miamuran envoy."

"Were any royal members in the envoy?" Danaray asked her captain.

"None," Greeneddy replied. "But they claimed to be selected by King Galledor himself."

"Where are they now?" Danaray queried.

"Audayin Creeksand has made them comfortable," Greeneddy reported. "But they requested I give you this promptly."

He extended to her a blue silk bag. Emblazoned on the side were two wide-spread white wings—the symbol of the city of Miamur. Every royal Miamuran mouse had the wings in his or her individual symbol, but when it was just the two wings, it usually meant a gift directly from the king himself.

"What's this?" she asked the general.

"A present from King Galledor."

Danaray took the bag, her brow knit worriedly. "Thank you," she said to Greeneddy distractedly. "Have someone inform the envoy that I will be with him directly."

Greeneddy saluted her again and left.

Danaray and Kermunda sorted through the various gifts inside until the chieftainess found the short note. She pulled it out and read it in an instant:

Kiarna is missing. We need a diversion to search for her.

Danaray extended the note to Kermunda. "It looks as if our enemy has made his first strike."

Galledor, king of Miamur, glared out the windows of his white palace. He was agitated, and not even his queen could calm him. Nor could any of his brothers or sisters, and they'd all tried.

It was night and raining hard. He stared hard out the window, hoping at least to see to the farms west of Miamur. But the rain and darkness made that impossible.

He longed to take off his crown—surely, that was the source of his headaches. But he knew better. It was a combination of a lack of sleep and worry over his sister.

The note was clutched in his paw, rolled up inside her ring. The crest on this ring was his sister's—the Miamuran white wings above a blue rose.

On an impulse, he spun around and hurried to his study. In the top drawer of his desk, he had a stack of medallions; on each medallion was a crest, each one belonging to one of his brothers or sisters. His was a sword in a tongue of fire flanked by the Miamuran white wings. But he pushed most of them aside until he found the one that was second to the bottom.

He drew his paw over the image tenderly. He had had it designed himself for his second youngest sister. It depicted a tongue of fire flanked by the Miamuran white wings, like his, but in the fire was a white lily. A scroll would have fit the personality of the sister this belonged to, but her name meant "lily." And he hoped that one day she would grow as bold as the radiant lilies.

He put down the lily symbol and picked up Kiarna's seal again and, to quell the worry in his stomach, pushed it under the others. The next one on top belonged to his brother Asherad—the Miamuran white wings above a pool of blue water. Under that was the seal of Lacritta, his blind sister, and beneath that his brother Orlian's. Lacritta's was a gray dove flying beneath the white wings, and Orlian's was a tree with wide branches on which the white wings were superimposed. Beneath Orlian's was the medallion for his third sister, Ressora, and here he paused. On hers was a brown hawk with folded wings diving between the white wings. The bird looked as if it were just about to pluck up a hapless creature. That certainly suited Ressora. Galledor shrugged and went on. Beneath Ressora's was Beshinor's, a black quill on a piece of paper that trailed through the white wings, followed by the fiery lily seal. The last one was a dagger entwined in small ivy vines, standing vertically between the white wings. This one was for Lochuran, his youngest sister.

He dutifully put them back in order and closed the drawer. Where was Kiarna?

The door opened sharply, and Asherad stood there, dripping wet.

"You have something?" Galledor asked hopefully.

Asherad nodded. His dusky gray fur was plastered to his head. "A message came. It's here."

He extended an envelope, oiled to protect it from the rain. Galledor took it with a nod. "Thank you, Asherad. You need sleep—get some."

"Do I have to?" Asherad asked wearily, swaying with tiredness.

"Yes, you do."

Asherad rolled his eyes and left.

Galledor hastily tore open the short message and read it urgently.

I received your message. I will look for Kiarna where I can. You'll hear from me soon. Zuryzel.

Part One

CONCH

Blend the river with the sea,
And one is lost among the waves.
To the e'er green lands I flee,
So greet the child that survived my grave.

~ *Kermunda Bluebrook*
Ballad of Anamay

The Shy Princess

Nurida was a princess of Miamur. Amber-furred and scholarly, she displayed almost no force of personality, perhaps because she was the second youngest of her siblings—there were six older mice in the Miamuran royal family—or perhaps because she was the only one who had actually been raised by her mother, who had an overbearing personality. It didn't matter why; she was quiet. Only her oldest brother Galledor really thought much about her, and as he was king, he was too busy to spend much time with her. Her oldest sister, Kiarna, spoke with her when they met, but she was always active and doing something, so their paths rarely crossed. Lacritta, the second oldest princess, often kept her company; but Lacritta was blind, so she relied on Nurida to be her eyes. In any case, Nurida was almost never in the company of any of her other brothers or sisters.

Late one fall, she went for a trip into the city surrounding Miamur's shining walls. She wore a small filigree crown about her brow topped with two white wings—the symbol of Miamur—but beyond that and her fine garment, there was nothing to distinguish her from the villagers. She wandered through the market, polite and almost utterly silent, with her servant behind her.

Galledor watched her from an upper window as Nurida, his forgotten royal sister, left the palace. Under their parents, the Miamuran court had been a typical royal court, always full of intrigue, and those that were trampled were trampled. Nurida had, by his ascendency to the crown, survived being trampled, but still …

"I don't know," he said aloud.

His mate, Elvinene, joined him at the window. "She has to find her courage somewhere," she whispered.

"She has courage," Galledor answered quickly.

Elvinene nodded. "You're right—she does not lack courage. What she does lack is confidence. There is a fire in her somewhere, and she must learn to bring it out."

"But in the wild?" Galledor murmured. "As it is now, she is harmless and not a threat to anyone. This … this storm brewing in the west will simply pass her by."

"No, it won't," Elvinene murmured. "You know it won't."

Galledor's brown fur glistened in the brilliant sun. "I am uncertain," he said finally. "But I will consider what you have said, Elvinene."

She smiled at him. "You know I won't let her get hurt."

He chuckled. "I am not afraid for anyone in your company," he said lightly. "At least, anyone but me."

She laughed. "You don't have to worry either—so long as you're nice to me." With that, she laid her head peacefully on his shoulder.

Nurida purchased a stack of new parchment and a bottle of ink. She handed them to her servant to be carried when she heard an unpleasant voice behind her.

"You're supposed to *bargain*, not just take it at his first price."

She turned around to see her third-oldest sister, Ressora, who was at least eight seasons older than she, if not more. "Then you can bargain next time I get paper," Nurida replied.

"I have better things to do than haggle over paper," Ressora retorted arrogantly.

"Then go do them and let me enjoy myself," Nurida suggested coldly.

Ressora's icy blue eyes locked with Nurida's emerald green. Galledor, Kiarna, Asherad, and Orlian, her four oldest siblings, never saw Nurida's anger because they never provoked it. Her three youngest siblings—Beshinor, Ressora, and Lochuran—sometimes witnessed Nurida's hidden fire. Ressora especially. Ressora was something of a bully and very arrogant, traits that provoked Nurida, yet she did not hate her sister.

"I don't suppose you've heard about what's been happening, have you?" Ressora asked finally.

"What do you mean?" Nurida asked coolly.

"Clearly not," Ressora smirked. "Never mind." And she disappeared into the market.

Conch swam carefully after his chief, Eagle, down the Bakkarra River. The sea otter was clammy all over and terrified for his sister.

He and Eagle had been out fishing, a common sea otter pastime, when they had heard a frantic voice shrieking their names. They'd dropped their fishing spears and darted in the direction of the cries to find Saline, Eagle's younger sister. There was a nasty gash on her cheek. Eagle had gripped her shoulder urgently. "What happened?"

Knowing who had been in Saline's company, Conch had added, "Where are Pearl and Starfish?"

Saline was a strong creature once she got her paws under her. She took a deep, steadying breath and managed, "Pearl's been hurt. I don't know about Starfish. We were looking for willows, and we—we split up. I heard Pearl screaming, and then an arrow came out of nowhere!"

"Who fired it? Where?" Eagle urged.

Saline shrugged, bewildered. "I never saw them. Pearl's by the old petrified tree, unconscious. Starfish went downstream."

The minute those words left Saline's mouth, Conch plunged back into the undergrowth, heading for the river. Eagle had paused only long enough to tell his sister to fetch Brine and some otters who could help get Pearl back to her home before racing to catch up with Conch.

They had already gone far downstream, past many willow-lined banks. Every few minutes they softly called out to Starfish, but there was no response. Conch wanted to swim frantically through the cloudy waters of the Bakkarra and shout his sister's name, but he knew he had to be quiet and careful, or he might miss danger lurking about.

Now the sun was setting, and they were nearing the edge of their territory. Eagle called out quietly, "Starfish? Can you hear me? Are you there?"

To Conch's relief, Starfish's voice called back, "I'm over here!"

And with that, the sea otter maiden slid awkwardly from a weeping willow onto the very edge of the river.

Both Eagle and Conch forgot their caution and raced toward her, scrambling in the shallows. A flicker of movement caught Conch's eye. It turned out to be only a twig floating on the river, but it reminded him to keep his senses alert.

Starfish turned a little, and Conch saw immediately that she had an arrow in her shoulder. "You're hurt!" he cried.

His sister shook her head impatiently. "Pearl and Saline? Are they all right?"

Eagle rested his paw gently on her uninjured shoulder. "Saline found us," he explained. "I sent her back for Brine. They should be all right. I think I could get that arrow out—would you like me to try?"

Starfish nodded. "Yes—please. It's hard to swim with that thing in my shoulder."

Eagle gripped her shoulder carefully. Starfish held perfectly still, her face tight with pain, but she didn't open her mouth as the arrow came out of her shoulder. As it turned out, the arrow had not gone deep at all. Starfish let out her breath as Eagle placed his paw gently over the bleeding wound. "Short arrow. Did you see who shot you?"

Starfish shook her head. "Not clearly, no. They didn't follow me in the river, so either they couldn't swim, or they had no way to protect their bowstrings in the water."

"So not river otters, then," Conch murmured. He grasped his sister's wrist. "Unless they lost you in the river."

His sister shook her head unknowingly. "I didn't see them, Conch."

"It's been a long time since we had to fend off Shorefish or some other otter tribe," Eagle mused. "I know Chieftainess Mudriver has a lot to do with that, but it seems our interim has run its course. Before we speculate further, we should get out of here." He glanced at Starfish out of the corner of his eye. "Whoever fired those arrows might come back."

As Starfish nodded, Conch bit his lip. It was sore from all the times he had bitten it to keep from grinning at the way Eagle sometimes looked at Starfish.

"Then let's get back home," Eagle added. "I bet no one else has anything so exciting to report."

Starfish inched her way into the river and swam gracefully beside Eagle, despite her shoulder. Conch swam on her other side, still trying to hide a grin. Starfish glanced at Conch, sighed, and whispered, "Wonder what Father will say about this."

The necessity to hide his smile vanished. Their father, Mollusk, was gruff and stern. He hadn't always been like that, according to Starfish, who had known their father before their mother died. He had loved her so much, despite the fact that she was a river otter princess. But when she died only a few days after Conch's birth, Mollusk had changed. He had become more somber and smiled a lot less.

When Danaray, their mother's sister, had been in the area, Mollusk had taken Conch and Starfish to meet her. Conch had admired her from the start. She seemed to be so full of strength, wisdom, fairness, and gentleness that he could not possibly forget her—not that he wanted to. Now, technically, she lived in a territory east of his, in a glade, but he rarely saw her these days.

Conch, Eagle, and Starfish reached their village to find no small disorder. Sea otters dashed to and fro, collecting their young ones and inquiring of their neighbors as to who had ventured into the woods. Mollusk was kneeling beside Saline, apparently pressing her for more information. When he saw the three slip into the village, he hastily stood up and hurried to meet them.

"You hurt, Starfish?" were the first words out of Mollusk's mouth.

His daughter touched her shoulder. "I got clipped by an arrow, but I'm fi—"

The rest of her statement was silenced as Mollusk wrapped her in a tight embrace. After a brief moment, Starfish pulled back.

"Are Saline and Pearl all right?" she inquired of her father.

Mollusk nodded, looking between the three younger otters. "Saline got back here fine, and we brought Pearl back, but Brine left the village this morning, and she hasn't come back yet."

"Brine's out there?" Eagle asked, worried.

Mollusk nodded, jaw clenched.

Eagle called to some of the nearby warriors, "Someone get out there and look for Brine!"

"Here she comes!" someone called out from the back of the crowd.

Brine had just entered the village, breathless and stricken-looking.

"Brine," Mollusk asked her immediately, "were you attacked? Did you see anything out there?"

Brine shook her head. "No I—I wasn't attacked. What happened?"

"Did you see anything out there?" Eagle repeated.

Brine's worried frown deepened. "Yes, I did. It looks like someone was injured very badly out there, but I couldn't get to them—he or she is under a fallen maple limb. What happened to Saline and Pearl?"

"Where was the wounded creature?" Mollusk pressed his sister.

Brine gestured vaguely. "Down by the bend in the Huakka Creek. I couldn't tell if it was a river otter or a mouse."

"I'll go look," Eagle decided. "Conch, Mollusk, come with me."

Fal'ne the mouse maiden stepped lighted-pawed beside her father and elder brother. They were on their way to Graystone! Oh happy day! Her father had two good friends in Graystone, and her mother had another. Her father had promised them for a long time that they would visit Graystone, but only a few weeks ago had they been able to. First they had taken a boat down the Keron River, well guided by a river otter named Kyka. Kyka had been delighted to have an excuse to sail on the Keron, but he had been extremely wary.

"It's the Keron Mice, you know," he had explained. "They won't hurt us, but it never hurts to be careful."

They had not encountered the wild tribe of the Keron Mice and soon had gone ashore to travel on foot the rest of the way to Graystone.

Her brother, Nathan'el, flicked her with his sack. "Hey, don't keep on dancing like that, or you'll have me at it!"

Fal'ne stopped dead and twirled on one paw. Her father stopped too and threw an affectionate paw around her shoulders.

"If your mother could see you now, she'd be laughing so much that even Nathan'el would laugh, too!"

Nathan'el, a sensible, taciturn young mouse, shrugged. "We need to hurry to get to Graystone—or we could set up camp and have dinner!"

Fal'ne let out the breath she had been holding. Not too many weeks before they had set out, her mother had disappeared. Her father never said much anymore, nor did he smile so often. When he did smile, it was always because of Fal'ne or Nathan'el. He never laughed anymore.

"I think that's a stupendous idea, Nathan'el," Ol'ver decided. "Let's find somewhere hidden."

That was another odd thing that had happened since Ran'ta's disappearance. Ol'ver always seemed to be looking back over his shoulder, as if he were afraid of being attacked. They ate and camped only in places well-hidden. But Nathan'el tried very hard not to let Fal'ne notice his odd suspicion.

They found a dip in the ground, shielded by fallen logs and huge clumps of salal bushes. Fal'ne dug into her pack and found some cold bread, while Nathan'el built a small fire and Ol'ver handed around wooden utensils. Fal'ne also found some cheese and mild, watered wine, and they had a fine dinner—at least as fine as can be had on the road.

Afterwards, Fal'ne fell asleep, leaning against Nathan'el. Ol'ver, too, fell into oblivion, exhausted from the day of travel. But Nathan'el stayed awake. His mind was, as it had been for weeks, on his mother.

Nathan'el had been watching his father almost unceasingly since Ran'ta's disappearance, hoping to hear a clue about what had happened to her. After two weeks of searching and not finding her, Ol'ver told his children she'd probably lost her way in the woods and perhaps died of starvation. And yet, he didn't act like it. He acted as if he knew something else. So far, he'd said nothing more, but Nathan'el thought, *It's just a matter of time.*

2

A MESSENGER

I t was late evening when Eagle, Mollusk, and Conch reached the spot where Brine thought she had seen an injured creature. An old tree had fallen over recently. Eagle noted grimly the mark of axes. Poking out from under the tree was a mass of brook-brown fur. Conch was reminded forcefully of Danaray.

"Brine *was* right for once," Mollusk observed. "Let's see if we can't get him out of there!"

Conch peered past the huge tree. "We could dig away at the mud over here; it's pretty wet."

"Good thinking," smiled Mollusk.

The three otters, even Eagle, went at it with a will.

The log began to groan, and all three otters jumped back. Then they scrambled to the other side and pushed the log toward the place where they had dug the earth away. The huge log groaned again and finally moved away enough that they could get a look at the creature.

It was a river otter whose tunic was ripped and torn, not to mention covered in soil and blood. He was clearly unconscious, curled up a little as though he had tried to protect his head when the tree fell. He was breathing shallowly and didn't stir as the three sea otters freed him from the log.

Conch's blood ran cold when he saw the wounded otter's face. He swallowed hard and said, "I know him."

Mollusk and Eagle looked to him in surprise. "Who is he?" Mollusk demanded.

"Audayin Creeksand," Conch replied quietly. "Danaray's aide."

Eagle looked back to the injured otter. "Her warriors don't cross into our land willy-nilly. What is he doing here?"

"Get some water from the stream, Conch," Mollusk ordered, scraping up a pawful of moss. "See if we can't revive him."

Conch did as he was bidden. As he dropped the moss in the creek, he glanced across. Then he smiled to himself hopefully. His aunt sometimes sojourned into that area. And he thought he saw the faintest outline of a river otter standing there.

But it could not be an otter. It was totally brown ... no; it was brown with blue dots that could be eyes. Wait ... they were eyes! The creature had moved. It drew a paw to its lips and then across its throat, shaking its head gently. Conch understood. The creature was signing, *I mean you no harm. Do not give me away.*

He did not. He simply soaked the moss and carefully toted it up to where the unconscious otter lay.

Mollusk wrung out the moss over the wretched creature's head, and the otter stirred. First his brown eyes blinked open, and then he winced. His lips formed words that Conch thought were Miamuran.

Mollusk spoke softly to the injured otter: "You're in no danger. This is sea otter territory."

The creature blinked and gazed around him without moving his head. "I was running from some strangers. I didn't realize that I crossed the boundary."

"You're Audayin Creeksand, aren't you?" Conch asked.

The otter nodded. "Who ... are you?"

"Chief Eagle," the sea otter chief answered. "Would your tribe be looking for you?"

The otter shook his head but winced. "Probably not. Not long ago, an otter came to our camp with a message. Danaray said we were moving out."

"*What?*" Conch exclaimed.

"Quiet, Conch," Mollusk ordered softly.

Creeksand continued as if Conch hadn't spoken. "All of us made ready to leave, and I was out scouting the way when I was attacked. I turned and ran, but I guess I got off course. The last thing I remember is the tree falling on me."

"What was in that message?" Eagle asked keenly.

The otter shook his head. "No idea. Danaray burned it."

"We should get him back to Brine," Mollusk said quietly. "It's too dangerous to be out and about."

Eagle nodded in agreement. "Conch, run ahead and tell Brine we're bringing him back."

Conch knew perfectly well the order was designed to get him back to the village safely, but he didn't argue.

"And if you can," Eagle added, "get Limpet and Abalone to bring a stretcher. If not, we'll get Creeksand back without one."

As Conch hurried homeward, he puzzled over the river otter he had seen.

Who was the watching otter if not from Danaray's tribe? There weren't many other tribes around. A few days north was the village of Kwang-ha`el, home of the river otter crew of Rain and Wave, brother and sister. *Is that one of their otters I saw?* Conch wondered. Perhaps she had been looking for Danaray. Perhaps she had heard something of the messenger and wanted to see what it was or meant.

Is it one of theirs, though? Couldn't it have been Streamcourse's? Shorefish?

That thought was worrying. Shorefish was Nighthawk's daughter. Admittedly, she had not turned half as cruel as Nighthawk had, but she was still a dangerous enemy of the sea otters. Conch knew virtually nothing about her, except that she had once aided the Wraith Mouse princess.

The Wraith Mice, black fur, except for their faces, which were like a full moon, supposedly had magic in their blood. They could vanish into the night like shadows.

And their princess ... she'd been famous for something once, but her name was never heard in those lands anymore. Conch doubted he could remember it ...

Zuryzel! That was her name.

But the last Conch had heard of Zuryzel was her disappearance.

3
ILL NEWS

Nurida was drawing—she loved to draw. She sat upon a grassy hill west of the Miamuran palace, a sheaf of parchment stretched flat on a clay tablet. With her was blind Lacritta. Nurida was trying to capture the early winter afternoon with its lingering traces of fall when she absently looked west.

What she saw made her sigh.

"What is it?" asked Lacritta.

"The Wraith Mouse," Nurida replied with no emotion.

The Wraith Mouse, whose name she knew only because Galledor had once introduced them, visited roughly once a month. He rarely spoke to her and always seemed to have information for Galledor. Ressora had spent no end trying to wheedle the information out of Galledor, but she had never been successful. Nurida thought of the Wraith Mouse with distaste—mostly because he always seemed to be in a hurry, and this irritated her. His blades never left his side. His name was Dejuday—but that meant little.

The Wraith Mouse crested the rise where Nurida sat; she swiftly stood, holding her head high.

"Your Highnesses," he greeted Nurida and Lacritta, dipping his head. "I must speak with your brother. If you could be so good as to take me to him?"

Nurida realized, not for the first time, that his accent was strange. As though speaking Miamuran was difficult. She dismissed the thought. "Of course," she said aloud, quickly packing up her drawing. "Is this meeting urgent?"

"Somewhat." Dejuday picked up the bottles of ink for her.

"Thank you," Nurida said. "This way."

She led him slowly down the hill, protecting her drawing with one paw and leading Lacritta with the other. Dejuday followed their easy pace, speaking constantly and politely. Nurida responded whenever his comments required a response.

Upon reaching the palace, they found Galledor in an airy meeting hall, bent over a table. With him were Elvinene, Ressora, and several nobles.

"Brother," Nurida said aloud. "Galledor."

He looked up and saw Dejuday. His face lit up, but Nurida detected a hint of worry in his smile. "Welcome, Dejuday," he said.

Dejuday bent at his waist. "I have news," he declared without preamble. "But by your leave, somewhere …"

Galledor nodded, and now Nurida was sure he was worried. "Of course." He turned to the courtiers and gave them various orders, each one designed to get them out and keep them out.

Elvinene eyed Dejuday's face worriedly. "Something has happened?"

He nodded wordlessly.

"Perhaps the small conference room would be a better place," Galledor instructed. His face softened when he turned to Nurida. "Would you keep Beshinor busy for the next hour or two?" he asked gently. "I know that is a lot to ask, little sister, but please."

Nurida smiled at her brother. "I will."

"Thank you," he said profoundly.

"And thank you for bringing me here," Dejuday added politely.

When he, Galledor, and Elvinene hurried to the conference room, Ressora murmured, "I wonder what they talk about."

"Is there any chance at all you'll help me keep Beshinor busy?" Nurida asked hopefully.

"No."

"There's no need," said a new voice. "His battle-teacher has him for the next three hours at least."

Nurida whirled around and found Lochuran watching them both. "Don't do that!" she exclaimed.

Lochuran shrugged. "Sorry."

Princess Lochuran was much absorbed by the allurement of stealth and sneaking and often appeared out of nowhere. She was the closest to Nurida in age, the only Miamuran princess younger than Nurida, and the closest in coloring and personality. Like Nurida, she had brilliant amber fur, bright green eyes, and was usually quiet. The difference was that she was like a snake, coiled and waiting to spring; Nurida was more like a fire hidden under a bowl.

"So shall we try to find out why Dejuday is here?" Ressora suggested eagerly.

"Why?" Lochuran inquired impatiently. "You'll just get caught again, get shouted at again, and find out absolutely nothing again!"

"There has to be a reason he's here," Ressora argued with equal impatience.

"Since there's no chance of finding it out," Nurida interjected, "why don't we pass the afternoon by going to the library?"

Her green eyes were hopeful. She loved the world of books and learning, almost to the point that she was indifferent to the rest of the world. Her sisters, however, didn't share that passion.

Ressora just sneered at Nurida. "How about *you* do that, and I'll go do something worthwhile."

She stalked off, her dress rustling. Nurida was stung by Ressora's coldness, but she tilted her jaw up and banished her sting with indifference. It wasn't practical to get angry or hurt around mice like Ressora.

"Let's go to the market instead," Lacritta suggested.

Lochuran touched her shoulder. "I'll go with you to the market," she said reluctantly. "Don't expect me to be much fun, but I'll go with you."

Nurida smiled, somewhat surprised by Lochuran's offer.

Nurida, Lacritta, and Lochuran passed some time wandering around the settlement, calling hello to various other shoppers.

Then, after a few hours, Nurida turned to Lochuran and faced her directly. "Why?" she said bluntly.

Lochuran shrugged, confused. "Why what?"

"Why did you come with us?" Nurida pressed. "Usually you avoid the city at all costs."

Lochuran looked away, making sure Lacritta couldn't hear, and then looked back. "I know why Dejuday is here," she said finally.

Nurida blinked in surprise. "How? Not even Ressora can find that out."

"Asherad tells me things, and I put two and two together," Lochuran explained softly. "Dejuday is here because Kiarna has gone missing."

Alarm filled Nurida's eyes. "Missing? I knew she was gone, but ..."

Lochuran nodded. "She left for the west on a diplomatic visit—I have no idea where—but she left last spring. She was supposed to be back at least two months ago."

Nurida tilted her head thoughtfully. "So they're trying to find her?"

Lochuran nodded. "I think so. And Dejuday might have seen her or have some information." She gave Nurida a sharp look. "But Ressora doesn't need to know."

Nurida sighed. Lochuran and Ressora always seemed to be at odds.

After two hours, they were met by Asherad. Like Ressora, his fur was charcoal gray and his eyes bright blue, but he was much warmer than Ressora.

"I need you two in the palace," he said quickly. "Something is about to happen."

Lochuran nodded, not giving away that she knew what was going on. "Such as?" she asked.

"Some sort of trouble with Kiarna," was all Asherad would say.

He led them back to the palace and told them briskly to go to Ressora's room. They were halfway there when they were hailed—or at least Nurida was hailed.

"Nurida!"

Nurida turned around. Her mother stood in the otherwise deserted corridor, looking regal in a golden gown and heavy crown studded with rubies.

"Mother," said Nurida, curtsying. Lochuran didn't follow suit.

"Lochuran, Lacritta, would you two go to Ressora?" Vindorra, the dowager queen, said. "Nurida, stay. I'd like to talk to you."

Obediently, Nurida paused while Lochuran and Lacritta went on. The queen mother waited until they were out of hearing and turned to the princess. "Nurida," Vindorra said regally, "your sister Kiarna is missing, along with two contingents of soldiers. Galledor is sending a few score trackers to try to find her. He has asked for you and Lacritta to go along."

Nurida blinked. "E-excuse me?"

The dowager queen sighed. "For some reason your brother has a notion that your upbringing won't be complete until you've spent time with the army."

"Who else is going?" Nurida inquired, hoping to hide her anxiety.

"Ressora, Beshinor, Orlian, Asherad, and a battalion of trackers, as well as Dejuday, the Wraith Mouse, as guide. Lochuran will be staying here." Nurida's mother spoke with a firmness that surprised Nurida. "And when you return," Vindorra added, "I will have a possible mate for you."

This news frightened the princess almost as much as her mother's first announcement. But Nurida knew if she wanted to get this latest decision reversed, she couldn't lose her countenance. "Thank you, Mother," Nurida said in her most respectful tone, secretly vowing to speak to Galledor at the first chance she got—both about this proposed excursion and this marriage their mother had arranged.

"Now go," Vindorra ordered firmly. "Go and ready yourself."

Nurida nodded briskly and followed after her sisters in her most princess-like manner. She went straight to Ressora's apartments.

Lacritta sat calmly on the bed with no expression on her face, listening to Ressora who, with eyes glittering wildly, was sitting on a chair facing Lacritta. Lochuran was there as well, standing instead of sitting, looking as she normally did, shunning the finery of the Miamuran royalty. She wore a short-sleeved tunic with no decorations that reached just halfway down to her paws. Around her waist, she buckled a corded belt with a knife sheathed on her left hip. Her shoes were made of toughened hazelnut bark, laced with more cord. *Why does she dress like that?* Nurida wondered, not for the first time. *She can wear so much better! Even the servants wear better!*

"Lacritta!" she exclaimed. "Guess what Mother told me!"

"Kiarna is missing," groaned Lacritta dryly.

"No," Nurida panted. "Not that. Mother said she'd have a mate chosen for me when we get back!"

The thrill racing through her voice was a thrill of alarm, but Lacritta apparently misinterpreted it because she burst into a smile. "That's settled, then! Do you know how many have asked to be your mate?"

"Wonderful," moaned Ressora. "I knew I couldn't be the only one."

"You could at least be pleasant about it," Lacritta muttered.

"Why should she be?" Lochuran scowled. "Nurida, have you heard about our mission?"

Nurida shook her head, glad for the distraction.

"We're supposed to look like another diplomatic assignment," Ressora said. "That's why Lacritta is going. But we're really looking for Kiarna."

"I don't know why Galledor insists on using the same tactic," Lochuran muttered. "It didn't work for Kiarna."

"So what would you do?" Ressora snapped.

"Not this." But she shrugged. "Either way, it won't be my call, will it?"

"You're not going," Nurida told her.

"Galledor's arranging it so I can."

"He's not going either."

"Who is leading the scouts?" Ressora asked, an interested gleam in her eye.

"Asherad, I suppose," Nurida guessed

Alarm flickered in Lochuran's eyes. "That's not good."

"Why?"

Ressora glanced at Lacritta. "You'll most likely find out tomorrow."

"Let's get kitted out," Lochuran suggested, her green eyes glowing.

Nurida frowned at Lochuran in sudden alarm. "You're enjoying this, aren't you?"

"Anything is better than staying here," Lochuran scowled.

What does she mean? Nurida wondered as she and Lacritta followed Lochuran out. *She is a* princess. *What more can she want?*

On the other paw, Nurida realized, in the woods, she wouldn't have to worry over being selected for a mate.

The sun was at its zenith when Ol'ver, Fal'ne, and Nathan'el stopped on top of an enormous rise. Stretched out before them was farmland, acre upon acre. A few mice were out toiling at the fields, with baskets at their side. It was the start of winter, so Fal'ne could only suppose they were pulling weeds. Their work songs trilled up to the three travelers. The sound of wind sighing and the cloying smell of disturbed earth wafted toward them like smoke from a fire. Beyond the farmland was an enormous wall of wood—a little ironical for Gray*stone*—that cast no shadow in the sun high. A pathway led from the hill to an enormous, crude gate made from lighter wood than the walls. It was wide open.

"Let's go!" laughed Nathan'el after a while. "Graystone, here we come!"

"You bet," Ol'ver agreed. "It's just as Feldspar described it!"

"Last one to the gates is a rotten leaf!" Fal'ne laughed, sprinting off.

"Go on, my son," Ol'ver laughed as Nathan'el glanced from his sister to his father. "I'll just enjoy the stroll."

Nathan'el laughed and took off after his sister.

Fal'ne had a good head start, and her paws were pounding the pathway. But Nathan'el was older and much, much stronger, and his strides were easily twice the length of hers. He shot in front of her, narrowly avoiding knocking her over. The two of them hurtled neck and neck, their sacks bouncing, their somewhat ragged clothing flapping behind them.

They were less than halfway to the gate, however, when a familiar mouse came trotting up the pathway to meet them.

"Fal'ne!" laughed Feldspar, their father's friend. "Nathan'el!"

Both siblings immediately quit their race to run to Feldspar. He laughed gleefully as Fal'ne threw her paws around him in a hug.

"Good to see you again, little missie. Great Cerecinthia, you're tall!" He released her to greet Nathan'el with a clap on his back. "Nathan'el, you're tall too. Glor'a's going to faint when she sees how grown-up you are. And can this possibly be Ol'ver?" he added as Ol'ver trotted up.

"Feldspar," nodded Ol'ver. "You look worse than you did in the Darkwoods prison."

"Hah, you're a fine one to talk; *you* look worse than you did after you were captured by the foxes. Had an eventful journey, did you?"

"Nope. Didn't even see Coll'n and his Keron Mice."

"Because he and most of his tribe are here. His deputy and the scouts are out somewhere else."

"What are they doing here?" wondered Ol'ver. "We're nowhere near the Keron!"

"Long story." Feldspar suddenly became a little more serious.

"Fal'ne!" the shout rang from the gates. A younger mouse maiden was racing along the pathway toward the friends. Her apron strings flew out behind her, and a crown of daisies adorned her head. It was Annor'a, Feldspar's daughter, roughly Fal'ne's age. She was as fine a friend as they got, Fal'ne thought often. Annor'a shot along the pathway into Fal'ne's embrace.

"Good to see you again, Annor'a!" Fal'ne exclaimed.

"Come on!" the child squealed. "Mother made some treats for us!"

Fal'ne glanced at her father, who nodded. Nathan'el muttered, "I'll catch up with you in a bit," and Annor'a pulled her along by her paw. As Fal'ne raced after the younger mouse, she kept glancing to the workers. This kind of farmland she had never seen, but Annor'a pulled her along so she could not really get a good look.

Winter was a bad season for the sea otters. They were not using Zurez, their fortress, during the winter but instead sheltered in the woods, and disease circulated unchecked through their gardens. Starfish had always feared the diseases terribly. Every winter, she would struggle to keep alive some plants in the back of their hut. Outside, by the makeshift chimney, she also grew a few herbs that Conch loved the smell of. He was helping her to gather them, stripping the leaves off the stems.

Starfish shot a glance at her brother. "You're awfully quiet."

Conch shrugged. "I'm thinking of Danaray. It doesn't make sense that her tribe would just *leave*."

"They used to be nomads," Starfish reminded him gently. "And they lived on a prairie. I suppose we shouldn't have expected her to stay here forever."

"Why settle there in the first place?" Conch asked softly. "It can't have been just because of us. She couldn't justify bringing her entire tribe here just to keep an eye on us."

"She's a river otter chieftain," Starfish reminded him. "She can do anything with her tribe she wants."

"Conch! Starfish!"

Conch and Starfish looked up to see Limpet and Abalone. Conch had grown up alongside them and never ceased to enjoy their company. "Finished your patrol?" Conch asked as they approached.

"Just got back," grinned Limpet, plopping himself down beside where Conch knelt. Abalone followed suit in a little more dignified manner. "It was all peaceful and boring, from start to finish."

"If your definition of boring is not having arrows shot at you from the bushes, I can't sympathize," scoffed Starfish.

"How is your shoulder?" asked Limpet sympathetically.

"Getting better," she answered, flexing it.

Abalone grinned at her. "Good to hear."

"So tell me, Starfish," Limpet said cheerfully, "if I offer up another set of paws in exchange, could we drag Conch away for fishing?"

"Whose paws?" Starfish inquired warily.

Limpet shrugged. "Oyster, of course. She was telling me before I left for patrol that she hasn't seen you in *so* long. If she comes and helps, can you spare Conch?"

"You could ask what Conch thinks," Starfish's brother interjected.

Starfish glanced at her small patch of earth. "I can finish this by myself," she replied neutrally.

Her brother shot her a concerned look—she hadn't been alone since she was attacked, and she wasn't looking forward to working by herself. That was her reason for enlisting Conch's help in her garden in the first place.

Maybe Limpet caught Conch's worried look because he said, "I'll go tell Oyster anyway. Be back in a minute!"

Abalone went with him to get Oyster, leaving Conch and Starfish still kneeling in the earth. After a moment, Conch reached for another plant. "Starfish?"

"Hmm?"

"Do you think the merchants will be by soon?"

Starfish looked at Conch. "I hope so."

Merchants were roving bands of creatures, usually otters, who bought and sold items for profit. Starfish loved it when they came because they always had news.

There was a muted staccato, quickly followed by Oyster's familiar voice calling out, "Starfish! Conch!"

Both siblings twisted around and chorused in unison, "Hi, Oyster!"

"Conch," Oyster said cheerfully, "my brother has commissioned me to tell you that he's waiting for you and your fishing spear at the river. He said you'd know the place."

Conch grinned. "He was right." Conch promptly stood up and inclined his head to both female otters. "I will see you both later."

As Conch disappeared into the house, Oyster knelt down in the earth beside Starfish and promptly asked, "How is your shoulder, Starfish?"

Starfish smiled wryly at her. "Better for your asking."

Oyster neatly yanked a leaf off a stem. "Does it need medicine?"

"Yes," Starfish answered. "But it isn't urgent."

Oyster sorted through the plants Starfish had gathered. "You know, none of these will help it."

"No. Those are to trade," Starfish answered.

"Oh." Oyster gently ran her paw across the arrow wound. "Can't I help any?"

Starfish had inherited her father's pride, and so she shook her head. "Not this time, Oyster. I've got it under control."

Oyster smiled. "You have the sea otter pride, you know?"

"Sea otter pride, river otter stubbornness," Starfish grinned in response.

"River otters aren't the only ones that can be stubborn," Oyster mused. "You do remember my father, don't you?" Oyster's father had been the chief after Crustacean.

"I certainly do remember him," Starfish laughed. "You're right, he was very stubborn. That's why he and my aunt could always see eye to eye."

"Mm," Oyster agreed. Then she tilted her head to one side. "Just like his successor."

She meant Eagle.

Starfish quickly returned her attention to her garden. "I don't think Eagle has ever met my aunt."

Thank the Bear King, Oyster didn't press.

Starfish and Oyster worked into the night, making sure the plants had enough water and heat from the chimney. Just as they were about to go home, snow began to fall.

4

FEAR

There was no sleep for Princess Nurida the night before she was expected to join a scouting party. Why—*why* was she supposed to do this? How could she survive in the wild when she had never in her life left Miamur?

How could she possibly be of any *use?* That was even more puzzling.

"Nurida?"

The princess turned to see her brother, Galledor, at the other end of the hallway. He strode up to her, his blue eyes kind and gentle. "You should be asleep. You have a long day ahead of you."

"I'm scared," Nurida confessed.

"You'll be fine," promised Galledor. "As long as you remember what I taught you with your dagger."

"Galledor ..."

"What?"

"I'm not a warrior," Nurida confessed. "I'm a scholar, and I'm certainly not built for this sort of thing. I can't do this! What makes you think I can? Why are you sending me on this mission or journey or whatever it is?"

Galledor surveyed her through bright eyes. Finally, he took a deep breath and said: "Follow me."

He led Nurida to the west wing of the palace, past dark bedrooms and out-of-use storage rooms. He turned to a door with a plain, dry appearance, and no handle. Nurida had never been to this part before. She curiously watched as he pushed open the door.

It led to a portrait gallery but unlike any Nurida had seen before. It did not have queens in splendid gowns or royally robed kings holding scepters as did nearly all the other portraits in the castle. These held images of … plainly dressed kings. Nurida had seen portraits of kings attired like kings who were nothing more than richly dressed fools. But these all were clothed simply and still exuded kingly bearing. All of them were Miamuran.

One of them depicted a dignified old mouse whose crinkly eyes showed him to be very scholarly. Another held a picture of a Miamuran knight wielding an enormous spear. A third held the image of an auburn-furred queen who could have been Nurida's twin. She looked at them with a smile.

"Queen Rosaya," Galledor murmured. "Our father's mother. Born a peasant, but she grew to be a truly great queen. After the wars that ended the Dark Ages, she helped pick up the pieces of the world."

He led her by the portraits, explaining each one. Every creature in that hall had done something important, and Nurida recognized every name from her books.

"They all started young," Galledor told her. "All of them started as you did. But when they were put in the right place at the right time, they rose to the occasion. All it took was their spark of courage."

Nurida shook her head dubiously.

Galledor sighed. Again. "Nurida, sister, have courage."

Nurida looked away and decided to change the subject. "Is Lochuran going?"

"Yes."

"So Asherad will lead the patrol."

"*No,*" was Galledor's fervent answer. "He won't be going at all."

"Then who will lead?" Nurida murmured, bemused.

"Elvinene."

Though Nurida trusted her sister-in-law, she was not completely reassured. "Galledor?"

"Hmm?" He started walking back along the gallery.

"Why are you sending me along?"

Galledor sighed. "Because I fear I have sheltered you too long. I fear … Nurida, there is a storm coming, and I want you to be ready for it."

Nurida blinked. "Ressora hinted that something was going on that I knew nothing about."

Galledor's eyes darkened. "And she didn't tell you what she so cleverly found out?"

Nurida shook her head, hiding her anger.

"Oh, Nurida," Galledor sighed. "The sweetest member of our family and not a single good brother or sister for you. I'm sorry."

"You've been a good older brother to me," Nurida protested.

"I do not think I have done a good job, though," he murmured sadly.

"Galledor?" Nurida pressed, determined to keep Galledor from this kind of sorrow. "Why do Dejuday and Asherad dislike each other?"

It was a straightforward question, but Galledor's sudden wariness showed the answer was complicated.

"They ... well. They don't. They ... both loved the same lady mouse. She chose Dejuday."

Nurida stared at him in shock. "Over *Asherad?*"

Galledor stopped and looked at her. He gazed at her for a long moment. Finally, he murmured, "You doubt he was a better catch than a prince?"

"Than *Asherad!*"

Galledor laughed. "In Dejuday's defense, he is honest and brave and generous."

"So is Asherad!"

Galledor inclined his head. "I will not argue there. But this maiden chose whom she loved best. I don't know her reasons, and I never asked."

Nurida sighed. "I suppose she ... made a good choice."

Galledor frowned. "You sound upset."

"Mother said she has a match for me when we get back," Nurida scowled.

Galledor's eyes narrowed. "I see," he said slowly. "Well ... I'll have to sort that out, won't I?"

"Don't worry about it," Nurida said hastily. "If not one courtier, it'll be another, and quite frankly ... they're all the same."

Galledor gave her a level look. "It doesn't matter. It's time I made clear to our mother that you are not her *toy.*"

Nurida blinked. Galledor put his paw on her shoulder. "Come," he said finally. "You do need sleep. I'll deal with the dowager queen."

A shadow invaded Conch's dreams. He wasn't sure what it was, but he knew it was dangerous. Whispers filled his mind as the unknown shadow began to grow. They spoke of danger in the north, of betrayal, of darkness. Darkness had always terrified Conch, but that was nothing compared to this shadow.

In his dream, Conch had been standing beneath a tree, pure silver of bark. He'd never seen one like this. Brilliant, it stood in a small circle of earth in a literally hard—almost solid—darkness. Conch had tried moving, but had been barred in as though by walls. Yet when he looked up, the moon—full—was shining brightly. Then the shadow covered it. The silver tree turned red. Conch could feel the malice. Then soft whispering of menace echoed in his ears, but it wasn't a warning. He couldn't decipher what the whispers were saying. Then, as if in panic, the whispering got louder and louder until it was a wailing. When Conch thought he would shout for panic, he woke.

He was shaking like a dried leaf, and his blankets were hot and sticky. Gasping for air, he threw them off and wrapped a light coat around his thin nightclothes. Then he staggered out of his room into the kitchen.

Starfish was already awake, flicking through the herbs she had gathered last night. Also in front of her was a book—she'd made it herself—of plants and what they were good for. Dried samples adorned every few pages.

"Starfish?" Conch asked. "Didn't you sleep at all last night?"

Starfish shook her head. "Couldn't."

"You look sick."

"When you and I were working out back," she explained, not looking at him, "Eagle met with Father. Eagle … he … he asked permission … to …"

"Court you?" Conch guessed, suddenly grinning.

Starfish nodded.

"That's bad?"

"No!" She looked up, looking astounded and, seeing her brother's grin, looked down again. "I'm just nervous, that's all."

"What did you say?" Conch grinned.

Starfish sighed. "I was thrilled. But now, I'm wondering if I'm one maiden Eagle would do better to keep away from."

"That's absurd," Conch chided. "He's been our friend our whole lives."

"I know, Conch, I know. But still, given where you and I come from—"

"If Eagle cared, he wouldn't have asked to court you," Conch reassured her.

Starfish sighed and turned a page in her book.

"Come *on*," Conch teased. "This can't be a surprise."

Starfish shook her head. "It isn't," she answered softly.

Conch leaned on the table. "I thought you'd be ecstatic."

Starfish finally looked up from her book, and her eyes flashed angrily. "What would be the repercussions?"

Conch blinked. "Excuse me?"

"Because of Mother," Starfish continued. "And Danaray."

"So you're the daughter of a river otter," Conch shrugged. "What do you care what unhappy, jealous sea otters mutter?"

"I don't," Starfish replied levelly. "I care about what Mother's enemies might do. To him."

Conch blinked. He hadn't thought of that. But before he could think of a reply, much less frame it coherently, Starfish dropped her gaze back to the book. "But Eagle's been my friend for so long … I can't just turn him down because I'm *afraid*."

"Families look after each other, Starfish," Conch murmured. "You don't *have* to be afraid."

His sister said nothing for a long while. She ended the silence with a determined, "I am not going to let fear control me. Not without a fight."

"*That's* my sister!" Conch grinned proudly. "Now, unless there's something else, I'm going to find Abalone."

Starfish raised her eyes to his face. "Why?"

"I was going off fishing with him for fish to trade with the merchants," Conch explained.

"Go for it," Starfish smiled. "I'm going to wash our clothes. I'll need a clean dress for when Eagle comes."

"Get it from the merchants with the fish we catch," suggested Conch.

"Maybe. But I think I need medicine first."

Conch sighed reluctantly. They were always short one thing that was next to essential. This time it was a fine dress for Starfish. Not only that, but they needed warm coats, food, medicine, blankets, bags for traveling to Zurez, tools, seeds, thread, needles, cloth, shoes, *and* cord. They barely had the things to trade for essentials. It got more expensive the older Starfish and Conch got. Conch promised himself he would get extra fish today.

He met up with Abalone at the exit to the village and, along the way to the creek, told him Starfish's good news.

Abalone's eyes shone with amusement. "You know, no one will admit it," he said, "but this will mightily disappoint more than one unmarried sea otter warrior."

"It's no one's fault but theirs," Conch replied promptly.

Abalone's expression grew reflective. "Hm. I guess. Makes you wonder …"

"Wonder what?" laughed a voice from behind.

Both the male otters twisted to see Pearl following them along the path. Her eyes sparkled with laughter. "What were you wondering?"

"Nothing, Pearl," Abalone assured her.

Pearl looked suspicious, but she nodded. "Where are you off to?"

"The river. Fishing."

"You'd probably catch a good price from what I've heard. There isn't nearly as much salmon fishing as usual."

Abalone frowned at her ominous statement. "What does that mean?"

Pearl lowered her voice. "I've been hearing things—things about trouble up north."

At the last two words, Conch's stomach clenched. The Wraith Mice were in the north. Trouble with them usually boded ill for the whole continent.

"The roads that were once well looked after lie in ruins," continued Pearl. "Old fortresses and garrisons and *cities* are empty. Fires have been seen in the great forests. Many signs of danger are there, but no one does anything about it."

Conch's mind was far away with her words, so distant he nearly fell into the river.

"Careful," warned Abalone.

"What else have you heard?" Conch panted, trying to regain his dignity.

Pearl leaned in closer, obviously about to reveal something important, but before she could do so, a voice hailed them from upstream.

"Pearl, you're telling them *without me?*"

Conch twisted around and grinned. "Saline! I thought you'd still be laid up."

Saline shuddered. "Fresh air is the only way to heal. But Pearl didn't wait for me to start gossiping? I'm hurt!"

Pearl smiled indulgently. "If you want, you can tell the rest."

Saline grinned at her; then her face darkened into the intensive look that Conch knew came when she had something particularly important to discuss.

"The kingdom of the Wraith Mice has gone silent. No one's had any news about the inside of their kingdom for months."

Conch's jaw dropped. Abalone frowned at Saline. "Where are their fortresses, again?"

Pearl drew a rectangle in the river mud to represent the continent. "Zurez is here," she said, making a mark on the bottom left. "Mirquis and Dombre are here," she continued, carefully marking two circles close to each other. "Dobar is here, and Kardas here," she added, making another pair of marks farther apart than the others. "And Arashna here," she finished, drawing a mark in the sea to show the island of Arashna.

"The Wraith Mice usually inhabit Arashna—their capital, not a fortress—and some always garrison Kardas. Mirquis and Dombre lie in the Ashlands, and after the war against Darkwoods, they were abandoned. Now they live in Arashna, Dobar, and Kardas. No merchants have been allowed into those cities for months, and no news about what's going on inside seems to be coming out. On top of that, there has been increased activity in the seas. Pirates now range the coasts instead of thieving in the deep waters. But those pirates who are friends of the Wraith Mice have disappeared!"

Conch felt himself shivering. Winters before this one had been terrible and life-taking, but before, all they had to deal with was the weather.

Saline wrapped up the foreboding speech. "The signs are there," she breathed. "Trouble is stirring in the north, in the very heart of ruling up there. Evil beyond the Darkwoods foxes is rising in the seas and coming closer to civilization. I have heard the elders speak of the Darkwoods foxes and their slow, unobservable rise to power. It will not be long before a terrible war is upon the whole earth. Just like last time."

KNIVES IN THE SHADOW

Nurida stood on a rise outside of Miamur. Her bright green gaze was unclouded with eagerness to see the woodlands. She had never seen any trees taller than she was.

A little ways down, the soldiers were milling about. A flame-colored mouse could be seen speaking quietly to each one of the soldiers. Nurida knew Lochuran was trying to get any information she might have missed before setting out.

Finally, Lochuran seemed to hear something. Her head tipped back, her shoulders slouched, and her eyes brightened. She hastily thanked the soldier she had been speaking to and strode up the hill toward Nurida.

"Any idea where Elvinene is?" she muttered nervously.

Nurida shook her head.

"What about any of the others?"

Nurida glanced toward the palace. "Here comes Beshinor."

Beshinor, a wiry gray mouse, only two seasons older than Nurida, was striding up the hill to join them. "All well?" he asked Lochuran, utterly ignoring Nurida. He had always been like that. He also missed the look of contempt that Lochuran flashed at the side of his face. He had not deigned to look at her.

"All's well, Beshinor," Lochuran muttered. "Where is Elvinene?"

"Don't know," shrugged Beshinor. "But Ressora and Lacritta are coming. Bringing a blind mouse on this journey is so fluff-brained! She should stay in the palace where she belongs!"

"Shut your fat mouth about Lacritta," Lochuran muttered. She also muttered some other things Nurida shut her ears to and watched as Ressora and Lacritta toiled up the hill.

Lacritta looked nervous beyond belief, but she had a right to. Ressora was gently guiding her. Lacritta was unarmed because she was going along merely for the appearance of diplomacy.

"Lochuran," Nurida whispered, "were you referring to whatever maiden Asherad loved yesterday when you said it would be bad if Asherad were to lead?"

Lochuran looked carefully at her sister and then nodded a few times.

Nurida took a step closer and whispered in her sister's ear. "He's not leading. Elvinene is."

Lochuran sighed in relief. "Thank the Bear King for that."

"I hope Elvinene gets here soon," Nurida added. "I can't stand Beshinor with all his swaggering."

"And his assumption of holding all the knowledge in the world," Lochuran agreed. "I wish I could gag him."

Nurida giggled. "His mouth is so big you'd have to have a pretty big gag!"

"He'd still manage to talk through it," Lochuran agreed, her eyes light with mirth.

Orlian was next up the hill. He had particularly long strides and dark, almost black eyes. His fur was gray, and he was tall, though not as tall as Galledor, who stood head and shoulders above the crowd.

Orlian nodded to Nurida and Lochuran, touching Lacritta's shoulder gently—he was always sensitive to her blindness—and began a low conversation with Beshinor, who pretty much ignored him. Orlian was dressed in brown, which looked strange against his dark gray fur, and carried a javelin over his shoulder. He did not speak much, but was usually quiet as a tomb.

"I'm scared," Lacritta murmured. "Orlian seems particularly cold."

"He does," Lochuran soothed. "But he's irritating Beshinor, so I can't complain."

Asherad was next, and to Nurida's surprise, Dejuday was a few steps behind him. Asherad looked as if he didn't want to go … wherever they were going, but Dejuday looked expressionless. He nodded politely to the princesses and murmured, "Good morning," for Lacritta's sake. It was all Nurida could do to keep from staring at his missing ear.

"Where in the name of the Bear King is Elvinene?" Lochuran muttered savagely as Beshinor began a new tirade at some soldiers.

"Right behind you."

Lochuran visibly jumped as Elvinene's voice sounded from behind Nurida and Lochuran.

Elvinene had come up the hill behind them, and her brown eyes glowed ruefully. "I think perhaps I should silence Beshinor."

"We all do," Lochuran agreed.

Elvinene straightened her shoulders and said something coldly to Beshinor. It looked as if Beshinor was taken aback, but Lochuran whispered to Nurida. "A princess missing. What *is* happening?"

Nurida shrugged.

"Lochuran, she's been missing for quite a while, hasn't she? What makes you think she didn't just get lost?"

"The last we heard from her was this time last winter from Pasadaga-vra," Lochuran agreed. "The last time Dejuday heard from her was a little after that in the area of Yoro, the city on the Wild River."

"The Keron River?" Nurida translated.

Lochuran's eyes widened. "Kiarna might have gone towards the coast."

"Pirates?" Nurida scoffed. "She would have had a heavily armed company. Pirates wouldn't *dream* of attacking her."

"Maybe ..." Lochuran looked helpless with unknowing. "We'll just have to see how this turns out, won't we?"

Nurida nodded. "After a princess goes missing, everyone gets a little jumpy. But it's going to be a long time before we find any trace of her."

"We don't know that," Lochuran murmured abruptly. "Kiarna might have been on her way back to Miamur and nearly here."

"Then why not stop at a city when we could have heard from her?" Nurida pointed out.

"Bringing secrets, maybe?" Lochuran suggested after a pause. "Or maybe she was being pursued and didn't want to be tracked too easily?"

"But who would follow her?" Nurida protested. "Someone who was able to track her through the wild?"

Elvinene began to speak to the soldiers, but Nurida and Lochuran kept up their conversation in the back, so quiet that not even Lacritta noticed.

"Or someone who caught her before she reached the wild," Lacritta guessed.

"I wouldn't think so," Nurida mused. "If she were being followed, she would have fled to the wild as quickly as possible."

"But someone tracked her in the wilderness?" Lochuran protested. "Not just anyone knows the wild well enough."

"Not just anyone could overwhelm a royal escort either," Nurida argued gently. "So we already know, if she is in trouble, it isn't from just anyone."

"I don't know, Nurida," Lochuran debated. "That just sounds so far-fetched. Last time, when the Darkwoods foxes rose to power, there were different signs."

"So?" Nurida asked.

"Well … we'd know if the Darkwoods foxes were stirring again. Ever since Burnish led his creatures back into Lunep Castle, there haven't been any dangers more serious than rogues."

"Who said it was the Darkwoods foxes?" Nurida exclaimed. "It could just as easily be some new conqueror."

"We'd hear," Lochuran argued. Elvinene was still speaking to the troops. Lacritta hadn't heard their conversation. The siblings were silent for a while before Lochuran broke the silence.

"That's funny," she murmured.

"What is?"

"We look so alike," Lochuran murmured. "We act alike sometimes. We're the only two in our family who even look this way, and we're practically identical. Yet how many times have we spoken more than thirty words a month to each other before?"

Nurida blinked. "I don't know. We're not all that alike."

Lochuran had a knowing look—a sadly knowing look—in her eyes. "I wouldn't be too sure," she said softly. "Maybe in our tastes and behavior we're different. But we have the same spirit."

Before Nurida could argue, Elvinene finished her speech. The tracking party—only two score trackers—began to move out. Lochuran gave her a quick piece of advice.

"Don't talk too much—save your breath for walking."

Nurida only nodded.

Lacritta and Ressora were somewhere in the middle, and Nurida didn't know where her other siblings were, so she stayed with Lochuran. Lochuran was quiet, and her steps were small and even.

Nurida should have known better than to try to talk to her, but she tried once. "Lochuran?" she whispered.

"Hmm?"

"How long do you think this will last?"

"I don't know."

"Whom do you think mother wants me betrothed to?"

"I don't know."

"Are you going to say anything else?"

"I don't know."

Nurida grinned. Lochuran was smiling slightly too.

That day, they skirted the prairie and moorland that had once been part of the squirrel Sling Tribe lands and kept to the flatter part of the prairie. Nurida knew this route would take much longer. "Why are we going this way?" she asked Lochuran as they paused to take a rest.

Lochuran sat back in the sparse shade of a withered tree. Nurida joined her as Lochuran began to speak. "Most of the soldiers—and probably most anyone in Miamur—believe that the Sling Tribe territory is haunted. When the Sling Tribe was obliterated in the war in Pasadagavra, creatures that passed that way heard strange things. There's *something* there if not ghosts, so we're just avoiding it. Besides, we could pass through Lunep this way and maybe find news of Kiarna there."

"Did Elvinene tell you that?"

Lochuran shook her head. "Nah. I deduced it myself." She closed her eyes. "I hope we don't find Kiarna anywhere near Miamur," she murmured.

"Why?" Nurida knew by now that Lochuran had a thirst for adventure, but surely she'd be worried about her sister.

"I don't want to go back to Miamur," Lochuran shrugged. "I just … don't."

"Really?" Nurida murmured. "I can't wait to go back."

Lochuran flicked an ear irritably. "Really. Because already, this has been good for you. Just yesterday you were—forgive me—a fluff-brained young princess whose nose rarely left a book and who hardly knew the difference between negotiations and threats. Just a bit ago, though, you were gladly talking strategy with me! Do you really want to lose that, Nurida?"

Nurida gave her sister a flat look. "I *like* my books," she said and then thought to herself, *And books can rarely get you killed.*

Snow was flying as a party of merchants trudged into the sea otter camp. Eagle, Saline, and Abalone had met with them and guided them into the camp. There were a dozen, give or take, in that particular band, and they were all laden down with merchandise.

Starfish had come to her front door when she heard the familiar voices. While her younger brother's eyes were on the bags the merchants carried and the cart two of them dragged, trying to guess if they held medicine, Starfish's brown eyes rested on Eagle. He was helping one of the older members of the band when his eyes rose a little and locked with Starfish's. They stayed like that for two long moments before Eagle tore his gaze away, but not before Starfish noticed a tiny little smile on his face.

As with all their visits to camps, two or three merchants would lodge in various willing homes. Mollusk always kept his home open to every merchant that needed shelter, and Starfish was just as eager to share what little she had, but her house was never graced by more than two visitors. It was not because her hospitality was stingy or her home was dirty or any failing on her part; Mollusk had told her once that he had heard some merchants "arguing ferociously" about who would get the opportunity to be Starfish's guest. They kept the visitors limited because they knew Starfish could not afford to keep too many and two was straining it as it was.

They also paid her excessively for her trouble.

The two who stayed with Starfish this time were Sh'vendi, a matronly gray-and-black mouse that kept the rest of that band in line, and Baklenne, a sleek-furred river otter healer. Starfish instantly went about her business making them feel at home. They both reclined at the table, their immensely heavy packs resting against the wall, and cups of steaming fragrant mint-and-chamomile tea in their paws.

Starfish sat down across from them. "What news?" she asked curiously.

"Starfish, *never* start a conversation like that," Sh'vendi scolded. "Especially not now. I'm going to ask you first. What news?"

"Oh, I've got nothing to tell there," Starfish answered ironically, shrugging her unhurt shoulder. "There was an earthquake a few weeks ago, it completely knocked over that tree that leans over the river. We have a bridge now, though no one uses it. Oh, and I was shot."

Sh'vendi sat up sharply. "*Shot?* By whom?"

Starfish shook her head. "I never saw them, and no one found any sign of them. I was out with some friends, and the next thing I knew, I had a short arrow stuck in my shoulder."

"Short?" Baklenne asked sharply. "How short?"

Starfish stood up. "I'll show you." She went back to her room, grabbed the arrow—she had kept it so Brine could test it for poison and hadn't gotten around to throwing it away—and returned to the table. "Here it is." She extended the black-feathered arrow to Baklenne.

As the river otter examined the missile, her face grew more and more serious. "This isn't an arrow," she announced sharply. "This is called a bolt. It goes to a crossbow, a very dangerous weapon. And a crossbow is used only by pirates."

Starfish gasped. "Why not by land-dwellers?"

"It's too heavy," Sh'vendi told her. "A longbow is much more convenient to carry on your back. But a crossbow weighs a bit more, and takes longer to fire. Pirates use it because it's steadier to fire, so on a rocking ship you have better odds of hitting."

"Can you not fire a bolt from a longbow?" Starfish asked, worried.

"Too short," Baklenne replied. "We'd better talk to Eagle. Pirates are so dangerous it isn't even funny."

"Just how dangerous?" Starfish asked nervously.

"Probably a gone danger by now," Sh'vendi reasoned. "Chances are that some ship wrecked in the mouth of the river during the storm. I'd strongly advise scouting the river for any debris, but if that is the case, then the pirates will move on soon."

Starfish felt herself relax. "That's good," she commented and turned the conversation to happier matters.

At the place where two rivers became one, Shorefish stood up from her fire. The others would be coming back soon. She despised the idea of what this band was doing, but she really had little choice. Her ancestral home was her everything, and nothing could keep her from regaining it—not even some things that made her conscience twinge.

Shorefish touched the two daggers she wore at her waist. One was the ceremonial dagger that belonged to her tribe. It had a fine hilt of spiraled bronze set with three pieces of amber. The other was a plain curved knife without a crosspiece. The hilt was made of heavy basalt, and a piece of smooth slate was the pommel stone. It was the weapon that belonged to a sea otter, the knife that killed Nighthawk, her father. A reminder that she had yet to avenge her father's death.

But still, she had not done it last time. Her blue eyes flashed with anger at the memory; she had seen the one who bore the deed of Nighthawk's death, and she had not been able to kill him. He had stood there, quite within range of her javelin, and she hadn't thrown it. That would never happen again. *Never.*

The soft crunching of paws on fresh snow announced that Moonpath was returning. Moonpath was another river otter who had lost both land and kin to the sea otters' conquest, but she bore her hatred not in the weapons that had killed her family—those had been irretrievable—but with bitterness in her heart. Her voice rasped and hissed frequently, and she had covered her face with a silken mask to hide her hideous scars. Shorefish oftentimes thought Moonpath was berserk—but berserkers didn't have that cold, calculating malice that Moonpath possessed. She was obsessed with the idea of revenge, and instead of clouding her thinking, it made her think more clearly. But her unclouded comprehension didn't make her any less mad.

"Did you find them?" Shorefish asked immediately.

"Of course not," Moonpath snarled. "If we had, you'd be the first to know."

Shorefish was about to argue but decided against it. "Where could they be?"

"If I knew, we wouldn't still be here," Moonpath hissed, stalking past Shorefish. The two warriors she had taken with her followed silently.

Shorefish was tempted to call her back and argue, but she knew it would be fruitless, pointless, and dangerous. Arguing with a fellow commander in a hostile territory was never smart. Reluctantly, she followed Moonpath back toward the fires that made up the makeshift camp where the warriors were preparing to attack.

Much though Shorefish longed to regain her ancestral home, much though she longed to discard her sea otter knife and avenge her father, fighting alongside Moonpath was not her idea of a good tactic.

Graystone—it was a place of peace, joy, and tranquility. Fal'ne and Nathan'el loved it there after only a week.

The first day, Fal'ne and Annor'a ran back and forth between the various places where the professions were performed. They peeked in the hospital and the blacksmith but spent a long time in the weaver's shed. Fal'ne had never seen so many looms; her mother had one, and her spun thread came from wool the wild sheep or goats left behind or, more often, soft bark fibers. Fal'ne had also been amazed with the dyes, colors so different from ones she was familiar with. Up north, they had almost no green, for green came from a very special plant. To her amazement, however, green was the most common color here. She did note, however, that there was very little red.

Then had come lunch. The two young maidens had skipped to the bakery and gotten some very nice bread. Just down the street, they made purchases from the cheese maker and spread some tasty cheese on their rolls.

That was where Nathan'el caught up with them. His face was ever so slightly amused. "Fal'ne, you'll be shocked to hear this," he informed his sister. "There isn't a glassblower in the town, as far as I can tell."

Fal'ne furrowed her brow. "Why not?"

"There isn't the right kind of sand," Nathan'el chuckled. "I did visit the bead worker, but believe it or not, all the beads are made from clay!"

Annor'a gave him an exasperated look. "Well, what else do you make beads from?"

"Glass." Fal'ne pulled out a silver chain that had but one bead on it, but one so beautiful. Glass of all colors had been melded together to make a winging bird that looked as if it was made from a rainbow.

Annor'a breathed in amazement. "That is a treasure," she gasped. She drew back. "But there *used* to be a glassblower in the town. The problem is that the whole settlement is made of wood."

"Despite the name," Fal'ne grinned.

"Exactly. The fires from the ovens spread to some of the buildings when I was much younger, so they moved the glassblower to a place near the river. I'll take you there someday if you like. The glassblower is enchanting."

That sounded good to Fal'ne.

Shorefish splashed heedlessly across a chilly creek too shallow to swim in. Her heart was racing, and her bright blue eyes excited. She had found them! This was it! The fun was about to begin!

Moonpath looked up from her fire as Shorefish ran into the camp. "Did you find them?" she asked sharply.

"I did!" Shorefish gasped. "I did! In *Graystone* no less!"

Moonpath might have frowned; Shorefish couldn't tell. "That's a good place to hide," she agreed. "But there may be a complication."

Shorefish wasn't prepared for that. "What is it?"

"Last spring when we were there, one of my warriors recognized a mouse living there—it was Feldspar. Remember him?"

Shorefish's expression grew worried. "Yes—from Pasadagavra."

"There's more," Moonpath continued. "My scouts saw three mice—Cliff Mice—entering Graystone a few days ago, a little after you saw Danaray's foolish aide get found by the sea otters. Believe it or not, two of them were recognized as well. The oldest one was Ol'ver—I'm definitely sure you remember him."

"Vividly," Shorefish snapped.

"The other male was Nathan'el," Moonpath added. "I remember a squirrel found a baby mouse called Nathan'el *in Pasadagavra* that she took care of when she was a captive."

Shorefish gave her a horrified look. "If they recognize her, we're in trouble."

"I don't think there's any danger from Nathan'el," Moonpath hissed. "But Ol'ver and Feldspar ... If I remember correctly, they were the mice that Princess Zuryzel rescued from Darkwoods. That being the case, we have to act fast."

"How fast?" Shorefish asked, though she was perfectly capable of taking charge.

"Tomorrow," Moonpath snarled. "Tomorrow we'll try to catch one of the Graystone brats, see if that takes the minds of our two friends off the princess."

Shorefish furrowed her brow in thought. "The glasshouse is outside the walls, like the fields, and I bet some young ones go to the glassblower sometimes." Shorefish had seen a glasshouse before, and she always considered them magical places. She kept that to herself, however.

"Maybe if we're lucky we'll catch Ol'ver's daughter getting the grand tour," Moonpath agreed.

"His daughter?" Shorefish echoed blankly.

"The third mouse with Ol'ver and Nathan'el," Moonpath snapped irritably.

You never said anything about a female mouse, Shorefish thought angrily, but again she remained silent.

"I'll send my warriors to the woods around the glasshouse," Shorefish sighed.

"I'll have my tribe cover the rest of the ground," Moonpath complied. "My tribe is much bigger."

Shorefish wanted to spit at her compatriot, but remembering they would be neighbors if they reclaimed their lands, she merely turned away. The comment about the size of Shorefish's tribe was an overused and stinging insult.

Moonpath took out her own chieftain's dagger; its blade was iron, its hilt made from smoky gray onyx. Strands of steel twined their way up the hilt like metal vines. The pommel stone was a piece of smoky quartz shaped like a leaf. The mad chief toyed with the blade, tilting it back and forth, watching as sunlight played tantalizingly over the quartz leaf, displaying its full beauty.

Shorefish heard Moonpath hiss to herself in pleasure and hunched her shoulders over in an automatic gesture of worry. The leaf was a symbol of words to river otters, and the other chief was enjoying the effect her "leaves" had on Shorefish.

The chief glanced over her shoulder to see Moonpath had her back to Shorefish and was staring transfixed into the gray pommel stone. *She's mad!* Shorefish thought, half-afraid and half-excited at what was to come.

Eagle looked up from examining the bolt. "You're sure of this?" he asked in an undertone.

The merchants Baklenne and Sh'vendi nodded. "Beyond a shadow of a doubt!" Baklenne exclaimed. "These feathers are puffin feathers, and they're found only on islands *far* out to sea. They don't roost in the mainland."

They were seated in Eagle and Saline's home, a plain but functional dwelling devoid of decoration. Eagle had lit a whale-oil lamp on the table and was inspecting the old arrow by its light. If not for the two merchants, he would never have suspected it came from a crossbow. Pirates never come here! "Why would pirates be on sea otter land?" he asked, shaking his head to clear it.

Sh'vendi shrugged. "I don't know what to tell you, Chief. I've seen these arrows in Cliff Mouse cities. A crossbow's bolt, beyond any doubt."

Eagle nodded slowly. This gave him much to think about. "Thank you for telling me this," he said to the merchants.

"Oh, if there are pirates about, it's nothing to thank us for," Sh'vendi reassured Eagle.

Baklenne leaned forward. "Tell me—have you seen much of Shorefish around?"

"What does she have to do with pirates?" Eagle asked.

"I know she's an enemy to the sea otters," Baklenne admitted. "But if there were pirates around, she'd know before anyone else. She might consider them a common enemy."

Eagle hesitated, not sure he shared Baklenne's optimism. Nonetheless, he said, "I will think about this."

Both the merchants took their leave, and Eagle stood up from his table. He needed to clear his head. The night was cool and crisp, so he grabbed his cloak and wrapped himself in it, planning on a walk. On his way out, he kissed his sleeping sister, who slept curled up by the hearth fire. She had fallen asleep reading again.

His paws had no real direction, but he realized he was ambling towards the river. He really wished there were some other well-known landmark in his territory; aimless paws always went toward the river.

What was left of the snow crunched under his shoes and the stars glittered in frosty majesty above his head, so he had to smile. "Danger cannot touch the stars," he was fond of saying.

When the river wove into view, he realized he was not the only one with a desire to take a midnight stroll. Wrapped in her cloak of soft gray, Starfish was dangling her paws over the water. She must have heard his steps because she looked behind her. And to Eagle's excitement, she smiled when she saw him.

"Good evening," she greeted him.

"Hello," Eagle replied for want of something better to say. "I didn't know you were here."

"The stars were so beautiful that I wanted to know what the rest of the night looked like," Starfish admitted. She scooted aside on her rock and patted the empty space.

Eagle joined her, feeling his heart pound. Starfish smiled at him one more time before tilting her head back to look at the stars. "Did Baklenne and Sh'vendi tell you about the bolt?"

"They did," Eagle told her. "Pirates. I'm having trouble wrapping my mind around it."

Starfish shifted her weight, balancing a little better on the rock. "Do you suppose someone could have hired them?" she asked. "Mercenaries might fight anywhere they could make a profit."

Eagle glanced at her in surprise. "Who would have hired them?"

Starfish shrugged. "It's merely a possibility. I suppose Shorefish could have."

"There are other hostile tribes besides Shorefish's," Eagle pointed out. "Baklenne actually suggested that Shorefish might consider pirates a common enemy."

"My aunt would disagree with Baklenne," Starfish mused. She dragged her eyes from the stars and looked at Eagle. "But someone else who might know are the otters at Kwang-ha`el. After all, if mercenaries are looking for profit, they'd attack any dwelling in the area."

Eagle tilted his head to one side. "I hadn't thought of that. Do you suppose it would be worth asking them if they know anything of pirates?"

Starfish nodded slowly. "I don't see why not—it can't hurt to ask. Conch or I could go—the chieftain there knows who we are."

Eagle frowned in consternation. "By yourself?"

"No!" Starfish exclaimed. "After getting shot, I'm not eager to go *anywhere* by myself!"

Eagle glanced at her old wound. "How is your shoulder?"

Starfish smiled up at him. "Healing nicely. Although, Brine told me that if you and Conch hadn't come so quickly, it'd be healing much slower. So I suppose I owe you one."

Eagle gave her a puzzled look. "One what?"

Starfish laughed. Eagle loved that laugh. He smiled with her, and when she shook her head despairingly, he said, "You don't owe me anything."

Starfish looked back into his eyes, and they were warmer than a hearth fire. "Still, thank you."

Her thanks both embarrassed and elated the young chief. He looked back at the river, smiling; when he was able to meet her eyes again, he looked back to her and said, "I'll send out some scouts tomorrow to see what they can see."

Starfish nodded seriously. "But don't let anyone else go out alone."

THE TRAP IS SPRUNG

The morning sun that woke Nurida glinted off Lochuran's fur. "Does my fur ever look as if it's made of pure gold as yours does?" she asked sleepily.

"Yours looks like sun shining through an amber globule," Lochuran replied.

"Either way, the sun feels warm for the winter." Nurida staggered to her paws. Elvinene had already roused the scouts, and they were rolling up their bedrolls. The prairie spread out indefinitely around them, except for the gray smudge on the western horizon and the bright flash of white light on the eastern horizon. The bright light was Miamur; the gray was the Ashlands.

Lochuran dug into her pack of supplies. "Want some of that tasty marching roll?" she offered.

"You should have woken me earlier," Nurida told her sister.

"Elvinene had to wake me up," Lochuran shrugged. She looked up secretively. "How about we share this?"

She took out a wrapped paper package and opened it. Nurida gasped when she saw the treasure therein.

"Dried trout? Where on earth did you get that?"

"Snuck it with me," Lochuran smirked.

The two sisters each had a piece of the treat, as well as a roll each. Nurida liked the rolls; they had been soaked in honey and rolled in flour. And were they good!

Nurida was surprised by the fast pace of packing up the small camp, but she knew by now that complaining would do no good. She was just slinging her pack onto her back when she looked up sharply. "Where's Ressora?"

Lochuran glanced around and stood up sharply when she saw no sign of the gray mouse. "Hiding somewhere," she whispered. "We'd be able to see her for miles otherwise."

As the trackers formed up, the two princesses watched for their sister. "I don't see her," Nurida murmured as they prepared to move out.

Lochuran hissed. "Kiarna missing, and Ressora disappeared! Where's Elvinene?"

"There!" Nurida pointed quickly off to one side.

"Is it just me, or does she look a little sad?" Lochuran whispered.

Elvinene was blinking more rapidly than usual, and her shoulders drooped. "She must know Ressora's not here," Nurida muttered to her sister. "Elvinene wouldn't miss a thing like that!"

Lochuran looked toward the place where Ressora and Lacritta had slept. "She hasn't been here for a while," she whispered, her voice shaking. "She must have left in the night."

"Look."

Lochuran turned to watch as Asherad strode past Elvinene. The two royal personages exchanged a sad, worried look—just a quick one. Asherad caught the eyes of his younger sisters and put his paw to his mouth.

Nurida and Lochuran exchanged a disbelieving look. "She ran away," Nurida surmised.

Lochuran sighed. "I don't know why I'm surprised. She talked about running away all the time. A lot of us did."

In the woods surrounding the glasshouse, Shorefish heard the signal whistle from Moonpath. Creatures were coming from Graystone to the glasshouse.

Shorefish balanced her ceremonial knife lightly in her paw.

Fal'ne and Annor'a were waltzing along the path to the glasshouse, paw in paw, totally unaware of the trap laid for them. After all, the sun streamed through the few breaks in the spruces, the day was warm for winter, and birds were singing freely through the trees—what was to fear?

The roughly hewn door of the crude hut at the edge of the woods was a welcome sight to Fal'ne and Annor'a. They quit their dancing and sprinted forward in a race.

Soon, Shorefish told herself. *Soon.*

The glasshouse was a magical place. Annor'a whispered *Shhh* as they entered and saw the glassblower, a tall otter, working on a glass flower. They knew he heard them enter, but he didn't look up from his flower. Fal'ne stared, enraptured, at the piece of glass. It looked like ice on fire, like a fallen star. Fal'ne knew her mouth dropped, and she knew she was staring, but she was unable to take her eyes from the swimming, morphing, fiery flower. Transfixed, her mind a blank, she would need a while for the spell to be lifted.

"How can they take so long?" Shorefish's second-in-command muttered.

"Patience," Shorefish breathed. "And silence."

A whole hour later, the door opened, and the two young maidens emerged. They were walking ponderously, their steps slow and uneven. *They're bewitched*, Shorefish thought. Watching fire turn into glass was a bewitching thing.

Perfect.

The mice got a hundred yards along the straight path when Shorefish nodded. Her second-in-command slunk forward behind the two young ones and thwacked Fal'ne hard across the head.

Annor'a spun around quickly and screamed before a hilt smashed against her skull. The glassblower banged open his door to see Shorefish's tribe surround the two unconscious maidens. The otters working made a perfect backdrop for Shorefish's part.

She stood, her knife held in exactly the right position, between the glassblower and her tribe, who were hurriedly binding the two captives. "Do not come nearer," she threatened. The amber and gold on her knife caught the single ray of sun and glowed like hot metal. She pointed her paw direly at the glassblower. "Stay there, or you will die."

Her tribe vanished into the woods with their captives, but Shorefish held her ground for a while. "Go back inside your *hut*," she told him with death in her voice.

The glassblower retreated slowly, but he did not close the door.

There was the sound of two warblers calling, and Shorefish stepped back into the shade cast by the trees. A moment later, she was gone.

The glassblower did exactly what the two chieftainesses wanted him to do: he ran to Graystone as fast as he could to raise the alarm. "It's Shorefish," he panted to an alarmed Opal. "I swear it. Her knife was very much in evidence."

And Opal—experienced, wise Opal—was also unable to avoid Shore-fish and Moonpath's trap. "Have all the warriors and able-bodied creatures in the city out to search," she ordered. "You two, run to Kwang-ha`el and try to find out if Wave and Rain can help."

Feldspar shook his head in disbelief. "What is Shorefish doing so close to Graystone?"

"I think she may want hostages," Opal whispered.

Ol'ver frowned. He was frantic. "Why?"

"This is between us," Opal told him in a low voice. "Two weeks ago, we found the wreckage of several boats in the rapids upstream. There were river otter spears in the dead and a fair number of dead river otters. The survivors were brought here. One of them, a female mouse, was dressed in *very* expensive cloth, and she had ornaments around her head made out of pure gold. We think she may be a mercenary chief from Eeried."

Ol'ver expression grew alarmed. "You think Shorefish was the one that attacked them?"

Opal hesitated. "Maybe, maybe not. It was a little far east for her tribe."

Nathan'el heard the whole exchange, though no one noticed him. Silent as a grave, he slipped away through one of the doors in Graystone's wooden walls, a knife at his waist and sword over his back. He *had* to find his sister.

From the woods, Shorefish watched as Graystone steadily emptied of all warriors. *Oh, this is too perfect,* she thought. *Patience. Silence.*

A group of warriors came within range of her ambush. She jumped to her paws and hurled her javelin with all her strength. She did not throw a mortal throw; it passed cleanly through both ears protruding over the head of the mouse in the lead. He yelped with pain and fell. *Hah,* Shorefish thought, *I could take a dozen wounds like that.*

"Shorefish!" yowled the fox behind the mouse. He aimed an arrow at her, but Shorefish ducked. Waving her knife, she beckoned the five with her away into the woods. Elsewhere, she knew, other searchers were getting the same surprise.

The five in her party stopped by a fallen log, and she allowed her warriors to rest. She picked up a hunk of moss and rubbed her knife blade.

At the sound of pawsteps, she froze. The rest of her party saw her freeze, and they too fell silent. Slowly, Shorefish turned to the log.

"Bring out the two maidens," she ordered softly.

From beneath the log, both young ones were dragged roughly out.

"Put your knives at their hearts," Shorefish ordered them.

As she heard her companions drawing their knives, she turned to face the pursuer.

This creature she heard was not a mouse from Graystone. Those from Graystone knew better than to let their paws slither on fallen leaves. This mouse was from a pine forest. Ol'ver—*or Nathan'el*, she decided.

The mouse came around a tree and stopped ten paces from her. Shorefish held her knife high and ready.

"Shorefish," Nathan'el growled.

"Nathan'el of Pasadagavra," Shorefish retorted. "Do you come after your sister?"

"Let them both go," he warned.

"Or?" Shorefish asked, her voice soft as honey. "You can hardly kill me without your sister getting stabbed."

"You can't risk that," Nathan'el told the otter. "In a fight, my sword would shear your tribe's knife in two."

Shorefish felt the brief flicker of doubt. For all that she was a river otter chief and the best fighter in the region, she knew that weapons took damage in a fight. And Nathan'el was more than capable of splitting her ancestral knife in two with his sword. Now Shorefish cursed throwing the javelin earlier. Throwing a weapon might kill, but it left you defenseless later.

A memory of a different fight broke out in Shorefish's mind. Again she saw her father die and remembered his fearlessness of death so long as his tribe endured. Shorefish could not let the ancestral knife be destroyed.

Wait, Shorefish thought, *Nighthawk's death!*

Very slowly, Shorefish placed her amber knife in her belt. Then she drew out the slate knife of the sea otters—the knife that Anamay, daughter of Mudriver, had thrown all those seasons ago. This knife was much heavier than her own, able to be thrown or deflect the kind of sword Nathan'el carried. "Take your knives from the maidens," she ordered her soldiers.

They complied instantly, and Nathan'el relaxed. *Good*, he reasoned. Shorefish didn't really want to kill him.

"Listen to me, Nathan'el son of Ol'ver," Shorefish told him intently. "I have no desire to hurt your sister. There is one thing in Graystone that I want. Go find the rest of the warriors and tell them that the maidens will be returned to them when they bring what I want."

"And what do you want?"

"Nothing of theirs. Bring a score of others here, and I will tell them that. Tell them to come unarmored and peacefully, and I will bear no weapons against them."

Nathan'el looked torn. His sister and her friend lay just beyond the river otter, hurt and probably in danger, despite what Shorefish said.

Shorefish saw his doubt.

She knew what to do. She lifted her canteen to her lips, unscrewed the cap with her teeth, and tilted it back, drinking deeply. Then she passed the canteen to one of her warriors. "Give the maidens some water."

Nathan'el relaxed even more as the obviously safe drink was splashed down his sister's unconscious lips. He lowered his sword.

"Very well," he told the river otter. "I will get them."

He backed away slowly. When he reached a bare ash tree, he glanced once more at his sister and ran back in the direction of Graystone.

Shorefish pressed the flat of the slate throwing knife against her heart in relief. "Thank you, Father," she whispered. "You saved my life and our tribe and quite possibly our land when you died."

As Nathan'el ran back with his message, what was left of Graystone's garrison donned armor and weapons, ready to march into the woods where Shorefish was. They had no plans of giving Shorefish anything but what she deserved.

Opal watched her friend's anxious face. "Ol'ver, you do realize that it could be *you* they're after."

Ol'ver turned to Opal. "If Shorefish is after me as well as Ran'ta, then I intend to be there and give her a piece of my mind."

Nathan'el was invisible to the two older warriors, but his pulse suddenly quickened. That didn't sound like what he was told about his mother … had Shorefish taken his mother, too?

Shorefish went back to the site of the ambush and retrieved her javelin. All river otter leaders carried javelins as well as the knives, and she wanted something a little more substantial besides two knives. She didn't believe for one instant that the warriors from Graystone would come to bargain peacefully. She sighed to herself. If they did, she would get what she wanted by bargaining. If they didn't, all their warriors would be gone, and her quarry would be hers anyway, along with the two maidens. She stopped and prayed fervently that the warriors would come unarmed and tranquilly, hoping for the sake of the two mice. She didn't want Moonpath anywhere near the daughters of Ol'ver and Feldspar.

Among the party, Ol'ver spotted Nathan'el. Ol'ver forced his way through the milling soldiers and gripped his son's shoulder. "Nathan'el, you stay in Graystone. I don't want you out there."

"Let me go, Father," Nathan'el begged, knowing the word "father" had a certain effect on Ol'ver. "I want my sister back too!" He looked pleadingly into Ol'ver's eyes. "Father, you taught me how to take care of myself. I'll be fine! I promise I'll be careful!"

Ol'ver's eyes were shadowed, but he nodded. "Stay well back."

Nathan'el nodded, fully intending to obey his father.

The trumpet sounded, and the throng marched out the city. They were not an army, but they knew how to fight.

Shorefish's tribe was congregated by the time the sound of pounding paws announced Graystone's warriors approaching. One of Shorefish's sentries slipped back to the log and whispered the headcount. She was a little surprised by the number but shook that away. They didn't have a clue what was going on.

Shorefish made some frantic paw gestures, and the rest of her tribe gathered behind her as a bulwark in-between the two maidens and the "army" from Graystone.

Fal'ne came slowly awake behind the army. She made a few strangled noises.

The nearest otter to her, a female, dropped to her knee. "Quiet," she whispered to the captive. "One way or another, you'll be taken back to Graystone. Just be patient, and be silent."

Shorefish heard the otter's rough but reassuring words. *Patience and silence*, she thought to herself. *That's the order of the day. And if this goes wrong, it may be the order of the remainder of my life.*

The warriors marched up to Shorefish and stopped, though not in unison. Shorefish thought to herself that it was a miracle the pikemice didn't spit some of their comrades with their disorderly handling of the long weapons.

"I said you would receive the children if you came peacefully," Shorefish began dramatically. Her eyes roved meaningfully over the chain mail and occasional breastplates.

"Graystone does not bargain with thieves," Opal growled from the front. Her sling began to whirl.

Shorefish raised her spear threateningly. "Slings! They take forever to launch. By the time your stone had enough momentum, you would be dead by my spear. Are you *now* ready to listen?"

Opal immediately saw the disadvantage she had against the battle-wise otter. "I'm listening."

"Life for life," Shorefish stated. "The mice you found in the rapids were prisoners of ours. Return them to us, and you will have your maidens back."

Shorefish saw Opal's paw inching towards the shoulder of her tunic of chain mail, and Shorefish realized Opal concealed a knife there. With a sigh, she realized there was no possibility of avoiding a fight.

"Life for life," Opal repeated. "And death for kidnappers." At once, swords, pikes, and knives all flashed. Opal snatched her knife out and flew at Shorefish.

And so the battle began.

Shorefish was a fighter, and her soldiers had fought with her since she could wield a sword. Though her group was smaller than the Graystone army, she had an enormous advantage: all her warriors knew exactly what to do in any given situation. They spent hours practicing various maneuvers so they could all react immediately and in unison to a single word from their leader. Graystone had no such practice, and most of their military training involved fathers teaching children how to use swords. They were woefully unprepared to stand up to Shorefish's ragtag and rogue army, which in a way was even more disciplined than the armies of the empires of old.

However, Shorefish didn't want to obliterate the army of Graystone.

She drew her sea otter's knife and used that to deflect Opal's first slash and then smashed the heavy hilt against the leader's knife paw. "Get the maidens out of here!" she shouted, knowing that one of her warriors would obey.

Opal switched paws with her knife, and again, she and Shorefish locked in knife-to-knife combat. Shorefish heard a warning behind her and spun just in time to smash the basalt hilt across the forehead of a charging Graystone fox. She then spun in equal speed and deflected another of Opal's knife slashes. The Graystone leader jumped back, gasping as Shorefish kicked her side viciously.

The rogue looked desperately around, trying to get a headcount of her remaining fighters. *Good*, she thought. She saw none down and the maidens were well away.

And then she heard a wild yell that froze her in her tracks.

As if in slow motion, she looked behind the ranks of Graystone.

It was Coll'n, that Keron Mouse and some of his band! Shorefish gasped. What were the nomadic Keron Mice doing so far from the Keron River where they lived? Even worse, Coll'n loathed Shorefish in particular.

This just got interesting, Shorefish thought.

The Keron Mice split simultaneously, running around the struggling armies of Graystone. They were going to hit Shorefish on the flank.

"Form a circle!" Shorefish shrieked above the melée.

As one, her fighters dodged around their adversaries and formed into a tight ball, and yet again, Shorefish had the upper paw, though she hadn't noticed it. Her tribe had spent arduous hours in the morning clearing out the area by the fallen log, and in the fading afternoon light, the Keron Mice, who were boatmice, couldn't make their way around the tangles of undergrowth outside the circle quickly enough. The otters had more than enough time to solidify their position in the circle. The Keron Mice had simply reached the flanks too late, and Shorefish had no objection to obliterating *their* army.

She realized then that she had the upper paw and whooped with triumph. Catching one dying ray of sunlight, she held her golden knife aloft where the sun and the light and the amber flashed briefly in a signal to a darkening world.

Moonpath saw the signal. Silent as could be, her tribe slithered from the woods on Graystone's back side to the postern in the far wall, well away from the open fields. The hospital wasn't too far away from here. She inserted her dagger into the lock on the postern, and the door clicked open. Her warriors filed in silently.

"Remember," she hissed savagely. "You're looking for a white building with a tall cedar tree in front.

Her tribe split up into their preordained groups and scoured the deserted streets near to the gate.

"There, chief!" whispered one of those with her.

Moonpath reached for the wooden whistles at her waist and chose the one carved like a sparrow. She blew a random-seeming patter, but one her crew knew well.

They all gathered around the door, and Moonpath opened it with her knife. None of the physicians was here; they had all been called to the battlefield in case they could be of help. The whole crew of warriors filtered in and began to search it, top to bottom.

Moonpath climbed up to the third floor where she saw a door at the end of the hall. The paper signs on the doors on the other levels all had the name of the patient, the age, and the aliment they suffered from. On this door there read *Unknown Name, Unknown Age, Amnesia.*

Moonpath opened the door slowly. *Amnesia, my tail.*

The white mouse inside was sitting on a stool gazing out the window and didn't hear the door open. Moonpath looked at the mouse for a long while, making sure this was the right one before she uttered the name. It wouldn't do for Graystone to know what she was looking for, and a body left behind would alert them to her presence.

Finally she was sure. Her voice changed from its hissing growl to a sweet, honey-smooth tone. "Good evening, Princess Kiarna."

The princess jumped and turned, her blue eyes wild at first. "Oh, it's just you, Moonpath," she sighed. Then her face grew anxious. "You haven't told those at Graystone who I am, have you?"

"I haven't seen them," Moonpath replied.

Kiarna looked confused for a moment before it dawned on her. "You snuck in," she whispered. "And you are kidnapping me."

Moonpath smiled behind her silk veil. "Guilty as charged." She pointed her knife coldly at Kiarna. "I do, of course, have permission to silence you."

Kiarna looked around the room desperately, as if trying to find any weapons. When she could not, she stood reluctantly. Unlike those at Graystone, she understood that it was sometimes wisest simply to go along.

Moonpath kept the dagger pointed at Kiarna the whole time the princess walked down the three flights of stairs. Kiarna tilted her head high with queenly dignity—she had once been, for all practical purposes, Miamur's queen—but she nearly faltered when they reached the bottom of the stairs. On the ground floor were gathered the nine of her company who had survived the attack by the river otter Doomspear and his tribe.

"Trying to get back to Miamur after they saw what they saw," Moonpath deduced. "And Doomspear wasn't fast enough—or dedicated enough. Well, no matter. All ten are here now." Then she whirled on one of her warriors. "Get them outside now! We must be gone before the Graystone army returns."

Obediently, the tribe bound the paws of the Miamurans and thrust them outside the hospital. No one from Graystone had thought their rapids survivor would be a Miamuran princess, and they might just assume that she had left on her own. Moonpath sent a couple of the warriors back up into the rooms to clear out all belongings to make it look as if they had left on their own.

The whole operation barely took an hour. Moonpath urged her tribe away from the city, and they melted into the woods heading back to the camp where the two rivers became one.

Moonpath found Shorefish already back at the camp. "You're back early," Moonpath observed to her compatriot.

"You should have been the one to cover the glasshouse," Shorefish snapped angrily. "Coll'n's mice were in Graystone. They were difficult to fight, even though I had every advantage I could want. *And*, as if the Keron Mice weren't enough, about an hour after the fight started, *Wave and Rain* and the otters from Kwang-ha`el showed up. My *cousins*, Moonpath! Opal must have sent to them for help."

"We have the princess, though," Moonpath purred. "And I see you still have the maidens."

"Who cares? We're letting them go anyway," Shorefish snarled.

Moonpath sat down, and she was smiling sickly. Shorefish could see it in her eyes.

"That's the little detail I left out," Moonpath informed in her nauseating voice. "We can't let go of any prisoners we capture. They come back to Dobar for slaves."

Fal'ne was bound to a tree, but she heard Moonpath's every word. *Slaves? Dobar? Since when did the Wraith Mice have slaves?*

"Not a chance," Shorefish snarled, leaping to her paws. "They're *my* prisoners. I caught them; I decide what to do with them. And *I* say let them go."

"Think, Shorefish," Moonpath smirked. "Did you really think the king would help us purge our lands if we didn't bring him something in exchange?"

"He demanded captives in exchange for helping us?" she gasped out. "You can forget that; I'm no slaver!"

"But what of that Cliff Mouse Ran'ta?" Moonpath argued smugly.

My mother? Fal'ne thought.

"That was different," Shorefish declared coldly. "She was dangerous."

"Shorefish, that's part of the mission," Moonpath said flatly.

"I knew there was a reason to ask the king himself before I accepted his treaty," Shorefish spat. She cursed savagely. "If he wants slaves, I won't stick with him."

"Shorefish," Moonpath interrupted sternly. "He offers to have his hordes help us regain our lands."

Shorefish spun around and faced Moonpath, her ceremonial knife in paw. "So did the Darkwoods Foxes! I trusted them to help me regain my lands, and Queen Demeda showed me a treaty by the Oracles and that bloody sea otter chief Current in which the sea otters offered to bring them any captives they caught! You yourself heard Current discussing the treaty!" Shorefish turned away and took several deep breaths; the memory of the Darkwoods foxes' betrayal still burned in her, igniting anger.

"It's the same, Moonpath!" Shorefish told her urgently when she regained her temper. "He's trying to get captives and slaves just as Oracle Hemlock did."

Who? Fal'ne thought in alarm.

"He's no more trustworthy than the foxes," Shorefish continued. "Think!"

"It's two maidens who you don't know," Moonpath said flatly. "Or your land. Your ancestral land. The home your father died for."

"Moonpath, I don't trust anyone who asks for slaves," Shorefish declared bluntly. Then her head lifted and her blue eyes brightened, and she turned around to face Moonpath. "Besides, the sea otters took slaves in exchange for the alliance. If we take slaves, what are we?"

"Desperate," Moonpath shrugged. "Our situations are very different."

"So what?" Shorefish snapped. "We have miles to go through dangerous territory. Let the maidens go, and we're home free."

"It's too late now," Moonpath replied. She turned so her eyes were locked with Fal'ne's.

Shorefish followed her ally's gaze and saw Fal'ne's alert, open eyes. Dismay stabbed at the chieftain's heart; the maiden had heard too much. She could not be allowed to go now.

Fal'ne stared back, unabashed, unaware what had just put her into trouble.

Shorefish held Fal'ne's eyes momentarily. Then she turned away and muttered to her tribe to take care of the maiden. "And try to wake the other," she added.

"What are their names?" Moonpath asked curiously.

"No idea," Shorefish lied. Of course she knew, but there was no way she'd tell Moonpath. That otter was crazy.

"Naturally not," Moonpath hissed smoothly. "You don't do interrogations the proper way."

"They've been out cold," Shorefish reminded Moonpath.

Moonpath's eyes crinkled; she was smiling a wicked smile. "Watch this."

She stood up and went to where Fal'ne and Annor'a were tied. From beneath her hood she drew a small crystal bottle filled with a bright red liquid. Shorefish's blood ran cold. That was a drug that pirates sometimes brought over from the east—a truth drug and very potent.

"Where did you get that?" Shorefish exclaimed.

"A pirate sold it to me," Moonpath replied. Her tone had the eager, anticipatory lilt that came when she was about to cause a certain amount of horror to someone.

As Shorefish watched, Moonpath drew the stopper out of the vial and gestured to one of her own tribe. "Tilt the maiden's head back."

Fal'ne watched fearfully as the unknown liquid drew nearer to her. The otter grabbed her ears and tilted her head back, holding her jaw open. Moonpath deliberately poured a few drops down Fal'ne's throat.

It didn't taste very bad. In fact, Fal'ne's mind, previously fuddled and confused, calmed down, and her body relaxed.

"Now, little one," Moonpath crooned. Her voice didn't sound at all threatening under the influence of the drug. "Could you perhaps tell me what your name is?"

Fal'ne saw no reason to withhold that information. "I'm Fal'ne," she replied, her voice dreamy.

Moonpath, thank Cerecinthia, didn't recognize the name. "And who is your companion?"

"Her name is Annor'a," Fal'ne answered.

Please! Shorefish thought desperately. *Bear King, please don't let Moonpath ask whose daughters they are!*

"Do you know who I am?" Moonpath asked.

On Fal'ne's ears, the voice sounded soothing and relaxed. To Shorefish, it sounded like the stroke of doom.

"You're Moonpath," Fal'ne replied apathetically.

"Did you know the name of the white mouse?" Moonpath pressured.

Bear King! Shorefish thought. *Thank you!*

"What white mouse?" Fal'ne asked unemotionally.

"You didn't know her?"

No! Shorefish thought in panic. *Please, no!*

"I don't know who you mean." Fal'ne's voice sounded dazed. The drug, hopefully, was wearing off. "Know who?"

"The white mouse," Moonpath urged the little one. Shorefish couldn't see her eyes, but she could guess the dawning understanding. "The one who was found in the rapids and brought to Graystone—probably three weeks ago. You must have seen her."

"I was on a journey to Graystone three weeks ago," Fal'ne replied, totally unaware.

Moonpath inhaled sharply. "On a—?"

She grew silent. Her breath became rapid and excited. Then she spoke again. "Whose daughter are you?"

Bear King, protect her! Shorefish screamed inwardly, her heart racing in the beginnings of panic.

"Ol'ver's daughter," Fal'ne answered.

No!

Moonpath had hit a goldmine. "And whose daughter is your friend?"

"She's the daughter of Feldspar," Fal'ne said.

Moonpath jumped to her paws and whirled to face Shorefish. "The Bear King has favored us!" she breathed. "Now how hard will it be to persuade Ran'ta to tell us what she knows of Princess Zuryzel!"

Shorefish stared long and hard at Moonpath in the flickering firelight. "You want to torture Fal'ne to convince Ran'ta?" she whispered incredulously.

Moonpath made a contemptuous noise. "You're so soft!" she hissed. With that, she spun on her heel and stalked away.

Shorefish's heart was racing. Just earlier that day, she'd been struck by how her father's death had saved her life. Now she was taking part in a scheme to torture a mother's love for her child.

Patience, she told herself. *Silence.* She didn't want Moonpath to suspect her; Moonpath's tribe was much bigger than hers. *Patience and silence. I must wait for an opening to release Fal'ne. And I must not say a word about my own plans.*

The setting sun bathed the cold forests of the sea otters in a sort of golden other-worldliness, and Starfish felt it with relief. There was no lack of comfort in glowing gold melting across the trees. She sat in front of her cottage, her day's work complete, with Sh'vendi and Baklenne.

"You look cold," Baklenne observed.

"I'm not," Starfish answered truthfully. "Just worried about what the bolts mean, that's all."

"Did the scouts see any sign of pirates?" Sh'vendi asked interestedly.

Starfish shook her head. "If they did, Eagle hasn't told me yet."

"We're leaving tomorrow," Sh'vendi announced sadly.

"I'm sorry to hear that," Starfish answered. The company of this group of merchants was a blessing from the Bear King himself.

"And we wanted to pay you for putting us up again," Baklenne picked up. There was a mirthful glimmer in her eye.

"That isn't necessary," Starfish insisted. "I enjoy having company."

"Nonetheless, we've done all sorts of trading and made quite a profit," Sh'vendi told her, putting a kind paw on her shoulder. "But your kindness is worth more than we can ever give."

"Anyone would be glad to help travelers," Starfish protested humbly.

"Oh, you'd be surprised," Baklenne snorted.

"We have something for you and your brother and father," Sh'vendi continued. "So as soon as they get back, we'll give it to you."

In the forests by Graystone, the scene was not so pleasant. Half of Graystone's army was celebrating its victory; Ol'ver, Feldspar, and Nathan'el were searching for any signs of Fal'ne and Annor'a but with no snow to aid tracking in the sheltered woods. The river otters Wave and Rain, the two chieftains of Kwang-ha`el, were trying to track down Shorefish, but even in the haste of her retreat, Shorefish had covered her tracks. She knew what she was doing.

After an hour of searching, Nathan'el decided that things had gone far enough. He drew his father aside and said, "Father, I have something to ask you."

"Go ahead."

"Did Shorefish capture mother?" Nathan'el asked very deliberately. "Like Fal'ne?"

Ol'ver held his son's gaze for a long time. "Yes," he admitted finally. "She did."

Nathan'el spun around and looked desperately into the woods. His baby sister was out there somewhere, and possibly his mother. "Why?" he demanded.

"I honestly don't know, except that maybe your mother knew something. Strange things have happened near Arashna, and I fear Ran'ta may have seen something."

Nathan'el stared hard into the forest, as if he could find his mother amongst the trees. "Father, let me go after Fal'ne."

"No," Ol'ver forbade him instantly. "It's dangerous."

"I'm also dangerous," Nathan'el replied. "Very dangerous. I can bring her back." He turned around and looked his father in the eye. "Father, I won't do anything rash, I swear. But I want my sister back, and you taught me how to do that kind of thing. Let me go!"

Ol'ver was tempted to go after his daughter himself, and bring Nathan'el along to boot. But his side hurt from a wound he'd received, and his son was unhurt. He could, he supposed, wait until he was healed, but by then

Shorefish could be anywhere. Nathan'el needed to follow her *now* while she could be found again. Shorefish had already proven that she could disappear for weeks on end. And Nathan'el *wasn't* a child anymore, no matter how much Ol'ver wished he was.

"All right," he relented. "But if you can, send messages back."

"Of course," Nathan'el replied.

He slung his sword onto his back, grabbed the cloak from where it had fallen, and with that was gone into the woods.

"Come home safely, my son," Ol'ver whispered.

7

SHADOWS FALL

Conch hefted a sack higher on his shoulder, trying hard to avoid Saline's gaze. He *had* volunteered for this expedition to Kwang-ha`el but not because he had expected to get some sort of enjoyment. No, Eagle had wanted one of Anamay Mudriver's children to accompany Saline, and Conch would far rather he go than Starfish.

As for Saline, she had to go. She was Eagle's sister, a fact the river otters would be well aware of. Conch was very fond of her, but he could tell she was nervous, and he could think of nothing to say to ease her mind.

Pearl, Abalone, and Limpet seemed oblivious to Saline's discomfort as they chattered blissfully a few paces behind.

"Rain and Wave will listen, won't they?" Saline asked when they were halfway to the city.

The sea otters had been following the Kyaagha Brook through the forest, and as Conch glimpsed its waters, he yearned to dive in. "They should," he murmured. "I think."

"But their mother was one of our clan's enemies," Saline fretted. "And so were their uncle and their cousin!"

"When Danaray talked about them," Conch murmured, "she always said something about pride. They didn't think much of their mother or Shorefish or Nighthawk. All their family's constant defeats embarrassed them. That's why they built Kwang-ha`el. The name is a combination of *kwanga* and *haeriel*. *Kwanga* means a place of defense, and *haeriel* is a new start."

"They'll listen to me if they don't listen to you," Conch assured her. "They wouldn't risk offending my aunt."

Conch had heard stories about their defense of Kwang-ha`el. Remnants of the Darkwoods foxes, hostile river otters, and even an Eerieden mercenary band had tried to wrest the city from Rain and Wave, but the river otters had successfully beaten off every advance. But he was fairly sure that Danaray *could* shake them out of Kwang-ha`el if she had a mind to.

"I hope you're right, Conch," Saline murmured. "I just wish my brother would have come."

"He's the chieftain," Conch reminded her gently. "He wants to be in the village if there's any more fighting."

Saline nodded again. "Bear King grant there won't be."

Indeed, Conch thought.

"I need a rest," Saline decided. "We've come halfway already."

"We could look for a shallow part of the river," Conch suggested. "There must be one at some point."

Saline twisted around. "Abalone, scout ahead for a shallow bend. We can rest there."

The warrior saluted her by pressing his paw to his opposite shoulder and proceeded to lope forward in search of a place to rest.

Redfin was a young river otter maiden under Shorefish's command. She was too young to remember Nighthawk, but her brother used to tell her stories about Shorefish's father. Nighthawk had sounded so brave to Redfin, but part of that was because her brother was such a wonderful storyteller.

Or he *had* been. His storytelling days were over. His body lay exposed in a forest near Graystone.

Redfin was given permission to search for some edible roots, but as soon as she was out of sight of other otters, she fell to her knees weeping.

One of Moonpath's otters, a veteran fighter called Treefrost, found her amongst the leafless bushes and immediately put his paw about her shoulder. "There, there now," he soothed. "What's this?"

"Let me be," Redfin begged. "Please, let me be."

Treefrost didn't leave her. "I'm scouting the way ahead," he murmured. "We have to look out for Rain and Wave, or they might ambush us. Why don't you come with me? A young set of eyes is always appreciated!"

Redfin struggled to her paws. "Thank you."

"What is your name?" Treefrost asked as they struck northwest through the undergrowth.

"Redfin," the younger otter replied. "You must be one of Moonpath's otters."

Treefrost nodded. "That I am. My name is Treefrost. For whom were you weeping, Redfin?"

Redfin burst into more tears. "My brother!"

Treefrost understood immediately. "Ah," he sighed. "Was he one of the dead left back at Graystone?"

Redfin nodded. "Just like my mother and father—they were left behind, long ago. Now my brother, too. I'm all alone!"

Treefrost wiped a tear from her cheek. "There, now. You must have friends."

"It isn't the same," Redfin whispered.

Treefrost laughed bitterly. "Survive enough hopeless battles, and they'll become the same quickly enough."

They pressed northwest and soon heard raised voices. Treefrost raised his paw, and both he and Redfin ducked down. They slithered between the undergrowth and soon saw the owners of the voices: five sea otters playing in the frigid river.

"Look at them!" Redfin hissed. "We could catch them easily! Knock out the maidens and get the males to carry them at spear point!"

But Treefrost had a different idea. "Redfin, do you see that one off by himself? Under that huckleberry bush?"

Redfin nodded. "I see him. What about him?"

"I'd know his face anywhere," Treefrost murmured, almost to himself. "He looks so much like his aunt. That is the face of the son of Anamay, nephew of Danaray Mudriver!"

Redfin hissed in quiet jubilation. "Chieftainess Shorefish has been itching to get her paws on him for as long as I can remember! She'd reward us brilliantly if we brought him back!"

"*No!*" Treefrost warned, pressing his paw on her shoulder. "Think of how Chieftainess *Mudriver* would reward us!"

"We can't just *leave* him!" Redfin protested.

Treefrost sighed. "Child, as you get older, you'll realize that there is a time for everything. Now is *not* the time to pick a fight with Danaray Mudriver. Best we say nothing to the chieftainesses of our seeing him." He smiled a slow smile. "The others, on the other paw ... would make quite a nice addition to the Miamuran princess."

Nathan'el had left sea otter territory long behind before he caught up to Moonpath and Shorefish. It was intensely difficult tracking them, although at least his pursuit wasn't hampered by chance encounters with other creatures. No one seemed to be in this area at all.

He heard them before he saw them and quickly realized, to his satisfaction, that they were arguing.

"Curse it all!" one female otter voice carried through the trees. "We are not slavers, and for the last time, it won't do any good to put our trust in this king!"

"Who says we should trust him? Shorefish, be sensible."

"*You* telling me to be sensible, Moonpath?"

"Never mind. We have to move! Graystone's army could come after us."

"And so? My tribe got away from them once. Twice shouldn't be too hard."

"Don't turn aggressive, Shorefish. Now isn't the time."

"Again, this from *you?*"

Just in front of him, a hollow log leaned up an outcropping of rock. Very quietly, he scurried into the log and climbed precariously through it until he could look through the opening. His vantage point gave him a view from above the undergrowth, and he thought it unlikely they would look up when looking for intruders.

The two tribes had halted in a rocky clearing and appeared to be recuperating from the battle of the previous day. Some polished weapons while others repacked bags, and Nathan'el spotted seven lookouts. He was sure there were more, but he couldn't see them.

In the center of the tribes were twelve mice: ten that he didn't recognize, and Fal'ne and Annor'a.

Can you see me? Nathan'el silently cried out to his sister. *Are you all right? Have they hurt you? I'll find a way to free you, I promise!*

Then another voice drifted in from the northwest. "Chieftainess!"

Shorefish—Nathan'el recognized her easily—turned toward the sound. "What is it?"

The undergrowth parted, and Nathan'el blinked in amazement. Two river otters led three sea otters, two female and one male, right before Shorefish.

"We found these to the northwest," the older river otter reported smugly. "*Far* out of the boundaries of their territory."

Moonpath released a triumphant hiss. "Were these the only ones you found?"

"There was only one more," the older otter answered. "He tried to kill young Redfin here, so she ran him through with her spear." (Which was not true; Treefrost had done the deed but decided to let the younger one take the credit.) "The others surrendered quickly."

One of the female otters promptly spat in Treefrost's face. For a moment he was stunned; then he recovered, and he drove his paw into the side of her head. She crumpled into a heap.

"No!" the male sea otter cried. He lunged for her, but two river otters grabbed his paws and held him back.

"Enough!" Moonpath snapped. "These three will come with us to Arashna. Make ready to move out!"

The river otters promptly rose to their paws, some binding ropes around the captives. Moonpath surveyed them with a satisfied gleam in her eyes while Shorefish maneuvered among her tribe mates, urging them to more speed. "Time is everything!" her voice carried to Nathan'el. "Everything depends on this!"

One of the ten mice from the tent threw himself violently against his guard but to no avail. He was weakened from the trauma of his journey.

"We need to go *now!*" Shorefish called. "Hurry!"

Nathan'el retreated into the fallen log, determined to follow them until he managed to free his sister.

The forests the river otters hiked through were primarily widespread deciduous trees. There were so many blackberries and ivy vines hanging from the branches that they almost blocked out the sky, even though there were no leaves on the boughs. Everything was brown and white—brown from the trees and brambles and white from the snow. They marched alongside the river, which made enough noise to cover the sound of their voices.

One of Shorefish's scouts slid through the water and got onto the shore beside his chief and out of sight of Moonpath. "There's a band of merchants about a mile ahead of us," he muttered. "Among them are a river otter and a silver-and-black mouse. I heard the others call the otter Baklenne and the mouse Sh'vendi."

"So?"

"The one they called Baklenne had a knife hilt protruding out of her pack," he muttered. "Silver worked into fancy art and studded with sapphires."

"And the top is a wave?" Shorefish whispered incredulously. "With a diamond set in its crest?"

"Exactly," the scout confirmed.

"Shinar?" Shorefish breathed. "What in the name of the Bear King is she doing so far from Arashna? Her tribe has been harassing the king's patrols for weeks! Why is she down here?"

The scout shrugged. "I don't know. But the mouse I recognized too. She had bright amber eyes and a thick green cloak."

"*Rainbow*? A Ranger out of her home?" Shorefish shook her head. "It looks as if our king isn't the only one executing secret maneuvers."

"His sister, you mean?"

They didn't notice one of Kiarna's soldiers listening carefully to the whole conversation.

Shorefish nodded slowly. "That's what it looks like. Lady Crow would gladly aid the princess, wouldn't she? I wonder if Shinar knows that Danaray just picked up and left her not-so-ancestral land?"

"Do we even know why Danaray camped there for such a long time anyway?" the scout muttered.

"To keep an eye on Anamay's children," Shorefish replied dismissively.

The mention of Anamay's children reminded Shorefish of Starfish and the crossbow bolt embedded in her. *Pirates ... what were they even doing inland?*

And thinking of pirates brought to mind Moonpath's truth drug, which she had bought from them. Finally, Shorefish realized ...

"Go back and keep an eye on Shinar, but don't let Moonpath know," she ordered her scout. Then Shorefish very deliberately slid through the tramping ranks of otters until she reached Moonpath's side. "What else did you buy from the pirates?" she hissed angrily.

Moonpath looked at her. "What do you mean?"

"The truth drug. What else did you buy?"

"A few weapons," Moonpath replied evasively.

Anger sparked in Shorefish's eyes. "I was tracking *you* the day I saw Danaray's aide found by Mollusk and his chief! There were pirate bolts all over that place, but no other signs of pirates—and no pirate could be stealthy enough to avoid detection from a river otter. You bought the crossbows, didn't you?"

Moonpath smirked, another thing Shorefish could see in her eyes. "I didn't expect you to catch on, Shorefish. Well done."

"Don't patronize me," Shorefish hissed. "Who did you buy them from?"

"Snowhawk. Captain of *Nygoan*."

"Snowhawk is one of the Wraith Mouse princess's friends," Shorefish reminded her acidly.

"You said yourself to not wholly trust the king. Did you think me stupid?"

Shorefish glared at her long and hard. Then she resumed her former place.

🐁

The first thing Conch became aware of was a throbbing pain in the back of his skull. The next was that his pelt was damp and water swirled around his tail. The third was a voice he didn't recognize murmuring his name. At least it *sounded* like his name, the name his aunt had given him when he was an infant.

Wren, the voice murmured repeatedly. *Wren, Wren, Wren ...*

Mama?

A moment later, cool water splashed over his face.

"Are you awake?" asked a new voice.

After a second, the water worked its magic. The voice he'd thought belonged to Anamay was really nothing but the river gliding over stones. His paws were still covered in Limpet's blood—his friend's body had rolled away when the young river otter had thwacked Conch's head with her spear.

"Who are you?" he mumbled to the creature who had roused him.

"Nathan'el, son of Ol'ver," the stranger murmured. "Were you with three other sea otters? Traveling somewhere?"

"Four," Conch murmured weakly. "They killed one—at least one."

"Three others were taken to Shorefish and Moonpath," the stranger filled in.

At the names, Conch's eyes snapped open. "When?" he demanded of the mouse on his knees in the undergrowth.

"Less than an hour ago," Nathan'el replied, sounding uncertain. "My sister is in Moonpath's paws, too."

Ignoring the pain in his skull, Conch struggled to sit up. He didn't recognize the woods around him or the creek he had been tossed into. "Where are they?"

Nathan'el twitched an ear. "Heading north towards a place called Nikor Mais."

*Kwang-ha`el.* "We were traveling to Kwang-ha`el. How far ... where ..."

"I've no idea where it is. I have no idea where we are. I'm just following Shorefish and Moonpath."

Conch rolled over and got unsteadily to his paws, ignoring the forest as it swam around him. "How far ahead are they?"

Nathan'el eyed him carefully. "No more than a league ahead."

Conch gave a slow nod, and the forest steadied around him. "Mind if I tag along?"

8

THE CAPTIVES' FRIENDS

Together, the two headed for the river otters ahead of them. Nathan'el was not the best at silent movement through the thickly overgrown forests that Shorefish and Moonpath traveled through. He and Conch stayed well back, Conch occasionally slipping into the river to watch the otters from there. That evening after hours of following the river otters, Nathan'el froze. "What's that?"

There was a thrumming in the distance. Not loud, probably not enough to attract Shorefish's attention, but Nathan'el heard it.

"What is it?" muttered Conch.

"I think it's the Keron Mice," whispered Nathan'el.

With that, he was flitting off through the trees.

Conch hesitated but went after him just the same. "Why are we going to the Keron Mice?" he asked irritably.

"Because it's better to approach them than to be caught sneaking past them."

The beating of the drum grew louder. Nathan'el paused several times to look through the trees. After Conch felt sure they would see the drum in just a few feet, a cold voice rang out. "Stop there if you want to live."

The mouse was speaking to Conch, not Nathan'el, and so the Cliff Mouse straightened and faced the Keron Mouse.

A long way ahead of Shorefish and Moonpath, the band of merchants stopped to rest. The leader of the group and a few others opened their bags to make sure nothing was missing. The mouse and river otter who had stayed with Starfish walked apart from the group to compile their information.

Shinar the river otter, known to some as Baklenne, shook her head indecisively. "I just don't know. Where would crossbow bolts and puffin feathers come from if not pirates?"

Rainbow the Ranger Orlysk (or ordinary soldier) was more convinced than Shinar, and she had shed the patience and idleness she assumed when pretending to be Sh'vendi. "What is there not to know? You yourself said there was no way pirates could remain unseen from the forest. It must have been river otters."

"But we didn't see any!" Shinar protested.

"Norya has been watching the forest behind us," Rainbow mused. "She might have seen them."

Shinar bunched herself together. "I don't understand why Zuryzel is so worried about the *sea otters*. They have long since ceased to be of importance."

"They hold Zurez," Rainbow replied firmly. "And Zuryzel is interested in what Mokimshim is interested in. It's sound thinking."

At that moment, a crow practically fell out of the sky and landed in between the two of them.

"What did you see, Norya?" Rainbow asked.

The crow gave Rainbow an unblinking stare. "Orlysk, I saw the same sea otters that I saw the last time I was down here. Current. Curse him! But more important things I saw. There is a band of river otters wending through the trees. Moonpath I saw easily. She is as mad as ever and as dangerous, but she never saw me. Shorefish was in the same group, but on the other side, speaking very quietly with one of her tribe. I would say the two have become allies but are fighting."

"Allies!" Shinar gasped. "What reason could Shorefish have to be allied with that cold-hearted dizzy-headed numb-pawed barbarian?"

"To regain her land," Rainbow replied evenly. "Remember how once she joined Oracle Hemlock? Then when Queen Demeda showed proof of Hemlock's treachery, Shorefish broke off that alliance."

"After she shouted herself hoarse," Shinar smirked. "I remember; I was there. And since then she's had various, desperate alliances. But I had no idea she was *Moonpath* desperate."

"Moonpath desperate?" Rainbow repeated quizzically. "What does that mean?"

"If you'd ever had to negotiate with Moonpath, you'd know," Shinar replied philosophically.

"Continue, Norya," Rainbow sighed.

"The news about Moonpath was not my important news," the crow declared coldly.

"Then forgive our interruption," Rainbow apologized.

Norya glared once more at Shinar and continued, "Marching in the center of the group of otters were several captives. There were some sea otters I didn't recognize. There were two young mice females—one of them looked to be from Graystone. But in the very center was Princess Kiarna."

Rainbow gasped, and Shinar bit her paw. "Kiarna knows so much," moaned Rainbow. "She has to be freed!"

"How?" Shinar cried. "I *knew* it was foolish to trust Miamur!"

"Zuryzel had to," Rainbow sighed. "Out of all the kingdoms in this world, Miamur has one of the strongest armies since they didn't fight in the Darkwoods conquest."

"There were dozens of others that didn't," Shinar argued.

"But we always knew what side they were on," Rainbow shrugged. "There aren't many rulers we can say that about. Galledor and Kiarna were always very stable, even if the rest of their family wasn't."

"The princess must be freed," Norya stated. "And soon. Moonpath has a truth drug. That was one of the things she and Shorefish argued about."

Rainbow stood up heavily and began to pace. "They're in dangerous territory," she mused. "But so are we. I have no idea how to contact the Keron Mice."

"Half of them are in Graystone, anyway," Norya added. "The others are scattered through the woods. They could be of no help to you."

Rainbow gasped softly, realization glistening in her eyes.

"Then what do we *do*?" Shinar groaned.

"I could try to pick most of the otters off with my arrows," Rainbow murmured. "But I'm not sure I could get them all."

"Truly," Shinar agreed. "We need a *diversion*."

"You think Moonpath will run after a diversion when her prize is in her paws?" Rainbow asked scathingly. "She'll guard Kiarna to the death."

"There *must* be a way!" Shinar insisted.

Rainbow thought for a few minutes. "Where are they headed?" she asked finally.

"Nikor Mais, I believe," Norya deduced.

"Then when they reach Nikor Mais, we will act," Rainbow decided.

"When they're in the deepest fortifications this side of Lunep?" Shinar asked heavily. "You can't break into Nikor Mais. And I'm bound by treaty not to fight other river otters there."

Rainbow smiled cunningly. "You won't be fighting, Shinar. But I will be."

"And how do you plan to hold off two tribes by yourself?"

The Orlysk chuckled. "You'll see."

The Keron Mouse was a paws-width taller than Nathan'el, and his eyes burned cold amber. The sword he expertly balanced was of the plainest, poorest steel Nathan'el had ever seen, and the scabbard at the mouse's waist had seen better days, but he wielded the sword as if he knew how to use it.

"Who are you?" the Keron Mouse challenged, his voice threatening.

"Nathan'el of Harboday," he answered calmly. "Moonpath and Shorefish have kidnapped my sister and her friend, and I was tracking them until I could get help freeing them. This is Conch, and his friends were also caught."

Conch swallowed hard and faced the murderous-looking mouse warily.

Then from behind them the sound of rustling salal announced the arrival of another Keron Mouse—this one a female as small as Fal'ne. "Jul'an, what's going on?" she asked.

"I was asking them, Nad'ne," the first stranger replied.

Nad'ne nudged Conch's paw cautiously. "It is an interesting question. What is a sea otter doing here, of all places?"

"As we told your friend," Conch replied patiently, "some of our friends and family fell afoul of Moonpath. We were trying to get them back. Why have you halted us?"

"The Keron Mice do not permit creatures to travel unwatched on their land," Nathan'el murmured to Conch.

"That is correct," Jul'an replied levelly. He lowered his sword.

"Could I ask a favor?" Nathan'el jumped in suddenly. "My father, Ol'ver, told me to send word whenever I could. Could you—please—go to Graystone and tell him I am all right? He can pay you for it."

Jul'an and Nad'ne shared a brief conference in a language Conch didn't recognize, but he knew from Nathan'el's musing look that he caught a few words. "What language are they speaking in?" he whispered.

"Eerieden," Nathan'el replied.

Finally Jul'an and Nad'ne turned to them. "This is what will happen," Jul'an declared. "You are seeking only to liberate your friends, so we will honor that attempt. Nad'ne is the swiftest, so she will take your message to Graystone. I will escort you as far as Nikor Mais, but not beyond. If you need my sword in freeing your sister or your friends, then I will help you. But if you are not ready to free them at Nikor Mais, then I will return to my tribe."

Nathan'el nodded. "Very well."

"Bear King go with you, Jul'an," Nad'ne murmured. Then without further ado, she was gone into the forest.

Jul'an glanced after her and then turned to Nathan'el and Conch. "Let's go."

NIKOR MAIS

Moonlight shimmered on the water of Nikor Mais when the warriors of Moonpath and Shorefish arrived. They dispersed among the caves behind the waterfall under the chieftainesses' order to rest, penning the captives in the farthest chamber from the entrance. Some of the warriors went out to forage for roots. Shorefish and Moonpath conferred in a quiet chamber, bent over a map of the territory they had to travel through.

On the cliff overlooking the camp, Shinar and Rainbow hid themselves in the shrubs growing where the waterfall spilled over. "Are you *sure* about this?" Shinar whispered. "There are so many of them!"

Rainbow rolled her eyes. "We've been over and over this," she replied impatiently. "I spent my youth running around with Lady Raven's secret messages. I've learned even more than Kiarna, or so Moonpath believes, so they'll come right after me."

"I'm not worried about *that*," Shinar argued. "You're free to fight here, but what about me? I can't kill other river otters at Nikor Mais, which means I can't back you up!"

Rainbow nodded. "That reminds me." She drew her own hard, sharp knife. "Use this," she shrugged.

Shinar took it in bewilderment. "If I kill other river otters, it will violate the security of Nikor Mais," she repeated as if Rainbow hadn't understood.

"I thought the rules say, 'No river otter *knife* may shed an otter's blood,'" Rainbow corrected.

"That wasn't meant to be taken literally!" Shinar protested.

"Shorefish *will* take it literally," Rainbow hissed. "Remember, she has that sea otter weapon that killed Nighthawk. Besides, if all goes well, you won't have to fight."

"Fine," Shinar protested, "but what if something happens to you?"

"Such as?" Rainbow snapped, her amber eyes glowing in the night. "Aspen and I survived the onslaught of the whole army of Darkwoods, remember? If I could survive that, I can fight my way around a bunch of tired otters."

"Darkwoods wanted you alive," Shinar muttered. "Moonpath will want you dead."

Rainbow bit hard on her tongue. "In the Darkwoods War, you were dangerous because you were so reckless," she growled. "Now you're dangerous because you're so indecisive! Bear King, Shinar, find the happy medium."

"*Someone* has to keep you Rangers in check," Shinar snapped.

"Moonpath wants me alive as well because she needs the information I have," Rainbow reminded the otter.

A large group of otters scurried into the surrounding woods, searching for food.

"Come on!" Rainbow urged. "Now or never!"

"I'd prefer never," Shinar muttered. But she eased herself into the water, holding herself against the current by grabbing a protruding root.

Rainbow pulled her hood up and swung her legs over the cliff side. She was nearly invisible in the night, and her footing was sure. She landed on firm ground silently and took her bow from her shoulder. Without missing a beat, she fit an arrow to the string and fired into the cave.

The arrow hit the wall of the room where Moonpath and Shorefish were convening. Both chieftains ran outside and froze at the sight of a Ranger so far from Oria.

"Rainbow!" Moonpath hissed. "What are you doing here?"

"Following my lady's orders," Rainbow shouted back. She fit another arrow to her bow and fired at one of the foragers running back to see what the shouting was about. Her arrow hit him so hard he staggered back a few paces before he fell dead.

As a group of other otters darted out of the woods, Rainbow took a few stutter-steps back. Her tail brushed against a tree, and she knew her back was protected.

Shinar watched the scrape, and when Rainbow obviously had the situation under control, Shinar released her hold on the root. Nikor Mais had been chosen as a famous meeting place because the waterfall was safe to ride over. That way, otters coming from the north could travel solely in the river and not have to hike around the cliffs, a journey of miles.

The trip over the waterfall didn't bother Shinar—the rapids near her home were much rougher—and once she reached the bottom, she forced her head above the water and tugged her soaked hood over her face. It was easy to pull herself out and duck in behind Moonpath and Shorefish, who were yelling angrily for their tribes to come out of the woods. No one was in the dank, cold cave except the prisoners, so it was easy to sneak back to the Princess Kiarna.

She raised her white head and peered into the hood, her blue eyes lighting up with relief. "Shinar!" she gasped. "Bear King be praised." Here was someone she had never doubted.

"You're not free yet," Shinar warned. With Rainbow's steel knife she hacked away at the ropes that bound the Miamurans at their waists.

Her actions roused the sea otters and two mice. One of them, a sea otter maiden—could it be Pearl?—held out her paws pleadingly. "Free us too!" she begged. She didn't recognize "Baklenne."

Shinar bent to work on another Miamuran's binding rope. "In your dreams, sea otter," she scoffed. Inwardly it saddened her to be so cold to Pearl, but they couldn't be allowed to recognize her. Moonpath couldn't know she'd been here.

The other female sea otter sat up straighter. "I am Saline, chief Eagle's sister," she declared with such imperiousness that no one could doubt it. "If you free me, he will reward you!"

Shinar finished with the Miamurans and answered Saline coldly. "There is nothing your brother has that I could want," she retorted. She kept her face hidden behind her cloak hood.

"Even land?" Saline pressed.

"Go!" Shinar said urgently to Kiarna. "And as for you, Saline, do you really think this is a petty war over stolen land? It is much more than that. A crown hangs in the balance, and with it, the fate of the western world." That was as much of a warning as she could give Saline.

Then she was gone after the Miamurans.

Fal'ne blinked after her, trying to make sense of what she had said. A crown? There was only one crown that dictated the fate of the western world. The west side of the Keron River was not like the east; it did not have great city-states like Miamur or Pasadagavra with many kings ruling over many acres of land. There were small villages that were oases in total wilderness. The only truly great kingship in the west was the Wraith Mice. Most of the west looked at the King of Arashna as their king.

How on earth did the crown of Arashna hang in the balance?

In the woods, Shinar pulled the Miamurans into the thickest cover she could find. Moonpath would send out searchers as soon as she discovered the princess was gone, but they had to rest for a minute. Shinar glanced over her shoulder, wondering if she had time to go back for the others, but knew in her gut that it wasn't safe to take one second more than absolutely necessary. Rainbow was good, but not invincible.

"Where are we going?" Kiarna gasped, leaning heavily on a tree.

"East to Lunep," Shinar replied curtly. "Your brother has sent out a scout party looking for you."

"I told him not too!" Kiarna exclaimed. "I told him that I was dispensable."

Shinar gave her a sidelong look. "What were you doing so close to Arashna that Doomspear caught you?" she asked.

"Reconnaissance," Kiarna sighed. "I was leading a diplomatic mission, and I wanted to see what was happening there."

"What did you find out?"

Kiarna put her paw over her eyes. "That Mokimshim isn't following the example set by his parents. Shinar, there were creatures in Arashna that didn't belong there—Eerieden war bands, river otters of shady reputation. I even saw old Oracle Hemlock, would you believe."

Shinar's fur stood on end. The last time she saw Oracle Hemlock, he was being hauled back to Dobar as a screaming, feeble, raving mad prisoner. "Did he look ill?" she asked.

"He looked ten seasons younger than in the Darkwoods War," Kiarna sighed.

Shinar realized the princess's shoulders were shaking. Of course. Demeda was more of a mother to Kiarna than her own mother, and Mokimshim was like a brother. The implications of Oracle Hemlock being seen in Arashna were not good.

"We knew most of that," Shinar explained. "About Mokimshim's alterations, I mean. Not about the foxes being there. I think Galledor was most afraid that you discovered something that made you dangerous."

Kiarna nodded and changed the subject. "We are ready to continue. Are we waiting for anyone?"

Shinar shook her head. "No. Rainbow will be traveling north. We will not see her again until she has shaken Moonpath off."

Rainbow hurried north through the woods, and then she circled back around south. Even though she couldn't see them, she knew Moonpath's warriors were on her trail. She was leaving as little evidence as possible, sometimes laying false trails, sometimes running through streams for several minutes. It was hard to trace a Ranger through any territory, even territory she was unfamiliar with.

When Nathan'el, Conch, and Jul'an reached Nikor Mais, it was a scene of total disorder. The three of them stayed hidden in the woods and watched as river otters rushed frantically around.

"They have been taken!" Moonpath was screaming, laying about her with a switch. "The Princess has been taken while you fools were running around like dimwits!" Her switch met Shorefish's onyx knife and was sheered in half. The next thing the vile rogue knew was that a knife pointed right at her eyes.

"*We* were the ones in the cave," Shorefish growled, "and thus the ones to blame for the infiltration. The point is Princess Kiarna is gone and probably with some Rangers."

Rangers? Conch mouthed at Nathan'el, who looked equally surprised.

Two of Shorefish's otters were muttering closer to the hidden trio. "It seems as if our friends Baklenne and Sh'vendi have gotten involved," one murmured.

"They'd be the only ones who could pull this off," agreed another.

"Who and who?" Jul'an whispered.

Conch was so stunned his mouth was hanging open. Jul'an nudged him and repeated the question.

"Uh—they're two merchants," Conch whispered back. "But I don't see—"

A paw landed lightly on his shoulder, and a familiar voice whispered, "Those who cannot see have not opened their eyes."

Conch whirled around. "Sh'vendi?" he gasped.

The mouse shook her head gently. "I'm afraid not. Sh'vendi was a guise among those south of Oria. My name is Rainbow, and I am a Ranger."

She glanced up at the scene of chaos. "But we must back away. It's only a matter of time before they find my trail. Come with me."

10.

RAINBOW'S WARNING

On the grasslands east of Darkwoods, Nurida lay half-awake, her mind practically asleep but her senses alert. She heard her sister's breathing beside her and realized that Lochuran was half-awake as well. Nurida tried to sink into the beckoning arms of sleep but didn't quite succeed.

After almost an hour of this, a dark shape loomed over her. She jumped into wakefulness, but it was only Elvinene. Beside Nurida, Lochuran stirred.

"Get up slowly," Elvinene whispered. "Something's not right."

Beyond her, Asherad was strapping on his armor, as was Orlian. Asherad looked alarmed, his fur prickling while Orlian just looked watchful. Lacritta slept on obliviously, but all around, the other trackers were upright and armed.

Nurida stood slowly and reached for the dagger she had taken to hiding under her pillow. Lochuran grinned at her and tugged out a similar one.

"What is it?" she whispered.

Lochuran listened for a few minutes and then whispered, "I think we're being watched."

"By whom, do you think?" Nurida whispered back.

"Otters," Lochuran guessed. "Maybe we should wake Lacritta."

Nurida shook Lacritta gently and stifled her mouth with a paw. Lacritta's sightless eyes blinked open, and she almost squeaked.

At that point, Elvinene slunk up quietly. "You three, head due south and get out now! Lunep is that way, and you'll be safer there. Hurry!"

Lochuran began to protest, but Elvinene shushed her. "Go!"

Nurida stared at Elvinene for a moment. Lochuran looked mutinous, but she pulled herself together and grabbed Nurida's paw and Lacritta's dress. They stood slowly and began walking south.

"Don't act as if you know you've been seen!" Elvinene whispered urgently.

They left the rest of the tracking party behind. Lacritta was still bubbling with questions, but Lochuran kept her firmly silent. Nurida led the way, her eyes being the keenest.

"There's definitely someone in these hills," she whispered.

The sun rose and outlined the trio's shapes, making Nurida nervous. She sensed someone watching them. But were they foes? She couldn't decide.

A piece of land had been hollowed by the wind with a shelf of land leaning over a gully. Nurida led them down into the ravine, hoping to protect them from being seen, but when the gully turned sharply east, she knew they had to get out. Lacritta climbed up first with Nurida close behind her, lest she fall. Lochuran stayed farther down, waiting for Nurida's word that she could come up.

Lacritta pulled herself up to the top of the gully. Nurida scrambled up behind her and looked around sharply, searching for any sign that they had been followed. But there was no one in front of them. "Come on up, Lochuran," she called softly.

No answer.

"Lacritta, stay down!" Nurida whispered. She peeked back into the gully and saw no sign of Lochuran.

Rainbow hurried the three trekkers into the shelter of the woodlands. When they were sheltered enough and she judged Shorefish wouldn't find them, she settled them down in a thicket and produced a pouch of nuts and a slice of old cheese. Nathan'el, who hadn't had any food with him when he left Graystone, eyed it hungrily, but he let Conch and Jul'an take from it first, as father had taught him.

After a moment, Rainbow spoke. "I assume you have a lot of questions. You especially, Conch."

Conch inclined his head. "You could say that."

Rainbow sighed. "I'm sorry, but—Nathan'el you go first."

Nathan'el nodded. "All right. Why did Shorefish and Moonpath capture my sister? How did Shorefish know who I am? And did she take my mother?"

Rainbow sighed. "She—yes, she took Ran'ta. And that ... that was my fault."

Nathan'el raised his chin. "How so?"

Rainbow fiddled with a hem of her cloak. "I was carrying a message from Princess Zuryzel, and I was caught in an ambush. I got away, but I was hurt very badly. It was your mother Ran'ta who found me and healed me. She kept me hidden away from the city. The night when I was ready to continue on my journey, she came to me and warned that someone was following her. I would have stayed with her, but I was carrying important information, and your mother wouldn't let me risk it. I tried to tell her to come with me, but she said no; she would talk her way out of a mess. It turned out to be Shorefish following her, who isn't much for talking, and she thought Ran'ta had learned some things from me. So to answer your questions, yes, Shorefish took your mother, and that is how she knows who you are. And as for your sister, I think Fal'ne was just an accident. Just caught in the way."

Nathan'el was quiet for a while. He turned to look away from Rainbow, his thoughts warring inside his head. Conch took the opportunity of his silence. "You're not a merchant, then?" he asked.

She laughed and shook her head. "No. I am a Ranger."

"Then why did you pose as a merchant?"

She shrugged. "So that I could gather information easier. All the times we stopped at your house and in your village, Conch, I was gathering news and rumor—not that there was much to gather, I confess."

"Were you waiting for something like that pirate attack to happen?" Conch guessed.

"Yes, and they weren't pirates," Rainbow replied shortly.

"But you said—"

"I said they were pirate *weapons*," Rainbow corrected him. "But they weren't pirates. First of all, you would have seen them if they were pirates since they can't hide in woodland to save their lives. Second, they would never have fired so many bolts as you described. You said there were many, yes?"

"Yes. At least fifty."

Rainbow nodded. "That seals it. Pirates never fire fifty bolts at a time. Those bolts cost a fortune to make; any good pirate knows that. And third, a good sailor wouldn't miss with a crossbow. Their accuracy is incredible. Conch, I think it might have been Moonpath and her otters who shot at you and Starfish. That, honestly, would be why she shot at *you*."

Conch lowered his eyes. "Of course," he murmured. "And Creeksand, too—he's a part of Danaray's tribe. Rainbow, I saw Shorefish in the woods just after that attack. She didn't hurt me; I think she just wanted not to be seen."

Rainbow nodded tiredly. "I think that *is* all she wanted. She and Moonpath don't seem to be getting along well. My guess is she just wanted to find out what Moonpath was up to."

"But how do you know all this?" Conch asked.

Rainbow was silent for a while.

Conch felt as if he was being evaluated.

Finally Rainbow sighed and murmured, "You seem to have been sucked into this, so you may as well know. There is … great corruption in the Wraith Mouse kingdom. Corruption and … and turmoil. There are several kingdoms and armies that are preparing to combat this corruption, and there is a desperate and very complicated plan that involves so many creatures. But so desperately important is this plan that only seven creatures know all its details. One of them is that white mouse who was captured by Moonpath—that's Princess Kiarna of Miamur."

Nathan'el inhaled sharply.

"That was the reason for the chaos you witnessed," Rainbow went on. "A rescue. She's too valuable to be caught."

"What about my sister?" Nathan'el interrupted.

Guilt washed over her face. "There wasn't enough time, Nathan'el, and we had to make *absolutely* sure Kiarna got away. I'm sorry."

Nathan'el inclined his head. "I see," he said icily.

"I had no choice, Nathan'el," Rainbow apologized.

"I understand," Nathan'el replied. "I don't like it, but I understand."

Rainbow looked as if she wished to say something but could think of nothing appropriate. She turned instead to Conch. "Conch, I know Pearl and the others are your friends, but is there any way I can convince you to turn around and go home?"

"You'd have to give me a good reason," Conch replied promptly.

Rainbow bit her lip. "Aside from the obvious."

"Yes."

She blew a sigh in frustration and then laughed. "You're a good creature, Conch."

She dug into her pack and pulled out some more food. "Nathan'el, you look famished."

He looked at the ground. "When I left Graystone, I didn't bring any food with me."

"Help yourselves," she offered. "Conch, could I have a word with you, please?"

She pulled him through the undergrowth away from the others as they fell on the food.

Making sure Nathan'el and Jul'an couldn't hear, she faced Conch and whispered, "Why are you traveling with a Keron Mouse, Conch?"

"We didn't have much choice," Conch admitted. "Two of them found us in the woods about two days ago. Nathan'el didn't want to get into a scrap, so he agreed to let the one come with us."

"He would," Rainbow muttered to herself. "No Cliff Mouse understands them." She shook her head. "Conch, I don't mean to scare you, but you *mustn't tell Jul'an who you are.*"

"What? Why?"

Rainbow gesticulated with her paws. "I've told you one of the seven creatures who knows about this plan. You know another—your aunt Danaray. Her father was a long-time ally of Miamur—now she's an ally of the Wraith Mice."

"But what does that have to do with me?" Conch protested. "I haven't seen her in ages!"

Rainbow sighed. "Oh, Conch. Your mother's … interesting story puts you in an equally interesting place." As Conch began to protest, she held up her paw. "I know you don't understand any of this; you were raised by creatures who hold you accountable for your actions alone. However, the majority of creatures you'll encounter on this journey haven't forgiven Anamay."

"What did she do that needs forgiveness?" Conch inquired angrily, ready to defend his mother's actions.

Rainbow sighed and put her head in her paw. "Conch, your mother did remarkable things to two tribes. She betrayed the river otters when she chose your father, or so *they* see it; however, she helped the Keron Mice when she saved one of their babes."

"But she's dead," said Conch blinking.

"Yes, she is," Rainbow agreed. "And her transgressions and heroism, both unpaid for, are passed on to her children." She leaned forward intently. "Conch, your life is in danger from Shorefish. She would love to rid herself of that sea otter knife, but to do that she must exact vengeance on her father's killer. Since her father's killer is dead, you and your sister have inherited the deed. *But*, the Keron Mice owe your mother a debt, which has also been passed on to you. In short, you have inherited a blessing and a curse from Anamay. And a secret from Danaray."

Conch stared at her. "I didn't know any of this. But Starfish must have," he added, thinking about her constant worrying about their standing in their tribe.

"The point is you're in danger," Rainbow added. "With Danaray's secrets, you will be a target."

"But Jul'an is from the Keron Mice, who supposedly owe my mother," Conch protested.

A shadow passed over Rainbow's face. "One thing I discovered on my journey is that half the Keron Mice are in Graystone under the rule of Coll'n; the other half are in the woods presided over by Al'ce, his deputy. Ask yourself why. Or better yet, ask Nathan'el. There is no way Shorefish and Moonpath should have been able to make their way through this territory without being detected."

Conch gulped. "They're allies with Moonpath."

"So it seems," Rainbow replied. "And that is just the beginning. Conch, I warn you, you'll meet many different creatures on your journey. Half of them, you shouldn't trust, but you won't be able to tell who you can and cannot. Nathan'el, I can vouch for, but not Jul'an or river otters or even any Wraith Mice."

Conch swallowed hard. "I didn't know it was this bad," he admitted. "Can you really not come with us?"

Rainbow shook her head sadly. "I am sorry. But I can tell you this: you cannot hope to free your friends by yourself. Leave off tracking Shorefish for a while and go to Pasadagavra. It's far to the east, but you could make it there in a few days if you hurry—and you must. The tribeking there is Rhonndan, and he remembers Nathan'el, I think. He will be able to help you. Also, along the way, you might encounter Tribeprincess Shaynnah; I can vouch for her as well. These plus Nathan'el are the only three I know for sure you can trust."

"What?" Conch exclaimed. "Pasadagavra and Dobar—they're in totally different directions! Shorefish and Moonpath will get to Dobar long before we can help my friends!"

"No they won't," Rainbow replied confidently. "After tonight, they'll spend at least a day licking their wounds. After that, they'll *have* to go after Kiarna. She's incredibly valuable to them. They know she's going east to Miamur, and that will bring them right by Pasadagavra."

"But how will we find them?" Conch protested. "River otters are really *good* at not being tracked! We might never find their trail."

"In the woods by your home, yes," Rainbow murmured. "But Pasadagavra boasts a completely different terrain where Shorefish and Moonpath will be plenty lost. In that area, I'd bet the Stone Tribe squirrels could track them down. You'd have the upper paw. Getting there before the river otters is your best bet."

Conch swallowed. "And yet you're letting me do all this? No, 'I wish you would go home'?"

"I wish you would," Rainbow smiled. "But I know you won't leave your friends to suffer alone. Be strong, Conch."

He smiled at her. "I will try."

She nodded. "Good. Now, let's join the others."

When they rejoined Nathan'el and Jul'an, she spoke briefly to Nathan'el in a strange language. Whatever she said, he didn't like much, but he nodded and accepted it. Then she stood up and said, "Good luck to all of you, and may the Bear King watch over you." She gave Conch one last, gentle look, and for an instant, she was Sh'vendi, the matronly mouse merchant who kept creatures together. Then she turned, was again Rainbow the Ranger, and was gone into the wild.

"This changes things," Nathan'el murmured.

"How so?" Conch asked.

"Rainbow suggested that we go to Pasadagavra and get help from Tribeking Rhonndan," Nathan'el said, a little louder. "The fastest way to get there is to track east until we reach the Keron River and then follow it north."

"Impossible," Jul'an interrupted, jumping to his paws.

"It's the only way I know where I can't get lost," Nathan'el answered mildly.

"That is Keron Mice territory!" Jul'an snapped.

Nathan'el faced him, and Jul'an recoiled slightly. "How exactly do you plan to stop us from following the river?" he inquired. "There're two of us and one of you. You can't call in for help from anyone around you—*can* you?"

Nathan'el was challenging Jul'an, Conch decided. Jul'an looked around in agonizing indecision.

"In that case, you have two options," Nathan'el went on. "You can come with us along the river, or you can go back to Al'ce and get help. The choice is yours. But whatever choice you make, I am going on to Pasadagavra by means of the river. Can I assume Conch will go with me?"

"Of course," Conch replied, surprised at his asking.

Jul'an's eyes lit up in alarm. He mouthed wordlessly for several minutes and then choked out, "You can't just go trespassing on my tribe's land!"

"My *sister* has been kidnapped!" Nathan'el exclaimed. "At the moment, I don't care whose land I have to cross to get to her!"

The ferocity in his voice startled Jul'an. He backed off a bit and then blinked. "I will come with you," he relented finally.

11

Starfish Learns
the Truth

When the dark walls of Lunep became visible, Nurida cried out in
relief. After looking for Lochuran for an hour and finding no trace
of her sister, she knew she had to move on with Lacritta. They ran as
quickly as the blind mouse could. Then when they reached the place where
Darkwoods had used to be, they found a field of felled trees and had to wend
their way arduously around each stump and trunk. It took them *two days*
to go from the gully to the castle, and the whole time Lacritta was no help.

When Nurida saw the castle, Nurida ran forward earnestly. She raised
her voice urgently. "Hail the walls! Hail the walls!"

When they finally stood before the mighty gates, one of the windows
in the gatehouse opened, and a voice called, "Who hails us?"

"Nurida and Lacritta of Miamur!" she cried.

The gatehouse door flung open. It was a bright-furred fox of Lunep.
"Princesses!" he cried. "Now three. Come through this way, Nurida
and Lacritta."

"Three?" Nurida exclaimed. "Who?"

But their guide put a paw over his mouth. "She warned us not to say
her name in the open. Come inside, and I'll show you."

Nurida followed the fox into the gatehouse and tugged Lacritta with
her. He closed the one door behind him and led them through the stone
building to another door. This he opened, and they were inside the palace
of Lunep.

The stone was still dark, even after the Darkwoods foxes had been driven out, but the sun shone through the windows, albeit feebly. Foxes bustled here and there. Nurida, who was much shorter than most of the foxes, pressed against Lacritta for support. Their guide saw this and grinned. "We won't eat you."

"It's not you I'm worried about," she murmured. It had suddenly occurred to her who the third princess was.

Sunshine fell over the sea otter lands. Ever since Limpet's body had been found, there had been a state of confused panic in the sea otter camp. Starfish had been in the center of it for a while, as had Oyster.

But now Starfish sought peace in the woods. She couldn't bear to see Eagle's face. She knew he blamed himself for the whole incident—why did he have to assume responsibility for everything that went wrong?—and he feared she blamed him for her brother's disappearance.

She suddenly realized that her wanderings had taken her to the fork in the Dellon River, where it became the Kyaagha Brook and the Huaaka Creek. This was where she had once met her aunt. *Danaray ... why had she left?* Danaray had sworn to be near her sister's children always. Starfish had repeated the oath to herself again and again when she was a child:

If you ever have need of me, I'll be there. If you ever wish to speak to me, I'll be there. Even when it seems that I'm not, I'll be there. Always. I swear it.

"Even if it seems that I'm not," Starfish said aloud. "Even if it seems ..." Her voice trailed off, but a fountain of excitement exploded in her stomach.

Even if it seems I'm not.

Danaray had not left after all!

Without further ado, Starfish dove into the Kyaagha and swam as fast as she could, southwest. Before too long, she reached the Othyrn River, which flowed at a strange angle to the Kyaagha until they met. She pulled herself onto the shore across from her clan's territory. Then she ran as fast as she could, going east.

"Please," she whispered. "Please."

In less than five minutes, she reached her aunt's city—or, rather, more a camp. Structures of varying sizes were arranged in a sort of circle around a long, open-sided shelter beneath which was a sort of market.

One of the female river otters at this market, looking up and seeing Starfish, cried out joyfully, "Starfish!"

Starfish hesitantly joined the others at the long market, and the otter who had hailed her inclined her head respectfully. "Are you here to see the chieftainess?" she asked.

Starfish nodded. "I am. Could you tell me where she is?"

"In her house," the otter replied brightly. "She'll be delighted to see you."

"Thank you," Starfish replied.

"Of course! Anytime."

Starfish hurried through the snow to the highest building—the only one in the city with real stairs. Starfish went up to this, noticing that the sun was fading. She didn't have much time. On the door was a gold knocker, which she carefully rapped.

The door opened, and an otter maidservant stood there. She quickly inclined her head and said, "Hello, Starfish. I believe you'll find your aunt in the upper meeting room."

"Thank you," Starfish replied, straightening her shoulders. As the servant let her pass, she noticed the difference in temperature immediately. Danaray always kept a warm house. The snow that clung to her fell away.

The stairs were plain but covered with colorful rugs. Starfish gripped the rail and climbed quickly. At the landing there was a table; here Starfish paused. There, on a flat slab of wood, was a sketch of her and Conch, with both their sea otter names and river otter names written beneath them. She smiled and continued on her way.

At the top of the stairs were hallways branching off in three directions. Starfish followed the middle one, which was covered with a long blue rug. At the far end was a door of very pale wood and beautiful metal designs. She timidly pushed this door open.

Inside was a wide room, and in three walls was a large window. In the center was a collapsible table strewn with maps and copper inkwells; there were other tables against the walls and heavily-cushioned seats, each with a wide back and carved pawstools. There was a woven rug, too, of olive green, and a roaring fireplace. Many lamps of bronze and silver cast light from the walls.

At the table in the center were several creatures. Closest to Starfish was Kermunda, Danaray's healer and primary adviser. Across from him was a mouse Starfish had never seen before. Standing at the head of the table was Starfish's aunt. All three looked up when the door opened. Danaray's grim face transformed into a wonderful smile. "Hello, Starfish," she said, as if it had been only a few days since they last met, not almost two months.

"Hello Aunt," Starfish replied quietly.

The mouse had jumped to his paws when he saw a sea otter enter, but when he heard her name, he sat back down with a knowing, "Ah." Kermunda stood and actually crossed the room to embrace her. "It's good to see you again, *kidanshar*," he said.

Starfish warmed with his tender "loved one."

"If it is the same to you, my friends," Danaray said, "we shall continue this conversation in a few hours' time. Kermunda, please ensure that our guest hears everything his son wished him to."

The mouse stood up obligingly, bowed to Danaray, and again to Starfish. Then he followed Kermunda out and closed the door behind him.

Danaray threw her chiefly dignity to the winds. She ran forward and wrapped her paws around her niece. "You remembered my promise, then," she said joyfully. "Oh, it's so good to see you!" She drew back and held Starfish at her paw's length. The beaming joy faded. "You look as if you've had a hard time," she said.

Starfish nodded. "In a way."

With a few words of gentleness, Danaray led Starfish over to a rich red sofa and poured two goblets of wine. Starfish sipped gratefully while Danaray watched her, as if trying to judge when best to speak. Danaray had never been as pretty as Anamay and, in the time since Starfish had met her, aged a little, but Danaray had certainly lost none of her dignity. A band of silver wrapped around her brow, and at her waist was her tribal dagger—heavy iron with a garnet set at the top. When Starfish had finished half of her wine, Danaray spoke. "Tell me everything," she murmured. "Tell me everything that is troubling you."

So Starfish did. She blurted out her worries about Eagle's attentions, the attackers in the woods, her wounded shoulder, and Conch's disappearance. When she finished, Danaray's face was grim and worn, as if she had taken all Starfish's burdens onto her own shoulders. It was some while before she spoke.

"There is always a time in a creature's life where everything seems dark, and light is but a distant memory. One thing I have learned is that in these times, the good in creatures shines more bright and fair."

Starfish nodded.

Danaray bit on her paw, trying to hide the depth of her anxiety. "You should have come to me immediately," she said abruptly. "The instant you were wounded. You know that I would have paid Kermunda to heal you." A smile flickered across her face. "Though I doubt he would ask for payment in your case."

"That same day, we had heard you and the tribe had moved out," Starfish admitted. She briefly described their meeting with Creeksand.

This time Danaray did not bother to hide her alarm. "Creeksand was carrying a message for me," she murmured. "He was told to say, if anyone asked, that this tribe had left. I wonder … well, I can't worry about that now." She lapsed into silence again. After a moment, she spoke even more abruptly than before. "I think I know what happened to your brother."

"You do?" Starfish asked nervously.

Danaray gestured at the door. "The mouse you saw in here earlier is a Cliff Mouse from Harboday called Ol'ver. His daughter, Fal'ne, was captured by Shorefish, and his son, Nathan'el, has set out after her. I think it possible that Wren might have done the same, if the others were also kidnapped."

"What if he was kidnapped too?" Starfish demanded, alarm filling her.

But Danaray shook her head. "Shorefish wouldn't dare. She knows what this tribe will do to anyone who dares harm either you or your brother. My tribe is the largest in the world; hers barely numbers a tenth of mine."

A combination of firelight and dying sunlight flickered over Danaray's face, and the fierce gleam in her eye made even Starfish nervous. "So you think Conch went after them without telling anyone?"

Danaray rolled her eyes. "He may have. It would have been stupid and thoughtless, but he may have." She sat back against the table, rubbing her eyes with her paw. "And as for the attack—I am certain they were not pirates."

"But Baklenne and Sh'vendi—"

"Must have been ordered to say things like that," Danaray cut her off. "They would have Eagle on the alert without him knowing exactly what is going on." She gave her niece a kind smile. "For that reason, I am not telling you several things. Eagle cannot know what is happening, but he might ask you."

"I would not tell him!" Starfish protested.

"Whether you would or not is not my concern," she said simply. "Whether you *can* or not is your safe-keeping." A sly smile lighted her face. "I am, I confess, playing a similar game to what I played with your mother. The less she knew, the less she could tell—whether or not she would—and thus … well, thus I know that no one can accuse her of treachery." When Starfish still looked resentful, Danaray added, "It's a terrible thing to have to keep secrets from one you love, child."

Starfish sighed. "I just wish … that I knew where my brother is."

"As do I," Danaray added. "He—mm—is the target for a number of creatures who search for information. Oh, he knows nothing," she said quickly, seeing Starfish's face. "But some might, in their desperation, think that I have passed my secrets on to him."

Starfish bunched herself up on the couch. "I'm scared," she admitted. "And I want to know … what is going on. Why are all these strange things happening?"

Danaray sighed and met her niece's eyes.

For a moment, Starfish was convinced her aunt would not answer.

Then Danaray spoke. "Do you know the names Mokimshim and Zuryzel?"

"I know the one," Starfish replied. "Zuryzel. She was a … a Wraith Mouse princess, right? The merchants talk about her often."

"Zuryzel is the second child of King Hokadra and Queen Demeda," Danaray went on. "Mokimshim is her older brother. He is—or was—the heir to Arashna's throne."

"Was?"

"Queen Demeda died several seasons ago," Danaray explained curtly. "That was a blow to any creature who lives outside the jurisdiction of Miamur or one of the Squirrel Tribes. Demeda was balance, and when any ruler as powerful as she dies, even a poor ruler, there is always upheaval. And Demeda was no poor ruler."

"So it was worse this time?" Starfish guessed.

"I can't tell you why it was worse," Danaray murmured. "But the results … I can tell you those. King Mokimshim made an alliance with almost every river otter tribe on the face of the earth; only a few are free from him. Wave and Rain's tribe remains independent; their aunt Streamcourse's is free; and three tribes in the north. And mine. Every other one has some sort of alliance to Mokimshim."

"But they're enemies, aren't they?" Starfish protested. "You told me once that Doomspear would never have anything to do with Shorefish!"

"They are united," Danaray replied tiredly, "by a common goal."

Anger kindled in Starfish's blood. "Our land?" she guessed.

"Precisely," Danaray replied neutrally.

"At their peril," Starfish vowed. "They won't find us easy to drive away."

"And you won't be fighting alone," Danaray added.

"I thought you would be on their side," Starfish admitted.

"Why should I be?" Danaray snapped. "If they were true leaders, they wouldn't be ruled by a predator!" She blinked. "That didn't make much sense. I've been saying this for so long that I've become incoherent."

She grinned at Starfish, who could not smile back. "You didn't used to care much for sea otters," she murmured.

"That was before you were born," Danaray replied firmly. "And it was entirely because of their indifference to the Darkwoods Foxes. But that war is in the past, and I am willing to let it rest in the past."

"And supposing the other chiefs aren't willing to give you the same courtesy?" Starfish asked quietly.

Danaray smiled. "Let me worry about that. And from now on, if anything goes wrong—*anything at all*—I want you to come straight to me. The smallest thing could be a part of this ... this war of shadows.

"But for now," she added, "it's getting dark, and your father and Eagle must be worried sick about you."

"Aunt—"

"I'll look for Conch," she promised. "Don't be afraid to care for Eagle, but be cautious about everything else. And if anything at all goes wrong, remember—"

"I'll come to you," Starfish promised.

"I'll walk with you as far as the Othyrn River, if you like," Danaray offered.

Starfish nodded. "Yes, please."

12.

A NIGHTMARE IS TOLD

Night came sooner on Lunep than it did in the snowy sea otter territory. It was pitch-black when Copper led Nurida to a room in the dark palace; she had instructed Lacritta not to accompany them. If there was one thing she had learned, it was that Lacritta knew nothing about this business and would not be able to cope if she did.

Copper left Nurida at the door. Nurida didn't even knock as she pushed the door open quietly.

A familiar white mouse was sitting in a corner, her head in her paws, the very picture of dejection. Her queenly dress was torn and filthy, her personal crest covered in dried mud, her shoes ragged. The remnants of black paint that usually lined the eyes were smeared across her face. Blood had dried at a wound on her side, and she sat gingerly. Nurida's heart swelled and wrung with pity.

"Kiarna," she whispered.

The mouse looked up with blue eyes, foggy from tears. She looked ten seasons older than she really was. For an instant, she didn't recognize Nurida, but when she did, her mask of pain altered to joy. "Nurida! Oh, Nurida, thank goodness!" She stood up painfully and hugged Nurida. As when she was little and had had a nightmare, Kiarna's embrace seemed to make everything all right. She was the best older sister Nurida had.

"My sister, my sister, oh, Nurida!" Kiarna was weeping again but this time from intense relief. "Oh, thank the Bear King." For a long time they stood like that, crying, Kiarna because the nightmare she'd endured was finally over and Nurida because Kiarna was.

Finally Nurida's new-found strength asserted itself and she drew back, holding her sister at paw's length. "Kiarna, what happened? Where have you been?"

Kiarna wiped her paw across her eyes, smearing the old paint even more. "Oh, Nurida … I was a fool. A reckless, air-headed fool."

Nurida grasped her sister's paw. "How so?"

Kiarna gestured at the two chairs. "Please, can we sit? I'm tired of standing."

It was another thing about Kiarna that Nurida loved—in spite of the many seasons' difference between them, Kiarna always spoke to Nurida like an equal. Nurida said quickly, "Of course. I'm tired too."

They sat and Kiarna put her paw on the wall, her shoulders shaking. "Nurida … what are you doing here?"

Nurida squeezed her sister's paw again. "You go first. How did *you* get here?"

Kiarna winced. "Are you really that curious?"

"I'm that concerned," Nurida replied firmly. "Please, Kiarna, tell me what happened to you."

Kiarna sighed. "Well then, if you insist. But, my … where to begin … where to begin …"

Nurida hugged her sister carefully. "Start from the beginning," she suggested. "That's always a good place to begin."

To Nurida's surprise, Kiarna laughed bitterly. "The beginning. Well, I suppose that's fitting, seeing as this is the result of my foolishness from beginning to end."

Nurida wanted to protest that Kiarna was never foolish, but she knew her sister wasn't able to hear something like that now.

Kiarna leaned her head back, rubbing her eyes, seeming to gather her strength. When she spoke, her voice was quiet. "Did you know I had gone to Arashna?"

Nurida blinked. "No—I didn't know that at all."

Kiarna nodded and wiped her eyes again. "I had been raised there. Before Father died, before the Darkwoods War. Nurida, Arashna was my childhood home, and the royal family there my dearest friends. I had always meant to go back … to stay there in peace. Zuryzel was my dearest childhood friend. Mokimshim always acted as if he was my brother. Their mother was more of a mother to me than our mother ever was—oh, how I wish you could have known her! It was my … dream, in a way. I thought when

Galledor finally married and then when you were married and settled … I planned to go back, to open paws and old friends—as if I could somehow go back to my childhood. Then I began hearing about things happening in Arashna. I … I should never have left Miamur. But Arashna was my home as well … So I took a group of warriors and used my authority as a princess to set out on a diplomatic visitation, only leaving word for Galledor. And when I got to Arashna—" her voice broke. She had to take several deep breaths before she could say, "Mokimshim has already been made king. And half of his kingdom is exiled."

"*Half!*"

"Give or take."

"For what?" Nurida demanded, still not quite understanding.

"One of them is exiled for being his sister," Kiarna sighed. "Princess Zuryzel—except she is no longer a princess, just an outcast. And her mate, too, has been exiled, and many citizens of the Wraith Mice. They were exiled. And his brother, Johajar—no, do not ask me about Johajar."

Nurida knew these names, and since she had never met any of them, they were to her nothing more than that, names. But to Kiarna, these were friends of a different life, a childhood she loved more than her adulthood. Exile … that was a capital punishment anywhere, but especially in the west. For in the west, the only places of true prosperity were under the domain of either the Wraith Mice or the Eerieden mercenaries. The mercenaries rarely let anyone enter their kingdom, so the only place to go was utter wilderness. Nurida squeezed her sister's paw, thinking hard. Finally she said, "What happened when you reached Arashna?"

Kiarna gave a great, shuddering sigh. "We were received like any foreign dignitary, and I had the *pleasure*," her voice was scathing, "of seeing Mokimshim and his queen. Karena. And my old friend—Nurida, I didn't even *recognize* him! We were lodged well and told we would be given further audience the next day. But then Eneng found us—"

"Who, excuse me?"

Kiarna sighed. "I forgot … I don't remember much of this because my mind was elsewhere (the height of my idiocy!). Mokimshim gave us a tour of the wharfs at Myanka, a Cliff Mouse city. Any ship with red banners, he told us, was in his service. There were dozens of them, but they were all pirates and mercenaries. He had paid them into his service, and Eneng was one of the mercenaries. I think he may have been trying to warn me to get out, but I didn't notice." She laughed bitterly. "Anyway, that night, after we had been left in peace, Eneng came and found us. He warned us to get out, that we were in danger. We had seen the ships, and Mokimshim didn't want anyone to carry word of his navy out past Arashna. So, in the dead of night, we snuck out of Arashna." Troubled, Kiarna sighed again. "If I hadn't spent my childhood in Arashna, we never would have managed it. But because I remembered so many half-used halls, we could sneak out unnoticed. Until the next day, anyway. When we were missed, Mokimshim guessed we had fled. He sent one of the otters in his service after us—Doomspear. They hunted us down for nightmarish weeks. We almost got away, but he caught us in some rapids. Most of my retinue was killed. That's when I got this," she added, pressing gingerly on her deep wound. "But Doomspear heard the war cries of the Keron Mice—or some of them—and he ran for it. I survived, obviously, and so did nine others. Before the Keron Mice reached us, I had enough time to warn the survivors to pretend to know nothing, to be lost. We pretended to be amnesiac. The Keron Mice took us to Graystone, where we were well cared for, but I wasn't sure if we were in friendly territory or not. Well, if I couldn't trust someone I'd known my whole life … Then one night, I heard a lot of commotion and almost all the grown mice left Graystone armed to the teeth. And that night, Moonpath got in and kidnapped us."

Nurida laughed tiredly. "Oh, Kiarna. You went from one enemy to another, didn't you?"

"As I said, I acted a fool," Kiarna sighed. "Anyway, Moonpath took us to someplace called Nikor Mais. There, a Ranger and a river otter called Shinar rescued us. Shinar brought us here, and that's my story."

Nurida squeezed her sister's paw more tightly, her mind whirling. This, then, was why Galledor was so worried. And what Dejuday must have discovered.

"But tell me," Kiarna said, wiping her eyes again. "Why are you here?"

"First," Nurida murmured, "tell me why you haven't been tended to." She gestured at the wound and the mess on Kiarna's face.

She smiled tiredly. "We got here only a few hours ago, and I told the healers here to take care of my retinue first. The least I could do, after I led so many to their deaths …" The lines appeared on her face again; it was as if twenty seasons had fallen on her in that one moment.

"You must forgive yourself for that," Nurida told her urgently. "You can't wallow in guilt."

Kiarna laughed. "I know, Nurida. And trust me, I am trying. Now tell me why you are here."

Nurida explained as if they had been investigating something odd, not as if they had been searching for Kiarna. Her older sister didn't need that kind of guilt added to what already burdened her. Then she asked, "Kiarna?"

"Hmm?"

"Why did Mokimshim want you dead?" Nurida asked gently. "It wasn't because of the navy, was it? That's barely more than harmless gossip, and it couldn't be kept secret for long anyway."

Kiarna stared at Nurida for a long time. Then she shook her head. "No, it wasn't because of the navy, and he didn't want me dead. He wanted me to talk. When he exiled his sister, she was out of his reach, and there weren't many places she could flee to. It was most logical for her to come to Galledor and me for help since we'd grown up best friends. Which she did—the instant she was exiled. With Wraith Mice and Cliff Mice who had been exiled with her. And he knew that she would tell us everything … and confide everything in us, just as her mother had done. Nurida, he wanted me for that." She sighed. "There are only six creatures on this earth who Zuryzel has confided her plans in completely. Galledor and I are two and then Lady Crow of the Rangers, a river otter chieftainess called Danaray, a pirate called Shartalla, and of course her mate—Dejuday."

Nurida gasped and stared at Kiarna in amazement. "Asherad is in love with *Princess Zuryzel?*"

Kiarna surveyed her knowingly. "Galledor told you why he and Dejuday aren't on good terms, then?"

Nurida nodded, and then pulled her paws up onto the chair. "Oh. Kiarna, you need sleep if nothing else."

Kiarna laughed bitterly. "I haven't slept peacefully since I reached Arashna. I keep having nightmares."

"I'll stay with you and drive the nightmares away," Nurida promised.

Kiarna laughed again, and this time her laughter was neither fleeting nor overlaid with bitterness. "Isn't that what I used to say to you when you were scared?"

Nurida nodded through tears. "You are to me what Zuryzel and Mokimshim were to you. Let me send for the physician, and then you can sleep." She phrased it like a request, but she didn't wait for Kiarna's affirmation.

13.
THE LETTER

If Nathan'el hadn't known exactly where to find Kyka the river otter, it would have taken much longer to make it up the Keron River. As it was, the skilled river otter piloted them up the river in only a week.

The day they left the river was highly eventful. Nathan'el estimated that Pasadagavra was only a day east and a few days north. He could see the mountain where Pasadagavra was built, and he led Conch and Jul'an on.

They reached a thicket of salal when Nathan'el heard a suspicious rustling. He froze and then dropped slowly to the forest floor, motioning for Conch and Jul'an to do the same. Then he inched one way around the salal while Jul'an snuck around the other way.

He wasn't prepared for what he saw.

Crouching there was a pale gray mouse with beautiful blue eyes. Her poor tunic was ragged, and there were several cuts on her paws. She started when Nathan'el walked up to her.

"Are you lost?" he asked mildly.

She shook her head. "N-no. I wasn't going anywhere."

He extended his paw to help her stand. "What's your name?" he asked as Jul'an and Conch emerged from their hiding places.

She looked anxiously at both of them before answering. "I'm Mar'e. Please, who are you?"

"Nathan'el," he answered. "These are Jul'an," he pointed at the Keron Mouse, "and Conch," he nodded at the sea otter.

"P-pleased to meet you," Mar'e stammered. "W-where were you going?"

"Are you cold?" Conch asked, noting her chattering teeth. Mar'e nodded.

"Come with us," Nathan'el offered.

"We'll make a camp and warm you up," Jul'an promised.

Her eyes grew wide. "I'm not going anywhere with you until you tell me what you're doing here!" she cried. "These are strange times … I can't be sure I can trust you!"

"We're trying to get to Pasadagavra," Nathan'el replied soothingly. "We need Tribeking Rhonndan's help."

"With what?" Mar'e whispered.

"That's a long story," Conch smiled. "Come on, let's make camp."

They went along a little ways and found a sheltered hollow. Mar'e watched anxiously, unsure what to do, while Nathan'el built a fire, and Conch and Jul'an dug into the packs they had borrowed from Kyka. Conch found a blanket and bade Mar'e sit, but she did so only with prompting. It took a long time for her shivering to stop.

"You told me your names," she said when it did, "but not who you are, exactly. So who are you?"

Conch gestured at Nathan'el, who went first. "I'm a Cliff Mouse from Harboday. My sister Fal'ne was taken by Shorefish and Moonpath, so I'm tracking them, hoping to get my sister back."

Mar'e shook her head. "You can't," she stated flatly.

"I know," Nathan'el replied patiently. "That's why I'm going to Tribeking Rhonndan." He nodded at Conch.

"My friends were taken by Moonpath and Shorefish, too," the sea otter said simply. "I met up with Nathan'el when I was sneaking after them."

Mar'e's eyes flitted to Jul'an.

"I'm just along because they're on Keron Mouse territory," he replied in a low growl. "As soon as they're off, I'm gone."

"Good," Mar'e replied promptly. "You have a sour face."

Conch snickered. Jul'an ignored them.

"What about you?" Nathan'el asked Mar'e.

She gave him a scared look. "I lived in a village that wasn't far away from here. I don't know which direction it was in, but it can't have been far. My village had several farmers that trade with the sea otters when they can, and I think that's why it happened. There was an attack last night from a river otter tribe ruled by Doomspear. They killed most of the fighters and took the females and children as slaves. But I was deemed too weak to be a slave, so they turned me loose."

"Slaving …" Jul'an mused. "That's what Shorefish and Moonpath were up to. I wonder why the river otters are suddenly taking up a new trade."

Nathan'el stared very hard at Mar'e for a while. Then he said, "Conch, come with me. We need to get some water."

He led the sea otter to a place where the roar of the Keron River would hide their words.

"Jul'an knows we're up to something," Conch warned Nathan'el.

"I want him to," Nathan'el replied. "I want him kept on his toes."

Conch shrugged. This was not his area of expertise.

"There's something wrong with Mar'e's story," Nathan'el said quietly. "And Jul'an's covering up for her. What she described was nothing like what Moonpath and Shorefish were doing. They didn't pillage anything; they just grabbed unsuspecting creatures and fled."

"This is a different part of the world than Graystone," Conch pointed out.

Nathan'el shook his head impatiently. "Look, after Queen Demeda died, a lot of odd things started happening. But all those things seem to be part of a … a war of shadows. Pillaging and destroying whole villages aren't shadowy warfare."

Conch pondered that for a while. "It makes sense," he said, "when you consider that these are two different river otter groups."

Nathan'el inclined his head. "True." He thought some more. "In fact, Shorefish and Moonpath might have done the same if they hadn't been right by the mightiest river otter tribe."

"Dana—Chieftainess Mudriver was gone at that point," Conch said.

Nathan'el gave him a bewildered look. "What do you mean?"

"A few weeks before that incident, we found a member of Danaray's tribe," Conch said. "He said that his tribe had left."

Nathan'el shook his head slowly. "He lied. I stopped at Danaray's city to leave a message to my father, and they were all there."

Conch stared at him for a long time. Then a slow smile spread across his face. "Then my clan isn't wholly alone. I was afraid they were stuck in the dark."

"But we're getting off subject," Nathan'el said quickly. "The point is, there is something wrong with Mar'e. We can't trust her too much. Otherwise, Jul'an wouldn't have covered up for her. He knows that what Doomspear allegedly did is nothing like what Shorefish and Moonpath did."

"You're right," Conch agreed. "Besides, river otters usually don't leave witnesses."

Nurida waited with Kiarna until the rest of the scouts arrived.

When Elvinene first saw Kiarna, she threw her paws around her sister-in-law and gasped, "You're safe!"

Kiarna pulled back from Elvinene, the shame of lost lives evident in every move the princess made. And Elvinene was not like Nurida, an equal and a sister. Elvinene was her queen, and Kiarna had to answer to her queen.

But Elvinene knew exactly what to say. "What did you learn at Arashna?"

Kiarna swallowed and glanced at Nurida.

"In my judgment, Nurida can stay," Elvinene said mildly. "But you are her sister. Your call."

"I want to stay, Kiarna," Nurida put in firmly.

Kiarna smiled wanly, like winter sunlight. "Speaking when not spoken to? Nurida, you're growing. But I'm not sure you are ready for what I have to say."

Nurida thought of Lochuran, missing, and suddenly she agreed with Kiarna. But Elvinene said, "In the last two weeks, she has seen two of her sisters disappear—yes, I've already spoken with Lacritta—and she brought a blind sister here by herself. She has proven herself ready."

But the last sentence flew over Kiarna's head, and a look of fear filled her eyes. "Who has disappeared?"

The door banged open at that point, and Asherad hurried in. His eyes found Nurida and Kiarna, and intense relief flooded his face. "You're all right," he sighed. Then he straightened and looked at his elder sister with keen eyes. "What have I interrupted?"

Kiarna looked as if she was having an internal debate for a minute, but then she nodded decisively. "Elvinene was telling me who disappeared."

"Ressora and Lochuran," Elvinene finished. "Lochuran just—"

"*Ressora?*"

The panic and terror in Kiarna's face caused Elvinene to take a step back. "She hasn't been kidnapped," she assured Kiarna. "I let her go."

"You—where?"

"Pasadagavra," Elvinene said gently. "Your mother has chosen a mate for her, and she has sworn to never marry someone she doesn't choose. She promised me that she could look after herself as far as Pasadagavra and find sanctuary in the court of Tribeking Rhonndan."

Kiarna shook her head, her mouth slightly open as she breathed heavily. "She hasn't gone to Pasadagavra." She reached into her tunic and took something out of a hidden pocket, which she extended to Asherad.

It was a scroll. Asherad unrolled it and read it quickly. As he reached the end, his eyes grew wide, and he looked up. "This is only a seal," he pointed out, his voice somewhere between desperate and insistent. "It can be forged or stolen."

"May I see it?" Nurida asked.

Asherad glanced at Kiarna, who reluctantly nodded. Nurida took the scroll and read it twice as fast as Asherad.

> To Mokimshim, esteemed King of Arashna, Lord of the West,
>
> Greetings.
>
> I know not what course of action my brother takes, but I promise you here that he knows the exact whereabouts of Princess Zuryzel. I have tried listening in to learn what I may but am largely unsuccessful. I think my sister Lochuran has some suspicions of what I am endeavoring to do because she seems to go out of her way to make sure I hear nothing from Galledor.
>
> I must point out that this failure is not permanent, and that my actions still fulfill our agreement. I have broken no part of my vow with you.
>
> Ressora,
>
> Third Princess of Miamur, daughter of the White Wings, sister of the Crown (for now)

Beneath these words was Ressora's seal: the hawk diving between the white wings.

Nurida wordlessly held it out to Elvinene, staring at Kiarna.

"It is heavy," Kiarna said softly.

"It makes sense," Nurida whispered. "Ressora always tried to get answers out of Galledor, and Lochuran always broke in. It … it's real."

Kiarna nodded heavily.

"But this is insane," Elvinene gasped. "'For now …' She can't actually think Mokimshim will give her anything!"

"Mokimshim is an artist of deception," Kiarna murmured. "And a Wraith Mouse cannot break a vow."

"Insane," Asherad whispered.

"At least she didn't tell him anything he didn't already know," Kiarna pointed out in a rallying tone.

"Yes, she did!" Elvinene exclaimed. "She said that Lochuran has a hint of what's going on. Galledor was counting on her and Nurida's ignorance to protect them. Now that's blown."

14

TRIBEPRINCESS SHAYNNAH

Keeping Mar'e at ease with the three trekkers was like blowing on a leaf to keep it airborne. After days with her company, Conch's nerves were frayed, and he was convinced they had lost all the time they had gained when Nathan'el had found Kyka.

On the fifth morning, Nathan'el rose before the others and walked slowly off into the woods. Birds sang in the trees around him, and the light was soft blue-gray. It wasn't as cold as it had been, and soft morning mist curled around his paws.

When he was completely alone, he said, "Hello, Shaynnah."

To the music of soft breezes and rustling branches, Tribeprincess Shaynnah dropped gracefully in front of him.

"How long have you known I was here?" she asked conversationally.

Nathan'el smiled, and a breeze lifted the fur on his head. "Two days."

Shaynnah grinned. "That's how long I've been following you."

They both threw their restraint to the wind and hugged.

Shaynnah was his oldest friend, from even before Ol'ver and Ran'ta adopted him. She had her mother Jaccah's black eyes and haughty bearing but a perky grin and clear laugh of her own. Her cheek was marked with the tattoo of the Stone Tribe, and an image of Pasadagavra hung on a chain around her neck. Small orbs of jasper graced the tips of her ears, and she sported a ring depicting a flute. Her ragged tunic bore signs that she had been in the wild for a long time.

"What brings you all the way over here?" Shaynnah asked.

"I'm looking to speak with Rhonndan," Nathan'el explained. "My mother and sister were kidnapped."

Shaynnah's eyes darkened. "I'm not surprised. These are strange times. Who's the she-mouse you drag with you?"

"She says she's a villager," Nathan'el replied, "and that Doomspear's otters destroyed her home but left her alive."

Shaynnah shook her head. "Impossible."

"How do you know?"

The tribeprincess twisted her ring. "Because Doomspear was near Graystone not long ago. I hear from travelers. 'Twas he who attacked Princess Kiarna. He's gone back to Arashna now, hoping to collect his dues."

"Which are?"

Shaynnah held her paws open wide. "For attacking a princess? Of Miamur, no less? Could it not be gold, silver, or jewels? No, it couldn't be. He wants the sea otters' land, and he can't take it without the army from Arashna."

Nathan'el frowned. "For one attack?"

"On *Miamur.*"

"Still ..."

Shaynnah gave him a wise look. "You forget. Just because river otters cannot drive off the sea otters does not make them mighty. Only a portion of King Mokimshim's armies need be used to o'erwhelm them."

"Not at Zurez," Nathan'el protested.

"The sea otters won't be there till spring," Shaynnah pointed out. "Which is how I know Doomspear is on his knees at Arashna now. He has little time."

Nathan'el suddenly felt as if he was trapped to his chin in earth. "So if he succeeds, the attack will come soon."

He never liked the sea otters much, but no one deserved the kind of retribution Doomspear and—Nathan'el shuddered at the thought—Moonpath would dish out.

"It gets better," Shaynnah added. "Your friend, Conch—you know who he is?"

"I would say he's Conch," Nathan'el admitted, "but I guess that's too obvious."

"He is Conch," Shaynnah agreed. "But who is Conch?" She shrugged and then answered her own question. "He is also Wren. In the east, that name is Danar. He is the son of Danaray's sister and child of the union that is an embarrassment to river otters."

Nathan'el's eyes grew wide. He had heard—everyone had heard—the story of Anamay, sister of Danaray Mudriver. He had also heard of Danaray's vow to destroy anyone who touched her sister's children.

"Indeed," Shaynnah agreed with his unspoken amazement. "Never thought that a story could become so real, right?"

"Some otters will do anything to have him dead," Nathan'el muttered.

"Doing so brings them within range of the vengeance of Danaray Mudriver," Shaynnah commented. "A region no one would want to be in. Hers is only slightly less vicious than Moonpath's or Doomspear's."

Nathan'el sighed. "This is getting complicated, Shaynnah. I would bet my life that Jul'an is an enemy, and Mar'e doesn't seem reliable."

"Trustworthy," Shaynnah corrected.

"Reliable," Nathan'el re-corrected. "She could very easily have mistaken another otter tribe for Doomspear's."

Shaynnah made a disgusted noise. "Have her bright blue eyes made a fool of your sense?"

"I don't intend to take any chances," Nathan'el promised.

"Good, 'cause I'd not go with you to my brother's city if you intended otherwise," Shaynnah scowled.

"Yes, you would," Nathan'el teased. "You'd say you had to watch my back if I was incapable of it."

Shaynnah's scowl disappeared, and she laughed. She had a beautifully clear laugh that filled the air around her. "You know me too well," she teased. "And it's been what—eight seasons?"

"Seven," Nathan'el corrected.

"I know," Shaynnah replied. Her mirth vanished. "I was going by the Miamuran calendar. And I wager your Mar'e will do the same."

When Nathan'el and Shaynnah walked calmly into the makeshift camp, Conch and Mar'e were sound asleep. Jul'an was awake, and he started when he saw Shaynnah.

"Hello, Keron Mouse," she said cheerfully.

"Who in the name of the river are you?" he demanded.

She laughed scornfully. "The river? When talking to squirrels, use an expression that *means* something to squirrels. Like trees, or storms. Not *the river*."

"Jul'an, this is Tribeprincess Shaynnah," Nathan'el announced calmly. "A friend of mine. She can take us to her brother's court."

"As if we couldn't get there ourselves," Jul'an muttered.

Nathan'el shrugged and grinned. "Now we've absolutely no chance of getting lost."

Conch stirred and woke. His eyes landed on the newcomer, and he jumped with a shout of, "Burning barnacles!"

He tried to scramble into a more dignified standing position and gave the squirrel a nervous look. "You must be Tribeprincess Shaynnah."

She grinned. "That I am. What are barnacles?"

"Uh—nothing," Conch mumbled. He attempted to look less ruffled. "Pleasure to meet you."

"Likewise," Shaynnah replied lazily.

Mar'e awoke at about that point, and she, too, jumped when she saw the wild-looking tribeprincess. "Oh my!"

"Oh you," Shaynnah retorted. "How is it impossible for any of you to come up with an intimidating phrase?"

"It's early yet," Nathan'el smiled.

"Not that early," Shaynnah frowned. "I'd say it's already two hours after dawn. Which makes it time to start toward my brother's city."

"Don't you ever say Pasadagavra?" Nathan'el inquired, smiling.

"*No!*" Shaynnah snapped. "Say *that city* in these parts, and creatures stop talking to you at all! The war left nothing good in the area."

"I thought this was all Squirrel Tribe land," Conch murmured.

"It is," Shaynnah replied, "or used to be. Don't forget that the Bow Tribe doesn't exist anymore, so lots of homesteaders moved in on their land. But the Ashlands—they're a little southwest of here, towards Mirquis and Dombre—they don't grow or support anything. Then, of course, there're all the problems with the river otters. They never tangled with anyone when Darkwoods and the Wraith Mice were strong in the area, but now they keep raiding the local farms. That's all the indirect result of the Darkwoods War."

"So talking about Pasadagavra is bad," Conch inferred.

Shaynnah grinned. "You're very intelligent for a male," she declared, making Mar'e giggle. "Now, onward to the stone city!"

The march through the forest took them half the day. It was high noon when they reached the edge of the open field that bordered Pasadagavra. It was an eerie sight for Conch: the trees stopped as sharply as if they stood on an invisible line, leaving a circular field of goldenrod-colored grass around Pasadagavra. In the distance, the pink alabaster walls gleamed, and the diamond dome at the top shone as clear as ice. A mountain rose up directly behind the city, and a range of mountains spread out behind it. Cold mountain breezes blew across the field and into the woods.

Shaynnah did not step into the open grassland but jumped onto a low branch and gestured for them to rest.

"We need to leave now if we expect to get there before night," Jul'an protested.

"We do not *want* to get there before night," Shaynnah hissed. "That would defeat the purpose."

Jul'an gave her a puzzled look.

"No cover out there," Nathan'el explained. "We wait for night to cross so no one will observe us."

"Who would be watching us?" Mar'e squeaked.

"Anyone," Conch replied with gritted teeth. "Eerieden mercenaries, river otters, thieves, or any number of other unpleasant characters. That's why we need cover of night."

"We camp here till nightfall," Nathan'el determined.

Conch sank down wearily, and Mar'e curled up beneath some ferns. Jul'an scowled but ducked down and dug into the food pack.

Shaynnah clambered up a tree and disappeared. Nathan'el readjusted his sword and slipped off into the woods.

Out of sight and sound of the others, Shaynnah dropped down and joined him on the forest floor. "I told you," Shaynnah murmured. "Not a local villager."

"I know," Nathan'el murmured. "She and Jul'an are up to something."

"Isn't that obvious?" Shaynnah murmured. "Wren, son of Anamay, is away from the protection of his aunt. If he dies out here, who will know? Who will she attack? He has more enemies than anyone else I know."

Nathan'el stared at her. "We left him alone with Mar'e and Jul'an."

"They are fine," Shaynnah shrugged. "I can hear them. But it is best that we return."

Nathan'el followed the route he had taken, and Shaynnah once more disappeared into the trees.

Nurida stayed with Kiarna until the healer from Lunep arrived. She left very strict instructions that Kiarna was to receive the best of care, whatever she said, and went to wander the halls of the almost-legendary castle.

In its days as the castle of the Darkwoods Foxes, Lunep had been dark and lit by stuttering torches, or so her guide said. Red had been a popular color; red velvet had been everywhere. Now the halls were brightly lit by metal lamps where polished copper and precious gems reflected light. Some of them even had light shining through glass, casting beams of blue, green, and orange over the walls. Doors were held in place by heavily decorated hinges, and their handles were extremely ornate, reflecting the renowned skill with the forge of the foxes at Lunep.

Nurida made all the right comments by rote, but her mind was elsewhere. Lochuran and Ressora were both gone. She was convinced Lochuran hadn't run off.

Ressora was a different story entirely. It wasn't just the letter that convinced Nurida she had run off; Ressora was such a rebel that it was *exactly* the sort of thing she might do. The question was, now that she had turned traitor against Miamur, what damage had she done?

Even though Nurida still wasn't exactly sure who the enemy was, it didn't matter. She loved Miamur dearly, not to mention that anyone who wounded her oldest sister was Nurida's mortal enemy.

Nurida knew what had to be done: someone had to find Ressora and Lochuran, get the truth from them, and bring them back.

When she rejoined Elvinene, the Miamuran queen gave her a faint smile. "Kiarna fell asleep a few minutes ago," she murmured. "For now, sleep is the best cure."

Nurida swallowed. "I want to go find Ressora," she said before she could lose her courage.

Elvinene didn't look surprised; she *did,* however, shake her head firmly. "Not a chance," she declared. "You were brought along on this mission solely for the purpose of bringing you to Lunep without arousing suspicion. It was considered safer for you here."

"I came as part of a tracking party," Nurida countered. "Armed to the teeth."

"Looking for Kiarna," Elvinene corrected. "Ostensibly. If you were just sent to Lunep, it would make it obvious that your brother knows a lot about what's going on."

Nurida tilted up her chin. "Your Majesty," she said formally, "my whole life, I've been the protected one. The little one, the studious one, the shy, quiet, safe one. My sister just risked her life to try to gather information. My brother Asherad has fought many times to protect Miamur. My sister Lochuran has been kidnapped. I believe it is time for me to do my duty to King Galledor and to the White Wings." All at once, she found herself blinking back tears. "Please," she whispered. "I want to help my sister. I want to help Kiarna."

Elvinene gazed at her for a while, then stood, and went to the window. Nurida knew she wasn't seeing anything; there was nothing to see except fallen trees and a little grass.

After three minutes, Elvinene turned around with a faint smile. "I expected you to say that," she admitted. "So did Galledor. Nurida, understand that if Ressora doesn't want to be found, there isn't much we can do to find her."

"I won't have to," Nurida replied instantly. "She'll find me. She'll want to taunt me."

Elvinene nodded tiredly. "Yes, I expect she will. She has no fondness for you, Nurida. You, like the lily you were named for, were always too pure, too radiant."

Nurida ducked her head humbly.

"But how can you be sure she won't kill you?" Elvinene pressed.

"I do not believe she will," Nurida replied. "She is a bully and a rebel, but everything she has done so far has no consequences that cannot be ignored. I do not think she would go so far as to kill her own sister with her own paws."

Elvinene rubbed her eyes. "This goes against all my better judgment," she admitted. "But my gut is telling me that you'll be able to handle yourself. You'll need all the help the Bear King can give you, Nurida. Tonight, start by going west. I'll show you where to go on the map."

With that night came a heavy fog. Shaynnah silently rejoiced at this and gleefully roused her companions.

Nathan'el watched Mar'e rise. Shaynnah was very right; this mouse was no simple villager. Most of the time, her act was convincing. But when she whispered to Jul'an, "Give me the bag," it was in the tone of one who expected to be obeyed.

Conch made a point of staying as far away from Mar'e as he could. He put himself on the outside of the group, noting that Nathan'el had his paw on his sword the whole time.

"We will make it, right?" the sea otter whispered.

"We don't know that there's anyone to try to stop us."

Conch shrugged. "We didn't know that Moonpath and Shorefish were in our territory. I didn't know Danaray Mudriver really was where she lived. I didn't know the river otters were starting to take up slaving. Just because you don't know something doesn't mean it isn't there."

"That's only reason to be cautious," Nathan'el replied. "Not worried."

Conch gave a brisk nod and readjusted the straps on his pack.

"Time to go," Shaynnah whispered. "Remember, swiftly but quietly."

For a squirrel, she was remarkably good at being unseen in an open field. Nathan'el and Jul'an were honest-to-goodness field mice, so it wasn't too hard for them. Conch was the real problem. He was tall, even for a sea otter, and his ability to duck down and crawl through grass was impeded by his tail.

Mar'e, to their surprise, was right at home on the grass. She was no field mouse, but she still glided confidently through the stalks and didn't make a sound.

As they neared the great city, the fog began to blow away. Conch looked up at the sky and nearly stopped dead. There were so many stars that he could never see in the woods by his family's winter home. One twinkled brightly, seemingly just above them. He glanced west and saw a constellation that looked almost like a bird, soaring jovially into the limitless sky. Looking at it, he somehow felt lighter.

"Keep going!" Shaynnah hissed, her eyes flashing in the darkness. "Can't stop now!"

With a reluctant sigh, Conch turned his eyes back to the grass and followed her.

The night was half gone when they reached the base of Pasadagavra.

Nathan'el would never cease to be awed by its vastness. It towered up so high that the top was lost in the distance. The ground began to slope up at the base, as it was built right up against a mountain.

"Wow," Conch whispered. "It's very big."

"How observant of you," Shaynnah muttered snidely. "Come on, quickly! Our presence is still a secret. For it to remain so, we must hurry and find a door."

She began running sideways along the wall, running the back of her paw against the pink alabaster. It made an odd clattering sound.

"What is she doing?" Conch murmured.

"Just watch," Nathan'el replied quietly.

Suddenly her ring hit a rock and let out a chime.

"Right here!" she whispered. She examined the stones carefully and then found one little circle that moved when she turned it; in the opening was an imprint of the flute on her ring. She pushed it into the opening, much as she would press a signet into wax, and they all heard a faint click. Impatiently, Shaynnah turned a circle of stone next to the impression, and a section of the wall opened.

"Hurry," she whispered. "Inside."

They all slipped into the doorway and looked around.

It resembled something of a greenhouse. Trees, plants, and grass grew profusely, and a little stream, no doubt fed by the big fountain in the highest dome, splashed nearby. There was an earthy, warm smell, not at all the kind of smell one would expect from an enclosed fortress.

Shaynnah closed the door behind her and twirled a lever. "Now it's hidden," she explained quietly.

She stopped and looked around, taking stock of their location. "Well," she said cheerfully, "I haven't the faintest idea of where we are."

"That," said a voice that stirred Nathan'el's oldest memories, "is because you spend too much time in the wild, my sister."

Nurida slipped out of Lunep at almost the same time Nathan'el and the others started out for the field. She heard Elvinene's instructions ringing in her ears: *Don't get into fights. Go west, then north, and you'll be in friendly territory. Trust her to find you, and don't take unnecessary risks. As for Lochuran, if you see any trace of her, sketch the place and give it to the first Miamuran you see. There should be some of our scouts in the area.*

The Miamuran princess briefly wrapped her paws around herself; then she dropped them to her sides and tilted her head up. Resolutely, she set her paws on the path before her.

15

DANARAY AT WAR

When Nathan'el had last seen Tribeking Rhonndan, they had been roughly the same height. Now Rhonndan, tall even for a squirrel, stood at about a paw's width higher than he. Unlike Shaynnah, Rhonndan resembled Jaccah from his nose to his tail—or would have, if not for his teasing smile. There was an imprint in the fur on his forehead where a crown usually rested, but he wore no crown now. Nathan'el wondered if he'd been watching for them from one of Pasadagavra's lookouts

Shaynnah rolled her eyes at her brother. "I stay here too long, I'm gone too long. Great Bear King, brother mine! I just can't please you, can I?"

"At least you remembered a way in." Rhonndan grinned. He dropped from the tree branch, landing confidently on the grass and bounded forward to embrace his sister. After which, he turned to Nathan'el. "Long time, no see," he said simply.

Nathan'el nodded, realizing that Rhonndan was trying to act grown-up. "A lot has happened in these last seasons," he replied.

Rhonndan knit his brow. "Like what?"

"My mother and sister have been kidnapped."

Rhonndan's eyes flew wide. "Doomspear?" he asked.

Nathan'el shook his head. "Shorefish and Moonpath."

Rhonndan shuddered. "Come with me."

Shaynnah cleared her throat. "Introductions, brother mine. It's embarrassing that I've been in the wild for so long, yet I remember my manners better than you."

"I assumed that part of Nathan'el's explanation includes that," Rhonndan retorted.

Shaynnah made a face. "Of course you did."

Rhonndan led them to a large prism-shaped stone four times as tall as any of them. Ivy crawled up the stone and left a curtain, but when Rhonndan pulled it back, he revealed a hollow chamber. Inside was a ledge spread with moss and faded blue velvet, creating a soft bench, while the floor was covered in soft, dry sand. There was a good supply of food in here as well, and a fountain bubbling in the back made enough noise to cover their voices from passers-by.

Nathan'el looked around and grinned. "I remember this place!"

Tribeking Rhonndan threw his dignity to the winds and grinned back. "Well, it worked. We were never found hiding here. After Tribequeen Jaccah retired, I decided to keep this place secret. It's proven very useful. Please, everyone, have a seat."

While most of his guests chose the ledge, Rhonndan pulled himself up to a higher pinnacle of rock projecting from the wall. He crossed his legs and leaned his elbows on his knees. "Now, to start with—who are you all?"

He was looking directly at Mar'e as he said it, and she found an uncharacteristic stroke of boldness. "I am Mar'e," she replied confidently. "I was living in a village not too far from here, but it was attacked and destroyed."

Rhonndan gave neither reply nor indication of his thoughts. After a moment, his eyes flicked to Conch.

Here, the sea otter swallowed. His eyes darted to Jul'an, and he took a deep breath to steady himself. Rainbow's warning about not letting Jul'an know who he was rang in his ears. "I am Conch, son of Mollusk," he said, and it was easier to say than "Wren." "Moonpath and Shorefish kidnapped some of my friends and might have killed another."

Rhonndan let out a small sigh. "My grandfather," he murmured, "would never believe that I could side with a sea otter over a river otter. So, Shorefish and Moonpath have dared to anger the sea otters enough to kidnap some of them? That ... is interesting. But it certainly confirms what rumors I have been hearing these last seasons."

He and Shaynnah exchanged sad looks. Then he glanced at Jul'an.

The Keron Mouse did not bother to reply with anything resembling respect. "I am Jul'an of the Keron River."

"Then what are you doing so far from the Keron River?" Rhonndan inquired. "It's almost two days away."

"I had a feeling they would return via the Keron River," Jul'an answered. "*My* land."

If Rhonndan was concerned by Jul'an's presence in a city the Keron Mice had never visited before, he did not show it. The tribeking turned to Nathan'el and said, "So—start at the beginning."

Nathan'el did, though Conch got the feeling that he left out bits so Jul'an wouldn't hear them. But when he reached the part about Shorefish and Moonpath heading for the area, Rhonndan shook his head.

"If they are," he murmured, "they're taking a very odd route."

Nathan'el tilted his head back. "What do you mean?"

"They're on the border of our territory right now," Rhonndan explained. "I've had my scouts watching them. But they didn't come straight there from Nikor Mais. At first, they started north, towards Dobar, and then turned around for some reason. There's an old raven called Craic that brings me reports, and he says they're crouching on the edge of the forest and have been there for several hours."

Conch could make neither heads nor tails of this information; nor, it seemed, could Nathan'el. "What are they doing there?" the Cliff Mouse demanded, the tone of his voice rising in surprise.

Rhonndan shrugged. "Apparently, regrouping. The reports I've gotten say they reached the forest north of Nikor Mais, then turned, and started northeast about there. They've moved at a double-time forced march and covered half the distance from there to here in only three days."

"That's faster than *we* were going," Conch protested "And we were on the river. What are they doing? Why didn't they go after the prisoner they lost?"

The minute the question was out of his mouth, he had an answer: *They didn't know where to look for her.*

"I have no idea what you mean by a prisoner they lost," Rhonndan replied. "But I do know that they were in a hurry to reach Dobar. They started into the forest; then they turned around and tried to go around it. I have no idea why—that's some of the easiest travel in the world, through those woods. Here, let me show you."

He reached for a niche in the wall and pulled down a rolled-up map. Then he landed on the earth and spread it out.

"Nikor Mais is here," he said, pointing. "The best route to Dobar is through this forest, going mostly north by northwest. There are some hills, but there's also a network of valleys that makes a smooth, easy trail. For some reason, they started on this trail and then doubled back and started going along the edge of the forest. This took them northeast until it brought them to our borders."

Nathan'el and Conch joined him on the floor and stared at the map. "Why would they do that?" Nathan'el asked, bewildered. "There's nothing there to stop them—no cities, no mountains, no rivers. No *obstacles!* And yet, they're trying to go around the woods."

"It doesn't make sense," Shaynnah agreed. "The woods offer shelter from prying eyes, but they've put their secrecy into a position of extreme vulnerability."

Conch hardly heard them as he stared at the map. Nathan'el was right—there was nothing on it to keep Shorefish and Moonpath from the woods. Looking at the map, there was no reason for them to leave the smooth, easy trail. But what if the map couldn't tell the whole story?

There was at least *one* kind of obstacle that wasn't marked on maps.

"An army," he whispered. "There's an *army* there."

He traced the river flowing down from Nikor Mais. It became the Othyrn River, which flowed right past his aunt's realm. A river otter could swim that distance in a matter of hours, not the three days it had taken Conch, Jul'an, and Nathan'el. Assuming Moonpath and Shorefish had waited a few days before leaving Nikor Mais, probably to bind their wounds …

Shorefish and Moonpath crouched as near to the Stone Tribe territory as they dared. As if the loss of Princess Kiarna hadn't been bad enough, they had been ambushed less than a day north of Nikor Mais. No one could tell who had attacked them; all the warriors wore masks. The size of their tribes was considerably lower than it had been at the attack in Nikor Mais, and Shorefish couldn't help feeling a little smug that most of the lost warriors came from Moonpath's contingent.

Moonpath was near the height of her madness. "Where did they come from?" she hissed. "How did they catch up so fast?"

"The river," Shorefish replied pointedly. "If we had dropped our captives back at Graystone, we could have followed the river ourselves and would be in Dobar by now."

Moonpath whirled around and would have smacked her if Shorefish had been a whisker closer. "We need that mouse brat," she hissed. "She'll make up for your losing Kiarna!"

"Oho," Shorefish challenged. "*I* lost her, now did I?"

From the shelter of some high grass, Kermunda Bluebrook watched them. He silently gloried in their position: Shorefish and Moonpath didn't dare slip out onto the open field for fear they'd be too easily seen. He, on the other paw, was born and raised in grassland very much like this, and he knew how to remain unseen.

If one were to travel a day back the way they came, one would reach the farthest edge of the pleasant woods that surrounded Nikor Mais; on the other paw, a little less than a day in the exact opposite direction and one would reach Pasadagavra. On the one side of the open grass were fine deciduous woods, the ones that made up Stone Tribe territory; behind him were pines. To go southeast, one would eventually reach the Ashlands, the burned remains of the forests that once were Bow Tribe and Wraith Mice lands.

Without making a sound, Kermunda watched Shorefish and Moonpath argue. If he moved, he might give his position away. He had to wait for exactly the right time. But then, he couldn't wait for the sun to clear the trees, either; this was going to be tricky.

His eyes fixed on Fal'ne, Annor'a, Saline, Pearl, and Abalone, who were in the dead center of the huddled tribes. Saline was acting very much the chief's sister, keeping the other two sea otters strong. She had received harsh treatment, too. Kermunda could smell the infections in her lash wounds from thirty paces away, and she was limping from a heavily bruised ankle. Perhaps worst, her right paw was dislocated, and no one had bothered to set it back. If she wasn't rescued soon, she would surely sicken and fall. Fal'ne and Annor'a, however, appeared to have escaped the most brutal treatment by the simple measure of pretending to be sick.

When Shorefish turned away, Moonpath following her a smidge closer to the woods, Kermunda took his chance and slithered farther back. The main camp of this army was several minutes away, but sentries and runners had been stationed around Shorefish and Moonpath, lest Danaray's tribe be caught off guard. They hid in the gold grass, all but invisible.

At the main camp, two generals and Ol'ver the Cliff Mouse were anxiously waiting. Kermunda spoke first to the older general. "Any sign of the chieftainess?"

He shook his head. "No, not yet."

Kermunda switched his eyes to the other general. "What did our rearguards report?"

The general shook his head heavily. "No one's following us that they could see. There aren't any traces of anyone in the area, besides us. No one's scouted into the Stone Tribe territory since we don't want to tread on their tails, but all other directions are clear."

Kermunda nodded. "All the camp's defenses are in place, yes?"

Nods from both.

Kermunda dismissed them both with a wave of his paw. When they were gone, he turned to Ol'ver. "I saw no trace of your son," he said apologetically. "Fortunately, Fal'ne is still strong. She's a smart young mouse, and she's taking very good care of Annor'a."

"When are we going to get them back?" Ol'ver asked. The lack of sleep he suffered from was painfully obvious.

Kermunda glanced at the rising sun. "Dawn. We have to. Saline, the sea otter chief's sister, has taken about all she can take."

Ol'ver scrubbed a paw over his eyes. "How did my family get mixed up in all this?" he moaned. "I meant to keep them out of it."

Kermunda shrugged. "When the Bear King blows a trumpet and calls us to war, there's nothing we can do but fight with honor and throw our backs into it. Try to get some rest tonight. You'll have your daughter back tomorrow."

When sun rose over the sea otter lands, Eagle followed Audayin Creeksand back to the Othyrn River.

"With your tribe gone," the sea otter murmured, "you'll be left to follow them."

Creeksand shrugged. "I'll be fine. They'll have left some trail for me to follow."

When they reached the river, Creeksand turned and bowed to Eagle. "Thank you for your kindness," he said sincerely. "Someday I will find a way to repay you." With that, he turned and dove into the river. At the exact moment that he disappeared, another river otter head popped up closer to the shore. Eagle barely had time to blink before the second river otter had pulled herself onto the shore and stood up straight.

"Hello, Chief Eagle," said Chieftainess Danaray Mudriver. "Will you talk with me a moment?"

She sat easily on a fallen log, disregarding the cold and the water dripping from her fur. Perhaps her thick pelt gave her the warmth she needed. Her dark eyes fixated on his, the look there a contrast to her light, casual tone.

Eagle inclined his head to her. "I was told you and your tribe had left the area," he said, predicting a very confusing situation.

"My aide was told to say to anyone he came across that we had left," she replied. "But Audayin Creeksand's injuries are of no matter. Your sister is missing, is she not—along with another warrior and my sister's son?"

Eagle looked at her in surprise. "Your knowledge is impressive," he murmured. "How did you know?"

Danaray smiled. "I had told my niece, long ago, that even when it seemed I was not nearby, I would be. She only just remembered a few days past and came to me for answers. I gave her no information she could pass on to you; I chose to speak to you myself."

"For what reason?" Eagle could not help but ask.

She shrugged. "The less she knows, the less danger she is in. What I can tell you is that your missing tribe members were kidnapped by Moonpath and Shorefish."

"*Kidnapped?*" Eagle blurted out. "*Why?*"

Danaray held his eyes. "To create chaos," she said bitterly. "I warned you once that sooner or later you would face a war against river otters. That time is coming, and their prelude is to stir up chaos and confusion, to have you chasing your own tails and stumbling in the dark."

"Then more will go missing?" Eagle guessed, feeling sick.

Danaray nodded. "This was just a bit of Shorefish and Moonpath entertaining themselves. Their true task was to capture a Miamuran princess who wound up in Graystone. When they are permitted to go full out against the sea otters, then chaos will truly reign."

"Task?" Eagle shook his head. "Permitted? By whom?"

Danaray gave him a sad smile and then replied, "Keep this in mind: river otters are not the only ones you will have to fight. The puppeteer pulling Shorefish and Moonpath's strings is wearing the same signet as a former friend."

Eagle frowned. "We have a worse enemy than Shorefish and Moonpath, don't we?"

Danaray nodded. "All the world does." She looked out towards the river and then back to him. "I have sent a part of my army after Shorefish and Moonpath. If all goes well, your sister and the others should be returned soon."

She stood up and her tunic shook, making a few gold disks on the hem jingle.

Eagle tilted his head sideways, and asked, "Why did you want to give the impression your tribe was gone?'

She shrugged. "Something else was going on—a princess had to be recovered. I was trying to draw all the attention onto myself so others could look for her unnoticed. It didn't work so well, but it still helped." She glanced once more at the river, then faced him again and bowed. "We will meet again soon," she promised.

Eagle bowed in return. "I am honored, Chieftainess."

She smiled lightly and then her face became serious again. "I should tell you," she said softly, "that Shorefish and Moonpath were not the only ones connected to this princess. Doomspear was the one who first drove her to Graystone, and his price was aid in attacking you sea otters—at least, that's my best guess. If I were you, I'd get your tribe to Zurez about as fast as you can."

Eagle gave her an incredulous look. "And leave behind Conch and Saline? And Pearl and Abalone?"

Danaray gave him a fleeting smile. "There's almost nothing you can do for them; once my army frees them, I'll send them along to Zurez. I swear it."

Eagle bit his lip. "I am grateful, but … why?"

She widened her eyes slightly, the river otter equivalent of raising an eyebrow.

"Why are you helping us?" he pressed. "Why have you befriended sea otters? What is your end game?"

She looked at him thoughtfully for a minute. "No one's actually asked me," she murmured finally. "Those who care know without needing to ask, and those that don't know don't care. Tell me, why would I ally myself to Shorefish and Moonpath?"

Eagle chose his words very carefully. "I had been told that—when Anamay lived—you were less inclined to be friendly towards sea otters."

Danaray nodded. "True—I was. The Darkwoods War was going on, and the sea otters insisted on ignoring the war. Ignoring evil is a policy I cannot abide. But times have changed—so alliances change, too."

Eagle nodded slowly. "I was sure it had to be something like that."

Danaray drew her knife and turned it over in her paws, as if reminding him that she was still a river otter chieftainess and she wasn't ashamed of it. "What matters now," she said quietly, "is that we are on the same side." She glanced at the sun. "I have to go. Were I you, I would start preparing your tribe to move."

He nodded. "I appreciate the advice," he said.

She made as if to dive into the water but then stopped and turned around. "Eagle," she said coolly, "understand this: you forfeit my friendship and warrant my enmity the minute you treat my niece with anything less than complete honor."

"Understood," Eagle replied quickly.

"Good," Danaray continued. "Because my death threat didn't extend just to river otters."

After Tribeking Rhonndan called for his servants to prepare rooms for his guests, he drew Conch aside. Once out of the hearing of the others, he tilted his head quizzically to one side and murmured, "I do not know who you are, but I do know my sister and her quirks. When I asked who you were earlier, she signed to me not to."

Conch swallowed. "That was because Jul'an was there."

Rhonndan nodded. "I expected as much. Tell me, who are you really?"

The sea otter still took a deep breath before plunging on. "I really am Conch, son of Mollusk," he replied. "But my other name is Wren—Wren, son of Anamay."

Rhonndan didn't say a word for some minutes. Finally he said, "My grandfather must be rolling over in his grave right now. But no matter."

He sighed and rubbed a paw over his eyes. "If your aunt truly has intercepted Moonpath and Shorefish, my scouts will know soon," he murmured. "Whatever the case, Shaynnah and I will accompany you to the site where they are camped. But tomorrow."

Conch nodded and bowed. "I appreciate this," he said. "But I do not believe I can repay you."

Rhonndan shook his head. "There is no need. This is welcome intelligence you have brought." After a pause, he added, "Mar'e has asked to stay here. I have granted her request."

"Good!" Conch exploded. A moment later, his fur felt hot with embarrassment.

Rhonndan's cheek twitched in a smile. "She was a dead weight, yes? Well, I'm not surprised." The tribeking gave a little shake of his head. "River otters really have been ravaging the countryside," he murmured. "But, as far as I know, Doomspear has not made an attack here for some time. My sister believes Doomspear is kneeling before his employer right now, demanding his reward for attacking a Miamuran princess." He gave Conch a very sharp look. "There is only one thing that could induce him to risk the wrath of Miamur: your land."

In a terrifying flash, the enormity of the whole situation dawned on Conch, and he was more afraid of Moonpath and Shorefish than he had ever been. "Then—what Moonpath and Shorefish did was a prelude to *invasion?*"

Tribeking Rhonndan nodded. "Most likely. If your chief is wise, he will move your clan to Zurez as soon as he can. It will take more than the combined powers of the river otter tribes to overpower Zurez."

Conch barely heard him. How had he missed it! Shorefish and Moonpath's common primary goal was to drive his kind away! Capturing the chief's sister had been a dead giveaway. How had he missed it?

He looked right at Tribeking Rhonndan. "I have to go back!" he exclaimed. "I have to warn them!"

Rhonndan shook his head. "You first need rest. Then, tomorrow, my sister and I will lead you to the place where your friends are. If Moonpath and Shorefish are gone, then Shaynnah will accompany you back to your land to help you warn them. She knows those woods well enough that you shouldn't have to follow the Keron River."

To avoid the legendary river with its horde of highly territorial mice was a welcome relief to Conch.

"Rest tonight," Rhonndan urged. "I can promise you this is one of the last safe places in the world, and I don't know for how long it will be safe. Enjoy this while it lasts."

It was upon that dismissal that Conch got to experience the wonders of Pasadagavra. He was led to a den made out of bent branches by a kind-looking, middle-aged, motherly squirrel. There seemed to be no rooms in Pasadagavra, but his hostess provided him with blankets made of linens finer than even those the merchants carried. She also brought a comfortable nightshirt and a goblet of a sweet drink made primarily from nectar. Mar'e and Jul'an had been given equally generous treatment for, as the squirrel murmured, "We treat our guests royally in this city." But Nathan'el had waved aside her attempts to offer him a bed, and he sat conversing with Shaynnah some distance away. Their heads were close together, and they were both drawing in the dirt, but Conch, exhausted by the journey and his impatience with Mar'e, fell asleep before he could wonder what they were talking about.

"Nathan'el, listen to me," Shaynnah hissed. "If Conch is right and Chieftainess Mudriver is there, then your sister is safe. Snug. Secure. But as for your mother, I don't know what to do. The Stone Tribe has very few warriors compared to the king of Arashna's army. Nathan'el, for the time being, there's nothing we can do to save Ran'ta!"

"There has to be," Nathan'el insisted.

"There isn't," Shaynnah repeated. "Not yet. Even if you could sneak into Dobar, or Arashna, how would you free her? If, as you say, she was kidnapped because of her connection to a messenger, then she'll be under tight security. If for some other reason, she'll *still* be under tight security.

There are hundreds of Cliff Mice—why capture your mother? She saw something, she knows something, she can tell something Mokimshim doesn't want told! He will guard her *securely!*"

"There has to be something I can do," Nathan'el repeated.

"If there was," Shaynnah snapped, "your father would have done so by now, instead of just fighting to keep you safe."

The fact that she was right didn't soothe Nathan'el's restlessness. He wanted to do *something*, something to help his mother and his sister. Not rest!

Shaynnah watched him steadily. Then she sighed. "Tell me something. If I take your sister back to your father, will you go on to Dobar? Alone?"

Nathan'el nodded. "*Yes*. My mother is there, Shaynnah!"

Shaynnah sighed again. "This territory is the strength of my brother's tribe. Within these borders, they are mighty, but beyond them, they are vulnerable. They cannot help you once you go too far out of our territory. But there is someone who can. Living in a network of caves on the shore south of Dobar is a tribe of river otters."

"Shinar's band," Nathan'el remembered.

Shaynnah nodded. "If anyone can help you, they can. Not immediately—too much is happening along the coast right now."

Nathan'el nodded heavily, resigned to being patient.

"Rest this day," Shaynnah added. "We'll leave when the moon is high."

The sun was setting in the west when the disguised warriors of Danaray Mudriver's army attacked. Kermunda, unlike Rainbow, had no objections to obliterating Shorefish and Moonpath's tribes completely, but he didn't expect to tonight. Surely they would flee when they saw the numbers arrayed against them.

With the blinding light of the sunset behind them, the river otters crept through the grass. Their quarry's first warning was a hail of thrown spears.

True to Kermunda's prediction, few of the river otters stayed to protect their captives. As a healer, not a soldier, Kermunda watched from the edge of the fight as his tribe's opponents scattered and ran. Some tried to grab possessions, and some just fled.

When the fight began to spread out and simmer down a little, he edged closer to the captives. He still had to duck between battling pairs and dodge projectiles, but in the bright blaze of the setting sun and the loud battle-sounds, no one noticed him.

Then he saw Moonpath dart up to the captives and grab two indiscriminately by the shoulder.

Kermunda loosed his knife and threw it as he vaguely remembered. He was aiming for Moonpath's veiled head, and considering how long it had been since he had last thrown it, he considered it a triumph that it hit her at all. Unfortunately, it was almost impossible to kill someone by hitting the tail.

But it was entertaining to see Moonpath jump and howl, clutching at her wound. When she ran from a pair of young masked warriors eager for distinction, Kermunda could not withhold a grin.

"Oh well," he muttered. "Next time."

He dropped to his knees and crawled toward the captives while the battle clashed around him. The two female sea otters pulled back, though Saline looked as if she could barely move.

"It's all right," Kermunda told them. "I'm from Danaray Mudriver's tribe."

Relief was the strongest-felt emotion by the five released captives. Kermunda stayed with Saline and kept one supporting paw around her waist. Fal'ne and Annor'a were both leaning on Ol'ver, and both weeping with relief. The other two sea otters, who identified themselves as Pearl and Abalone, resolutely walked on their own.

When they reached the camp, Kermunda flat-out refused to let them move out yet. "There will be no attack for at least an hour," he pointed out. "And these five need medical attention. The chief's sister especially."

He led the five former captives over to his fire and opened his traveling case, which contained medicines and bandages. "All right, Saline. You're first."

Saline sat down awkwardly, and hardly seemed able to sit upright without wincing. Kermunda inspected her bruised paw to find infected cuts; he rubbed some salve on them and then wrapped her paw in bandages. "Walking on that will still hurt," he warned.

Saline gave a dismissive flick of her head.

Next he attended to the whip marks on her back to find that the whip had been braided poison ivy and thorns. Whoever whipped her must have worn thick gloves. Kermunda first washed her back with a combination of alcohol and herbal water to clean out all the infection and poison. She clenched her jaw the whole time and breathed through her teeth.

"I'm sorry," he kept saying. "But this will be over soon. It will hurt worse if it is left any longer."

Saline nodded and fought back tears.

After he rubbed salve on and bandaged *those* wounds, he decided to give her a little breathing time. He prepared the bandages for the splint and sling he knew he would need, then turned to face Saline.

"This is going to hurt," he said, "but I have to set your paw." And he did not relish doing so in the faint light of the fire.

"Can't you put me to sleep or something?" she begged.

"I can't," Kermunda replied regretfully. "If Shorefish and Moonpath counterattack, we may have to up and move at any moment, which we can't do if you're asleep or groggy."

Saline sighed and nodded. "Then do it."

To her credit, the sea otter only yelped when Kermunda yanked her paw back in place. For a moment, he thought she might faint with pain, but she bit her lip and held on.

"You know, I can do that to any number of seasoned warriors, and they'd all scream louder than you," Kermunda told Saline, which was only partly true. "There now, hold on; I just have to splint it."

The other two sea otters were watching with faintly sick expressions, but the worst they had to endure at Kermunda's paws was some bandages and salve.

"See if you can make a stretcher," Kermunda ordered a few of his tribemates.

They obeyed with alacrity—fearing, perhaps, that failure to do so would result in retribution from the healer the next time they were wounded.

Ol'ver walked Fal'ne and Annor'a over to Kermunda as he was finishing with Abalone. The healer looked up anxiously. "Any sign?"

The Cliff Mouse shook his head. "Not a trace."

Kermunda sighed. *Lucky me. I get to tell my dearest friend that I can't find her sister's son. Bear King, I'll need help with this task.*

"I'll send out a few scouting parties," he promised. "The smart thing to do would be to go to Pasadagavra, which is only a day away. If they're around, we'll find them."

Ol'ver nodded. "I have faith in your tribe," he replied softly. "And I have faith in my son. But this is a big, dangerous world. Sometimes brains aren't enough to keep you safe."

"They should be fine," Kermunda replied. "No one would dare offend Chieftainess Mudriver, and if Nathan'el is with Wren, he will be under her protection as well."

Ol'ver sighed. "I pray it works out."

"It will," Kermunda replied with conviction. *Bear King, make it so.*

At first Saline refused to be carried on a stretcher, but Kermunda assured her that she would only slow them down if she tried to hobble along on her bandaged paws. "Tell the scouts to follow our trail back to our camp," Kermunda murmured to one of the generals. "If they find a trail for Wren, they are to follow it."

"If I may make a suggestion," one of the generals requested.

Kermunda smiled. "As far as military matters go, your orders stand, not mine."

"I would suggest the scouts sweep the area for several days," the general replied. "In a large area, it is possible they have gotten lost. Also, unless they acquired a boat, chances are they haven't reached Pasadagavra."

"This is why your orders stand," Kermunda chuckled. "I hadn't thought of that. I'll accompany these patients back to Graystone or Zurez. You, generals, please do what you do best."

Kermunda's sole leading responsibility was to report to Danaray when this thing was over; he was happy to leave the rest to those who knew what they were doing.

CROSSROADS

While Nathan'el, Conch, and Jul'an prepared to set out with the squirrels, Mar'e tremblingly approached Nathan'el. He looked up with a pleasant smile, courteous as always around her. "Yes?"

"I wanted to thank you for helping me," she blurted out. "And for bringing me here. And for being so nice to me."

"You're welcome," Nathan'el replied. "It was a pleasure."

Conch stared. *Speaking of a lie through teeth.*

Mar'e reached for something around her neck. "This is the most valuable thing I own," she said, lifting a chain over her head. "But it's no use to me anymore. Will you take it, please, as a token of my gratitude?"

She held out a chain with a circular pendant dangling from it. Nathan'el took it with a smile and a thank you.

She smiled back prettily. "Maybe you could use it to find me after you find your sister," she suggested shyly.

Another smile and a nod. "Maybe I will."

Conch rolled his eyes.

Without Mar'e, Nathan'el, Conch, and Jul'an could travel much faster. They were led by Rhonndan, Shaynnah, and one of Rhonndan's scouts. It was a longer journey than Conch had anticipated, especially because Shaynnah insisted they change course once or twice to make sure they weren't followed. Once they got out of the field surrounding Pasadagavra, the route was entirely through gray, leafless deciduous trees.

They traveled through the night and the early dawn, but when the sun was first visible through the trees behind them, Shaynnah stopped and held out her paw.

The squirrel scout tilted his head sideways, as if listening. "Hm. They were near here. We should hear them by now."

"Maybe they're asleep," Rhonndan suggested.

Shaynnah nodded slowly. "Or gone. They are on the run. But it's a good place to start looking."

The mice and the otter crept through the trees, and the squirrels took to the branches. But before they had broken out of the trees onto the grass, they heard the rustling of bushes as Shaynnah dropped from the trees.

"There's no point in slinking," she called. "There are none here to see."

The others hastened out of the trees and stopped and stared around them.

"By the heavens' mighty thunder," Rhonndan whistled.

There was a long row of dead river otters stretching out on the grass. They were laid side by side, their faces covered by their cloaks, weapons in their paws.

Shaynnah touched the nearest one. "Not been dead a day," she whispered. "His fur still has a little warmth."

"Well," Rhonndan observed, "it looks as if you were right about Chieftainess Mudriver, Conch."

Nathan'el stared at the carnage for four long minutes; then, as if pushed, he ran forward and began examining the dead bodies.

"There's no mouse or sea otter among the dead," Shaynnah called. "No mice, anyway. There are three sets of mouse prints leading away from here. Two small, one large. Your father, perhaps."

Nathan'el carried on searching as if he hadn't heard.

Conch just walked down the long line of dead otters—there were at least fifty. All of them were ragged. "I don't see any from her tribe," he murmured.

Nathan'el stood up, his face haggard. "Great Bear King, what am I to do?" he whispered.

They spent another several hours examining the bodies, making conjectures as to what had happened and who went where. Rhonndan's scout followed the tracks that appeared to belong to Shorefish and Moonpath's bands. He came back panting.

"Shorefish, Moonpath, and the other survivors have definitely turned west," he reported. "They gathered up at a river about half an hour north and then followed it west. There was some blood among the prints; I also saw a thorny branch with blood on it. Someone was whipped."

"Or someones," Shaynnah muttered. "Were there any mouse prints among them?"

The scout shook his head. "None."

Nathan'el said hardly a word for several minutes. His eyes darted back and forth, and Conch could almost hear the desperate words running back and forth in his brain—*What do I do now?*

Conch sat down and stared at the bodies. No sea otters among them—Pearl, Saline, and Abalone were probably safe with his aunt. All he could do was hope—he had to get back to warn his family about Shorefish and Moonpath!

With renewed determination, he stood up and turned to see Shaynnah watching him.

"I have to get home to warn my chief," he stated. "To warn him of danger."

Shaynnah nodded. "I expected as much. The fastest way back is along the Keron River. If you wish, I will go with you. Nathan'el will have me make sure his sister is safe, anyway."

"Why are you so quick to offer help?"

Shaynnah shrugged. "I'm not really considered sane enough to help my brother in ruling my city," she said cheerfully. "So I help his allies outside Pasadagavra. Besides, he'll want to know what's going on in that region."

"Thank you, I think," Conch replied.

A smile flitted across Shaynnah's face. "Besides, you'll need someone to watch your back in Keron Mouse territory, and Jul'an doesn't count."

"What about Nathan'el?" Conch pointed out.

Shaynnah looked away so the sea otter couldn't see the troubled look on her face. "I think he's going after another prisoner of Shorefish's."

Nathan'el stood beyond the line of dead river otters, staring west, paw on sword. His posture and the agitated switching of his tail told Shaynnah exactly where he was going.

He was going to Arashna.

Part Two

NURIDA

A kingfisher dips o'er the foamy roars,
An eagle flies for hours and hours more,
But above all else,
The Lily of the White Wings soars.

~Miamuran Poem

ALONE IN THE WOODS

What in the name of the Bear King am I doing? Nurida thought as the sun rose over the plain.

She stopped when she reached a river and leaned back against a rock to survey the scene. If Ressora was anywhere near here, she could find Nurida with no trouble at all. Nurida had left a trail a blind child could follow, and Ressora was no blind child.

Lochuran sometimes entered her thoughts, and more than once she thought she heard her younger sister's voice. Sometimes she wondered if it was Ressora who had kidnapped Lochuran, but she really didn't think so. Ressora wasn't so much stronger than Lochuran that she could have kidnapped Lochuran without Nurida hearing. Was she?

It was late afternoon when she started following the river west. Ressora wouldn't have gone near Miamur; she would have fled in the opposite direction. Most likely, she would have fled to Arashna.

Elvinene had told her to go west; she had not specified how far. Perhaps she hadn't thought Nurida would go as far west as Arashna. It was sure to take forever, she reflected, and odds were that Ressora would find her long before she got that far.

"All right," she murmured as she started west. "This river should take me through the Ashlands, but only through the narrow part. This should be the Dellon River. It meets the Eupharra River, eventually, which comes out north of Diray. If I stay by the river, I can't get lost ... So I really do talk to myself. Ressora wasn't lying."

After an hour of traveling, she reached the trees. Much though she liked the open grasslands around Miamur, she also liked the shelter of the pines. There was no snow under these branches, and there was plenty of undergrowth.

When night fell, the temperature dropped steeply. Nurida found a sheltered hollow beneath some stretching tree roots and built a small fire. She covered the entrance of the hollow with some branches, leaving just enough of a hole to allow the thin wisp of smoke to spiral out.

Inside the hollow, the tree roots made a crisscross pattern on the ceiling. It was dry and earthy-smelling, and it made her think of the upcoming spring. There was also a bit of a wood smell that tickled her nose. It brought of warmth to the tip of her nose and ears.

She dug into her pack and took out her blankets. It was cold, but not as cold as she knew it could get. She burrowed into her blankets and watched the small tongue of flame, her ears attuned for any nightly noises.

She had almost dozed off when a strange voice reached her ears.

"There's a running river over here!"

She started and then crept toward the opening.

"How observant of you," sneered another voice. "As if I couldn't hear it a mile away."

"Then why didn't you say anything?" snapped the first speaker.

"I thought you heard it, too."

From beneath the screen of branches, Nurida stared hard out into the night, searching for the speakers.

"I can't hear nearly as well as I used to," the first stranger snapped.

Two dark shapes crossed right in front of Nurida, not noticing her. As they passed, freezing air swirled down into her hollow. Even as close as she was, she heard no sound of paws on the ground.

The two shapes walked to the river and knelt down; the minute shadowy paws touched the water, the shapes became more distinct. Nurida recognized the outline of two mice, both slender and wiry.

"You've been waspish lately," the second speaker observed. Nurida thought it might have been a female. "Why?"

The first one, who was definitely male, was silent for a while. Then he took a deep breath and exhaled heavily. "How can your conscience live with what we're doing?"

"What are we doing, Dikiner?" the female sighed. "We're carrying out the orders of our king."

"But you know what's going to happen once they're found," he argued. "And it isn't right."

"Then we'll just have to make sure we don't find them," the female answered with near indifference. But Nurida was sure she detected an odd note of apprehension in her voice.

Dikiner did not reply.

"Look," his companion said earnestly. "If we find Johajar, we don't have much choice. We were ordered to capture him and bring him back to Arashna. As for Zuryzel, where she is hiding is anyone's guess."

"How can you be so calm?"

Outlined against the silvery river, Nurida saw the female shrug. "Johajar needs me to be calm and to not find him. I haven't let my friend down yet, and I don't intend to. So, where else shall we look that we know they aren't?"

"Can't we stop for the night?" Dikiner suggested.

"Not yet," replied his companion. "We have to tell Mokimshim that we put all our effort into this. Come on, let's head upstream."

Both mice stood up; their outlines became blurry and almost invisible again, and they walked upstream. Or rather *glided* upstream.

Nurida slithered further back in the hollow. She knew what she had just heard, and it made her fur burn with anger. The two were Wraith Mice. She thought she might know the name Dikiner—hadn't Galledor mentioned him once or twice? Now that Queen Demeda was dead, they were in the employ of King Mokimshim. Zuryzel and Johajar were names she knew as well, and it seemed as if Mokimshim was hunting down his brother and sister.

And Ressora had really joined him? Did the idea of triumphing over her other siblings appeal to her? Now Nurida was beginning to find her older sister positively sickening.

She curled up close to the fire and forced her breathing to even out. Her eyes drifted closed, and she felt sleep encroaching. But before she slept, she swore silently that she would not let Ressora get away.

She woke to sunlight filtering through her branches, shivering all over. With shaking paws she rebuilt her small fire, making it a little larger. She found some wild potatoes and cooked them over the flames; they warmed her through in a heartbeat.

When she was finished, she buried the last of the firewood and scattered her sheltering branches so no trace of her presence remained. Then she crept back to the river and again began following it.

I need to get Ressora's attention, somehow, she thought. *I need to do something big. Something she'll notice. But what will she notice that no one else will?*

She was nearly lost in thoughts when someone moved up ahead.

Startled, she stopped and then slipped behind a bush.

It was almost twenty minutes before the other creature moved again. When he did, Nurida's first reaction was powerful pity.

He was a mouse with a black fur and a white face—a Wraith Mouse. But he crawled on all fours, his dark eyes darting madly back and forth. When he reached the river, he stood up but still looked ready to flee back into the shelter of the undergrowth. After looking around for several minutes, he dropped to his knees, drank straight from the river, and then turned and fled back to the woods.

Nurida was startled, her mouth hanging open. The Wraith Mouse looked as if something was wrong with him.. The way he darted around indicated he had some kind of battle-shock, but what was he doing in the wilderness instead of being cared for?

The Miamuran princess, whose sole asset in the whole affair was sheer determination, slunk forward and resolved to follow his tracks. It wasn't easy. The forest earth didn't imprint very well, and Nurida had no idea how to track in woodlands, anyway. She spent the better part of an hour following possible trails into the woods and running back to the river to try a new tangent. At the end of an hour, she sat down on a log.

"Bear King," she prayed again, "what am I doing? If I ever needed your help before, I surely need it now."

She gazed at the ground in front of her, completely out of ideas. The snow around here was hardened by many pawsteps, so probably the mad mouse visited here often. She could wait for him to come back, perhaps.

On an impulse, she straightened and stared very hard at the ground. If he came here frequently, he must have a trail.

On this new inspiration, she stopped searching for pawprints and broken twigs and started looking for packed snow, which might indicated the frequent treading of paws. This wasn't much easier, but when she reached a clump of salal bushes, she saw a path barely wide enough for paws going straight ahead, like a white line through the light green. Eagerly she ran forward, the cold almost forgotten.

Somewhat to her surprise, the trail led to a burned-out shell of a small wooden building, half-hidden by encroaching ivy. Nurida heard nothing from inside, so she ducked down into a nearby bush to watch.

For a long time, she waited, and still no sounds. She did not have the patience born of experience for a stakeout, so she drew her dagger and inched forward, half-bowed.

There was a piece of wood where the door used to be. She tapped the handle of her dagger on this three times.

There were several seconds of silence, and then a high-pitched, reedy voice screamed, "Begone, spirit!"

That was not the response Nurida expected.

"I-I'm not a spirit," she stammered. "My name is Nurida of Miamur."

"Get thee gone!" cried the voice from inside again.

"I promise, I'm not going to hurt you," Nurida repeated. "But I need to know who you are."

There was a startled silence. "You—you don't know who I am?" the voice exclaimed.

"No, I don't," Nurida replied.

To her right, one of the shutters on the window banged open. "Get inside!" hissed the mad Wraith Mouse's voice. "Hurry, before they see you!"

Nurida had done her fair share of climbing through windows to get outside the palace without her nurse knowing and readily fit herself through the window frame and shut it tightly behind her.

"No," said the voice behind her. "No, you're not one of them. You're too bright."

Nurida turned around to see the Wraith Mouse.

In the faint light slanting through the openings in the roof, she could examine his features. He used to be very handsome, but now his fur was ragged and unkempt, and his eyes jumped out of his head. Even though he shivered compulsively, he stood straight and held his head as if he were used to wearing a crown.

"One of whom?" Nurida asked, puzzled.

He licked his lips, looked anxiously back and forth, and whispered, "The portal demons."

18

PATROLLED

"The what?" Nurida asked, hoping for some clarification.

He gestured at the walls. "Portal demons! They haunt the outside of this building, but they're very sleepy creatures. You can avoid them if you run past them fast enough, but you don't want to be caught. Trust me, they're vicious. But they all know who I am, which means you're not one of them. What did you say your name was?"

"Nurida," the princess replied. "And yours?"

"Eyixid," he replied but whispered it. "I had another name once, but I don't remember. Anyway, what are you doing in this part of the woods? No one ever comes around here."

"I'm looking for my sister," Nurida replied. "She ran away."

Sadness filled Eyixid's eyes. "Ah," he murmured. For a moment, he was silent and then spoke.

"I came into these woods looking for my sister too," he said. "But I haven't found her. Maybe your sister is with her."

"Maybe," Nurida agreed.

"I remember it was a pirate who first noticed my sister was missing," Eyixid rambled on. "I think she had red fur, but I don't remember her name. She was a friend, though."

Nurida nodded, as if it all made sense to her, though the only reason she knew he meant the pirate had red fur, and not his sister, was that all Wraith Mice had black fur. "Have you seen a gray mouse with blue eyes out here, maybe?" she asked. "It would have been in the last few weeks."

Eyixid shook his head. "No, I haven't. But then, you're the first I've seen since the last time the moon was full."

Nurida sighed.

"You must love your sister," Eyixid observed.

"Yes," Nurida replied blandly. "Yes, that's why I want to find her." She took a deep breath. "Perhaps I should stop bothering you. I should go look for my sister."

"Don't go!" Eyixid cried as she started to turn away. "The portal demons know you're here. They'll be waiting for you!"

Nurida turned back around. Everything Eyixid had done showed he was crazy. But there was a glimmer in his eye that didn't look insane at all. It looked to Nurida as if this might be a precious moment of lucidity.

So what was he warning her about?

"Maybe I could stay awhile," she allowed. "I mean, if it's dangerous."

"Good," Eyixid replied. "It is dangerous. You don't want the portal demons to catch you. Come with me, I'll show you the living room."

The "living room" left Nurida with a thought: he was not right in his mind, but he hadn't always been like this.

It was really more of a basement cellar, but it was warmer than the area above. A fire burned in a pit in the dirt floor, but the walls were fine gray stone. There were shelves and alcoves built into the stone, some of which had blankets, food, or glass bottles. The stone walls were decorated with crude paintings done by no artist. Probably Eyixid had done them. There were different images—a mountain, a castle, and some flowers. But in each drawing was a star. Not many stars, just one star per drawing.

"You like stars?" she asked, looking around.

Sadness descended on Eyixid. "Not especially. I just feel they're important."

He went to one of the alcoves and reached for a wrapped package. "Here," he said, cheerful again. "Some food. I believe you must be hungry."

"You could say that," Nurida replied.

But when he held out a piece of dried fruit, she didn't accept it.

"What happened to you?" she asked, unable to keep the question back. "How did you end up here?"

His paw dropped back to his side. "You really want to know?" he asked his voice wavering.

Nurida nodded.

He frowned. "I angered someone. I stood up to him. He beat me up and held me in a dark, wet room. But I got away. I came here thinking I could avoid him." He cackled. "Now I have to run from the portal demons. But they're not hard to avoid."

Nurida nodded, though she had to fight against tears of compassion.

Nathanel slung his pack onto his back and tied his cloak one more time.

"You could at least rest before you take on the King of Arashna," Shaynnah suggested blandly.

"Not happening," Nathanel returned. "You're going to take care of my sister, right?"

"I will," Shaynnah repeated her promise. "But I won't explain a thing to your father. That is your trial."

"I understand, Shaynnah," Nathanel replied. "Thank you."

She smiled at him and then looked back toward the sea otter and the Keron Mouse. "I'll try to catch up with you after I've seen them back," she added.

Nathanel threw his paws around her and hugged her. "Thank you, old friend," he murmured.

She patted his back with one paw. "Cheepers, Nathanel, no need to get emotional about this."

What he didn't know was that she was blinking hard to keep from crying.

When she yanked back, she jerked her eyes away so he couldn't see her face. "Ready to go?" she called to the sea otter and the Keron Mouse.

"Ready as we'll ever be," Conch replied.

Jul'an just scowled.

"I'm ready to go, too," Nathanel sighed. He straightened his shoulders and turned around, going north. He would then end up by the river, the one otters had followed, and from there he would go west.

"Time for us to go our way as well," Shaynnah decided, refusing to show her concern over Nathanel. She strode between the otter and the mouse and started directly south.

Mercifully, Shaynnah's charges were silent for a few hours. Then one of them decided to start talking.

"Shouldn't we be going more southwest?" Conch called.

"I know where I'm going," Shaynnah called back. "We want to avoid a local band of river otters."

"And the river," Jul'an added importantly.

"I love how you Keron Mice talk about the Keron River," Shaynnah shouted over her shoulder. "Just simply 'the river,' as if it's the only one on the continent. And how you make oaths on it, as if it's somehow sacred or powerful."

"It's the home of the Keron Mice!" Jul'an snapped. "It has been for generations, and it will be until the ending of the world. It holds the blood and the heart of every one of my tribe that has ever lived. We fight for it and would gladly die for it. The river runs through all our hearts!"

"Why would you die for the river and not your tribemates?" Conch asked mildly.

It sounded as if Jul'an smiled as he replied, "Who said we wouldn't die for our tribemates?"

Shaynnah snorted. "Besides, it's not as though the river will in any way be affected by your dying for it."

Though Nurida left to scout the area for Ressora, Eyixid begged her to come back. She promised she would, thinking both that she couldn't leave Eyixid alone and that his derelict house made a perfect base for her to return to. Even though she wasn't afraid of his supposed portal demons, she humored him by running very fast through the opening.

Still … his references to these demons was not something she could shake off. Even now in daylight, she thought there was something sinister in these woods—although, maybe that was just her imagination.

She knew where in the world she was—she was in the woods between Dombre and Pasadagavra. The Ashlands could be reached if she went five days south, and Dombre in six. But she had no intention of going all the way to the Ashlands; after going south about a mile, she turned west.

She fully intended to spend the day exploring and gathering information. It might take her awhile to find Eyixid's house again, but she knew she could pull it off.

It was high noon, and having gone west for most of the day, she knew she was past Pasadagavra by now. She didn't think she was far enough north to see the city, even if she could see past the thick branches. Maybe it was the trees that felt sinister.

She remembered once, when she was very little, she'd stolen into her father's room and snatched up his royal robe, throwing it completely over her head. At first she'd thought it was a great game, but that changed rapidly when the heavy material bore down on her, pressing her to the ground. She'd felt as if she was suffocating. That feeling pressed on her chest now, and she was sure it came from the trees.

Then a voice drifted through the woods: "Besides, it's not as though the river will in any way be affected by your dying for it."

Clearly a bad time to walk in on the conversation, Nurida thought, her heart fluttering nervously.

She drew herself up to full height and prepared to meet the newcomers.

A moment later a bush was thrust to one side, and a wild-looking squirrel stood in the cavity. "Who are you?" the squirrel demanded, looking startled.

Behind her, to Nurida's great surprise, emerged a sea otter and a rugged mouse. "I am a traveler on the way to Myanka from Miamur," she invented. "Am I on the right trail? So many of the old roads are inaccessible now."

The ragged mouse gave her a startled look, looking as if he'd just walked into an invisible wall, but he said nothing. The squirrel looked at her suspiciously. "Most traveling to the coast from Miamur go by Pasadagavra," she said.

"I wished to avoid all major cities," Nurida replied casually. "It is hard to know who may be trusted these days."

"Amen to that," the squirrel agreed. "Why go to Myanka?"

Nurida gave her a guarded look. "What does it matter?" she asked. "At least, to you? Tell me, am I on the right path?"

"Such as it is," the squirrel replied.

"Who are you?" the sea otter asked.

"I did not ask you your name," Nurida returned. "In return, do not ask me mine."

Still the rugged mouse stared at her in astonishment.

She addressed her next question to him. "Tell me, have you met any other Miamuran travelers on your way?"

"Yes," he blurted out. "I mean, no. I mean … she wasn't Miamuran, but yes, she was another traveler."

"Was this creature perhaps traveling to the coast as well?" Nurida asked. "I might like some company."

"No, she's at Pasadagavra," the rough mouse stammered back. "And she wasn't going to Myanka. Why are you?"

Nurida inclined her head to them. "I see you have somewhere to go, and I will not detain you. Have a fine journey." She continued in her same direction through the undergrowth.

"Wait!" the rough mouse cried after her. "Who are you?"

"You will not meet me again," Nurida whispered under her breath.

Shaynnah stared after the mysterious mouse in a combination of consternation and surprise. "Who was *that?*" she demanded of thin air.

"I got the feeling she really didn't want us to know," Conch murmured.

"How very observant of you," Shaynnah retorted, still staring after her. "'I will not detain you?' Who uses the word 'detain'? My brother doesn't even use it in official documents!"

"Does it really matter what word she used?" Conch asked dryly.

"Have you ever used that word?" Shaynnah challenged.

"No."

"What about your family?"

"I don't think so."

"What about anyone you've ever spoken to?"

Conch racked his brains. "Well … Chieftainess Mudriver, maybe."

"And she's royal," Shaynnah elaborated. "But I've never heard anyone else use that word! Well, except for poets."

"So maybe the mouse was a poet?" Jul'an suggested.

Shaynnah rounded on him angrily. "'No, she's at Pasadagavra, and she wasn't going to Myanka?' Seriously? One pleasant smile from that stranger and you drop all your barriers?"

"I did not drop any barriers," Jul'an snapped. "What did I say that was important?"

"If she was after that simpering, fluttering idiot Mar'e, she now knows exactly where to look!" Shaynnah snapped.

"I thought you didn't like her," Conch interrupted, furrowing his brow in confusion.

"I don't like *him,* either," Shaynnah exclaimed pointing a dire paw at Jul'an, "but that doesn't mean I want to see anything happen to him! And if Mar'e was running from that 'poet,' then she surely isn't hidden in Pasadagavra anymore!"

"So … what happens now?" Conch asked.

"My brother will take care of her," Shaynnah replied firmly. "We keep going towards Graystone. And now I am thinking we should follow the Dellon River instead of the Keron."

"What's on the Dellon River?" Conch asked.

Shaynnah suddenly smiled. "It is the most pleasant of all rivers, I think. A few days west of here, it makes a sharp turn due south and splits into several tributaries. One goes due west, and it's called the Gal Dar'An River, or Midnight River. Another one of the tributaries splits into the Kyaagha Brook and the Huaaka Creek, which go through your territory. Another one goes over Nikor Mais and becomes the Othyrn River, but the nearest one joins the Keron River. The Keron Mice consider it part of their territory. We'll go by the Othyrn, since that one will be the safest route."

Strangely, Jul'an said nothing to this.

Conch asked, "What makes it the most pleasant?"

Shaynnah chuckled. "The word *Dellon* means *clear*, and clear the Dellon River is! It's ten feet deep in places, but you can see the sand in every part of the river. There aren't a bunch of water weeds in it or tangled weeds falling into it from the bank. There's no rotten smell or squelchy mud. Rocks line the banks, and there are ferns on each side to hide in. Moss, too. I know where to find a hidden canoe, so we can have a swift, pleasant journey. I also know an inn to stop at where we can pick up supplies, so let's pick up the pace. You two will be home in barely more than a week. Just think of the reception you'll get."

She saw Conch wince. Satisfied, she turned around and led the way southwest. They would find the Hidden Glade Inn later in the week and reach the Dellon soon enough … if they could avoid getting followed by anyone hostile …

Nathan'el reached the river where Shorefish and Moonpath had fled as night was falling. The bank was made of brown mud, and there were trees about two miles away both upstream and downstream. Everywhere were otter prints and blood spatters. The mud also had odd ridges and dips, probably sculpted by the river. On one of ridges, Nathan'el sat down heavily and stared at the water.

Little though he wanted to admit it, Shaynnah was right. How was he supposed to get his mother back? At the very least, he needed a plan.

He reached for a piece of flint in his pocket, about to strike it, but then stopped. From now on, he had to consider himself in enemy territory; that meant no fires at night. Not as though there was any dry wood, anyway.

The western sky was lit up with fire and scudding clouds, and he felt a little leap in his heart. He would get to see at least the ocean again, if not his home in Harboday. He would hear the waves crash against a rocky shore and watch as the seagulls soared above. He would smell salt on the wind instead of river mud. The thought of going home lightened his heart.

He was about to stand to find a place to sleep when something caught his eye: a mouse print.

He scooted closer and examined it. Rhonndan's scout had said there were no mouse tracks by this river, and the print looked fresher than the multitude of otter tracks here, there, and everywhere.

Another mouse had been here!

Nathan'el tried to fit his paw into it, but found it was smaller than his. Careful not to ruin any other prints, he crept around the scene searching for more. There were only a few mouse prints—but there was one print he couldn't identify at all.

What is that?

It looked a little like a squirrel, he supposed, but it was too wide. There were only three of these tracks evident, and all three of them led to the river. It was deep and bubbling here, but right at the water's edge was a deep gouge in the earth.

A boat docked here, he thought. *And there were two creatures in it: a mouse, and—could it be a ferret?*

A pirate?

From the top of the bank, a voice called, "Let's get some water."

Nathan'el whirled around and stared at the edge of the bank; then he darted for an outcropping of rocks and hid behind it.

A heartbeat after he was hidden, four creatures appeared at the top of the bank. There were two mice, both looking like Eerieden mercenaries, and two creatures that were undeniably ferrets. The Eerieden mice walked casually to the river's edge and ducked down to drink; the ferrets lingered on the bank.

"You ain't our bosses," called one, a female.

One of the mercenaries wiped his mouth and turned to leer at her. "King Mokimshim seys I am. You wanna contest it with him, Wi'terblade?"

The ferret glared back but said nothing. After a moment, the two mice chuckled and turned to walk upstream.

The two ferrets walked to the water's edge, but instead of drinking, they waded right in. The female muttered softly, "She's askin' a lot."

The other gave her shoulder a reassuring pat. "It's as much for our freedom as hers. Be patient, 'Blade."

"Easy fer you to say, Eneng," she muttered back. "Yer a pirate for the fighting, not for the ocean. I *miss* my seas."

The other sighed. "Patience, little sister, or you won't ever get yer seas back. C'mon, let's follow the others. The way these patrols keep gettin' in each other's way, it'll be a miracle if any of us actually finds anything."

They continued upstream, still wading in the water.

As soon as the coast was clear, Nathan'el darted off the beach and into the cover of the woods. He found a small hollow that was mostly screened by bushes and dug in there. It looked as if he would have to do a lot of sneaking over the next few days. This area was patrolled.

19

A SMUGGLER'S HAVEN

"Come here and look at this!"

Nurida left off sharpening her knife and hurried to the window where Eyixid stood. The moon had risen beautifully over the tops of the trees, and Nurida somehow felt warmer for it.

"The moon always reminds me of my sister," Eyixid said. "What reminds you of your sister?"

Nurida was about to say *hawks,* but then she thought of Kiarna. "Roses," she replied. "My sister always likes to sit in our rose garden. She'll have some of her projects with her and always someone playing music. She invites me to join her and talk with her, but I … I never did as much as I should have."

"It's always like that," Eyixid reflected. "We never spend nearly enough time with those we love."

He gazed at the moon awhile. After a few moments, Nurida stood up and went back to sharpening her weapon.

"You need a sword," Eyixid said out of the blue.

"I don't know how to use one," Nurida replied, still focusing on her dagger.

"I can teach you," Eyixid answered dismissively. "I used to be very good."

"Swords won't do any good against the portal demons," Nurida observed, breathing gently on the metal.

"It would if you got one by itself," Eyixid shrugged. "Anyway, it can't ever hurt a pretty young mouse to know how to use a sword."

Nurida sighed heavily. "My brothers know how to fight with a sword, but I never learned. I just know how to use a dagger because my oldest brother insisted on it."

Galledor had given her this dagger, too. The blade was inscribed with the Miamuran letters that spelled out *lily*. Only there, written in steel, did the word seem powerful.

"You need a longer reach," Eyixid commented. "If it's a thrust between you and someone with a long sword, you're going to lose."

Nurida paused in sharpening her knife. "I don't expect I'd survive anyway. I barely know how to use the knife."

Eyixid clicked his tongue. "You need to learn. In times like these, everyone should know how to use a knife."

"Where am I to learn?" Nurida asked.

"I can teach you," Eyixid repeated. "It's not as though there's much else to do around here. Right outside the living room is a door, and past that is a flight of stairs. It leads down to the cellar. Pick out a sword from there, and make sure you can lift it. Then come back up here, and I'll start teaching you."

Nurida laid her knife aside and stood up quickly. "Are you sure? I—I'm not that tough."

"How do you know?" Eyixid asked, a tiny little smile quirking at his whiskers. "It's hard to tell how tough you are until you've been tested. Go on."

The princess slipped through the arch that led to the living room. Immediately to her left was a door she'd never paid attention to before. She lifted the bar and opened the door carefully.

She saw the first few stairs, but the rest descended into darkness. With one paw on the wall, she stepped down slowly, afraid of falling forward. The stairs were wood beneath her paws, and they creaked restlessly at her step.

But about halfway down into the darkness, the wood became stone. The wall at her sides also became stone. Two stairs after this, a faint orange glow reached her eyes below her, and a wave of warmth washed over her.

It was only another eight steps before the ground leveled out. Nurida stared at the "cellar" with wide eyes. "Great Bear King," she whispered.

The faint orange glow came from a forge in the far corner of the room. It was a tall thing with a bellows ready to fan the flames to greater life. Right now it was nothing more than a few tiny flames dancing over a bed of bright coals, but the warmth resided in every corner of the room. Hanging on the wall, bathed in the glow of the forge, was a staggering array of swords. They rested by the hilt on pegs, each one unique and powerful and somehow *beautiful*. One had a crosspiece as wide as Nurida's waist, but it was shaped like a pair of eagle's wings reaching out. Another was shorter, slimmer, and finer, but the hilt was made to look like the head of a roaring lion. One had almost no crosspiece, and the pommel stone was an emerald. Another pommel stone was a blood red garnet, and it looked as if it was held in the claws of some great bird of prey. There were some swords that probably weighed more than Nurida did, and others that looked as light as a feather. Some were just plain swords, but still beautiful, while others must have taken months to create.

Nurida's eyes were drawn to one of blue-silver steel. There were jagged designs where the hilt met the blade that made Nurida think of icicles, but no other artwork graced the sword. When Nurida lifted it from its peg, it was almost as light as her knife. When she swung it experimentally, it balanced perfectly in her paws.

Snatching the scabbard that lay beneath it, she turned around and hurried back up the stairs. The door fell shut behind her, and she grabbed onto the wall to make the tight turn into the living room at top speed.

"What's that forge down there?" she panted, her chest heaving.

Eyixid smiled. "I don't really know how best to use it, but I keep it going. It keeps the house warm, and the portal demons don't like it. So which one did you choose?"

Nurida had almost forgotten about the sword in her paws. She held it forward and Eyixid bent close to it, inspecting it but not touching.

"Hmm, I remember this one. It belonged to a wise warrior, a long time ago. I think her name was Demeda. She was brave and very smart."

Demeda? Nurida wondered. *Not* Queen *Demeda!*

As Eyixid straightened up, she noticed sadness in his eyes. But he was quick to turn away, and there was no trace of it in his voice when he said, "All right, first lesson. You picked a good one to learn on, because Akuwair has ideal grip. We may have to rewrap the hilt, though …"

"Akuwair?" Nurida repeated.

"That's the name of the sword—though, I don't know how it got here," Eyixid explained. "In the old days, great swords bore names that reflected the wielders. *Akuwair* is Simalan for *The Far-seeing One*, so presumably the wearer—"

"Had good eyesight?" Nurida interpreted.

"Well, maybe," Eyixid replied. "But don't you know lore, Nurida? Interpret The Far-seeing One as if it came from lore."

Nurida thought back to the epic poems she used to read in the Miamuran library. She thought about the heroes and heroines and their titles. In the world of lore, sight didn't just apply to the eyes.

"She—could see one step ahead," she murmured. "Could see more than what was right in front of her face. She could predict what her opponent was about to do."

"Indeed," Eyixid replied. "It's most likely that is what was meant by Akuwair. It's also a good name for a sword because part of a sword fight is being able to plan for your opponent's next move while concealing yours from him. But I'll get to that later. For now—just some basics."

He crossed the room to the far corner that was hidden in shadow and picked up another sword, this one plain. He strapped the scabbard around his waist and drew the blade. "First and foremost," he said, "don't think of this like a science. It can be, but you'd do best to learn it as a piece of lore. This is a bit of legend you're learning, like a key to a story. Don't try to memorize anything; the true sword fighter doesn't just fight with the paws but also with the heart."

Nurida nodded. "Got it."

She knew about putting a piece of her heart into her work. She did so every time she opened a book.

"Now, a sword battle is about leverage," Eyixid continued. "You can overpower anyone, no matter how strong he is, if you know where to put your sword. We'll start there. When I bring the sword around in a slice, intercept it with your hilt as close to my blade as you can. Remember, neither of these has been sharpened in a while."

Nurida nodded, taking a deep breath to help herself focus.

Eyixid brought the sword in an uppaw slice against her head. To her it seemed blindingly fast, though actually it wasn't especially swift, and she nearly panicked. She reacted on bare instinct and lifted her sword up desperately.

She met the stroke with the hilt a good six inches from Eyixid's blade. It would have been passable, but she had flinched away from the stroke, which weakened the force behind her block. And, perhaps worse, she met his strike with the sharp edge of her sword.

Eyixid nodded. "Good, you didn't freeze. That's promising. But in the future, turn the sword so you intercept with the *flat* part of the sword."

"You didn't tell me that," Nurida murmured.

"I know," Eyixid replied unabashedly. "I'm telling you now. Also, *don't flinch* when you meet the strike."

Nurida nodded.

"The only way to cure this flinch is to practice, practice, practice," Eyixid continued. "When something sharp and deadly is coming at your head, your instinct is to flinch and flail. Practice is the only way to overcome instinct. Now … again!"

They did the same stroke thirty times. Then Eyixid tried to surprise her by swinging another blow at her legs. But Nurida had been waiting for that, and though her defense wasn't especially strong, it caught the sword.

"Good!" Eyixid exclaimed. "Oh, not your defense—that needs work— but good that you weren't surprised!"

Nurida grinned.

"Now, when you try to block one going down, it's important to block it as soon as possible," Eyixid continued. "Again, more of the leverage. So we'll work on your speed as well as your strength with this block."

He showed Nurida how to block a downward swipe without exposing herself to an attacker's blade. By the time he decided they had finished with that practice, Nurida was panting heavily.

"Well done," Eyixid murmured. "Well done, indeed. You have a reflexive mind, Nurida."

That bit of commentary confused the princess. "What does that mean?"

Eyixid smiled. "It means that what you lack in natural gift, you make up for with your cleverness."

Nurida sighed and looked away.

"You didn't think so?" Eyixid asked, and Nurida didn't miss the wisdom tinting his voice.

"It's just …" She searched around for the right words. "Practice is one thing. I'm worried—I doubt I'll be able to think when it's for real."

She glanced back to Eyixid to see that he was smiling.

"Nurida," he soothed, "have faith in yourself."

Nurida shook her head. "I cannot."

Eyixid rested a paw on her shoulders. "Everyone wonders how they'll react in trouble. But I have seen troubles, Nurida, of all kinds. Every time, I always watched those that are most afraid, least sure of themselves. Well—they never accomplish great feats of legend. But neither do they fail. Creatures like you have a way of rising to the occasion."

Nurida looked up in wonder.

"I've always been annoyed by those epic legends," Eyixid continued. "They speak of great kings with the strength of thirty foxes. They are wonderful stories, I suppose, but they never tell the best parts. They never tell of creatures like you—creatures who have lived peaceful lives and then find their courage when need calls. It's the most irresponsible omission in the whole world of stories."

The Miamuran princess hardly dared believe it. She was no warrior; but then, Eyixid hadn't spoken of sword skills, he'd spoken of courage.

"I still enjoy reading those legends, though," he added humorously, as if trying to make her smile.

She did smile. "Who wouldn't?"

"Those whose imagination is less capable than yours, Nurida," Eyixid replied cheerfully. "Those who cannot journey into the wonderful world, all within a paw's touch."

Nurida shrugged. "With a good imagination, you don't even need a book to be somewhere else."

"Ain't that the truth," Eyixid said fervently, his ears twitching. "If not for my imagination, I'd have gone insane waiting here day after day with all the portal demons lurking outside!"

Nurida managed to stifle her laugh, but she couldn't conceal a grin.

Eyixid raised his sword once more. "You should smile more often," he said. "It's good for you. But for now, back to work."

The Hidden Glade Inn made Conch nervous from the moment he saw it.

"Is this really safe?" he muttered to Shaynnah.

She nodded. "Yes, if you don't talk too much. I come here all the time."

That didn't exactly ease Conch's worry. Jul'an looked just as dubious. "It looks like a smuggler's haven," he said nervously.

"That's because it is!" Shaynnah exclaimed in a whisper. "At least, smugglers use it sometimes. But trust me; it's the safest place around."

After the last four days of trekking along in Shaynnah's wake, Conch had learned she had an interesting definition of "safe." Two nights ago they'd camped in a cave with an entrance covered by stinging nettle. Last night they'd slept on a muddy island in the middle of a creek.

"What about smugglers is safe?" Jul'an asked icily.

Shaynnah rolled her eyes. "Use your head, Keron Mouse. Smugglers don't want to be caught by anyone either, and especially not by the creatures we're avoiding. That means they won't blab about us being here."

"But what will they do *to* us?" Conch queried nervously.

"Nothing, if you don't bother them," Shaynnah replied promptly. "Come on. Inside."

The building was a three-level wood building covered in ivy vines. The trees made a tunnel leading right to it. As the three journeyers approached the inn, Conch saw numerous tiny paths that could lead to a quick getaway. Was that why Jul'an had said it looked like a smuggler's hideout?

Then he realized what had really made Jul'an think so: there were no windows in the building, but numerous doors. Again, helpful for a quick getaway.

"Who rules this area?" he asked.

Shaynnah snorted. "No one. This has been the wild for as long as anyone can remember." She started for the door but, just before knocking, paused and turned. "Oh—one more thing. While we're inside, don't draw a weapon for *any reason* except to defend your life."

With that, she knocked thrice on the door.

It was opened by the oddest creature Conch had ever seen. Something about it was reminiscent of a squirrel, but not much. It had gray fur and pointed ears. And, at first he thought it had a black mask around its eyes—but then he realized this was fur, too.

"Hello, Una," Shaynnah said pleasantly. "Hoping there's room for three."

"Tribeprincess Shaynnah," Una said coolly. "You're not exactly welcome here anymore."

"Ah, come on, Una," Shaynnah said winsomely. "My money is still good, and I bring *guests* this time!"

Una frowned. "Last time you were here, you started a brawl that upended tables."

"Well," Shaynnah said casually, "you have my word that *that* won't happen again."

Una's eyes swept past Shaynnah and took in Conch and Jul'an. Finally she said, "No trouble from you, Shaynnah. This is your last chance."

"But of course," Shaynnah replied cheerfully.

Una scowled at her and stepped back, but to Conch and Jul'an she said, "Welcome to the Hidden Glade Inn."

Immediately inside the door, the Hidden Glade Inn didn't look too different from the outside. Potted trees everywhere released a sweet smell. It was dark inside, as most buildings were, but there were tiny lanterns hanging from the tree branches. There were some on the ceiling, too, making it look a bit like the night sky.

Immediately to their left were rows of doors that could only be rooms; they stretched out into a hallway that was lost in darkness. In front and to their right was a small reception room with nothing more than a locked chest and a table, on which sat an open ledger. Una walked around behind this, and picked up a stick of burnt wood.

"How many rooms?" she asked with a sort of weary mistrust.

"Three," Shaynnah replied confidently. "Right next to each other."

"On you, Shaynnah?" Una added.

"I still have gold on my tab."

Una nodded and rubbed her eyes. "Yes. That, you do. Lots of it. How many nights?"

"Not sure yet," Shaynnah answered easily. "Two or three, maybe. But don't worry about writing our exact names down, either."

Una gave her an irritated look. "You know I never reveal my customers' names."

"I know," Shaynnah agreed. "But you don't walk around with that ledger chained to your paw, either. And I don't want the wrong creatures opening it up to find the Tribeprincess of the Stone Tribe was here. I'll pay extra for it, but put in three fake names."

Una rolled her eyes. "I don't need extra pay, Shaynnah. Three fake names."

She reached into a pouch at her waist and drew out three copper keys. She handed one to Shaynnah, one to Conch, and one to Jul'an. "Follow me."

She led them back down the dark hall, until she stopped at three beige doors. On each one was written a word in blue ink: *surim* on one, *akor* on another, and *liliar* on the third.

"The names of the rooms are written on the keys," Una informed them. "If you need anything, I'll be at my desk. Otherwise, please make yourselves at home."

She turned around and started for her desk. Shaynnah gestured at the doors for Conch and Jul'an's benefit, then darted after her. "Una, wait! I have something to discuss."

The strange creature didn't stop; she just beckoned over her shoulder with her paw. Shaynnah caught up to her and began to speak in a low voice.

Conch frowned after her, not happy to be left alone with the Keron Mouse, but Jul'an had already figured out which room he had the key for and gone in. Conch followed his example, at which point he discovered— and he didn't think it was by coincidence—that Shaynnah had the room between him and Jul'an.

The room that greeted Conch's eyes when he opened the door made his jaw drop in surprise. The floor was solid rock covered with fresh juniper branches. The bed was connected to the wall, but there was no mattress. It consisted of rope strung taut between the wall and two posts; the rope was covered in cedar branches. Across the room from the bed was a nightstand and a washbasin—except the stand was a tree stump growing right out of the floor and the washbasin was simply cut into the wood. The far side had a glassless window, but instead of being hidden by curtains it was concealed by willow fronds and ferns. The walls were reddish wood, unfinished and unpainted, giving a feeling of being inside a tree. No wonder Shaynnah liked this place so much.

Conch sat down carefully on the edge of the bed; the rope sagged but did not give completely. The door had swung shut of its own accord, and now Conch saw there was something like a mini door set in at about eye level—probably to peek out and see who was knocking.

He lay back, completely alone for the first time in ages, and began to think.

All right, he thought. *Shaynnah, I can trust. Sh'vendi said so. I mean, Rainbow said so. Oh, whatever. But Jul'an, she didn't trust, and Nathan'el wasn't sure about him either. And yet … Shaynnah didn't trust Mar'e very much, but she does seem to trust Jul'an. Or at least, she hasn't passed judgment on him yet.*

He began to make a mental list in his head. *Item one: find out what Shaynnah knows about Jul'an that makes her hold back judgment.*

He rubbed his eyes and began to think again. *I have to get back soon. And when I do, Eagle won't be too happy. Nor will Father …* That thought left him feeling rather gloomy. He knew perfectly well that they would say he should have gone back for help—but if he had done that, how would they have found Shorefish and Moonpath's trail again? They could have disappeared, and Conch doubted even his aunt would be able to find them.

He lay back on the bed for a long time, wondering what his punishments would be when he got home. When Shaynnah knocked, the stars were out in the velvet sky and fireflies winked outside his window.

"Such a gloomy look for one who's nearly home," the tribeprincess observed.

"Never mind," Conch muttered. "What are our plans?"

Shaynnah closed the door. She went to the window and looked casually out, searching for a listener. "Oh, good old Una. She still grows the blackberries beneath the windows." Assured but still wary, Shaynnah returned to the middle of the room and sat down on the floor.

Conch slipped off the bed and sat across from her.

"We'll leave in six days," she whispered. "And then we'll—"

"*Six days?*" Conch exclaimed. "Why so long? We have to get back to warn the sea otters!"

"I know," Shaynnah replied coolly. "Una has two canoes she rents out. The last users are expected back five evenings hence. We leave before dawn on the sixth day. If we were to travel overland, it would take two weeks. We only need one canoe, and we'll get back to your lands in three or four days—and that's only if we have rough sailing. But we won't go all the way by river. We'll have to carry the canoe around Nikor Mais—that will be fun—and get back in the water once we're sure we're out of hostile territory. That river becomes the Othyrn River eventually. We should be safe from the Keron Mice and the river otters. But understand this: if we are to encounter trouble, it will come at one of two places. It will either be at the fork where one of the rivers leads to the Keron River or at Nikor Mais itself."

"How dangerous is this?" Conch asked nervously.

"Until we get to the Othyrn River—it's dangerous," Shaynnah said simply. "Our greatest assets will be speed and concealment, and our best bet—maybe even our only bet—is not to be seen."

Conch nodded. "I understand."

Shaynnah snorted. "I doubt you do. But that's actually quite all right. You probably will understand by the end of this."

"Shaynnah," Conch began, "you didn't trust Mar'e at all. But even though Nathan'el didn't trust Jul'an, you trust *him*. Why is that?"

Shaynnah surveyed him for such a long time Conch was beginning to think she hadn't heard the question. But then she murmured, "That's for me and me only to know—at least right now. Keep in mind, Conch, that the world you've walked into is a complicated one."

20

PORTAL DEMONS

When Nurida awoke one morning in Eyixid's home, she caught a strange scent in the air. Struggling to her paws, she slipped out the window. She caught herself running quickly away from the house and chuckled to herself.

Now Eyixid's got me worrying about the portal demons.

She followed the path off to the river, still sniffing the air. When she reached the stream, she recognized the smell.

Spring.

But it couldn't be spring yet. Could it? Had it really been almost three months since that day she'd stood on a hill and seen Dejuday coming? No, it couldn't be. They'd been on the road for only four weeks, and she'd been at Lunep only five or six days. How long had she been out here? A week? It had been only two months since she'd learned Kiarna had gone missing! So why did it all smell like spring?

"Hello!"

Nurida turned at Eyixid's voice. His brow knit when he saw her face. "You look troubled."

"It smells like spring," Nurida murmured. "But it can't be spring yet, can it?"

"Oh, it will be in two or three weeks," Eyixid chuckled. "The forest stirs to spring more quickly than anyplace else. Besides, the wind is coming from the west, and it's always warmer when it does that."

I'm missing spring in Miamur, she thought regretfully. *Well, as long as I'm back for summer and fall.* Summer was the best time to see Miamur. The sun struck the white towers and made them gleam brighter than any diamonds. The flags would be floating high in the air, and golden trumpets would cry out the time of day instead of the bells of every other season. The roses in Kiarna's courtyard would be alive with every color known to rosekind, and her garden pool would be just the right temperature for cooling paws. Nurida, who had seen the sight many times, could still stand and stare in awe at the highest tower shining at high noon.

Eyixid noticed the look on her face. "Missing home?"

"Every day," she replied.

Eyixid bent down and splashed water on his face. "Anyone in particular?"

"My oldest brother," Nurida murmured. "But he's the only one still home."

She sighed and sat down on the river bank and gazed at her reflection in the water. No one would recognize her, she thought. No one would think that she was the invisible princess who burrowed into books.

"What was your sister like?" she asked Eyixid.

Eyixid sighed and looked at the trees. "Beautiful. Smart. Brave. Everyone respected her. She loved her family, loved her mate, loved her friends. They all loved her, too."

Just like Kiarna, Nurida thought, her heart constricting.

She stood up. "I'm going to go look for signs of my sister," she said softly. "I'll see you later today, Eyixid."

He smiled up at her. "See you."

Conch knew there would be trouble the minute he awoke that morning. There was the sound of arguing voices outside.

Wishing he had more than a carving knife, he crept out to look in the main room and saw that Jul'an had done the same. To his alarm, the main room was filled with river otters, none of them from his aunt's tribe.

"It's Streamcourse and her bunch," Jul'an murmured. "They're arguing about something Doomspear has done. They're saying he was reckless."

"Which one's Streamcourse?" Conch asked softly, pressing back in the shadows.

"The one with the blue band tied around her head," Jul'an murmured back. "She's got the tribal knife. Among others."

Conch singled her out and winced. This, he recalled, was Shorefish's aunt. She definitely resembled the otter that had kidnapped his friends, except her eyes were pale gray instead of blue. Her fur was gray, too, and Conch guessed she was older than his father. Well, actually she had to have been—after all, Shorefish had become leader of her tribe when Mollusk was still courting Anamay. But age didn't seem to slow Streamcourse down. She was carrying an impressive array of knives and two swords beside her tribal knife—a clear steel blade and a curved steel hilt set with emeralds—and now she had a knife in both paws, though they rested on the table.

Jul'an apparently sensed his discomfort. "Don't worry," he said dryly. "She won't attack. I don't think she's actually started a battle in my lifetime, even with the sea otters."

The sea otter wasn't convinced. "The stories I've heard about her say that she murdered her *sister*."

Jul'an snorted. "From what *I've* been told, by creatures who were actually *there*, Sky was killed in a skirmish with Current's tribe of sea otters, and Streamcourse wasn't even *in* that skirmish."

Conch nonetheless stayed well back. "Are they planning on staying here?" he asked, unable to understand the language they were arguing in.

"Unfortunately, yes," said Shaynnah's voice above them.

Both tilted their heads back to see that Shaynnah was clinging to the rafters from where she spied on the river otters unnoticed. She had a grim look on her face, but she gave a vague calming gesture in Conch's general direction. "Nothing to fear from her. Not now. She knows nothing about us. She is angry about the bargain Doomspear made."

Conch licked his lips. "What bargain?"

"Doomspear failed to deliver the Miamuran princess to him," Shaynnah murmured. "So he is asking for another captive of equal value. Another one of royal blood. And Doomspear must hurry if he means to get help before the sea otters traverse to Zurez."

"Who?" Jul'an hissed. "Who has he made the deal with?"

Shaynnah turned to look right at him, an unsettling glint in her black eyes. "Don't you know?"

Jul'an swallowed and looked back at the otters.

Conch turned his face to Shaynnah in confusion. "But why is Streamcourse so angry?"

"Because Doomspear is making it obvious how far river otters will go," Shaynnah explained. "Now anyone who seeks to make a bargain with them can demand whatever is wanted. By not negotiating, Doomspear makes the river otters appear too desperate to bargain."

Conch inhaled. The river otters were desperate, yes, but they weren't weak. He could imagine the havoc they would wreak if unleashed upon lone settlements or villages like Graystone. Two underpopulated tribes had already done their fair share of damage in Graystone and the sea otter lands.

Shaynnah narrowed her eyes. "Now Streamcourse is wondering who Doomspear will go after. She doesn't like the possibilities. All are allies of her tribe."

They listened for a while longer. Then Shaynnah said, "Lie low today. Tonight, we get the canoe, and tomorrow we'll push out."

Nurida returned to Eyixid's hiding place late that night. She had seen no sign of Ressora and was beginning to think she ought to move farther west. She'd been at Eyixid's for nearly two weeks! But something she couldn't explain prompted her to stay. Perhaps it was the curiosity about Eyixid's story—she'd have to ask him if he ever got more than a few seconds of lucidity.

After she crept through the window and bolted the shutter tightly shut, she sagged against the wall. Exhaustion burned through every limb, and she wanted nothing more than to fall asleep right where she lay. But then a soft voice murmured from the shadows, "Nurida?"

"I'm here, Eyixid," she replied wanly.

A moment later, his paw jammed up against her mouth.

"*Shhh!*" he hissed.

She jumped into wakefulness, aware that something was wrong.

With his other paw, Eyixid passed the sword, Akuwair, to her. "Someone's out behind the house!" Eyixid whispered. "And it's not the portal demons."

Nurida listened intently, and after a few moments she heard the whisperers.

"*Someone's* been around here!"

"Can't be, fishbrain. There's no way to live."

"Anyone can live here if he knows how to live in a forest," said a voice different from the others. Where the first two were harsh and rough, like sea rocks, this new one was as smooth as a pebble polished by the waves. "But I think our esteemed mercenary friend is right, Winterblade. In all his wisdom and experience, he has noted that there is truly no sign of fire in the area. No smell of smoke. And all the dead wood is still lying around, so none has been gathered for fuel."

"Right!" hissed the first voice. "Yah, Winterblade!"

"If you knew all that," Winterblade snarled, "why didn't y' just say so?"

There was the sound of tramping—*very* loud tramping—through the brush. Then came a moment of quiet, and then the smooth-talking whisperer quietly said to Winterblade, "I just love traipsing around with loud, obnoxious Eerieden mercenaries."

"Really, Arasam," Winterblade growled in response.

Arasam's voice lost all pretense of smoothness. "Arr, they think they're so 'igh 'n' mighty. I'd love to poke that 'n's eyes out with a dull *stick!*"

"Why dontcha?" Winterblade asked dryly.

"B'cause then we'd be lost," Arasam returned. It sounded as if he was scowling.

"How'd y' know about the wood?" Winterblade inquired, sounding curious.

There was a reflective moment of silence. Then Arasam replied, "Princess Zuryzel mentioned that a time or two when I came out here with 'er. I 'membered it from then."

"Y' used t' fight alongside 'er," Winterblade said neutrally. "Now y'er fightin' t' kill 'er."

"Pirate's life, Winterblade," Arasam replied jovially. "Pirate's life. C'mon, let's make sure our guide doesn't cut 'is 'ead off with that sticker 'e's got."

"Right be'ind y," Winterblade replied.

There was more loud crashing and some even louder cursing, and then Arasam and Winterblade were gone.

Eyixid removed his paw from Nurida's mouth. "Well," he said, in a low voice she didn't recognize at all.

"Who were they?" Nurida whispered.

"I don't know who Winterblade and the Eerieden mercenary were," Eyixid scowled, his voice returning to normal pitch. "But Arasam was a one-time ally of the Wraith Mice. He came when Princess Zuryzel summoned him to help at Pasadagavra."

"He must be awfully old," Nurida murmured.

"Oh, sure," Eyixid replied. "But, unfortunately, he isn't decrepit. Nurida, you need to stay around here for a few days. Just to make sure the danger's passed."

"Danger?" Nurida whispered. "Why would they hurt me?"

"They're pirates, Nurida," Eyixid scowled. "They'll hurt you for their own amusement. Best you stay here until they're gone."

But I have to find Ressora! Nurida thought in panic.

Although, if she were killed, she wouldn't find Ressora at all. It was with that knowledge that Nurida nodded slowly and said, "I'll stay here awhile, then."

A PLACE OF PEACE

onch awoke only a few minutes after he'd fallen asleep. Shaynnah was shaking him gently.

"Wake up!" she whispered. "We've got trouble. Get your things and be ready to make a dash for the canoes!"

"I thought you said we wouldn't get into any trouble before Nikor Mais!" Conch hissed, only to find that Shaynnah had already darted out of his room.

He snatched up his knife and hastened out after Shaynnah.

To his concern, he found the tribeprincess and Jul'an crouched in the shadows on the edge of the main room. Despite the lateness of the hour, Streamcourse was sitting at a table in the main room without any of her tribe.

"Where's her tribe?" Conch whispered.

Shaynnah waved her tail. "Outside somewhere. River otters don't like being inside too much. Odds are they're camped by the river."

Una sat beside Streamcourse, and the raccoon was pleading with the otter.

"Streamcourse, please!" she said urgently. "You and I have never been enemies. Whoever is out there, please just tell them to go away!"

"I can't do that, Una," Streamcourse replied softly. "This is neutral ground. So long as the chief of a tribe is in this inn, there can be no battle concerning that chief's tribe. So long as I remain in here, there will be no battle, I promise. But because of the truce, I cannot tell them to leave. You know that."

So that's why Shaynnah said this place was safe, Conch thought. *And why we weren't supposed to draw weapons. River otters won't attack in here!*

He thought back to the other places they'd stayed on their trek and realized that Shaynnah must have chosen such places with that in mind.

"Streamcourse, please," Una said pleadingly. "I do not trust anyone lurking outside my inn!"

"Then trust me," Streamcourse said soothingly. "Trust me one more time, gentle innkeeper."

At that moment the door opened, and Conch's heart very nearly stopped. Shorefish and Moonpath stood silhouetted by the starlight.

"What's the matter, Moonpath?" Streamcourse asked coldly, very differently from how she'd just spoken to Una. "Afraid to go back to Arashna without a prize for your master?"

"You," Moonpath spat. "I might have known."

"Known what?" Streamcourse snarled. She drew her tribal knife and laid it on the table.

A warm smile glided up Shorefish's face. "Hello, Aunt."

Streamcourse gave a faint and reserved smile to her niece. "Hello, Shorefish."

From her tone it was obvious she was disappointed with the younger otter, and Shorefish's smile slid away like mud washed off a wall.

Streamcourse looked back to Moonpath and indicated the tribal knife on the table. "Will you hold peaceful discourse with me? I know how challenging you find that, Moonpath, but as we are in neutral ground, it's the only option open to you. Unless you leave."

Moonpath released a furious hiss, but she nonetheless strode forward and slammed her knife on the table across from Streamcourse's. The older otter didn't flinch or even blink.

Shorefish followed Moonpath more slowly, and she chose a seat that was on a third side of the square table. She laid her bright knife lightly on the wood and looked expectantly at her aunt. Una remained beside Streamcourse, eyes lowered and paws clenched.

"These are dark days," Moonpath observed, and all three hidden in the shadows winced at her tone. "Our land lies in the paws of invaders, and our dead are restless in the earth because one of those wronged will not rise to vengeance."

"And this is why you say our days are dark?" Streamcourse countered. "It has nothing to do with you serving a tyrant?"

"I serve no one!" Moonpath spat.

"Then why are you here?" Streamcourse inquired, ice coating every word. "Both of you," she added, flinging a look at her niece. "Have you both taken leave of your judgment? Do you not see that he will keep you doing whatever he wants? Promising help in obtaining that territory, dangling that land in front of your noses, while you scurry to do his bidding like blind fools?"

Moonpath reached for a knife, but Streamcourse held her gaze unflinchingly.

"They used to be friends, once," Shaynnah murmured sadly. "During the Darkwoods War, they were close friends, before Moonpath was driven insane by the enticement of revenge."

After those tense moments, Moonpath dropped her paw.

"So what are you after now?" Streamcourse pressed on. "Are you, like Doomspear, looking for a royal prisoner?"

"No, actually," Moonpath replied harshly. "We're looking for leverage. Fal'ne, the daughter of one of the prisoners at Arashna, was in our grasp. She was taken from us."

"By whom?" Streamcourse asked. "And whoever they are, I'll offer them an alliance."

Conch stuffed his paw in his mouth to stifle the soft sounds of his breath.

"Mudriver's tribe, of course," Moonpath grated.

Conch's heart began pounding in his chest, but then Shorefish spoke.

"You don't know that, Moonpath," she said sharply. "We have no idea who they were. They were masked. It could have been anyone."

"Like who?" Moonpath shrieked, making Shorefish jump. "Who else would have taken them?"

"Others who would do to them what you would do!" Shorefish shouted back. Then she winced.

She had seen Streamcourse's expression of disappointment and disgust. Conch imagined that look on his own aunt's face and felt an unexpected wave of sympathy for Shorefish. Unexpected and fleeting.

"Well, we shall see," Moonpath declared, her voice erratically changing pitch. "If Mudriver *did* ruin my chances at getting my pay, then I will make *her* pay!"

Streamcourse burst into mirthless laughter. "Moonpath," she choked, "how—exactly—do you plan to do that? Her tribe is ten times larger than yours—maybe eleven times larger after this little scrap you got into!"

Moonpath sighed with a sick pleasure. "I will take away that which she values most," the mad chieftain answered, stroking the blade of her knife.

"Her sister's children?" Streamcourse inferred. "You mean the members of a sea otter clan that you've been trying to destroy your whole life—without being *able* to? You might stand a better chance against Mudriver herself, numbers notwithstanding. Besides, I hear that Anamay's daughter is being courted by the chief of that tribe. He won't let anyone get near her if that's true."

"And stay away from Anamay's son," Shorefish added suddenly, her eyes blazing.

Moonpath turned to her compatriot. "Why, pray tell?"

"Because he … is … *mine*," Shorefish returned, baring her teeth. "His mother killed my father, and I *will* have his blood for that!"

Conch managed not to look too afraid. It wouldn't have mattered since Jul'an wasn't looking his way, but Rainbow's warning about not letting Jul'an know who he was still rang in his ears. Then he thought it might be foolish to be more afraid of Jul'an than of Shorefish.

Streamcourse looked at her niece full on for the first time. Conch couldn't see her face, but he heard disappointment and frustration battling in her voice when she spoke.

"Are you that easily bought, my niece?" she asked, her voice grim and urgent. "Can't you *see*? The rest of the world looks at your vendetta as nothing but a means of another controlling you! The sea otters are not the problem anymore—the problem is the creature who has used them to turn you into a moth following a candle! You've sold your warriors and your honor over to a slave master—and to this gutter parasite!"

Moonpath jumped to her paws. "How dare you!" she hissed. "Rich words, coming from a spineless flower! If you insist on aiding the princess, Streamcourse, then you and I *will* meet in battle, and you will *not* like the result!"

Una winced, pulling her paws off the floor. Moonpath's eyes blazed from behind her mask. Shorefish stared in amazement at her aunt, but whether in awe of her courage or in incredulity of her statement, it was hard to tell.

"I'm shivering in my fur," Streamcourse retorted sarcastically.

Moonpath reached for her knife. "Shall we see if your blood is as gray as your fur?"

"Please!" Una burst out in a panic-stricken squeak. "Please, everyone has agreed that this is a place of peace! No threats, please!"

Moonpath turned a look of disgusted disdain on the raccoon. "This is not your conversation, innkeeper."

There was a scuffle behind Conch, and he turned; Jul'an had trapped Shaynnah against the wall. The squirrel made a fearsome sight, with her teeth bared and her eyes blazing.

"We need to go!" Jul'an whispered. "We need to get to the boats, and now!"

His urgency must have penetrated Shaynnah's fury because she jerked back and started retreated down the hall. Jul'an twitched his paw, and he and Conch followed.

"We have to make sure to avoid Shorefish and Moonpath's tribes," Jul'an murmured nervously. "They'll be out there, staking out the inn."

"They can't," Shaynnah snapped in an undertone, still hurrying to the other end of the inn. "This is a place of truce."

"After what Moonpath said, I'm not sure any of them care," Jul'an growled.

"Do you think they'll attack Streamcourse?" Conch asked.

The squirrel shook her head. "No. Shorefish would never let Moon-path attack Streamcourse. She's the only one of Shorefish's family who talks to her anymore."

The end of the corridor turned out to be a secret door; Shaynnah pulled a certain board and the wall moved. All of them snuck out, keeping their heads low and bending at both the waist and knees.

The door had barely swung shut behind them when Shaynnah dropped completely to the ground. Conch and Jul'an followed her example, and what they saw made them all sick to their stomachs.

"Unbelievable," Shaynnah whispered. "They're really breaking truce. Moonpath, you fool!"

There was a ring of river otters hidden in the trees and bushes, armed to the teeth. Most of them sported bandages, and all of them sported weapons.

"We can't fight them," Jul'an murmured. "We'll have to sneak past them."

Conch twisted enough to stare at him. Sneaking unseen past river otters? That was a near-impossible feat.

But Shaynnah's eyes gleamed. "What you need," she whispered, "is a diversion. Leave that to me. Jul'an, you know what to do."

The Keron Mouse nodded quickly.

Shaynnah reached for the branch over her head and silently lifted herself into the trees. Jul'an and Conch waited for a few seconds; then they heard a loud yelp.

"Help!" shouted a voice with an unmistakable river otter accent yet also unmistakably Shaynnah's.

A moment after the shout, all the sentries left their posts and hurried toward the yelling. As they were moving, Jul'an started forward and Conch followed. The rustling of the river otters' paws and Shaynnah's yelling muffled the sounds of the pair's passing.

Jul'an sprinted behind the back of the inn, Conch immediately behind. As they passed the building, Shaynnah dropped from the trees and literally hit the ground running.

"They're still chasing a damsel in distress," she panted, leading the way.

There were sounds of shouting behind them, and some of them definitely sounded indignant, as if the river otters realized they had been tricked.

"Hurry!" Shaynnah gasped. "The river is close!"

A few minutes later, Conch heard the sound of a swift river. The next moment, Shaynnah turned a corner around a tree and suddenly all three of them were face-to-face with a river otter.

Shaynnah jumped back, startled, and Conch and Jul'an narrowly avoided colliding with her. Before any of them could draw their weapons, the otter said, "Tribeprincess Shaynnah, the boats are at the dock. My chief has instructed us to cover you while you and your companions get away."

Shaynnah almost melted in relief. "Thank you," she said, breathing heavily. "Tell Streamcourse I owe her one."

The otter inclined his head in acknowledgment, and the three travelers again started running.

The dock extended a few feet out into the river, and two canoes were tied to it. The sounds of pursuit coming closer behind them, the three travelers jumped in the one farthest downriver. Jul'an hastily undid the rope tying it down while Shaynnah and Conch grabbed paddles. Pulling with all their might, they paddled the canoe out into the middle of the river. Then the current took over.

For all Shaynnah's talk about the Dellon being clear and beautiful, Conch realized she had another motivation for choosing this river. The current was far swifter than any creature could possibly run. With the sounds of the conflict fading into the distance, the canoe began its journey into the night.

Danger on the River

Conch insisted on taking the first watch with Shaynnah while Jul'an slept. He didn't want to appear to be any less capable than the other two. While he was the least experienced, he could still paddle a canoe. The sun was rising when Conch repeated a question.

"You trusted Jul'an," he said to Shaynnah. "But not Mar'e. Why?"

Shaynnah was in the very back of the canoe, so Conch couldn't see her expressions. She was silent for a minute, presumably watching the willow-lined bank pass by. When she answered, she sounded tired.

"Mar'e pretended to be something she was not," the tribeprincess explained. "She said she was from a village near Pasadagavra, but she talked like a Miamuran. So did that stranger we met in the woods. It's unusual for creatures to want to leave Miamur, especially now that Galledor is king."

"Maybe her village spoke Miamuran," Conch suggested.

"Maybe," Shaynnah replied. "But I know for a fact that Jul'an has made no such pretensions."

Conch gave an especially fierce dig with his paddle. "You were right," he sighed. "This is a complicated world."

They drifted on in silence for a minute. Then Shaynnah mused, "You sea otters will have to be very careful for a while. Never go out alone, never leave your borders unwatched, and that sort of thing. After Moonpath and Shorefish, I guarantee there will be more raids."

Conch scowled. The more he knew about this scenario, the worse it got. So many powers were involved.

"Hopefully one day it will be different," the squirrel murmured. "But—well, until then, don't be stupid."

Soon after the sun rose, the canoeists switched off. Although Conch offered to stay awake with Jul'an, Shaynnah said she didn't want to sleep, so Conch gratefully fell asleep in the middle of the canoe.

He soon realized why Shaynnah didn't want to sleep; images of the looks on Streamcourse's face as she gazed at her only brother's only daughter plagued his mind. When he didn't see that look emerging on his own aunt's face, he dreamed that the otter from Streamcourse's tribe that had covered their retreat was actually from Moonpath's and two tribes of angry warriors were close on their heels.

He awoke a little bit around noon and feigned sleep, not wishing to talk to either of his companions.

Bear King, he prayed, *can't I at least dream of something a little less unpleasant?*

He dozed off again not much longer. Unfortunately his next dream, though far less terrifying, was intensely more painful. He dreamed that his mother was still alive.

In his dream, she hadn't died in childbirth. She was sweeping the inside of their house, which was far less shabby than it was in real life. Mollusk was sitting at the table, which wasn't only clean and well cared for but was bright and new. His father seemed to be taking a break from his daily labors, which he never did these days. They were talking about something serious—Conch would never remember exactly what they talked about. He basked in his mother's voice, even though it probably wasn't her real voice; it sounded like a cross between Danaray's and Starfish's.

The door to his house opened, and Starfish came in. Conch's throat tightened most especially at the sight of her because she was completely free of the burden he usually saw on her. She looked carefree and bright, laughing and giggling. She stopped abruptly when she saw Mollusk.

"Something funny?" he asked suspiciously.

"Oh," she said vaguely. "I was just talking with my friends."

"Was Eagle there?" Anamay asked, partially hiding a smile.

Starfish's eyes grew innocently round, and she shook her head. "No. He just stopped by for a minute."

Mollusk grunted and returned to his conversation with his mate, apparently missing the conspiratorial smile that flashed between mother and daughter.

When Conch woke up, he was sure he'd never be able to shake the regret that his dream had ignited. His father, happy. His sister, freely following her heart. His mother, alive. It was all so different from what life was like in reality. The next moment he realized what had wakened him—someone was jabbing the back of an oar into his back.

"Wake up, wake up, wake up," Shaynnah chattered. "It's your watch."

Conch pulled himself into a sitting position. "I'm awake."

Shaynnah jerked her paw towards the back of the canoe. "Come on. You're paddling in the back this time."

Conch crawled towards the bench and picked up the oar Shaynnah had dropped while she curled up in the center where the wood was warmest. Jul'an glanced back at her and said, "It's called the stern."

"Stern applies to a *ship*," Shaynnah replied, chuckling derisively, "and not even the proudest boatwright can possibly make this little thing out to be a ship. It's not even the size of a dinghy. And ships usually require sails."

"Stern applies to *any* kind of watercraft," Jul'an called back. "Not just a ship."

But Shaynnah was asleep before she could reply.

Conch and Jul'an rowed on for a few minutes in silence. At least, Conch rowed in silence; he sometimes thought he heard Jul'an muttering things along the lines of "deluded, indeed."

Eventually Jul'an half-turned back to Conch and asked, "Bad dreams?"

"Not really," Conch lied. "I was thinking of my family."

Jul'an jerked his head in acknowledgment. "Family is quite important," he observed.

Conch dipped his paddle back into the water. "What about yours?" he asked.

Jul'an shrugged. "I … really don't have a family. My mother was killed when I was very young. Her sister raised me—sort of—but mostly it was just me. Me and Nad'ne—she's an orphan too."

It took a moment for Conch to remember that Nad'ne was the Keron Mouse who had first found him and Nathan'el in the woods. He'd nearly forgotten her—and suddenly something occurred to him.

"You were awfully far away from the Keron River when we found you," he observed in as unaccusatory voice as he could manage. "Why?"

Jul'an shrugged. "We were following some prints. They probably belonged to a river otter tribe. Otters almost never go near the Keron, so we were curious about them."

Conch did some math in his head. Streamcourse and Moonpath hadn't gone that way—they'd been too far east; Doomspear had been in or near Arashna, if Shaynnah was correct. It might have been his aunt's tribe, he supposed, but they'd been awfully close to Current's territory, and she disliked going so near. Jul'an could be lying, but if he wasn't—then what other tribe was lurking so close to sea otter land?

Almost immediately after, he thought of a possible answer. There *were* other parties interested in that land besides Shorefish and Moonpath.

The trip down the Dellon would have been pleasant, except all three of the voyagers were worried about being followed.

Shaynnah seemed the most concerned. She would glance sharply at the bank for no apparent reason; perhaps she saw or heard something. Conch always hastily followed her line of sight, but when Jul'an saw him doing this, he murmured, "Don't look at the bank straight on. Trust the side of your eyes to see movement."

It was difficult to spot movement when the canoe was moving so swiftly. Sometimes Conch thought he saw a branch shake or a vine twitch, but they passed the sight so fast that he couldn't get a good look.

The second day of their journey, Shaynnah murmured to Jul'an, "Should we travel closer to the bank so as to not be seen?"

Jul'an considered it for a minute; then he shook his head. "No. It's faster in the middle. Even if we're seen, we can get away from anyone following us."

"I'm worried about floating into a trap," Shaynnah replied concernedly. "If we're closer to the bank, we can get away by land if we have to."

"Others can't have gotten ahead of us to set up a trap," Jul'an pointed out, "even assuming they knew we were at the Hidden Glade Inn in the first place."

"If they didn't suspect anything, then why did they stop there?" Shaynnah fretted.

"Remember how Moonpath said 'you' to Streamcourse when she first came in?" Conch interjected. "It seemed she thought something was going on and wanted to find out what. Although," he added, "how did Streamcourse know we were there?"

"Una," Shaynnah replied immediately.

"Una said she wouldn't tell anyone who we were," Jul'an observed.

"She did …," Shaynnah agreed slowly, "but … I won't lie, Una is a good, decent creature, but she is not brave as fire. She has no idea how to survive a face-off with Moonpath. When she heard angry river otters approaching, she probably went straight to Streamcourse to beg for help. Streamcourse is far more adept at dealing with Moonpath than Una is."

"Why is she all by herself in such a defenseless place?" Conch asked.

"It didn't use to be," Shaynnah replied, sounding irritated. "Queen Demeda once encouraged Streamcourse to protect that general area. It was outside the Wraith Mice's jurisdiction, so she couldn't send Wraith Mice there, but she could offer favors to Streamcourse in exchange for her protection."

"How so?" Jul'an queried.

Shaynnah grinned. "This is an example of her true genius. You see, there are some things the Wraith Mice have enormous influence in, but not always directly. Demeda didn't have any real power over the area near the inn, but she had *huge* influence with river otter tribes near Arashna—some of them even offer service to the Wraith Mouse crown. Long story short, Demeda told Streamcourse that if she would agree to keep watch over the area around the Hidden Glade Inn—and the trade routes around it—she would persuade some of the local chieftains to patrol some of the northern areas, such as the mountain passes Eerieden mercenaries liked using to attack Streamcourse's tribe. Una would be safer because Streamcourse could protect her, and Streamcourse could protect her because she only had one side to worry about, not two. Furthermore, since the trade routes were safer, more of Graystone's produce and other goods made it further north, even to the northern river otter tribes. Everyone was happy."

"They were willing to risk their lives in a fight to get a few more luxuries?" Jul'an snorted.

"There was never really any fighting," Shaynnah replied. "The only ones who threatened that area were gangs of thieves—dangerous to Una, but not dangerous enough to risk attacking a whole river otter tribe. As for the Eeriedens, they would attack river otter tribes, but not tribes backed by the might of the Wraith Mice. Demeda knew that. Sometimes the greatest weapons never see any action because no one's stupid enough to challenge them."

Conch was somewhat amazed. He had always heard that Queen Demeda was a wise ruler, but that was the first time anyone had ever laid out for him why they thought so. "But why does that make it so dangerous now?" he asked.

Shaynnah sighed. "Demeda's dead. Different ruler. Different laws." After a few minutes of silence, she added, "Streamcourse's base of operations isn't far away, so she still tries to keep Una's place a little protected, but she's got her paws full with other matters—like Eerieden mercenaries. She just can't do everything."

"Who's sending mercenaries against her?" Jul'an asked. "I thought she was very well-liked."

"Warriorqueen Zinntah of the Moor Tribe, maybe?" Shaynnah suggested sarcastically.

"All right, fine," Jul'an snapped. "What reason could the king of Arashna possibly have to send mercenaries against Streamcourse?"

"Because Streamcourse was one of Zuryzel's friends," Shaynnah loudly retorted in the tone of one stating the obvious.

"Keep your voice down," Jul'an admonished her.

Shaynnah didn't reply, but she cast a worried look at the bank and the water behind them.

The next three days on the river were anxious at best. When Shaynnah, Conch, and Jul'an drew near Nikor Mais, they dragged the boat ashore, and Conch and Jul'an lifted it over their heads to carry it through the thick foliage. Shaynnah darted into the trees and guided them by gently nudging the boat one way or another.

Nikor Mais, as Conch had learned earlier, was in the middle of a set of cliffs. It was possible for a creature to ascend or descend them, as Rainbow had done when she confronted the two river otter tribes, but it was impossible to move something as large as the canoe up and down the precipice. The nearest trail that could be used to bring the canoe to the lower level was two miles away; carrying the canoe would take half a day's travel. But Shaynnah dismissed that trail as too open, and she insisted on going around the cliffs completely.

As they struggled west—away from the Dellon River—they came across the place where Danaray's tribe had first ambushed Shorefish and Moonpath. There were signs of carnage similar to the place on the edge of the Stone Tribe territory, but no bodies. They paused to rest for a few minutes here, although Shaynnah was against stopping at all.

"We're only making ourselves a target!" she chattered. "This is a heavily traveled road!"

Jul'an looked toward the gullies that would lead eventually toward Arashna. They were completely void of travelers, fresh tracks in the snow, lost items, or anything that would indicate anyone had been there before or after the battle. "So I see," he said sarcastically.

"There are creatures who can travel here without leaving any signs of their passing," Shaynnah whispered, nervously scanning the surrounding area.

"River otters?" Conch guessed.

"Birds," Jul'an corrected. "She's worried about hawks and ravens. But they're a constant everywhere nowadays."

"True," Shaynnah agreed. "Still, they come here *expecting* to find unwary travelers."

"Why should ravens hurt us?" Conch asked, confused. "They don't usually hunt living things."

Jul'an shrugged. "They're still big. You're right, though, the hawks are our biggest problem."

With that, he flopped back in the snow, his eyes on the sky.

"They'll go after Shaynnah first," he said, sounding amused.

Shaynnah raked her claws along the tree branch she perched on. "Watch it, Jul'an. I could have dumped you into the river at any time if I thought you were slowing us down."

"Ah, Shaynnah," Jul'an smirked. "If you had, you'd be left to explain everything to Conch on your own. I know how much you just *hate* talking." After a moment he added, "A few hawks might prefer mice over squirrel, but not enough to warrant ending our rest early."

Conch glanced toward the sky. "I guess hawks don't like otters much," he murmured.

Jul'an sat halfway up and gave him a curious look. "Why do you say that?"

"Because I've never seen one near my home," he explained. "And I haven't heard of any bothering river otters."

Jul'an frowned thoughtfully. "Maybe it's got something to do with how thick otter fur is?"

Conch shrugged. "Could be."

"But hawks must like the nutty flavor of squirrel," Jul'an added with a completely straight face. "That's why Shaynnah's not allowed to live in Pasadagavra. She's such a nut that she'd attract too many hawks."

Shaynnah chattered angrily at him, apparently too annoyed to form words. Jul'an's straight face broke into a grin. He had an infectious smile, on the rare occasion he used it, and Conch couldn't help but grin as well. Their journey had been so grim and dangerous, it was a relief to smile.

The three travelers didn't quite reach the edge of the cliffs that day, and Conch and Jul'an were so tired of carrying the canoe that they refused to travel once they could no longer see their paws. When they gratefully hid the canoe amid some fallen logs, Conch finally noticed something. "No snow," he said. "We're getting closer to the sea."

Jul'an gave him a confused look that he didn't see.

Shaynnah asked the question the Keron Mouse didn't. "Why should being near the sea mean less snow?"

"There's a warm current coming up from the south running parallel to the coast," Conch explained. "It brings warmer weather with it. Not *warm* weather, just warmer."

"Warmer and wetter," Jul'an sighed as they felt the first few drops of rain.

"Find a cedar tree," Shaynnah advised them. "The rain drips to the edge of a cedar tree."

There was only one nearby, and they collapsed gratefully beneath it while Shaynnah scurried into the branches. Conch was asleep almost immediately. Jul'an wasn't surprised, but he also noticed with approval that Conch gripped his knife as he slept.

The Keron Mouse himself leaned back against the tree and sank to the ground. He didn't stir from the moment his head rested against the wood. But he was not asleep; his sharp ears were attuned for any sound of movement and not from the sea otter.

Before an hour passed, his patience was rewarded. He heard a faint scratching noise and then a soft brushing.

"I wondered how you could be so tired when you hardly did any work in the canoe, Shaynnah," he murmured. "You don't sleep."

The squirrel crawled slowly down the trunk until she was close enough that she could murmur in his ear. "I trusted you more than anyone else would have," she muttered. "Cut me some slack."

Jul'an opened his eyes enough to glare at her. "Why shouldn't I be trusted?"

"Why didn't you tell Nathan'el exactly who that stupid gray mouse was?" Shaynnah shot back.

Jul'an didn't flinch. "Why didn't you?"

Her eyes narrowed. "I asked first."

Jul'an shrugged. "Nathan'el was a stranger to me, and to her. He didn't need to know her secrets. Your turn."

"You're a complete stranger to me," Shaynnah parroted. "You don't need to know my secrets."

Jul'an smirked. "You didn't trust him."

Shaynnah was accustomed to being alone in the woods and so had very little ability to control her expressions. She bared her teeth at Jul'an and hissed, "I trust him fine."

Jul'an gave her a skeptical look.

Shaynnah did not back down. "More than I trust you."

"But you hadn't seen him in such a long time," Jul'an filled in. "Since before Mokimshim took the throne. You knew Nathan'el's sister had been kidnapped, but you didn't know why. Perhaps she was a hostage to make sure he did what he was supposed to. Perhaps he was acting under Mokimshim's orders even as you spoke to him."

Shaynnah did her best to show an expression that said, *Oh, really?* But her semi-rational mind knew she failed.

"So then," Jul'an continued quietly, "you were always willing to trust him a little, but you drew the line at revealing anything of earthshaking importance. I'm guessing you warned him not to trust Mar'e, to make sure he was safe, but you didn't tell him why you knew she was lying."

"Is that why you were so insistent on traveling with him and Conch?" Shaynnah guessed. "To make sure he wasn't a threat to your tribe?"

Jul'an closed his eyes again. "That reminds me of another question," he murmured. "Why exactly *do* you trust me? You've made it so plain you don't *want* to, and yet you do."

It was Shaynnah's turn to smirk. "I know who you are," she whispered.

"And who am I?" Jul'an asked. Outwardly he was completely relaxed, but inside an alarm bell was ringing.

"You're the son of Dan'elle," Shaynnah murmured.

Jul'an did not open his eyes. "What has that got to do with anything? She's dead. I can't remember her."

"She? Nothing. But you know who rescued you, right?"

Jul'an nodded once, shortly.

"And you know what Al'ce, everyone's favorite betrayer, did to the one who rescued her sister's son?"

"I repeat," Jul'an said through gritted teeth, "what has that got to do with anything?"

"It seems incredible to me that anyone would have followed the lead of a creature like Al'ce," Shaynnah murmured. "That mouse betrayed everyone who ever did her a favor, and she's a murderess to boot. But what is hardest to believe is that *you* would join her. You of all creatures should know what she is."

Don't you remember why I needed rescuing in the first place? Jul'an silently asked Shaynnah. *And that Al'ce is, in fact, my mother's sister—the only family I have?*

"And yet," Shaynnah continued, "Conch and Nathan'el found you in the woods while Coll'n and the remaining faithful Keron Mice were inside Graystone. I can't add it up."

Jul'an shrugged. "Why weren't *you* in Pasadagavra?"

"Because I'm not *wanted* inside Pasadagavra," Shaynnah countered.

The Keron Mouse flicked an ear, dismissing the squirrel. "Say what you like, Shaynnah. By your logic, I'm no less trustworthy than you."

He could tell the tribeprincess hadn't considered that. He heard her sharp intake of breath, but no corresponding words. A few moments later, Shaynnah skittered back up the tree to the branches where she slept.

Jul'an fell asleep not much longer, but the conversation with Shaynnah revived nightmares that hadn't haunted him in a long time. He didn't cry out—he'd learned to control what he said even in sleep—but his rest was fitful. He awoke completely when the rain eased off and the world was beginning to lighten.

Conch apparently hadn't slept so well either, because the sea otter was already awake. He offered a smile and said, "At least we'll be dry marching under that canoe."

"And the timbers won't dry out," Jul'an agreed.

They couldn't climb the tree to wake Shaynnah, and they didn't want to yell her name too loudly. They considered the problem of rousing her for a few minutes; then Jul'an reached for a smooth pebble, tossed and caught it a few times, and then threw it up in an easy arc. It hit Shaynnah squarely on the shoulder, causing her to jump awake.

"Time to keep going," Jul'an called quietly.

Conch grinned. "You know," he said, "you're not so bad when you're not going on about the river."

Jul'an grinned back. "And you're not so bad when you make an effort to discover things on your own."

23

So Close to Home

On the march back towards the river, Shaynnah knew they were being followed. She saw a number of low branches moving against the wind. Even though she never caught sight of their pursuer, she was fully aware of his—or her—presence.

Or maybe it was more than one.

They reached the river, hearing the sounds of the waterfall in the background, and carefully shoved the canoe into the water. Conch and Jul'an both collapsed in relief into the boat, rubbing their shoulders.

"Oh, for pity's sake," Shaynnah scolded. "It was easier than paddling."

"But at least when we paddle, we can see where we're going," Conch retorted. He took up one of the paddles without being asked. Jul'an thrust the other one into Shaynnah's paws.

"We can't sleep this time," Shaynnah warned. "There could be a tribe of river otters near. Besides, this river goes near the Keron, and while that may be fine for Jul'an, it won't be all right for the rest of us."

"It wouldn't be fine for me, either," Jul'an muttered. "They'd wonder why I was with you. If Nad'ne's told them how I ran into Conch and Nathan'el, they may ask questions before they attack. If not, then their reaction is anyone's guess."

Conch frowned at him. "They're your tribe. Can't you guess what they'll do?"

Jul'an grinned fiercely. "They're wild, Conch. How they'll react depends on some of the circumstances, and I've been away too long to know the circumstances."

Conch shuddered. He knew that if Eagle saw him coming home in the company of strangers, or even enemies, the sea otter chief would always ask questions before attacking.

Jul'an clambered up into the prow of the canoe while Shaynnah sat in the back to keep watch behind them. "We'll reach the Othyrn River by tonight," Jul'an told Conch conversationally. "I don't plan on going too far into your territory. No reason for me to."

"That's probably for the best," Conch allowed. "But if you ever find yourself *near* my land, look me up."

Jul'an looked over his shoulder and chuckled. "And if you ever need to travel *near* my river again, give me a shout."

"It's a deal," Conch grinned.

"What," Shaynnah grumbled. "Can't I give either of you a shout?"

"No," the otter and the mouse replied simultaneously. Then both of them laughed.

"Quiet," Shaynnah hissed. "Someone may be following us."

Conch glanced over his shoulder and saw nothing. Then he glanced at Jul'an who smiled faintly and nodded once. His eyes were far away.

It was an uncomfortable afternoon. Just as afternoon shadows were turning to evening, they all heard a very loud whistling coming from the bank. Conch and Shaynnah almost ignored it, but Jul'an's head shot up in alarm. For a moment, he listened carefully; then he whistled three times.

Whoever was on the bank replied with a series of whistles and then was silent.

"Shaynnah, Conch," Jul'an said quietly, "we need to get the canoe to land, take everything out of it, and continue on paw. The Keron Mice are just ahead. That was Nad'ne whistling."

"But the fork is so near!" Shaynnah hissed.

"And they're guarding the fork to both the Keron and the Othyrn Rivers," Jul'an whispered back. "Let's land on the east bank. Then we can get around them into Mudriver's territory."

Conch was all for that, so he obediently began paddling for the bank. Shaynnah did so as well after a moment's hesitation.

"Why was Nad'ne warning you about them?" Conch whispered to Jul'an.

"Most likely because Al'ce is in a bad mood," Jul'an replied quietly.

Conch swallowed his fear, and a moment later, they reached the bank. They all climbed carefully out, taking everything that had been lying in the canoe except the oars. Then, cautiously, they slipped off into the undergrowth.

They hadn't gone far when Conch began to hear drumming, much like the day when he and Nathan'el first encountered Jul'an.

"They're close," Shaynnah murmured.

"And they're together," Jul'an added, frowning. "That's odd."

"Why aren't they on the Keron River?" Conch muttered.

"I told you that part of this river splits and joins the Keron, while the rest of it becomes the Othyrn," Shaynnah muttered. "They're guarding what they see as a gateway to their home."

Jul'an murmured something in Eerieden that Conch didn't understand, but he caught the words *Bear King*.

The tips of the branches were just beginning to swell with new leaves, but the undergrowth was already thick and bushy. Conch knew that Jul'an and Shaynnah were grateful for this, but the sea otter found it irksome and somewhat worrying. He couldn't slide silently through the bushes the way the mouse and the squirrel could.

"Couldn't I swim past them?" he murmured to Jul'an.

The Keron Mouse shook his head. "No. They'll have nets in the water."

Conch refrained from rolling his eyes. "To catch *what*, exactly?"

"Otters, of course," Jul'an replied.

Jul'an took the lead, sliding through the bushes with ease. Shaynnah scrambled into the trees to scan the ground from there. Conch lagged behind Jul'an, allowing as much of a space between him and the Keron Mouse as he could without losing sight.

His mind was fixed with hope on his aunt's domain knowing that it was near. She had very clearly established borders—the Othyrn River on the west side and a line of partially-stripped trees on all the other sides. Conch kept lifting his head a little above the bushes, trying hard to spot one of the trees that was without most of its bark, even though he knew it would be at least an hour before he spotted one. And, at the rate they were crawling, it would likely be more than an hour.

When they had been crawling for only a short time—ten minutes at best—Conch heard a twig snap off to his left. He dropped to his stomach and froze, listening hard. For a moment, all was silence. Then–

"Let *goooooo!*" Shaynnah yelped.

Then the bushes erupted. There were high-pitched, blood-curling war screams and bloodthirsty cries. Conch looked over his shoulder and saw Shaynnah jump a branch higher like an arrow from a bow, hairs from her tail spiraling down. Six ragged mice, clutching knives between their teeth, scrambled up the tree after her. Two others emerged from the bushes with short recurve bows and took aim at her, probably meaning to drive her to the ground.

Conch saw all this in the blink of an eye; a moment later, he heard one of the Keron Mice near him. Without thinking he swiped his tail in an arc and caught his attacker's paws, sending him sprawling. The sea otter scrambled away on all fours, trying to avoid being seen in the undergrowth. He heard the thrumming of paws pounding the earth near him, drew his tiny knife, waited a heartbeat, and then lashed out, catching his assailant on the hip. He was rewarded by a loud squealing and a clear sight of Shaynnah; she was still free, high above him in the branches.

Until she ran right into a net.

"*Ruuuuunn!*" she screamed.

Conch froze, still hidden in the ferns. Shaynnah was twisting madly, shrieking, probably meaning to keep all the attention on herself. Then a new, harsh voice shouted, "*Quiet!*"

Shaynnah ignored the command. Over her thrashing and yelping, the harsh shouter yelled, "Archers!"

At least twenty mice stood up from the undergrowth, aiming recurve bows at Shaynnah.

"Whoever else is there, come out now!" shouted the voice. "Or she gets it!"

Conch didn't move. Shaynnah was trying to make enough noise for him to get away, and he meant to just as soon as he could see a clear path. He would run south and get help from his aunt's tribe. They wouldn't shoot Shaynnah—she was too valuable a prisoner to risk losing.

That was Conch's train of thought, and had his enemies been anyone else, except maybe Moonpath, it would have been sound reasoning. But he wasn't facing anyone else. Only four or five seconds after threatening Shaynnah, the speaker—Conch decided it must be Al'ce—said in a lower voice, "Put an arrow in her leg!"

Conch hoped Shaynnah didn't hear; but a moment later Shaynnah's shouting and struggling was cut abruptly off.

"Idiot!" shouted Al'ce. "I said shoot her leg, not kill her!"

There was a heavy *thwack*, and one of the archers fell forward. Conch didn't catch a good look at whoever hit him because a drop of Shaynnah's blood dripped into his eyes. He blinked it away and looked up, seeing the tribeprincess moving feebly. The arrow protruded from the narrow space between her lungs and her gut, so maybe it wasn't fatal. But it must have been painful, because Shaynnah started whimpering.

"Whoever's there, your friend isn't going to last long!" Al'ce called out. "You'd better get up, or she takes another arrow!"

"Is that necessary?" demanded another voice. With a jolt, Conch realized it was Jul'an's.

"Probably not," Al'ce agreed. "But it does the eyes good to see one of such wildness at our mercy!"

There were amused chuckles.

"Last warning!" Al'ce shouted. "Get up or your friend dies! And it *won't* be a quick death, either!"

Conch swallowed hard and stood up.

There were more Keron Mice than he'd realized. He'd thought this was only a small war party, but he very quickly counted at least sixty mice half-hidden among the ferns and salal bushes. Their armor was both old and ill-kept, but their blades and arrows were wickedly sharp. Their eyes gleamed with malicious amusement, gloating silently.

Conch ignored all of them and glared straight at Jul'an, whom he had begun to trust. Jul'an didn't quite meet his eyes, but other than that, he didn't look all that ashamed.

The sea otter glared silently at him for a moment and then switched his gaze to the female mouse Jul'an stood by.

If Al'ce had been wearing the finest, queenliest gown ever created and the richest crown ever worn by the stateliest empress, she would still bear no resemblance to any true leader. Something about the arrogant set of her mouth and the belligerent, smug gleam of her eyes took away any semblance of leader-like dignity that she might have possessed. She wasn't a ruler because of wisdom or virtue; she was just the strongest, loudest bully in the woods, and so other bullies flocked to her. Conch found it almost impossible to look at her with any respect, no matter how many sharp knives she wore at her waist, in her boots, on her shoulder, and—for some strange reason—behind her ears.

She wore a black bandana around her head, which was decorated with gold beads and other trophies. Her shirt and trousers were black, torn, and mud-splattered. Her boots were the most well-cared-for thing about her. She wore bands of cloth around her wrists and a gold choker around her neck.

When Conch first stood up, her eyes glinted triumphantly. Then they darkened, and she knit her brow in surprise. She strode forward, pushing aside her followers as she did so, and came to a stop about ten pawsteps in front of Conch. It seemed she didn't want to get closer—perhaps because

Shaynnah's blood was dripping down faster. But she squinted her eyes and scowled at Conch for several minutes.

Her eyes were the same shade as Jul'an's. And her fur—beneath the mud and paint—was the same hue. She had his stocky build, and if not for the score of earrings in each ear, her ears might have been Jul'an's. She curled her left paw into a fist the same way he did and opened her mouth just a little when she contemplated something, as he did.

For a long few moments, Al'ce stared at him. Then, all at once, she began to laugh. Her teeth were broken, and her tongue had been pierced by a tiny bird's claw.

"Well done, nephew!" she exclaimed. "Well done indeed!"

Jul'an frowned. Al'ce, apparently expecting some response, turned around in surprise.

"You didn't know?" she asked. Then she laughed again. "Of course not; you're too young. You wouldn't recognize this sea otter's face."

Jul'an shook his head. "I don't know what you mean."

Al'ce chuckled. Then she spread her paws dramatically wide.

"See, Mice of the River?" she declared. "My sister's son has brought the son of Anamay Mudriver to our paws!"

The ragged mice erupted into laughter, cheers, and jeers. Only Jul'an was silent; he looked at Conch in astonishment and disbelief. Shaynnah whimpered faintly, and Conch remembered Rainbow's warning of not letting Jul'an find out who he was. But now, as Shaynnah's blood dripped to the ground at his paws and the Keron Mice mocked and jeered them both, Conch found that he didn't care.

Al'ce took a few steps nearer, examining Conch through narrowed eyes. "Yes," she snorted. "Definitely Anamay the Fool's son. He has the same glare she had when I told her she was throwing in her lot with the enemy. Do you remember that, Keron Mice? You older ones? Do you remember how she glared at me?" Al'ce laughed. "That's all she did, of course. She didn't say anything. Just glared. I wonder if the fool was still glaring when she died."

"Let Shaynnah down," Conch said suddenly.

Al'ce blinked. "What?"

"Shaynnah's dying," Conch replied, his voice calm but underlain with anger. "She'll die for sure if she's left up there much longer. Let her down. Let her live."

Al'ce strode forward and smacked his face.

He had expected that and hardly flinched, even though it stung.

"Oh yes, just like his mother!" Al'ce yelled to her mice, less amused now than angry. "So very uppity he thinks he can tell *me* what to do!"

"I told you not murder an innocent creature in cold blood!" Conch shouted back, his blood boiling. "*Every* creature has the right to ask that of any other he comes across!"

Al'ce glared at someone behind Conch. "Gag him," she ordered, and a moment later, someone looped a vile-smelling rag around Conch's mouth.

"And cut down the squirrel," Al'ce added. "Her brother's the richest creature on earth. He'll pay a fortune for her body, and I don't want any vultures making off with it."

A weight settled in Conch's stomach, and for a minute, he was afraid Shaynnah was already dead. Then she whimpered as the net holding her was cut down.

PLUNGE INTO THE RIVER

The Keron Mice force-marched Conch through the woods for almost a mile. Nettles caught in his fur, and thorns and sharp branches scraped his cheek. He didn't care. His last vestige of concern was for Shaynnah. Other than his worry for her, he felt nothing but a simmering anger.

Whoever had cut the net must have been one of Al'ce's kinder followers. He wasn't dragging Shaynnah across the ground but carrying her over his shoulder, like a sack, still caught up in the net. Her wound ceased bleeding, but the arrow hadn't been removed, and Conch was terrified the mouse would decide she was too much of a burden and drag her across the forest floor. Such a rough journey would kill her for sure.

They stopped by the Keron's bank at a place where dozens of boats like long canoes were moored. Conch was tied roughly to a tree by a rope around his neck, and Shaynnah was dumped on the ground beside him, hardly moving.

Conch wriggled around until his bound paws were in front of him; he managed to remove his gag and then scooted closer to Shaynnah. Gingerly, he untangled her from the yards of net. He didn't dare draw out the arrow, but he stroked her brow until she managed to speak.

"It's not as bad as it looks," she whispered. "But, Bear King, it hurts."

"They want a ransom," Conch replied gently. "That means they have to send word to my aunt soon. She'll bring medicine and healers. Her friend Kermunda is really good with battle wounds."

Shaynnah nodded. "So I hear. But you'd be more useful as leverage against your aunt's enemies. And I … my brother has enemies."

"No one's going to risk attacking anyone shut up safely in Pasadagavra," Conch soothed her. "He could pay more than anyone else. I heard Al'ce mention that."

Shaynnah feebly moved her paw. "You … I failed you. Forgive me, Conch."

"You didn't fail," Conch reassured her. "It must have been Jul'an—he led us into a trap. That must be it."

"And Nathan'el," Shaynnah whimpered, as if she hadn't heard. "I failed him, too. I couldn't find his sister. We shouldn't have taken the river."

Conch looked around him at their captors, who were busily loading things onto the canoes. "Tell me about Al'ce," he suggested. "Just to pass the time."

Shaynnah shuddered. "I hate her," she whispered. "Evil mouse. Evil, evil mouse. Her family was small. Only she, her parents, and her sister, Dan'elle. Her parents died when she was very young, still a child. They were taken in by Coll'n, who was childless. The sisters grew up as rivals, always scheming to supplant the other. Dan'elle wasn't a fabulous creature, but Al'ce was worse. So much worse. She worked against Coll'n behind his back. The creature who saved her from starving on the riverbank, she only fought to gain what he had. And creatures who helped her ended up losing everything. Some even wound up dead. Al'ce is ruthless. She even tried to kill Anamay once. Yes, Conch," Shaynnah added, as if she could see Conch's face. "Anamay once did Al'ce a favor, and Al'ce repaid her by trying to poison her. But Anamay knew what kind of creature Al'ce is and got away.

"Al'ce's sister, Dan'elle, was less … less ruthless, less heartless. All her plotting involved making sure Al'ce got nothing of Coll'n's when he died, not hurrying his death and her sister's. But then she fell in love with a well-respected archer. They married. All her scheming stopped being about ambition and became about keeping her family safe from her sister. Only a few days after her son was born, her mate died. I don't know what killed him, but Dan'elle was sure it was her sister, so she fled the Keron Mice, certain her sister was coming for her next. But she and her son wound up in the paws of the sea otters."

Conch jerked his head back. "And she was killed," he murmured. "Current and Crustacean killed her. But they just left her child to die. And Anamay went to the Keron Mice and told them about the child."

"Yes," Shaynnah whispered. She opened one black eye and smiled weakly. "*This* is why I trusted Jul'an. Your mother saved his life. I thought

… I thought, if he was half a decent creature, maybe we could trust him to show back some kindness." She sighed. "I see I was wrong. I should have sent him away before we reached the Hidden Glade Inn."

Conch looked around him. The mice were busy, tying ropes, loading bags, dragging things to and fro; some were going through garbage, and Conch had a feeling that some of that garbage would end up in his and Shaynnah's fur.

He tried to spot Jul'an in the throng—there must have been more than a hundred mice in this clearing—and saw him at Al'ce's side. He seemed to be arguing, although Al'ce was laughing at whatever he was saying. Conch wondered if he was trying to get Al'ce to release him and Shaynnah, but somehow he doubted it.

"They'll take us to Coll'n now, won't they?" Conch murmured.

Shaynnah coughed. "Coll'n? Conch, no! The Keron Mice are split in half. Al'ce led this bunch, I guess, away from the others. Conch, Al'ce … is … evil."

"How did she pull that off?" Conch murmured.

"Wasn't there for it," Shaynnah murmured. "From what I've heard— Conch, how much do you know about the state of affairs in Arashna?"

Conch shook his head. "Nothing, I guess."

"Demeda's oldest son was Mokimshim," Shaynnah said wearily. "After she died, Mokimshim became king. But his sister was more popular. More renowned. The Wraith Mice trusted her more because she proved herself a better leader. Wiser, more just … you get the idea. Her twin brother, Johajar, openly said she would be a better monarch than Mokimshim. Foreigners trusted her more, too, because she could meet anyone on his or her level. When Mokimshim became king, Zuryzel was in charge of some patrols along the eastern edges of Wraith Mice influence. He … he ordered a regiment to the east to take her captive. One of the princess's friends—a pirate called Ksheygha, I think—got wind of it. Ksheygha is famous for being a gossip in the ports; I think that's where she heard it. Ksheygha sent a messenger to Zuryzel, and the princess just … disappeared. I thought she must have gone to Miamur—she's close friends with King Galledor and Princess Kiarna, but Galledor insists she she's not there."

Conch suddenly remembered what Rainbow had told him about some great scheme that his aunt was involved in—Princess Kiarna had been part of it, hadn't she? And that scheme had had something to do with the Wraith Mice. Conch looked away from Shaynnah, unwilling to let her see his thoughts.

"In the time since Zuryzel disappeared," Shaynnah continued, not noticing Conch's silence, "Mokimshim has been searching for her. He can't find her or her mate, and no one knows where they've gone."

"What has this got to do with the Keron Mice?" Conch asked softly.

Shaynnah chuckled weakly. "Mokimshim is a great believer in mercenaries—well, he has to be since his kingdom knows he's exiled his own sister. He has to rely on soldiers who're not bothered by conscience. He sent an envoy to the Keron Mice. What do you think he promised them?"

Conch glanced at their nearest guard. "Better armor?"

Shaynnah chuckled. "Heh. Good guess. Most likely. Armoring requires resources they don't have, so they have no way to make decent armor. They're restricted to pretty much what they can scavenge or buy, and they can hardly repair it at all. But Coll'n refused to sign on with Mokimshim. The Keron Mice weren't mercenaries, he said, and even if they were, someone who tried to kill his own sister was not a worthy employer." Shaynnah sighed heavily. "I wish the old fool had taken a better look at whom he'd adopted. Al'ce immediately wanted to side with Mokimshim. The Keron Mice who'd been unswervingly loyal to Coll'n up until then were disappointed, and Al'ce offered them an alternative. She used the issue to stage a coup, and almost half the Keron Mice followed her."

"So they're in Mokimshim's service," Conch murmured, gazing at the horde of mice. "Mokimshim's going to tell them to ally with the river otters who support him."

"I think so," Shaynnah murmured. "And, I'll tell you this—there are no lines Al'ce will not cross. Truthfully, she's already crossed them all."

Conch shook his head wearily. "Where is Coll'n's faction?"

Shaynnah managed a shrug. "Graystone, probably. I rather imagine they're offering protection in exchange for shelter and better equipment. Not that Graystone is a high step up from the river, but still ..."

Conch stared at the mice, imagining them tearing through his home. *No. Bear King, please, no.*

Jul'an hurried after his aunt, but he was unsure how best to argue his case. He had already tried bargaining, cajoling, and insisting—the three methods that usually worked best on Al'ce—and now was left wondering what had gone wrong. He knew Al'ce better than anyone else, and he knew she had few weaknesses. Unlike Shorefish and Doomspear, she had no desire to regain lost property. Her one driving force was greed, and Jul'an wasn't sure how to play off that.

His stomach was full of loud, burning guilt. He silently wished his journey with the sea otter had been shorter, wished Conch had never come to rely on him. Then he wordlessly mocked himself. Even if Conch had never trusted him, he was still honor-bound to help the otter. He owed Anamay Mudriver his life, and he had to put that debt to rest somehow.

But Al'ce didn't see it that way. She saw only that she held captive a creature who would be valuable to many rulers as a bargaining chip.

"How much do you think Mokimshim would pay for Anamay Mudriver's son?" Al'ce asked Jul'an gleefully. "Think what power he would have over Shorefish if he had the creature she seeks in revenge. Of course, we would have that power over her too, but Mokimshim could do much more for us than Shorefish could. I think I'll negotiate with Mokimshim."

Jul'an's heart sank. Mokimshim was sure to offer Conch up to Shorefish, and then she would kill him. Unless, of course, Mokimshim never actually *did* give Conch over. But Shorefish wouldn't be stupid enough to go along with that for long.

Jul'an looked around desperately, searching for some inspiration, but he could think of nothing.

Conch looked up when Al'ce approached. She spared only a brief glance for Shaynnah, who was feigning unconsciousness, before addressing Conch. "You'll be pleased to know," she said ironically, "that I've decided what to do with you."

The sea otter glared back silently.

"I'm sending you to King Mokimshim," Al'ce continued, undaunted. "You'll be very valuable to him as a bargaining chip, and Mokimshim can do all sorts of things for these mice. The squirrel will be valuable to him, too—she might be the key to Pasadagavra."

Shaynnah didn't move, but Conch could sense her despair.

"So you two be good until I hear from Arashna," Al'ce finished. With that, she turned and walked away.

Conch waited only until she'd gone two steps before calling, "Mokimshim is a good choice. Best choice you could make."

His voice dripping sarcasm got Al'ce's attention. She turned around, tilted her head, and returned the same. "You have something to say, sea otter?"

"My aunt could do better than Mokimshim," Conch smirked. Then he closed his eyes and leaned his head back against a tree, as if sleeping.

He was rewarded with a solid kick in the ribs, and he grunted in pain and rolled on his side. But it was worth it; Al'ce stared down at him and demanded, "What could Mudriver possibly give that a *king* couldn't?"

"I thought you'd already made up your mind," Conch grumbled.

Al'ce gave another kick, this one to his gut.

"He is his insolent mother's son!" Al'ce snapped. "Sea otter, what do you mean?"

If Conch heard *one* more insult about his mother, he would cut out the insulter's tongue! "Ironic you whine about my river otter mother and then call me 'sea otter' in the same breath," he gasped.

He gasped again as Al'ce aimed one final kick to his stomach. "*Answer me!*"

"Armor," Conch choked out. "Better armor."

"The Wraith Mice have armor, fool!" Al'ce exclaimed. But she sounded puzzled rather than angry.

"Not *Miamuran* armor," Conch panted. "My aunt grew up by Miamur and Lunep. Her smiths learned the Miamuran secrets. They have better materials and better skills than the Wraith Mice do."

He actually had no idea if that were true, but there was almost no mining in the Wraith Mice cities and plenty of mining in both Lunep and Miamur, so he reasoned their techniques must be more refined.

"Besides," Conch added, "she's closer. You wouldn't have to wait as long to hear a reply from her."

Jul'an, standing behind Al'ce, gave Conch a look of encouragement. Conch sneered at him. Al'ce didn't notice the exchange because she was mulling over what Conch had said.

"Mm," she murmured. "It would be a risk. Mudriver's threatened to kill anyone who lays a paw on her sister's children ... But if we were to tell her we *rescued* you instead ... She'd reward us handsomely and probably stop ambushing our patrols ... hmmmm."

Please, Conch thought fervently, *please, Bear King, let her take the bait!*

But before Al'ce made up her mind, another mouse ran up to her.

"Chief!" he panted. "The patrol's back, and they have news!"

"Go on," Al'ce murmured absently.

"Doomspear ambushed a part of Mudriver's tribe!" the mouse exclaimed. "Ten warriors! They were traveling south from Nikor Mais through the woodland, instead of on the river, and Doomspear hit them then! They were being led by Mudriver's captain Greeneddy—her senior captain!"

Conch closed his eyes. *Oh, no.*

Al'ce snapped out of her reverie. "How many are dead?"

"All ten of Mudriver's otters are dead," the mouse reported. "But they were escorting prisoners."

Shaynnah gave up on her pretended unconsciousness and let out a wail of despair.

"Who? How many?" Al'ce demanded, ignoring the squirrel.

"Three," the scout answered, and Shaynnah's eyes opened hopefully. "They were sea otters, and they'd been tortured. The scouts spoke with Doomspear—apparently the sea otters were taken by Moonpath and Shorefish in a raid. They were snatched by some masked raiders that Shorefish couldn't identify, and then they were taken by Mudriver's otters. Moonpath thinks it was Mudriver who took them in the first place, but Shorefish says it was someone who was trying to beat them to Arashna with their prize."

"Why does Shorefish say that?" Al'ce asked.

The scout shrugged. "This is all stuff I've heard second-paw from Doomspear, so I don't know how reliable it is. Doomspear said Shorefish said they had two mouse maidens with them, one of whom was the daughter of a captive in Dobar who knows something important but won't share it. Shorefish was going to use this captive's daughter to make her talk. But there were no mice among the dead in Mudriver's tribe, so they must have changed paws at least once."

Al'ce nodded slowly. "That would explain the masks," she mused. "If it was someone else in Mokimshim's employ, she would bring an accusation against them."

Conch closed his eyes and released a silent sigh of relief. He knew in his heart that Danaray had ordered her warriors to attack Shorefish and Moonpath—perhaps she'd been searching for him, but he didn't think it was that simple. After what Shaynnah had said—about the rift between Mokimshim and Zuryzel—he knew which side Shorefish and Moonpath fell on, and he also knew what side his aunt fell on.

"Does Doomspear have the three sea otters?" Al'ce asked.

Conch opened his eyes in time to see the scout nod.

"All right," Al'ce muttered. "Doomspear will get out of here faster than you can blink, which means, if Mudriver starts scouting the area, we're the only hostile force she'll find."

She paused, and for a minute, Conch saw that she was scared of Danaray. Well, why shouldn't she be?

"Where was Doomspear's attack?" Al'ce pressed.

"South," the scout answered. "He's currently camped south and east, but he's leaving before evening."

Al'ce hissed in frustration. "That clinches it—we're going to Mudriver's. Fast. Don't worry about the boats—we'll walk. It'll take too long to get them prepared."

She raised her voice and shouted orders. "Keep preparing the boats, but everyone not involved in that, get ready to move out fast!"

Al'ce turned around and sneered at Conch. "Your aunt better pay up, sea otter. Or else you'll pay with your life."

Conch glared back coolly. *Not likely.*

He was hauled to his paws, and Shaynnah was hoisted over another mouse's shoulders. Two guards tied ropes around Conch's front paws and then to their own paws, so he couldn't escape. Conch kept looking at Shaynnah, making sure she was alive. The squirrel made a few feeble sounds, but mostly the only thing he had to prove she was alive was her twitching tail.

"Let's move!" Al'ce shouted.

Jul'an tried to catch Conch's eyes, but the sea otter ignored the Keron Mouse.

Focus on Shaynnah, Conch told himself. *Think about Shaynnah. Watch her. That way …*

He didn't continue the thought, lest his guards should read it on his face.

The Keron Mice kept to the bank of the Keron River. Walking was slow; the boatmice were unused to marching across land. They tripped over everything. Conch puzzled over how smooth and hidden they had been in the ambush and decided they must have had many ambushes at that place before.

The mice marched single-file along the river edge. The Keron River had little bank—partly, Conch assumed, because the river was so fast. Shaynnah was carried by the mouse in front of him. Conch was at the very back between his two guards. He kept his eyes fixed on Shaynnah, saying her name once in a while. The two guards tied to him marched at his side, saying nothing. Conch almost felt sorry for them.

As he focused on Shaynnah, his peripheral vision scanned the nearby terrain. After only a few minutes of marching, they reached a place where the bank dropped sharply into the river. The water looked deep.

Without any warning, Conch threw himself to the side and plunged into the water. He heard the two guards gasp in surprise before he submerged. The Keron River's current took over, and he plunged as far down as he could, dragging his two guards completely underwater. He felt them struggling as the river swept them south, and he glanced off a couple of rocks.

Shaynnah stared at the water where Conch had disappeared with her jaw hanging open. She didn't say anything; Conch had been at the back, no one had noticed his disappearance except her. She whimpered once, and because her chest was right by her carrier's ear, he couldn't hear that the guards behind him were no longer tripping over branches.

The Keron Mice might have been boatmice, but they were *not* otters. Conch could hold his breath three times as long as his two guards. As the river whipped him along, he searched for sharp rocks, and saw one soon enough. Using his hind paws, he braced the rope against it and sawed ferociously back and forth. One guard had already gone still; the other one continued struggling but weakly, and Conch freed him first. The dead one simply floated to the surface once Conch cut that rope. *Free!*

Mother, he thought, *your blood runs in my veins. Help me. Teach me how to use the power of the river.*

As he thought of her and as he twisted around to follow the river, something awoke in him. An instinct he had never honed among the sea otters took over. It was as if he could sense every eddy, every turn, every rock, branch, and fish in the river. He knew how fast he was going, and how far he had gone. The water seemed to whisper in his ear. New energy awoke, and he swam tirelessly.

When he finally needed a breath, he broke the surface and paused to check his surroundings. He still hadn't passed his aunt's borders, and he knew Doomspear had to be around here somewhere.

He listened hard and thought, maybe, he heard some shouting to the west. He clenched his jaw and determinedly set off after Doomspear.

FACE TO FACE

Shaynnah had almost drifted off—it was quite rhythmic riding along like a sack of potatoes, and she was very tired. Her limbs ached, her head spun from blood loss, and she was just so tired of fighting pain and fear that she was willing to consign herself to sleep.

She was almost asleep when there was a loud shout of, "Halt!"

Her ears pricked. That was no mouse.

"Chieftainess Mudriver!" Al'ce's voice carried back to the tribeprincess. "It is an honor, truly, to see you ag—"

"What are you doing here?" Danaray Mudriver's voice cut across Al'ce's.

"I've got a bit of business to conduct with you, Chieftainess," Al'ce replied. "A transaction, of sorts."

"I have no interest in getting involved with your 'business,'" Danaray retorted. "So if that's all, you can turn back."

"Really?" Al'ce inquired, a sneer creeping into her voice. "Not even interested in your sister's son?"

There was a moment of shocked silence; then Danaray said, "The only *business* I do with anyone who threatens Wren and Warbler involves blades and bloodshed."

"But there's no need for any of that!" Al'ce cajoled. "I brought him along. He's unharmed. Tribeprincess Shaynnah's here too, and she's less unharmed, but you can have her too—for a price."

"A ransom?" Danaray asked with distaste.

"I was thinking of it as thanks for my not turning him over to Mokimshim," Al'ce replied smoothly. "Or any of your other enemies. Or your sister's. I could get quite a ransom from *them*."

Shaynnah held her breath. Was Danaray alone? Were there others with her? Shaynnah couldn't hear any, but that didn't mean they weren't there!

"Show him to me," Danaray ordered. "Show them both."

At that point, every captor turned to look towards the back where the prisoners were—or had been. And every one of them saw only Shaynnah.

The tribeprincess lifted her head, daring to look around. Danaray had not come alone—far from it. She must have had a whole regiment with her, although it was hard for Shaynnah to count from her upside-down position.

"Where's the otter?" Al'ce screeched, hurting Shaynnah's ears.

"He was at the back with his two guards!" insisted one of the mice.

The mouse holding Shaynnah spun in a half circle, giving the sole captive a better view of Danaray's face. She looked *furious*.

"Squirrel!" Al'ce cried suddenly. "What happened to the otter?"

Shaynnah considered playing dumb, but she realized that she couldn't get beaten anymore and hope to survive. "The river," she said calmly.

At least, she *tried* to say it. It came out as a faint whisper.

"She's hurt!" Danaray snapped. "Put her down!"

Her holder gently lowered Shaynnah to the earth, rolling her onto her back so that the wound wasn't aggravated further. Even so, the treetops above Shaynnah began to spin.

"Kermunda," Danaray said curtly. An otter hurried up from behind Danaray and knelt down beside Shaynnah.

"What happened to the sea otter?" Al'ce demanded.

"While ago," Shaynnah whispered. "Jumped in the river with his guards. Pulled them under. Swam south."

"Was he hurt by these mice, Tribeprincess?" Danaray asked coldly.

Shaynnah shivered. "Kicked."

The healer, Kermunda, took out a canteen of water and a cloth and gently began to sponge away at Shaynnah's wound. It stung, but she did not cry out. Instead, she closed her eyes and gave up any effort to keep awake. But in spite of how exhausted she'd been a minute ago, she couldn't fall asleep.

"An interesting insult, Al'ce," Danaray observed. "You kidnap my nephew and demand a ransom without bothering to ensure his safety. I can't decide if you're unreasonably arrogant or just incompetent. Although, from Shaynnah's story, you sound more incompetent."

"How dare you insult me!" Al'ce shrieked. "You lousy, arrogant, …" She launched into a series of insults that Shaynnah tuned out.

Danaray waited until Al'ce ran out of breath before retorting, "You're pathetic."

"*Pathetic?*" Al'ce shrieked.

"Where did you capture my nephew?" Danaray shouted, even louder. "And when?"

"I could have killed him!" Al'ce shouted in the tone of someone using a clever counterpoint. "And if you want the tribeprincess, you still have to pay up."

"No," Danaray snapped. "I don't have to."

"Don't treat me as if I'm dirt on your paws," Al'ce sneered. "You think your fancy armor and fine ways make you so much better than I am. Well, here's the deal—I want armor in exchange for the squirrel!"

"*Armor,*" Danaray snorted. "You think I call you pathetic because you have poor *armor*? It has nothing to do with *armor*. And you aren't getting a single armor plate from me, but the tribeprincess *is* coming with my otters!"

"Ha!" Al'ce sneered. "Not likely. I don't know if you can count, but I have more warriors here than you have."

"I can count," Danaray retorted icily. She didn't sound impressed.

"Then you're in no position to be making demands," Al'ce sneered.

For a long moment there was silence. Then Shaynnah heard the call of a bird she'd only heard near Miamur, and Danaray's mouth curved up in a smile.

"Neither," she said softly, "are you."

Shaynnah knew then that there was someone else in the forest, but Al'ce apparently didn't. "I fail to see why."

"Do you?" Danaray smirked. "Then look behind you."

From her prone position, Shaynnah saw Al'ce look over her shoulder; for a minute there was silence. Then she shrieked, "*You!*"

After that, Shaynnah only saw a confused blur of movement. Kermunda knelt protectively over her with a knife—*how humiliating!*—but after only a few minutes, everything was still again. The rebel Keron Mice were ringed in by more otters and—*wait, what?*

There were other mice amidst the otters.

No. Shaynnah had to be seeing that wrong. Keron Mice fighting alongside Danaray? But there was no fighting. Everything was still.

Everything except Al'ce, anyway. She was held between two otters, throwing herself angrily in every direction, trying to break free, and screaming like a banshee. And she was being made to face an old mouse, who looked as if the encounter was more of a trial for him than for her.

"So," Danaray said, walking behind Al'ce and resting her tribal knife on the violent mouse's shoulder. "We were speaking of my nephew."

"Chieftainess," the old mouse said in a soft, sad voice, "it is against me they have offended. Not you."

Danaray gave him a jaundiced look. "They took my nephew, Coll'n. She offended against me as well. Now then, baitfish …"

The word sent Al'ce into another fit of rage, but this one was shorter; clearly she was losing energy.

Danaray waited for her to grow quiet, and then finished her command. "Tell me again what happened to my nephew."

"You should die," Al'ce spat. "As your sister did. As her son will, no doubt."

Danaray stiffened. "Explain yourself."

Al'ce licked her lips. "What would you pay to know where he went?"

Smack!

Shaynnah couldn't tell if it was Coll'n, Danaray, or someone else who slapped Al'ce's face. But something clicked in Shaynnah's memory. She swallowed hard and croaked out, "*Chieftainess.*"

Kermunda echoed her plea in a louder voice.

Danaray glared at Al'ce one more second before turning and kneeling down beside Shaynnah. "What is it, Tribeprincess?"

As quickly as she could, Shaynnah relayed what the scouts had said about Doomspear and the three sea otter captives. The ambush of her warriors was the last straw for Danaray. She didn't reply for a moment. Then she murmured, "Coll'n, would you be so kind as to bring these captives back to my city? You have my word who has jurisdiction over them will be determined there—we are pressed for time. I want ten river otters to go as well, to show you the way."

"Of course," Coll'n replied instantly. "And we'll take the tribeprincess back, too."

Danaray nodded respectfully. "Thank you, Coll'n."

Then she raised her voice. "Doomspear is to the south on the other side of the river. Let's get him before he can escape north!"

FREEDOM

onch knew he couldn't get his friends out by himself—or so he had
thought until he saw Doomspear's camp.

Great Bear King, he thought. *They're guarding only* one *entrance!*

And he knew that because he knew this clearing. This wasn't quite
within sea otter borders, but it was very close—maybe a mile away, perhaps.
It was right on the Othyrn River, and the river was being watched by warriors
with spears and bows. The trees ringing the clearing were cedar, and their
branches dipped low, touching the ground. Conch knew that behind the
branches were thick bunches of salal, virtually impossible to get through,
except at one point. It was the farthest point back from the river. The cedar
branches were thick enough to conceal that what lay behind them was not
salal, but a pond.

And the best part? Saline, Pearl, and Abalone were being held right
in front of that section.

They were being treated well, at least. They were seated on three stumps,
their front paws bound, but their bandages—Kermunda must have put those
on—were being checked by an old otter who looked like a healer. Saline's
eyes were red, from either exhaustion or grief, and they sparked with hate.
Pearl sat on her right, and her gentle silver eyes were both concerned and
angry. Abalone was staring straight at the ground. Conch prayed fiercely
that his friend wasn't blaming himself.

The river otters were all hurriedly preparing to leave, though they
clearly still had quite a bit of preparation to do before they were ready to

move out. It looked as though some food packs had split, or maybe a tent bag. Conch knew they must be edgy; they were *very* close to Danaray's forces. If Conch snatched even one of their prisoners, it would delay them further, maybe enough for his aunt's armies to find them.

Conch crept carefully through the woods; he lost sight of the clearing, but he could still hear the otters within it. Every move he made was slow, careful, and he listened earnestly for any sign of an outpost or a sentry stationed in the woods.

He saw the murky brown waters of the pond—*what was it called? Brown Banks? Dark Shores? Something like that*—without seeing a single sentry. The same instinct that had awoken in the river guided him silently through the trees. Still, he froze when he saw the pond, listening, for several minutes. When he was satisfied that no one was watching, he slid into the cloudy waters.

This pond was where he'd learned how to swim, and he could reach the point behind the clearing with ease. There were only a small patch of land and some ferns between the pond and the clearing. Conch would have to be careful—but maybe he could do it!

He crawled silently from the pond and ducked beneath the ferns; he was screened by the cedar branches, but he could hear what was going on in the clearing. And his stomach jolted when he realized his friends were being interrogated.

"You say your brother is a chief," a low, quiet voice said. "Which chief?"

"Why would I tell you that?" Saline's voice snapped back.

"Because if you do, I can let your friends go," the low voice replied firmly. "But if not, they must come as well."

"*Come?*" Saline echoed. "You mean *be taken.* I don't know what use my brother's name is to you, but I do *not* make deals with kidnappers!"

Conch saw a flicker of movement on the other side of the screening cedar branches; a minute later the interrogator asked, "Who was it who tortured you?"

His voice had softened, but Saline's voice did not as she retorted, "Shorefish and Moonpath."

"Shorefish?" the interrogator exclaimed. "She actually took part in torture?"

"She stood by and watched it happen," Saline growled. "There is no difference."

This resulted in another stunned silence. It was broken by the interrogator's voice, this time sounding uncertain.

"I have no idea what insanity prompted Shorefish to allow such a thing as torture to happen in front of her," he murmured. "And you are right to not trust Moonpath. She has abandoned all reason and dignity. But I have not—and I will prove it to you."

There was the rasping of a blade being drawn; Conch nearly shouted in alarm, but then the interrogator said, "I swear upon the knife of my tribe, that should you give me your brother's name, I will release your friends. I have no interest in them—only in your true identity."

Conch realized what was happening, that Doomspear understood the value of his royal prisoner—Eagle's sister.

Saline, no! he thought in panic. *Don't tell him!*

"My friends will be free," Saline put in. "Immediately. And they will not be recaptured."

"Yes," Doomspear replied. "I swear all this."

Don't give in, Saline! Conch though urgently.

Saline's voice was silent for a time. "Will you let me consult with them?" she asked finally, sounding defeated.

Doomspear's voice held a bite of impatience. "Very well. Consult quickly. Time is wasting."

There were a few seconds of silence; then Saline demanded sharply, "Time to do *what?*"

"Don't tell him, Saline," Abalone's voice answered. "It can't be good."

"But if he lets you go…," Saline's voice trailed off.

Conch willed up his courage. If the river otters were busy breaking camp and guarding the river, then maybe he could get his friends away. He swallowed nervously, pressed as closely to the ground as he could, and wriggled forward.

He emerged right behind the tree stump that Pearl was sitting on. Praying that no one was watching the captives, Conch hissed Pearl's name.

She jumped a little, turned around, and gasped. But she had the good sense to look around immediately, lest any of her captives see her looking over her shoulder.

"How did you find us?" she demanded out of the side of her mouth.

"Long story," he muttered back.

Saline looked over, and her eyes widened. "Great Bear King, Conch, what's going on?"

"Saline," Conch whispered back. "You *can't* give him your brother's name. You have to stall him."

"What? What are you talking about?"

"You're near my aunt's territory," Conch rushed on. "But listen—Doomspear needs a captive of royal blood, someone equal to a captive he lost. If he gets this captive, he'll have help to invade the sea otters. My guess is that if he goes back not knowing what your connection is, his ally's help won't be guaranteed. He has to know your connection. You have to stall."

He stayed crouched behind the stump, hoping against hope that no one could see him. Saline had a neutral expression. She leaned around, pretending to talk to Pearl, but really addressing Conch. "How do you know all this?"

"Long story," Conch blurted out. "Is anybody watching you?"

Saline glanced up, then shook her head. "No one. Conch, listen to me—take Pearl and get out of here. Find my brother or your aunt—whoever is closer—and come get us."

"What about you and Abalone?" Conch asked worriedly.

"You can't get all of us away all at once," Saline replied firmly. "I can't really walk, much less swim, and Abalone has an infection—he's too sick to move fast. Take Pearl away."

Conch thought of Shaynnah—was she being punished for his escape? He hoped Al'ce wouldn't notice his absence until she ran into Danaray, and the odds of *that* were high. And his friends … he worried that if Saline didn't reveal her brother's name to Doomspear, the river otter would begin pressuring Pearl and Abalone to do so.

"Fine," he muttered. "But Abalone's coming too. Doomspear can't have any leverage against you."

Pearl twisted so that she was facing Saline, as if they were having an intense conversation; really, it was a subtle way of preparing to follow Conch.

Saline glanced back at Abalone, and Conch could tell Saline didn't want to be alone, but before she could say a word, Abalone spoke up. "Conch, I'm not going anywhere. I won't leave Saline alone."

Saline shot him a grateful look.

"It might be better if you did," Conch warned.

"I'm willing to take the risk," Abalone muttered back.

Conch nodded—he'd expected something like that. "All right. Pearl, is anyone watching you?"

"They're glancing our way," Pearl explained quietly. "Hang on—you might want to back up."

Conch obliged; he slid back under the cedar branches. Pearl glanced after him to see where he'd gone, and then went back to her ostensible conversation with Saline and Abalone.

It was several minutes before she rolled off the stump and crawled after Conch.

"Come on!" Conch hissed. "There's a pond—" A moment later his paws hit the water. He shifted so Pearl could slide in before him and then plunged in after her.

It was so blessedly quiet underwater. Conch could barely make out Pearl's dark shape, but he tapped her shoulder, indicating she should follow him. Then he led her to the southern edge of the pond where they cautiously poked their heads out.

"We have to find Danaray," Conch whispered in her ear.

"Why are we looking for your aunt instead of Eagle?" Pearl whispered back.

"Because Eagle's probably gone on to Zurez by now," Conch muttered. He heaved himself out of the water. "Come on—we have to hurry."

No sooner had he said that than they heard shouting coming from the river otter camp.

"Yeah," Pearl agreed, emerging onto land. "Let's run."

Conch grabbed her paw and they took off.

First they ran south to avoid any lookouts or scouts; then they turned west. They raced through the narrowest passages they could find, getting twigs and leaves caught in their clothes. When they were near the river, Pearl let out a yelp and stumbled.

Conch risked stopping, but she was upright in the blink of an eye. "I'm fine!" she gasped, hop-skipping forward. "Rolled my ankle, that's all."

She limped forward a few paces until she could run again. This time, Conch heard the sounds of pursuit behind them. The river was close, but it sounded as if their pursuers were closer.

"Pearl, keep going," Conch muttered. Then he pressed behind a juniper bush. A few seconds later, a yelling river otter came into view, chasing after Pearl. At the last minute, Conch sprang up and plunged his knife into the otter's throat.

He didn't stop long enough to see the results; instead he ran after Pearl, catching up with her in a matter of seconds.

"Not far now!" he panted.

He'd barely spoken when they saw the strip of water that was the Othyrn River. They put on an extra burst of speed and submerged in the river before anyone saw them.

They swam south, but only for a minute or so. They emerged at a place that Conch knew well and struggled up onto the bank.

"But they're on this side!" Pearl whispered frantically.

"So are my aunt's patrols," Conch replied. "Come on, hurry!"

They didn't run far this time. They'd barely left the river behind when Pearl let out a startled shriek. Conch turned toward her and saw river otters emerging from the woods. A quick look showed they were surrounded.

Then a female otter pushed her way through the throng to face the two sea otters. "Conch! Great Bear King!"

Conch managed a tired smile. "Hello, Aunt. I'm glad we've found you."

Pearl sat wrapped in a blanket, sipping from a wooden mug filled with tea that Kermunda the healer had provided. Conch glanced at her from time to time, but mostly he was listening to Danaray. At first he'd wanted to go with her warriors to chase Doomspear out and retrieve Saline and Abalone, but his aunt's expression had killed that question before he'd asked it.

"What," she said quietly, "were you thinking?"

It was the third time she'd asked that, and Conch answered the same way he had the other times.

"I didn't want to lose the trail. There's no way we could have tracked them."

He'd already told her about Nathan'el and Shaynnah—she'd waved aside the news about the squirrel without any explanation—and so she seemed to have no more questions.

"Conch, I—that was—"

"Stupid?" Conch filled in for her.

Danaray nodded. "That's one word for it, yes. Don't you *ever* go chasing an entire *tribe* by yourself again, no matter what the stakes are!"

"I thought maybe I'd find help on the way," Conch offered. Then he laughed bitterly. "I didn't expect it to be a Keron Mouse traitor."

Finally Danaray's eyes softened. "He was a traitor, Wren," she said gently, "but not to you. He meant to lead you away from Al'ce and her ilk. He'd been … installed, I suppose, by Coll'n as a spy. Against Al'ce."

Conch turned to his aunt in surprise—and maybe relief. "Really?"

She smiled wryly. "Really. He has more honor than Al'ce does."

"So why did he insist on accompanying me and Nathan'el?" Conch protested, puzzled.

Danaray shrugged. "He wouldn't answer that question while I was in attendance. But if I had to guess—possibly because he felt he could no longer keep spying. Al'ce is—"

"His aunt," Conch filled in. "Shaynnah told me." Then he sat up sharply. "*Shaynnah!* Where is—"

"She's fine," Danaray smiled. "Currently in Kermunda's care. She passed out a little bit after we found her."

Then Danaray's eyes grew serious again. "Conch, I'm glad you're safe," she said. "But I never—*never*—want to hear of you doing anything like this again. You have no idea how lucky you were that you weren't killed!"

Conch swallowed. "I've been told," he admitted.

"And I hope it's stuck in your mind," Danaray added sharply. "You caused a lot of worry. Following Shorefish and Moonpath—it's something you should never have done!"

Conch lowered his head humbly. "Yes, Aunt."

Danaray sighed. "Having said that, well done."

Conch smiled and murmured, "I won't ever do it again."

"Hmm," his aunt murmured. "*Ever* is a long time."

"Not for a long, long time, then," Conch offered, grinning.

She smacked his head fondly. Then she stood up. "Part of your clan is waiting for you at your home," she said. "Waiting for you, Saline, Pearl, and Abalone to come home so you can join the rest of your clan in Zurez."

ROYAL PREY

Nurida had taken to slipping out at night and sleeping during the day. Evening was falling when she awoke. But she hadn't wakened gently; Eyixid had forcefully thrust his paw in her mouth.

"Wake up but be quiet," he breathed in her ear.

Nurida swallowed and nodded.

Eyixid crept back, allowing her to get to her knees. "What is it?" she whispered.

In response, he touched his ear.

Nurida held her breath, and she heard shouting.

"It has to be!" one voice cried. "It has to be!"

"Why? Why does it have to be?" another shouted. "We're wasting time!"

Nurida closed her eyes in dread. "Who are they?" she whispered.

"I don't know," the Wraith Mouse replied heavily.

It was then that Nurida noticed his voice wasn't squeaking. It had become strong and sure. It was hard to tell, since he was whispering, but he definitely sounded different. She looked at him, scared, and after a few seconds, he returned his gaze to hers. The wild, frayed look that had filled his eyes was gone.

He held her gaze for a few minutes; then he sighed in resignation. "Come with me."

They crept out of his living room, and he held the door to the forge room open for her. She hurried down the stairs, and he followed her, closing the door softly.

When they reached the forge, Nurida turned around to face Eyixid. "What's happening?" she asked, her voice calmer than she thought it would be. "You've been acting, haven't you?"

"Most of the time," the Wraith Mouse said wryly. "There were times— well—yes, I was acting."

"Why?" Nurida exclaimed, no longer calm. "Why've you been—"

"Because I knew that a Miamuran princess was in league with the creature trying to kill me, and at first I thought she was you," the Wraith Mouse answered in a rush. "But now—well, I have to make sure you're safe."

Nurida blinked. "Kill you—who *are* you?"

The Wraith Mouse sighed. "My name—my real name," he said reluctantly, "is Johajar."

It took a moment for the full impact of his statement to penetrate Nurida's confusion.

"*Prince* Johajar?"

He laughed hollowly. "Not prince. Not anymore. I've been … I've been stripped of that title by my *dear* brother." He laughed, and it was the first time Nurida had ever heard a laugh sound angry. "Apparently I threatened his right to rule."

Nurida was too surprised to do more than stammer. "What—how— what's happening?"

Johajar sighed and shook his head. "Sit."

Nurida promptly dropped to the floor, looking up at him anxiously.

"When my mother, Queen Demeda, died, Mokimshim inherited her place," Johajar explained, pacing. "I was—well, I was disappointed. I'm not sure there's anything my mother could have done, since the laws of the Wraith Mice are so complex and specific, but I really hoped he wouldn't become the next king. He did. My sister, Zuryzel, was commanding the patrols along our eastern borders, about two days away from Arashna, when Mokimshim became king. As I said, apparently I was a threat to Mokimshim's rule because he was waiting for an excuse to arrest me. I didn't know it, so I was … careless. I told some creatures in court that I wished Zuryzel would inherit the throne instead. Within the hour, I was arrested and thrown in a dungeon."

Nurida was stunned. "But … how did … how did you get out?"

Johajar's eyes softened, and so did his voice. "Karena—Mokimshim's queen. Bear King bless her courage. She slipped down to the dungeons herself, carrying the keys, and let me out. She told me to get away and hide, find Zuryzel if I could, but not come back to Arashna while Mokimshim was king. Well, I got out, but I-I couldn't find Zuryzel. So, I wound up here."

Nurida swallowed hard. "The creatures outside—and the pirates a few days ago—they're hunting for you, aren't they?"

Johajar nodded. "Well—Zuryzel and me both. But that doesn't mean they'll leave you alone. Trust me, Princess, they won't. Which is why," he continued, "you have to do exactly what I say. You have to trust me. And, most important of all, you have to find this *sister* you keep talking about."

"Ressora," Nurida sighed. Then she straightened. "Wait—you knew who I was?"

Johajar gestured at her knife. "I recognized the writing on the blade—Miamuran for *lily*. When you said your name, I recognized that too. And—your bracelet."

Nurida glanced at her paw. She'd completely forgotten about this bracelet. It was a braid of cord with a small metal plate embossed with her symbol. She'd worn it every day for quite some time. Galledor had given it to her.

Nurida twisted it so the metal was hidden. "All right—why is it most important for me to find Ressora?"

"Call it a hunch," Johajar replied. "You said you're looking for her, and you haven't left the area, so I assume you think she's still around here. If so, then Mokimshim's got plans that no one knows anything about. That's very disturbing, but she might know what they are. Information, Nurida. This is a strange type of war we're in—its decisive weapon will be information. You must find your sister."

Nurida stared at him. "And you?"

His face twisted into a grim smile. "You don't want to know."

Nurida said nothing.

He sighed. "Nurida—I'm going to be getting out of here. Those searchers out there have found something that makes them sure I'm here. I doubt it's anything you did," he added reassuringly. "Because there's no way on earth for them to connect me to you. And that is exactly how it must stay. You cannot be found with me."

"What if I get caught?" Nurida whispered.

Johajar surveyed her steadily. "I pray you won't be. But I plan to be seen, so that when I get out, all the searchers should be pulled out of the area following me. You're smart enough to hide from anyone left behind."

Nurida shook her head. "What if *you* get caught?"

"I get put back in a dungeon," said Johajar indifferently. "Mokimshim needs me alive. I'm valuable to my sister, and he *loves* using other creatures' loved ones against them. But you, Princess—you must be safe."

"I won't know what to do!" Nurida panicked. "I—Johajar, I have no idea why I volunteered to find Ressora. I have no idea what I'm doing! This is so absurd!"

Johajar's harsh features softened. He stepped forward and embraced Nurida gently, much the same way Galledor used to.

"Don't worry," he murmured in her ear. "The greatest weapon in any situation is common sense and quick wit. You have both. Maybe more wit than sense, but more of both than most creatures I know. You have a part to play in this, too, Nurida. Otherwise you would never have found me."

Nurida took a deep breath and forced herself to relax.

Johajar pulled back and gave her a warm smile. "Remember three things—never let your weapon out of sight, never let go of your sense, and never let anyone you come across sense your fear. You can do that. I know it—I've seen you. Be strong, and you'll be fine."

He had so much faith in her. But she wasn't a fighter, and she said so.

"I know," Johajar replied. "But, Nurida, here's the secret—you don't *have* to be one. The world is full of all different types. What you lack in aggressiveness and battle instinct, you make up for in cleverness."

He believed in her. She owed it to him to put aside her self-doubt. She took another deep breath and raised her chin. "All right."

"When I get out, you lock the door to the forge," he instructed. "Stay down here. Don't say anything. Bank the fire and let it go out. When it's daylight, or as near to it as you can guess, then sneak out carefully. Don't come back here, but if you're looking for your sister, try going northwest. I know you haven't searched there yet."

Nurida tilted her head to one side. "How did you know?"

Johajar chuckled. "I followed you part of the way. I know the woods well enough to guess where you went. Now, stay here, and don't make a sound until morning."

Nurida nodded. "Bear King keep you safe."

Johajar kissed the top of her head. "And you. I will never be able to describe what a comfort it has been to have you here, Nurida. See you again someday. And—Nurida," he added, drawing back and looking her sternly in the eye, "remember to watch out for portal demons."

Nurida laughed helplessly, and so did he. Then she hurried over to the forge and began scattering the coals with a rake. When she looked back, Johajar was gone.

The youngest child of King Hokadra and Queen Demeda had a powerful sense of déjà-vu. Once before he'd been cornered in a dark place, although that time it had been by Mokimshim himself instead of his creatures. And of course, that time Mokimshim had been running with him. The then-prince had turned on his brother in the blink of an eye. Johajar had believed that to be nothing more than an act of temper and stress at first, but after some time passed, he began wondering if it was more than that. Still, he'd never said anything to Queen Demeda. It had crossed his mind that maybe his mother could change the succession if she had known, but it would be his word against Mokimshim's, and everyone would wonder why he had kept it to himself, only bringing it forward at the last minute. So he had said nothing.

But now that he was repeating the experience, he really wished he'd said something.

These creatures pursuing him were no pirates or Eerieden mercenaries. They were light on their paws and could apparently see very well in the night. Johajar thought with a sinking feeling that they were Wraith Mice.

His bravado in front of Nurida had been all a fake. He believed Nurida could manage just fine if she kept her wits about her, but something told him that *he* was going straight back to the dungeon in Arashna.

Well, he thought grimly, *home sweet home.*

He made for the river as quickly as he could, but before he caught sight of it, he turned and hurried east. If there were river otters here too, the river was a bad place to be. East it was, then.

All at once, he heard voices shouting to the south, so he veered north. Then he caught sight of shadows in the trees northward, and he knew he was surrounded.

So be it, he thought wearily. *Not without a chase.*

But the chase didn't last long. Someone slipped up behind him and hit him over the head, sending him spiraling into darkness. His last coherent thought was of Nurida.

The Miamuran princess heard the shouting from her hiding place in the forge room. The fire had gone out quickly, so now she sat in darkness. She crept over to a corner near the source of heat and wrapped herself in her cloak. There was nothing to do now but wait until daylight.

Nurida did not get an instant of sleep the whole night. When she judged it to be near daylight, she snuck up the stairs and paused to listen at the locked door. She couldn't hear anyone, but still she was wary about creeping out.

She listened at that door for an hour and then some. After all that time, she had heard no sound. Steeling her nerves, she cracked the door and peeked out.

Sunlight swirled through the cracks in the ceiling and the gaping windows. Nurida tip-pawed to the edge of the room and peered out a window; no one was there. Quiet as a shadow, she crept out of the house and into the woods.

Northwest. Northwest, Johajar had said. So she steeled herself and started northwest.

She knew she was west of Pasadagavra when she stopped. She had reached a river of some kind, but she didn't recognize it. Her stomach was empty; she hadn't brought any food from the house.

When her steps reached the water, she dropped to her knees, buried her face in her paws, and cried.

Part Three

NATHAN'EL

A love that binds, a love that burns,
That heals, strengthens, and inspires.
A warrior's heart unto it turns
And ever races to its fires.

~Old Cliff Mouse Song

STRANGERS

Nathan'el was so tired of the area by the river. He had been trapped there for over three weeks, hiding from all manner of interesting creatures. He was able to sneak about and grab food, but he didn't dare travel too much.

In the morning, the river was busy with boats, piloted by ferrets and foxes, traveling up and down the waterway. At noon, they unloaded patrols, which spent the afternoon and early evening sweeping the forests. The patrols consisted mainly of sneaky, cunning, but somewhat clumsy mercenary mice.

The nights, though, were the spookiest. The air in the forest turned cold as Wraith Mice by the score searched the woods. The river swarmed with river otters scanning the banks. They were looking for something— actually two somethings—and when Nathan'el listened, he could hear what they were searching for—

Prince Johajar or Princess Kiarna.

Nathan'el had *had* it with palace politics. He wanted his mother back. He wanted his family returned to normal. To the Serpent with monarchs.

He made camp in a ring of bushes, a different one each night. Weariness dragged at his eyelids, but he refused to let himself fall completely asleep. He had to be semi-alert, able to move if someone got too close. Sometimes, he would play with the little necklace Mar'e had given him. Every once in a while, he entertained his memories of her clear blue eyes and her timid smile. Mostly, however, he watched the searchers.

It wasn't longer than a week before he noticed certain patterns to the search routines. He began to find safe places to watch from (always in daylight; hiding from the mercenaries by day was much easier than hiding from the Wraith Mice by night) and mentally cataloged his observations.

Two weeks in, he though the numbers of creatures haunting the place was lessening. Three weeks in, he was sure of it; the bulk of the searchers was moving east.

Much of the snow was melting, which helped to disguise his tracks. That late afternoon, he snuck along an outcropping of rocks that he had gotten to know quite well.

He managed to wriggle in-between two of them, his eyes and ears just poking above the stones. His ears were completely attuned to the sounds of the forest. There was some yelling in the distance, some of the mercenaries grumbling and some shouting in frustration.

But as he was listening, a flicker of movement caught his eye. Someone was creeping along amid the trees, bent low and light-pawed. Nathan'el blinked; whoever it was snuck south to north, and Nathan'el was looking at him or her from the east. He waited until the creature had gone farther north before squinting for a better view.

It was a mouse with fur the color of honey. Nathan'el thought maybe it was a female. She moved very slowly, her paws sliding through the grass. Nathan'el could tell that she must be making sounds as she walked—twigs cracking, leaves brushing—but she was quiet enough that the shouting mercenaries would never hear her.

She clearly wasn't one of them; too quiet, but too unskilled. Nathan'el wriggled out of the crevice and slipped after her.

The stranger made her way toward the river. When the murmur of the water became clear, and the shouting of the boat crews was overwhelming, she dropped to her knees behind a huckleberry bush.

Nathan'el crept up behind her and wrapped his paw around her mouth.

She reacted faster than he would have expected; her paw flew to her waist and emerged with a knife. Nathan'el barely caught her paw in time.

"I'm not going to hurt you," he murmured directly into her ear. "I'm not one of them."

He released her mouth; her immediate response was a venomous, "You have a funny way of showing it."

"Desperate times," he muttered. "I'm sorry."

"Then release my knife," the mouse snapped.

He very carefully released her knife-paw. She twisted around, which put her in a vulnerable position, but the glare in her green eyes told him she didn't care.

"Who are you?" she snapped.

He crouched so that he was level with her but ready to spring up at a moment's notice. "A Cliff Mouse," he said as calmly as he could manage. "I'm trying to get to Myanka without attracting all the attention around here. But they're looking for someone."

As he said that, her eyes filled with tears. She blinked them back ferociously. "And the thinking behind sneaking up on me?"

"I didn't want you to scream," Nathan'el admitted.

The mouse scowled and twisted around so she was looking at the creatures by the river again.

"Where were you going?" Nathan'el asked her softly.

"Northwest," was her bitter reply. "I'm waiting for them to clear off."

"What makes you think they will?" Nathan'el persisted.

She glared at him over her shoulder but gave no other reply.

Nathan'el was slightly taken aback. She was angry and still seemed on the verge of tears. He'd seen his sister like that.

"There's a path a little further back," he whispered. "There should be a few moments we can get through before their night searchers come."

The mouse twisted around again. "Show me. Please."

He stood up, and she followed suit, sneaking behind him. Her paws weren't adept at woodland travel, but she was so light and graceful that she was naturally quiet.

Nathan'el led her west, then sharp north on a pattern he'd memorized. He was right—the lessening of searchers meant that this area had been neglected first. There would be a quick dart across a field, but then they would be safe in woods that were lightly patrolled, if at all. Woods that he knew, woods that were within a week of the coast.

They reached the field without incident; he twisted around to glance at the stranger and saw her looking at the field in something like relief. He scanned the grass and saw no one, so he murmured, "Come on."

She seized his paw and hissed, "*Wait!*"

He looked at her perplexedly, and she jerked her chin. "There—off to the left—he'll move again soon."

Barely had she finished speaking when a mouse on the other side of the field straightened up. He began jogging south. Nathan'el looked at his companion and murmured, "Any more?"

She shook her head and led the way out onto the grass.

If Nathan'el had been surprised by her grace in the woods, it was nothing like the subtle smoothness with which she glided through the grass. When the evening wind blew through the grasses, she seemed to move with it. Nathan'el knew he didn't have half her grace or ease out here.

But once they reached the far trees, she turned again to him to take the lead. He didn't know these trees as he knew the ones that had imprisoned him for the last three weeks, but they were tall evergreens—firs and cedars, mostly. Nathan'el noticed one cedar whose branches touched the ground like a tent. He listened very carefully for a moment and then led the newcomer to the space under it.

The minute she was concealed she dropped to her knees and put her face in her paws. She took three deep breaths, as if calming herself.

"You're Miamuran," Nathan'el said abruptly.

She looked up at him. "What is it to you?"

"Miamurans are supposed to be very adept at traveling across flat, treeless places," he answered.

"Miamur isn't flat," she answered stiffly. "It has an abundance of hills."

"Who are you?" Nathan'el asked her.

He stood to his full height, no difficulty even beneath the boughs, and as he did so something changed in the newcomer's expression. A wild light lit her green eyes and she inhaled sharply.

"I think a better question," she said coldly, "is who are *you?*"

She stood up as she spoke, moving her limbs slowly and painfully.

"How come?" Nathan'el asked, surprised by her aggression.

He was even more surprised when, in one swift motion, she stepped close to him and pressed her knife point against his throat. "Because of what you carry," she whispered.

Nathan'el grabbed her wrist and with blinding speed pushed her back until she was pinned against the tree trunk. She gasped, but her eyes sparked defiantly.

"I just led you out of a network of searchers," he hissed. "Pulling a knife on me was rude. I prefer creatures remember their manners."

He had so had enough—enough of the fear, the weariness, the caution. But it seemed the mouse glaring back at him had had enough as well.

"I don't particularly care what you prefer," she snapped, eyes blazing furiously. "Especially not if you killed a princess of Miamur!"

29

PRINCESSES OF MIAMUR

The accusation was so unexpected that for a minute Nathan'el could say nothing. When he found his voice again, he managed, "I have never in my life even *seen* a princess of Miamur. I certainly never killed one."

The honey-furred mouse reached up with her spare paw and touched something on his neck. "Then where did you get her symbol?"

She lifted the chain that Mar'e had given him.

"This belonged to a traveler that I met in the woods," he answered, calm and still bewildered. "A mouse."

Green eyes glinted wildly in triumph. "This mouse was gray-furred, was she not?" she smirked. "Icy blue eyes. Young—about your age. Older than me. She was as skilled on a grassland as I was, probably even more so."

A weight settled in Nathan'el's stomach. He lessened the pressure on his captive's knife paw. "Who was she?"

The mouse captive twitched the necklace. "The White Wings. A hawk diving between them. Gray fur, blue eyes. Where is she now?"

Nathan'el scowled. "Who *was* she?"

The mouse tilted her head back. "Ressora, Daughter of the White Wings, Third Princess of Miamur. Where is she now?"

Nathan'el lessened his grip a little more. "Pasadagavra."

The anger and bitterness vanished from his captive's face to be replaced with utter confusion. "*What?*" she whispered.

"Pa-sa-da-gav-ra," Nathan'el repeated more clearly.

The captive looked away, mouth open slightly. She looked so bewildered, so lost, that Nathan'el's heart softened.

"But that makes no sense," she whispered to herself.

"Who are you?" Nathan'el asked gently.

She shook her head minutely.

Nathan'el released her knife paw and instead touched a braided bracelet on her free paw. He turned it carefully until a steel plate was visible. Embossed on the metal was another symbol. "I think you are a princess of Miamur, too," he murmured.

The symbol was beautiful—wings on either side of a tongue of flame. A flower—*maybe a lily?*—stood amid the flame. It had two leaves curling out, clearly unharmed by the fire.

The mouse looked away, shoulders drooping. "Nurida," she murmured.

"I beg your pardon?"

"My name. Nurida."

Nathan'el did not completely release the paw that pinned her against the tree. "And what are you doing here?"

"What business is it of yours?"

"I did just get you out of a very sticky situation," Nathan'el reminded her. "And how do I know *you* didn't kill a princess and take her signet?"

Nurida twisted in his grip. "Traveling," she said bitterly. "And looking for my sister. For Ressora."

She pushed away from the tree and managed to get past Nathan'el. "Thank you for getting me out," she said abruptly. "But I have to go back to Pasadagavra."

"Back past all the searchers?" Nathan'el challenged.

She laughed mirthlessly. "They aren't looking for anything anymore. They found what they were searching for."

She sounded so bitter and angry that Nathan'el was confused. "She's in Pasadagavra," he repeated.

"Did you actually see her in Pasadagavra?" Nurida challenged.

"Yes," Nathan'el replied firmly, offended by her skeptical tone. "I saw her inside it, and she was still there when I left."

"Then she left after you did," Nurida scoffed.

"Tribeking Rhonndan was having her watched," Nathan'el countered. "He and his sister were both suspicious of her. I doubt she's been allowed to leave."

Nurida shrugged indifferently. "Then I still have to go back," she said. "I have to see her and return her to Miamur."

"If I were you," Nathan'el snapped, "I would at least wait until morning, and give the search a chance to die down a bit more."

Nurida twisted around and gave him an angry glare. "And yet you are not me," she retorted. "Thank you, again, for your help. If you happen across any Miamuran soldier, I am sure he or she could reward you. But I must go, and I do not have the means to reward you at this time."

With that, she spun around and darted back toward the field.

Nathan'el slapped his paw against the tree in anger. *What a reckless fool!*

He watched the tree branches she'd pushed aside stop shaking, and didn't turn away immediately.

No, he told himself. *No, I am not following her. I offered her help, and she ran off. I am not helping her any more.*

Nurida stopped in the middle of the field and collapsed. She knew no one could see her—the grass was much too high. But she was so cold. And so hungry. And so tired.

But mostly, she was angry. Angrier than she'd ever been at Ressora or anyone else. Johajar had made no transgression except a slip of the tongue, for which he'd been driven to isolation in the wild, and even *there* he was hunted!

And *Ressora wanted a part of this!*

Nurida was so angry. She was also hungry and thirsty.

Once in the woods, she resumed her bent-double position and listened carefully for the sound of water. She heard it before too long and slunk toward the sound. There was a little rivulet crawling in the general direction of the river, and here Nurida bent to drink. She cupped her paws and lifted her head to look around—Lochuran had taught her that while they were still with the tracking party.

Lochuran. Hm. Nurida hadn't thought much about her younger sister in weeks. When Nurida bent back over the rivulet, she saw her reflection and gazed contemplatively at herself for a bit. *I almost look like her,* she thought. *Almost. I'm still nowhere near as strong as she is. Not in the eyes. But I look like her in every other way.* She continued to regard herself, thinking of Lochuran. She wondered if her little sister had been taken by the same creatures as Johajar.

And as she wondered, something finally stirred in the tired princess's mind.

When Nurida had asked Johajar why he had acted crazy when he wasn't, what was it he had said? *I knew that a Miamuran princess was in league with the creature trying to kill me, and at first I thought she was you.* But her? Why her?

Elvinene—or Kiarna, she couldn't remember which—had said back in Lunep that Galledor had made a point of keeping Nurida away from the notice of political players. Yet Johajar had thought *she* was the Miamuran princess in league with Mokimshim? It didn't make sense.

It didn't—unless he had caught a glimpse of this Miamuran princess, or heard some description of her, and she had resembled Nurida.

Or if he had seen an example of scholarly work—a written letter, for example. One with far lovelier language than Ressora could use. One that would point to a scholar.

The princess sat back hard on her tail, mind spinning. Lochuran was wily. Why would it be beyond her to forge that letter and Ressora's seal?

Ressora *was* in Pasadagavra. The Cliff Mouse had confirmed that. And that was where Ressora told Elvinene and most likely Galledor she would go. She was going to Pasadagavra because she didn't want to be married. It was hardly inconceivable that Ressora would have left Pasadagavra after the Cliff Mouse had, but why give him her necklace? And why agree to go to Pasadagavra in the first place?

If Ressora *had* written the letter Kiarna had found in Arashna, then her disappearance could be attributed to her fear of Kiarna discovering it and being punished. But if she *were* afraid of Kiarna finding the letter, then why go straight to Pasadagavra? She must have known that some Miamuran official would get there as quickly as Elvinene could send him to make sure she was there. It made no sense.

Lochuran, on the other paw …

She had vanished without a trace. Vanished when Nurida had been busy leading *blind* Lacritta. Nurida had seen no sign of another creature, and Lacritta had heard no one.

Maybe that meant there had been no other creature.

Nurida was so stunned. She pulled her tattered tunic around herself and rested her head on her knees. No. It couldn't be. Ressora, Nurida could believe. Lochuran?

The amber-furred princess bent over the stream again, seeing herself but imagining Lochuran.

And she knew it was true.

Good, Nurida thought. *Because I know how to find Lochuran.*

THE LETTER WRITER

Princess Lochuran, fifth daughter of the White Wings, was glad when the boat she rode in finally landed. She loathed water travel and usually felt nauseous. She'd never lost her composure in front of anyone, but the relief of sinking her paws into ankle-deep, icy cold river mud was one of the strongest sensations she'd ever felt.

She'd barely stepped onto the ground when the ferret piloting the boat sneeringly called, "You all right, Princess?"

Lochuran turned about patiently. "Yes, thank you." Then she turned away before he could see her queasiness.

The sailors were all in very sour moods. Lochuran didn't know it, but they were surly about being forced to transport shore creatures. Their skills were invaluable, and they were paid accordingly, but they missed the rolling of a ship's deck and the salty wind of the ocean. Lochuran, even if she had known the source of their gruffness, wouldn't have understood it.

She pulled herself out of the mud and started up the shore. This was a small encampment, with no more than a dozen creatures and half as many tents. She longed to sit down, but she thought that maybe walking around a bit would dispel the motion of the boat from her head. She'd already visited two other encampments along the river and knew her escort believed her to be slow-witted, so she didn't bother following them as they reported to the highest-ranking officer here. Instead she wandered to the trees on the edge of the encampment.

She was chafing with impatience. Kiarna was sure to have discovered some trace of her treachery in Arashna, and Mokimshim had promised her asylum whenever she chose. They could have *been* at Arashna by now if Lochuran's escort hadn't insisted on taking so infuriatingly *long*. Three weeks—three weeks!—to get from Lunep to here, and they hadn't even reached the evergreen forests characteristic of the west coast.

The trees were skeletal, but the tips were beginning to grow with new leaves. Lochuran paused to examine the branches, inhaling their fragrance. It was fresh and less crisp than snow or the grasses of Miamur. She pushed away a wave of homesickness, contenting herself that she would be well-treated in her new home. Lochuran wandered east around the clearing, closely examining the branches. She so loved looking at new leaves!

"Don't wander off, Princess," shouted her escort, with yet more sneer.

She looked over her shoulder and imperially replied, "Thank you for the advice."

She was turning back when something on the next tree caught her eye. Glancing at the others in the clearing, she casually stepped closer and examined it. Her blood ran cold.

It was a braided cord bracelet, adorned with a single metal plate. Lochuran knew the design on the metal very, very well.

Nurida?

What was *she* doing out here? She should be safe in Lunep!

Lochuran stole another glance over her shoulder at her escort. None of them was watching her. Without a sound, she dashed into the woods.

Nurida had waited two days, watching her bracelet from the trees. She had snuck in during the night, wrapping her cloak tightly about her and covering her face with a mask made from the hem of her cloak ripped off. She'd hung the bracelet on a branch where only Lochuran would spot it. Then Nurida had retreated to the woods where she could watch and wait. She was as still as stone, only stirring to get some food. She slept lightly, watching for Lochuran.

On the second day, Nurida's patience was rewarded. She saw Lochuran step unsteadily off the boat and into the river mud. Nurida inhaled excitedly, knowing that Lochuran would at least look at the trees. And if she did the same thing she'd done every spring in Miamur, then she would surely spot the bracelet.

Sure enough, Lochuran examined the branches for new buds. As soon as Nurida saw her moving toward the bracelet, the hidden princess crept backward through the ferns. Lochuran would find her—Nurida had dragged a stick through the snow in a line from the bracelet to a glade far enough away that they wouldn't be heard by anyone at the river. Hopefully, there were no patrols or search parties, but since they now had Johajar, Nurida doubted there would be any. Nurida ran straight to the glade where Lochuran would find her. It was just a matter of time.

Nurida was seated on a fallen log, her back to the direction Lochuran would be coming from, cloak wrapped about her but her mask abandoned. Her hood was down, too, so Lochuran would see right away that it was she. Nurida was taking deep, calming breaths when she heard Lochuran's voice.

"Nurida?"

She twisted around and adopted a pleasant smile. "Lochuran. It's been quite some time. Won't you sit?"

Lochuran didn't move. Her face was shocked, even frightened. "What are you doing here?" she asked in barely more than a whisper. "You should be safe in Lunep!"

Nurida had meant to keep up her pretense of pleasantness and serenity, but she was tired and angry. "I was," she answered, her voice hard. "Do you know who else was there?"

Lochuran said nothing.

"Kiarna," Nurida answered her own question. "She had a letter, ostensibly from Ressora, written to King Mokimshim and speaking of a kind of pact."

Confusion covered Lochuran's face, but Nurida saw through it. "But I don't think it was Ressora who wrote it," she continued, burning with anger. "I think it was the princess who slipped away from the tracking party *without* Elvinene's permission. I think it was the sister who was riding so calmly in a boat owned by the very creatures Kiarna just escaped from!"

Lochuran looked steadily at Nurida for a while, saying nothing. When she finally spoke, her voice was calm.

"You're right. And so?"

"*And so?*" Nurida snapped, struggling not to shriek. "You've betrayed Miamur, and you framed Ressora for it!"

"Ressora was asking for it," Lochuran sneered. "You know that better than anyone. As for betraying Miamur, so what? This was my chance to get *away* from it all!"

"From *what* all?" Nurida hissed. "Peace? Freedom? "

"Peace? Have you looked around you lately? Where is this peace? And freedom, my tail!" Lochuran snarled, her face distorting with rage. "Only for Galledor and Mother. They still haven't given us—you, Ressora, and me—the freedom to choose our lives!"

"What are you talking about?" Nurida exclaimed.

"The reason Ressora ran away in the first place," Lochuran scoffed. "Arranged marriage. I don't know if you knew this, and I doubt you did, but mother arranged a marriage for her when she was very young, before either of us was born. The mouse is twice her age and highly unpleasant. Galledor never intervened in Ressora's defense. Nor yours and mine. We're still to be married off when our mother feels like it. Didn't she tell *you* that you'll be married as soon as you get back to Miamur?"

Nurida had forgotten it, but she did not blame Galledor. "He said he would speak for me. If he truly didn't care about us, he would never have let Ressora flee to Pasadagavra."

Lochuran's green eyes glowed violently. "A *very* kind brother he is. He knows exactly where Ressora is, so when he needs her for something else, all he has to do is pick her up."

"So you threw your lot in with Mokimshim," Nurida said disbelievingly. "Who *exiled* his brother and sister. Who is *clearly* a tyrant. That's so much better."

"Mokimshim is a means to an end, not an end itself," Lochuran replied with dignity.

She would have said more, but Nurida jumped to her paws and raised her voice. "So you walk away from your family and throw in your lot with our enemy! With Kiarna's tormentor!"

"Kiarna walked into it herself!" Lochuran spat back.

"Yes," Nurida agreed. "And you set a trap for her, didn't you? You warned Mokimshim, I take it?"

Lochuran sneered. "I asked Mokimshim not to hurt her. I never bore *her* any ill will."

Nurida's anger faded—or at least, retreated from complete control of her mind. "Come back with me," she pleaded. "Galledor will bury this. If you're willing to do this, then you have the strength to fight Mother and any arrangement she might push on you. Lochuran, please."

Lochuran tipped her head to one side. "Why should I?"

"Because I will return to Galledor and tell him everything that happens here," she replied. "Whether or not you come."

"I don't care," Lochuran sneered. But there was a flicker of anxiety in her eyes.

Nurida saw it and seized on it. "You'd be gone from Miamur forever," she pressed. "If you ever decide that you want your family again, you'll be cut off from them. If you come with me, Galledor will forgive you. You can have your family back."

Lochuran didn't hesitate for more than a heartbeat. "And my enslavement back," she hissed. "I think not."

Nurida sighed and turned away. "Then you are lost from Miamur orever."

"So are you," Lochuran said sharply.

Nurida turned. "How do you mean?"

Lochuran strode forward, and now she was the confident one. "Here's the thing: Ressora knows different snippets than I do. Galledor knows what both of us know and what we don't. As long as he thinks Ressora is the one turning on Miamur, he won't know what Mokimshim knows. Which means you can't go back and tell on me."

Nurida's blood ran cold. "What do you have in mind?"

Lochuran held out her paw. "Come with me."

Nurida didn't budge.

"Nurida," Lochuran urged, her eyes suddenly enticing, "*come.* You are still my dearest sister—that hasn't changed."

"And is Galledor your dearest brother?" Nurida challenged.

"Don't be silly," Lochuran retorted. "You're not he. Nurida, please, come."

The older princess blinked. But she didn't move beyond that.

Lochuran sighed. "All I have to do is shout for my escort. They'll drag you back in chains, if they have to."

"They can't hear you," Nurida replied smoothly. "That is why I chose this spot to meet you. You'd have to run back and find them, and I'll be gone by then."

Lochuran considered this. Her eyes darkened. "You give me no choice."

Nurida crossed her paws. "You're going to kill me? I thought I was your dearest sister."

"You are," Lochuran replied earnestly, and Nurida saw that she meant it. "But nothing and no one is dearer to me than my freedom. Nurida, please! You need not be a prisoner. You can be free as well!"

Nurida smiled then, humorlessly. "You want me to turn my back on Galledor and Kiarna? No. Never."

"So you are willing to be given away to someone in the name of the White Wings?" Lochuran cried.

"No," Nurida replied, surprising even herself. "But I'll take on that fight when I come to it. And any king who aids me in that fight is no tyrant."

Lochuran shook her head. "Nurida, you give me no *choice!*"

"Of course I do," Nurida retorted. "You can come with me, or you can kill me. Choose. Just make sure that whatever you choose, you can live with it."

Lochuran stared at her for several minutes, and Nurida held her breath. She didn't really believe Lochuran would kill her, but she still feared it.

Her fears proved wiser than her heart because all of a sudden Lochuran pounced.

Nurida was quick, and she dodged out of the way, but Lochuran was quick too. She caught Nurida's ear and jerked her head back.

"I don't want to do this," Lochuran hissed.

Nurida smashed the back of her paw into her sister's head. Lochuran fell back with a yelp, and Nurida kicked out wildly. Blind luck was on her side as her paw made direct contact with Lochuran's stomach. Nurida reached wildly for her knife, but her sister's paw wrapped around Nurida's wrist before she could find it.

Her weeks in the wild, especially her past few days of little food, had drained her of her strength. Lochuran was easily stronger than she. The grip Lochuran had on Nurida's paw was all that was needed to throw her hard. She came down on a protruding rock and would have screamed in agony had the breath not been driven from her. She tried to rise, but her sides hurt so much she had no control over her limbs.

Lochuran glided into view, holding Nurida's knife. Her face was twisted in pain, her paw pressed against the side Nurida had kicked. She held the knife a few inches above Nurida's neck, showing neither aggression nor impatience. "Nurida, please. I don't want to do this. Come with me. Be free with me."

"I … will … not …" Nurida gasped out.

Lochuran extended her other paw. "*Please!*"

Nurida shook her head.

Lochuran tightened her paw around her dagger, tears forming in her eyes. "Nurida—I won't stop asking. It'll be hours until you're well enough to move, or my escort gets out here. But please, how will you survive in the wild hurt like that?"

Nurida couldn't even shake her head. She was so weak. So tired. So ready to give in.

"Nurida," Lochuran whispered.

Thwack!

Lochuran crumpled to the snow.

A moment later, a sturdy paw slipped behind Nurida's shoulders, helping her sit up. She gasped in pain, fearing her ribs were broken. Then she heard a strange voice murmur, "Easy, easy. No deep breaths. Just relax a minute."

Nurida turned her head just enough to see her rescuer. His face was vaguely familiar, but in her state of dazed pain, she couldn't quite place it. "Who are you?"

"We met a couple days ago," he replied dryly.

Oh, that was it. The Cliff Mouse. Nurida nodded a little to show she understood.

"Don't move a minute," he said firmly. "Catch your breath."

Nurida heeded his advice. When she could breathe evenly, she asked, "Did you kill her?"

"I have never yet killed anyone who wasn't facing me," the mouse replied. "She's unconscious."

Nurida nodded gratefully. "Thank … you."

She sat a moment longer, pain receding. At least her ribs weren't broken. But her heart ached. Why had it been easier to believe Ressora capable of treachery and not Lochuran?

"What now?" she whispered.

She sensed the Cliff Mouse look away. Then he murmured, "You're not well enough to go off on your own. I have business to take care of. You'll have to come with me." He sounded reluctant.

"I can manage," Nurida hissed. But the effort of hissing made her sides ache.

"It won't be for long," the Cliff Mouse reassured her. "Just a week."

Nurida shook her head. "Too long."

The mouse looked her right in the eye; he had mahogany-brown eyes and fur the color of maple branches. "I won't hurt you," he promised. "You have my warrior's oath on that."

That might have meant something to a Cliff Mouse, but to a young princess of a kingdom half a world away, that was little more than worthless. Especially when Nurida could see the unconscious Lochuran. But as Nurida drew breath to tell him to let her be, there was another stab of pain, and her vision swam. She didn't have much choice.

"I know of someone who can get you back to Miamur," the mouse continued reassuringly.

Nurida nodded. Now that she had accepted the fact she needed this stranger's help, the last thing she wanted was to hear more reassurances.

"But we cannot take your sister with us," he continued.

Nurida nodded again. The full impact of Lochuran's attack was beginning to settle on her, but she refused to cry.

"Are you all right for a minute?" the Cliff Mouse asked again.

Another nod. Then she figured speaking would reinforce her point. "I'm fine."

He let her sit by herself for a few minutes. She closed her eyes, the better to prevent tears, while he did something that made several scuffing sounds. When she reopened her eyes, he had propped Lochuran up against a tree and secured her by wrapping her paws backward around the tree and tying her paws together with a belt. He was in the process of tying a ripped-off strip of his tunic around the tree and her throat.

"When she wakes up, she'll be able to call for help," he explained. "But she can't get away before someone comes by. It will be a while before anyone comes out here.

Nurida nodded and pulled herself to her paws. He extended a paw toward her, but she didn't accept. She did not want him to think they would be friends, and she made up her mind never to let her guard down near him.

"I don't—think I caught your name," she mumbled.

"Nathan'el," he replied. "And we should get out of here."

WITHIN REACH

Sunlight slanting through the trees woke Nathan'el a little earlier than he'd been used to, and he realized that spring wasn't far away. He had fallen asleep beneath a Douglas fir, surrounded by its sharp, pungent smell. When he roused himself enough to remember the Miamuran princess, he first thought she'd run off. Then he recalled that she'd fallen asleep by a nearby tree, out of his line of sight.

However annoying he found her suspicion, he couldn't really blame her. In truth, he was also somewhat pleased with her for her wisdom. It got under his fur only because he knew perfectly well that he would not harm her.

He pulled himself to his paws and crept softly around her noble fir. She had pushed slushy snow out from between the roots and curled up into a tight ball in the resulting cavity, paws wrapped around herself as if she were very cold. Her face, which had been taut with pain and grief the day before, was now relaxed and just weary.

For a while, Nathan'el did nothing but look at her. She almost looked like a pool of sunshine herself. But he didn't remain still for long; he knelt down and gently tapped her shoulder.

She opened her eyes groggily, not reacting with honed reflexes. "Time to go?" she mumbled.

He nodded. "We have a long way to go today."

She got to her paws more swiftly than he had and shifted her cloak easily about her shoulders. "I'm ready."

🐁

They'd traveled for two hours before Nurida spoke her first words since he'd roused her. "Where are we going?"

Nathan'el glanced back at the Miamuran princess. "To a place near Arashna," he replied. "Do you know of a river otter called Shinar?"

At the name, the princess's eyes flickered in recognition, and the dull, beaten weariness dissipated somewhat. "I know of her, yes."

Nathan'el returned to looking forward, keeping a wary eye for any blackberries or nettles. "Her tribe lives in caves south of Arashna and Dobar. I was going to ask for their help with … something."

He was reluctant to reveal the details about his mother to this princess.

"I know Shinar to be a friend," the princess murmured. "But I have never met her."

He didn't press—after all, he didn't want anything more to do with palace politics. Between the insanity going on in Arashna, the drama with this princess and her sister, and that rescue at Nikor Mais—

Nathan'el glanced back over his shoulder at Nurida. She was Miamuran, too. Was Kiarna, then, her sister?

Maybe that would account for the weariness in her eyes.

They stopped to rest far from any rivers, and still Nurida had barely spoken. They built no fire and scrounged for any kind of food to take the edge off their hunger. Only after Nurida had munched on some pinecone seeds did she speak.

"You mentioned earlier that you were seeking the river otters' help in something," she observed. "What is it?"

Nathan'el shook his head. "Nothing, really."

She was silent, but it was a disbelieving silence. When he looked up to reassure her that it was nothing, he met her green eyes. They were deep and steady, fully expecting him to speak, and far more intelligent than he had thought earlier. Almost before he knew what he was saying, he answered, "My mother was captured. I need help getting her back."

Nurida tilted her head a little. "A Cliff Mouse seeks help from a coastal river otter tribe and yet is closer to Pasadagavra than Arashna?"

He smiled faintly at the irony. "It's kind of a long story."

Nonetheless, he found himself telling her all, from Ran'ta's disappearance over three months ago to the attack in Graystone to his journey to Pasadagavra and then his weeks trapped by the river. She listened attentively, absorbing every word.

When he had spilled out the entire story, her face had lost all traces of weariness or defeat. "Someone told me," she murmured, "that information is in high demand. It seems as though rulers are doing anything they possibly can to get their paws on some."

Nathan'el let out a silent sigh of disappointment. He'd somehow hoped that explaining his situation to the princess would lead to some idea, some inkling as to what he should do next. But her response stifled that hope.

"Except," she murmured, "that everyone I've known has been going after … um, officials. But a messenger … I wonder why they went after her. They must have been desperate."

"Why desperate?" Nathan'el asked calmly. "Messengers have access to a lot of information."

Nurida ran a paw over her brow. "I think perhaps your mother may have had some as well. Some that maybe did not come from the messenger."

Nathan'el frowned. "Beg pardon?"

The princess looked up calmly. "When we first met, you asked me how I had known the searchers would be leaving. The answer is, simply, that I knew they had found what they were looking for."

"Prince Johajar?" Nathan'el guessed.

Nurida looked at him in consternation. "How did you know?"

"I heard them talking about it when I was holed up by the river," Nathan'el explained. He left out the bit about them mentioning Princess Kiarna.

Nurida nodded slowly. "I see." She cleared her throat. "In any case, when I first happened upon Prince Johajar, there were only a few searchers in the area. When I last saw him—at his hiding place—there were many more."

"You think someone may have told them?" he asked sharply.

"Perhaps," the princess replied. "When—when was your mother captured?"

Nathan'el gave a little shake of his head. "She disappeared three months ago. If that was when she was captured, or if she were in hiding for a while—that, I do not know."

Nurida's shoulders sagged. "Ah," she murmured. "I had been thinking perhaps your mother knew something that she didn't hear from the messenger, but Johajar was in captivity three months ago, so they cannot be connected."

Nathan'el sighed and shrugged. "To be honest, I don't care why she was captured. I just want her out."

Nurida nodded understandingly. "But how will you get in?"

Another shrug. "Guess I'll figure that out when I get to the coast."

🐁

If Nathan'el had been thinking properly, it would have occurred to him that the coast was sure to be patrolled. Moreover, he would have realized the area around Shinar's land would be under surveillance.

But none of those thoughts crossed his mind. He wasn't prepared at all when, during the seventh day of his travel with the Miamuran princess, they heard the shouts of a patrol. A big one.

Nurida was paying better attention; she heard them first and jerked his cloak.

Then Nathan'el heard the shouts and recognized the accents as Cliff Mice. They were less than two hours from the shore, and this area had to be very familiar to them.

"South!" Nathan'el hissed. "Quickly!"

Nurida obeyed him without question, but her paws, even though they were quiet, left a trail through the snow. Maybe a Cliff Mouse could spot it, maybe not.

As it turned out, it didn't really matter. The sounds of the patrol began to move away north. Nathan'el breathed a sigh of relief and hurried after Nurida. The patrol must have been moving south-to-north and had already scoured the area.

Nathan'el glanced at the sky, and then he was hit with an awful realization: judging by the sun, it was only a little after twelve hours past dawn. Dawn was the central time unit on the west coast, the way high noon was to Miamur. Patrols usually lasted six hours, which meant they had just passed the second patrol of the day. Either they were farther south than Nathan'el had thought, and that was the southernmost patrol, or there was another company of soldiers moving south to north. Given that the patrol was Cliff Mice and would most likely guard only areas they knew well, he and Nurida had to be near the Cliff Mice cities.

"Nurida, stop!" he hissed, and she froze. He looked at the woods and sniffed the air, thinking frantically. "West, then," he muttered. "We have to keep going west."

"There will be more patrols further west," Nurida whispered. "King Mokimshim has two siblings he fears as rivals. If he expects them to be gathering armies against him, then he will have his fortresses prepared for war. The defenses will only get thicker as we get closer to his base. We would do better to slip into Shinar's caves from the south."

Nathan'el blinked. She was right, of course. "*Infernal scheming.*" He hadn't meant to say that out loud.

The ghost of a smile flitted across Nurida's face. "You get used to it, or you get trampled," she said simply. "South?"

"Yes, quickly," Nathan'el agreed. "You take the lead, keep your eyes open."

She grinned at him and hurried forward, knife ready.

He stayed a little behind her, the better to listen for pursuit behind them. She slipped through the forest at a swift walk, sometimes almost a jog, saving her energy should she need to run—more common sense than Nathan'el would have expected from a princess. They had covered about a mile, maybe more, when she suddenly stopped, then ducked down into a patch of ferns.

Nathan'el bent double and slipped into the ferns beside her. She put a paw to her lips, green eyes wide. Nathan'el had to listen for a while before he heard what had spooked her.

"The king expected a messenger," a rough voice said so quietly that Nathan'el wouldn't have distinguished his voice from the wind if not for the hissed *s* sounds. "Or *something*. We have to wait this out."

There were indistinguishable murmuring replies, but all were from the south. Nathan'el wordlessly pointed west between the ferns, and Nurida crawled carefully between them. He slipped after her, moving very slowly. Before long, their way was blocked by a fallen log.

"We should just hide and wait for them to be gone," Nathan'el muttered in her ear.

Nurida nodded and bunched herself into a ball. Her emerald eyes were wide and terrified, but her fear was tinted with determination. Nathan'el squeezed her paw reassuringly and felt it shaking. Then, all at once, her eyes widened even more, and she had to stifle a gasp.

Nathan'el looked over his shoulder and up in the tree branches. There was a mouse sentry sitting on a branch. He appeared to be dozing, his eyes closed and his paws folded across his chest. Nathan'el pointed and Nurida crawled south deeper under the ferns. He followed her past the fallen tree. But something hard—maybe his sheathed sword, maybe her water canteen—struck the log, which must have been hollow since it announced their presence like a drum. Nurida put a paw over her mouth and they both froze, but the quiet patrol had heard the sound.

"Who's there?" the leader of the patrol shouted. Nurida fell flat on her stomach and Nathan'el reached for his sword. There was silence for a minute, before the leader shouted, "Whoever's there, answer! We're from the Guard of Arashna!"

Nurida's ears pricked at that, and her brow knit.

"Patrol, out swords!" the leader shouted. "Start chopping at the undergrowth!"

There was the terrifying sound of swords being drawn and then of their slashing through plants. Nathan'el felt a heavy weight of failure in his stomach. He had come so close!

Nurida turned around and whispered, "You need to get into Arashna?"

"Preferably not as a prisoner," Nathan'el replied quietly.

Nurida nodded. "Then follow my lead!"

The soldiers were only a few feet away at this point, enough time for Nathan'el to ask the princess what she meant.

But before he could do so, she sprang to her paws.

"Please don't hurt me!" she cried, tears in her voice.

THE BROTHERS' FEUD

Eneng the pirate had been in Arashna a few times when Queen Demeda ruled it. The last time had been something of a farewell dinner, right before Zuryzel had been sent to command the eastern patrols. That had been such an interesting event—pirates mingled with Wraith Mice gentry, and yet Zuryzel had treated them all with undiffering respect and pleasantness. So had Queen Demeda. She had been a little feeble—the fever that would eventually claim her life had already taken a slight hold—but she'd been in good spirits. Mokimshim hadn't been there, away at Kardas for one reason or another, but Johajar had been present. That was the last time Eneng had seen Johajar.

Until today, anyway.

Arashna had changed a lot since Queen Demeda had ruled—it was no longer the jewel of a powerful, free kingdom but had become filthy and stagnant. The air reeked of fear and grief, and oppression stained the stones.

The worst part? Mokimshim had made certain offenses punishable by *enslavement*. Eneng was sure that would be Johajar's fate.

His first sight of the exiled prince was a boat rowing south toward Arashna. The capital of the Wraith Mice was built on a rocky island, connected to the mainland at low tide by sandy tidal flats. But the combination of sharp rocks and tidal shallows meant it was rare for a boat of any kind to be approaching Arashna, much less a heavy old dinghy that probably couldn't turn five degrees in ten seconds. It was riding low in the uncertain waters and approaching a narrow lip of sand between the shallows and the rocks. If they actually managed to land it there ...

Eneng was on the bridge when he saw the watercraft. The bridge was a long, low affair made of black stone and inlaid with silver. The waves lapped at it during high tide, but it remained steadfast and defiant. Its edges were shaped like dragon scales. This bridge was the only convenient way from the mainland to Arashna during high tide, and it was guarded by Dobar.

The pirate saw the craft between two of the "scales," and even from that distance, he recognized the red flag that Mokimshim had employed. It was just red, nothing more, but it was easy enough to see from a distance. His first thought was how perilous it was to attempt that landing with the tide changing and the wind blowing from the east.

Then he realized it was riding so low because everyone inside it was armored. Great whispering winds, had *no* sense been employed in the loading of that craft? If it tipped, every armored creature would sink.

And why was the craft necessary in the first place? The bridge was *right there.*

But the boat was going through a peculiar landing—using both the tide and the wind to steer more than the rudder. That was one of Arasam's tricks. Likely he was the only one in there without any armor on, the smart fox.

Huh. Winterblade came back yesterday, and her search was fruitless. Wasn't Arasam part of her search too?

"Oh, no," Eneng whispered, blood chilling in his veins.

He began running toward Arashna. Before he went more than a few steps, someone slammed into him from behind.

"Sorry!" exclaimed his sister's voice.

Eneng would have gotten angry with Winterblade under any other circumstances, but this time he just steadied her for a minute before they both took off for Arashna again.

A crowd of creatures—mercenaries and the like—had gathered by the little lip of sand, climbing on the rocks that surrounded it and standing on the paved stones that led more or less to the bridge. There were no Wraith Mice here. None of them wanted to witness further friction between their king and his brother.

Prince Johajar sat in the bottom of the boat, and four armored Eerieden mercenaries surrounded him, swords pointed straight at his head.

"Why bring him in on a boat?" Eneng muttered to the ferret in front of him.

He regretted it when a moment later she turned her head and he recognized her as Snowhawk, Winterblade's archenemy. Her black eyes flickered once in Winterblade's direction before she answered Eneng's question. "Victory lap. Maybe t' make him scared. No logical reason though, to be sure."

It wasn't more than a few minutes before there was more shouting and then Wraith Mouse guards cleared a path through the crowd. Eneng made absolutely sure that he and his sister wound up on the opposite side of the path as Snowhawk. After everyone had stopped moving, King Mokimshim himself stalked across the paving stones and picked his way down the sand to where the boat waited.

Johajar raised his eyes to his brother's face; his glare would have killed a jellyfish, but he was wisely silent.

Mokimshim's face always looked as though a thousand different thoughts chased behind it, so his expression rarely gave away what he was thinking. Like his mother, like Demeda, he had a propensity for absolute stillness and a golden talent to make creatures listen when he spoke.

Eneng had no idea how the Wraith Mouse king could play an audience as well as he did. The pirate found himself holding his breath, even though he knew what was coming, as did everyone there, Still, all were caught up in suspense.

After seemingly endless seconds, Mokimshim ordered, "Bring him out."

Johajar did not cease glaring at his brother as his four guards dragged him from the boat. Arasam the pirate, who had been in the stern at the tiller, wore an expression of frustrated relief as he was allowed to scurry to the prow and tie the boat to some rocks. Mokimshim's mercenaries had no clue of what was important aboard a watercraft.

Johajar was forced to his knees in the sand, still glaring furiously at his brother. Mokimshim met the glare in a calm, borderline amused fashion, but again he was silent.

Eneng made sure he wasn't holding his breath.

"I'm a bit curious how you escaped the dungeons in the first place," the king finally said.

Johajar's expression did not change. "Secret tunnels," he retorted sarcastically. "Old ones the Darkwoods Oracles knew about."

Eneng found himself repressing a sigh. He knew perfectly well that Johajar suspected Mokimshim of betraying Wraith Mouse secrets during the Darkwoods War. But antagonizing the king was unlikely to help Johajar's case.

On the other paw, could it *really* hurt?

Mokimshim smirked at his brother. "What were you doing so close to Pasadagavra and yet not within its walls? So close to sanctuary, yet so far away. You could have hidden in Tribeking Rhonndan's good graces forever. So what was there to find in the wild? For whom were you looking?"

As the king had phrased his last question, there was a soft stir among the watching crowd. Eneng glanced toward the city and saw Queen Karena descending toward the king and the prince. As she passed, Eneng saw her expression: hard as rock and cold as ice. She swept past, glancing neither left nor right, stopping just short of the sand.

But Mokimshim and Johajar both ignored the queen. "Why in the wilds?" Mokimshim pressed. "Why not Miamur? What reason could she possibly have to be there?"

Johajar again gave no more response than a smirk. Eneng refused to let himself think, *Dombre*.

"You knew something," Mokimshim persisted. "She had told you something that made you seek her out in the wild." Now all traces of good humor had vanished and were replaced by a driven, obsessed kind of fury. "Why? *What did she tell you?*"

"That she would never give in," Johajar answered, his voice calm compared to his brother's. Like Mokimshim, he had a talent for making creatures hang on his every word. "That she would be strong, no matter what. You won't find her, Mokimshim. I didn't find her. Nor will you." He gave another insolent smirk. "Not until it's too late."

Mokimshim did not explode at his brother's response. He just looked to the guards and said coldly, "Take him to a cell."

"Which one?" one of the mercenaries asked.

"*Not* the one he escaped from," Mokimshim retorted as he turned away and swept back towards Arashna. Karena followed him without a glance at Johajar.

Once they were gone, the crowd blossomed into noise. Johajar's captors dragged him up the shore to the city, and the guards that had cleared the path fell in behind them, leaving the crowd of hired mercenaries and pirates to either follow or mingle again on the shore.

Throughout the scene and its aftermath, Eneng, Snowhawk, and Winterblade remained silent. Snowhawk glanced again at Eneng, her expression hard to read, before she turned and disappeared into the throng, presumably returning to her ship. Eneng found himself staring at the spot where she'd disappeared.

Mokimshim's campaign to locate Johajar—and Kiarna, for that matter—had been a painful experience. Snow, trees, and everything else that pirates hated had been bad enough; but the creatures they were expected to interact with only made it worse. There were over twice as many mercenaries as Wraith Mice in Mokimshim's employ, and Mokimshim had gone very far afield to find some of them. They provided him all kinds of valuable information, mostly about terrain or the creatures who governed their homelands, but most valuable to Mokimshim was the chance that they might know where his sister was hiding. Mokimshim was terrified of Zuryzel.

When Queen Demeda had died and Mokimshim had ascended the throne, Zuryzel had been days east, commanding the string of patrols that guarded the western edges of Wraith Mouse influence. Their primary purpose was to hunt down thieves or any remnants of the Darkwoods foxes that had escaped the Wraith Mice during the war. Almost as soon as Johajar had been imprisoned, Mokimshim had sent soldiers eastward to capture his sister.

Eneng had been in Mokimshim's service at that point, and when he got word of the soldiers going after Zuryzel, he'd gone straight to Ksheygha, the gossip-loving captain of the *Wideprow*. She'd dispatched some of her crew to find Zuryzel and warn her. It must have worked, because when Mokimshim's soldiers reached the place where the patrols were supposed to be, there had been no trace of them. No tents, no food, no fires, nothing. The patrols—about a hundred creatures combined, Eneng guessed—had followed Zuryzel rather than serve Mokimshim.

Johajar had escaped less than a month after he was imprisoned. Since then, Mokimshim became obsessed with the idea that he must have been working with Zuryzel, must have known something. He hired every mercenary he could find—sometimes with gold, sometimes with other bargains—and launched a search for both Johajar and Zuryzel. Kiarna's unexpected arrival and swift departure guaranteed that her name had been added to the list as well.

Eneng did not know what would happen now. Most likely, Mokimshim would demand information from Johajar while launching a military campaign to tear the world apart until he found his sister.

"Well, Blade, at least military campaigns are more interestin' than search campaigns," Eneng murmured to his sister.

Then he looked and realized his sister was no longer there.

"Winterblade?" he called, alarmed.

He spotted a ripple through the crowd where it looked as though someone had just shoved a way through. Holding his breath, the pirate hurried through the crowd, hopefully following his sister. If Winterblade's temper got the better of her *again* …

He found her when he reached the edge of the throng, starting into Arashna. Eneng called her name again, but she ignored him. That was a *sure* sign of trouble.

A group of river otters were crossing the bridge; Winterblade got in before them, but Eneng was forced to wait until they had vacated the bridge and cleared the gate. *Stupid land beasts!* Seething with frustration, he hurried in on their heels and sprinted for one of the nearest towers, the one that contained Mokimshim's strategy room. Mokimshim would surely be there, and maybe Winterblade too.

He had to climb three flights of stairs, but he heard his sister's shouting while he was still on the second flight.

"I am a *ship's captain,* by the great fire-topped mountain, not a general!" she was yelling. "An' now y' want my crew t' be under *Snowhawk's* command? My crew signed up t' fight as a whole, not t' be scattered between other captains!"

"You signed your crew up to *fight,*" Mokimshim snapped in response. "Your contract does not specify where or under whom."

Eneng's jaw dropped as he ran. *What?* Mokimshim wanted Winterblade's crew to take orders from *Snowhawk? He can't do that!*

"I am not your creature!" Winterblade shrieked. "Contract or no contract, I am not a slave! I am a *captain,* an' my crew fights with *me.*"

Eneng burst into the room just as Mokimshim said, "I am paying your crew good gold to fight, and as long as I am paying them, they will fight where *I* command."

That was not how mercenaries fought. They were paid for the service of fighting, and to some extent, they followed the orders of their employers, but they maintained their own autonomy. Winterblade was right that Mokimshim had become too high-pawed with the pirates he paid—no amount of money for mercenaries was enough for them to follow orders of any captain other than their own. But Zuryzel was counting on them.

Before Eneng could utter a word, Winterblade snapped, "Then y' c'n quit payin' us. My crew will *not* be subject to Snowhawk!" She turned on her heel and started for the door.

"If you walk out of your contract, I will have no choice but to banish you from all places within my influence!" Mokimshim snarled after her.

"Do yer worst," Winterblade snapped without turning.

Eneng stared after her, fear tingling through his fur. He wanted to call after her, but if he did so, it would be too obvious to Mokimshim that she was needed here—and by *whom.*

"Captain Eneng," King Mokimshim snapped, "are *you* willing to place your crew under the *temporary* command of another captain?"

Eneng looked back at the king. "Why?"

"Call it a special favor," the king growled. "I need someone to make a contract with Captain Immihg of the *Redsea*. He is currently in Denirna. Go there, convince him to enter my service, and Captain Snowhawk will have command of your crew until you return."

The arrogance of that order—the implication that the king could do whatever he liked with Eneng's crew—made the pirate's stomach writhe in fury. But it had just hit him hard that Winterblade had left, and he was Zuryzel's only friend here. So he kept his voice calm as he replied, "That's the job of a first mate. T' be in command till the cap'n returns."

"Your first mate has not signed any contract," Mokimshim replied icily. "Snowhawk has. Therefore, *she* will take command of your crew until your return."

If Zuryzel hadn't needed Eneng there—an inside pair of eyes—then he wouldn't have agreed to it. He had no choice.

Winterblade ... patience, you never knew, my sister.

"Double the pay for those days," he said coolly.

"Done," Mokimshim growled.

Eneng nodded once, shortly and coldly. "I'll leave in two days."

33

Dobar and Arashna

The Guards of Arashna had not been expecting an unarmed female mouse, particularly not one who stood shivering, her weapon dangling uselessly from her belt, and her eyes wide with panic. They stopped in their search, staring at her in surprise.

Nurida took advantage of their surprise and pretended to pull herself together. She lowered her paws, straightened her head, and said in a shaky but calmer voice, "I have h-have come to speak with King Mokimshim. Be-be so kind as to take me to him."

"Who are you?" the captain of the guard asked, surprise evident in every hair on his face.

"I have no words for you, guardsmouse," Nurida replied stiffly. "Take me to Mokimshim, if you please."

"Before I do," the guard answered coolly, "you'd better give me a very good reason to. And your name."

"What is my name to you?" Nurida protested.

"Your name may be your opportunity to speak with the King of Arashna," the guard retorted, sounding even angrier.

Nurida shifted her shoulders and her stance. "Very well," she said in her best spoiled-princess voice. "My name is Nurida, sister to the King of Miamur, and Fourth Daughter of the White Wings."

The guard clearly didn't believe it. "Can you … verify that?"

Nurida drew her dagger and awkwardly extended the blade. The guard stalked forward and carefully grasped the blade without looking at it. "When you give a knife to someone, you extend the hilt, not the blade."

"Oh," said Nurida carefully. "I didn't know that. Well—the writing's on the blade, not the hilt."

Surprised, the captain looked back at the knife. Apparently he could read Miamuran because he scanned the writing and Nurida's symbol, embossed near where the blade met the hilt.

"Have you a retinue, Princess?" he inquired, his tone surprised and a little more respectful.

"No," Nurida answered in a small voice. "Just my servant."

She glanced over her shoulder at where Nathan'el crouched in the undergrowth. Taking his cue, he stood up.

"A princess travels alone with one servant?" the guard inquired, clearly suspicious.

Nurida's tone was colored perfectly with embarrassment. "He ... well ... he was the only one who agreed not to tell the king I was here!"

The guard looked less suspicious but more concerned. "Why would you care if your brother knew you were here?"

Nurida straightened her shoulders. "That is what I have to discuss with His Majesty of Arashna."

The guard nodded slowly. "I see." He seemed to consider for a moment; then he said, "I am General Dikiner, commander-in-chief of King Mokim-shim's armies. I will escort you and your servant to His Majesty, but I must ask you to give me your knife."

"No!" Nurida cried out impulsively. "I will not give my only defense over to a guard!"

The word *guard* clearly got under the commander-in-chief's fur, but he just said, "Princess, I swear, we won't hurt you."

Nurida wordlessly pressed her knife hilt against her shoulder.

The Wraith Mouse hesitated but eventually inclined his head. "Very well. If you wish. Follow me, please."

He turned and barked to the rest of the patrol, "Muryda is in command until I return. Follow the search pattern closely."

With that, he again faced Nurida and Nathan'el and said, "Follow me, Princess."

From what Nathan'el could see of Nurida—which wasn't much, given that he was behind her—she never let her act drop. Her shoulders shivered a little, and she kept her paws either crossed or wrapped comfortingly about herself.

The walk through the forest made Nathan'el nervous, but they encountered no one until he caught the smell of the ocean.

Bear King, he hadn't realized how much he'd missed it.

The three of them emerged from the woods about a mile south of Dobar, and Nathan'el heard Nurida's exclamation of surprise. He didn't blame her. They stood on a set of respectably high hills, and below them, waves threw themselves against the rocks in a frenzy. The sun had just touched the water, casting everything in a blaze of red and gold. Dobar—a black square fortress at least four thousand strides long—stood on a rise overlooking the only sand in the area, and facing Arashna.

Nathan'el's home in Harboday was too far away to see the island city of Arashna; he'd seen it once or twice when he was young, but he had never become completely accustomed to its beauty. Unlike Dobar, it was circular and tall. It was as dark as night, but the towers were accented with brilliant, polished steel that gleamed like stars. Except now, of course—now they glowed red in the sunset.

"I had no idea a place could look like this," Nurida whispered in absolute awe.

Nathan'el was equally breathless, but Dikiner just laughed bitterly. "Like what, Princess?"

His tone did not invite further conversation, and Nurida wisely did not pursue any.

Dikiner led them along a pawpath that ran by the edge of the hills, and as they neared Dobar, the path sloped down. Nurida slipped and stumbled more than she actually walked, and Nathan'el didn't think her exhaustion was an act. He considered holding out a paw to help her, but since she was ahead of him, there was no way he could do so conveniently.

Just as the pathway leveled out, with ground sloping high on either side, the earth beneath them became paved. Not far beyond that, the ground to the left fell away, and as it did, Nathan'el's heart leaped.

The sea was right there.

It was high tide—it had to be, because the water was barely ten strides from the black paving stones. The shore was pebbly, and caught in the stones were pieces of seaweed and shards of old crab shells. The combined smells of seaweed, salt, and forest earth flooded Nathan'el's nostrils, and for the first time in months, he felt elated.

Nurida had stopped and blinked in wonder at the sea. She was breathing deeply, no doubt inhaling the smell, her eyes wider than an owl's as she stared, transfixed, at the horizon. The sun itself was gone, but two half-discs, one of clouds and sky and one of water, were still ablaze. Above the aerial half-circle, the sky was velvety black, and three stars were just visible. Beyond the edges of the marine semicircle, the water was dark and appeared fathomless.

"Please keep moving," Dikiner called abruptly.

Nathan'el did not think the Miamuran princess feigned her reluctance to pull herself away from the breathtaking tableau. The Cliff Mouse had seen thousands of sunsets much like this one, and his breath was stolen every time. How could Dikiner be so indifferent?

He was even more confused by the Wraith Mouse's coldness when he looked away from the sea and at Dobar.

The fortress was never meant to look inviting, but in this light it looked downright menacing. Nurida wrapped her paws around her as they approached along the paved stones, and Nathan'el didn't blame her. The windows were narrow, and most were covered with heavy shutters. Dull bronze lamps hung from some windows, but instead of giving off a light of warmth and welcome, they looked more like torches held by prison guards.

Nathan'el had to swallow hard in order to keep up his courage. He had no idea how Nurida kept putting one paw in front of the other—but maybe she had more courage than he gave her credit for.

The paved pathway led to a heavy wooden gate in the side of the fortress. Dikiner rapped the hilt of his sword against it three times. It opened slowly, and the Wraith Mouse guard holding it open looked weary and careworn. Or maybe fear worn.

"General," he murmured, ducking his head.

Dikiner ignored this sign of respect and led Nurida and Nathan'el inside. This was a corridor largely reserved for war, so it wasn't pleasant, and Nathan'el hadn't expected it to be. But his recollections of Dobar were quite different—sounds of bustling, laughing, and brisk productivity. Now all he heard echoing down the hallway were shouted commands and the grinding sounds of heavy things being rolled or dragged across flagstones.

Dikiner led them up a flight of stairs and into the square, central area of the fortress. When Nathan'el had been here before, there had been a fair. Most creatures who lived in Dobar were soldiers and their families, and it was Queen Demeda's policy to hold carnivals and events to honor the soldiers frequently. King Hokadra had done so as well, although Nathan'el had no memories of that king. When Nathan'el and his family had attended the one fair to sell some wares and enjoy themselves, the place had been merry and lovely. Now, it was nothing but a war preparatory room. Heavy siege machines were being pushed across the floor, no doubt en route to the walls. Creatures hurried by, rolling vats of oil, carrying jugs of water, or lugging coils of rope. Nathan'el's heart wept silently to see the change.

"Is there a war on?" Nurida asked in a horrified whisper.

"I think this is a drill," Dikiner replied. "If war does begin, Princess, we will be ready for it," he said grimly.

The architecture of Dobar's central room was just as impressive as Nathan'el remembered. It was estimated that four generations had been poured into the building of the fortress, and its designer's love and skill showed in every stone. There was a high ceiling over the whole area, and though it wasn't domed, it narrowed as it soared upward. It was so high that the peak was lost in darkness. As one followed the stones from the top toward the floor, it looked as though they had been falling in a spiral and been frozen in time. There were sixty doorways leading to various places from the main room; each doorway was bare of a door and arched in a way both strong and graceful. But the beauty of the architecture only accented the grimness around him.

Nurida looked considerably less impressed by the fortress than Nathan'el was—but then, she'd grown up in a castle. *Still ...*

Dikiner led them along the edge of the staggering room until they had gone a quarter of the way around it. At the east and west edges of the room were two particularly fine doors, twice as tall and wide as the others and edged with designs of the night sky. The one in the east wall went towards Dobar's main gate; the one in the west hall must have led to the bridge.

Nurida will love the bridge, Nathan'el thought, and in spite of the grimness surrounding him, he was a little pleased when he thought of Nurida being excited.

The door Dikiner chose opened onto a structure resembling a great stone dock. There were towering walls on either side, and gimlet-eyed sentries atop the walls, as well as on either side of the bridge. There were no walls on the seaward side, which left a view of the bridge, Arashna, and the western horizon. The fire was gone now; there were more stars visible, and the clouds were dark purple.

It was so windy that when Nurida set paw on the dock, she gasped and shielded her face. Nathan'el could see wind-tossed waves even in the shallow waters between Dobar and Arashna. They crashed against the dock and the bridge, beautiful and wild.

Before Dikiner led the way onto the bridge, he turned around to Nurida. "The bridge is perfectly safe, Princess," he said curtly. "Step along."

Nathan'el wanted to tell him off for using such a tone with someone frightened, but just in time, he remembered that Dikiner thought he was Nurida's servant, and the Cliff Mouse didn't know whether or not palace servants spoke to generals. So, instead, he discretely touched Nurida's shoulder to reassure her and urge her forward.

She didn't even glance over her shoulder, but she did relax her paws.

Crossing the bridge was a long walk—maybe ten minutes. At first Nurida jumped every time a wave crashed against the side and saltwater sprayed over her. But halfway across, she stopped to look out northward. Her paws rested on the scales of the bridge, and Nathan'el saw her suck in her breath. For the first time since they'd run into the patrol, she turned to look him in the eye. There was a kind of calm confidence beneath her nervousness, and Nathan'el realized that she had a plan for once they reached the palace.

"Thank you," he murmured.

For the first time since he'd known her, she smiled. It was a smile that gleamed with intelligence, wit, and courage.

"Come along, Princess!" Dikiner called over his shoulder.

Nurida turned away and hurried after Dikiner. As she did, Nathan'el realized he was short of breath. Must be the wind.

Or maybe it was fear. As Arashna grew closer, his stomach clenched, and he broke out into a sweat. He had no idea what he would do when he set paw in the imposing city. All he could do was hope Nurida's plan would work.

Arashna was alike to Dobar only in its coloring—black and silver. It had a rounded wall and rounded towers, and it soared higher than the mainland fortress. At the edge of the bridge was a flat platform of black rock; the closest word Nathan'el could ascribe to it was a patio, but it was part of no home. A pathway wound up to it from the north—no doubt where some creatures went at low tide to search for clams. He didn't know it, but this was the same pathway that Prince Johajar had been dragged up only hours before.

Less than twenty strides from the bridge was Arashna's gate. It was a pointed arch, trimmed in silver and polished obsidian. The gate itself was made of sturdy oak; it was closed now, and silver patterns played across it. At the very center, split between the two doors, was a gleaming crescent moon.

Nathan'el had never actually set paw here before, but he was fairly sure that the red banners hanging from the parapets were a new addition. Traditionally, the Wraith Mice had little to do with the color red because it was the color of an eclipse of the moon, an event that hid their beloved moon. So much did they love the moon that the last queen had given her only daughter a name that meant *moon*.

There was a series of shouted orders from the wall top, and the gate opened slowly. It opened wide enough only for one creature to squeeze through, and again Dikiner led the way without a word. Nurida took a deep breath and plunged after him. Nathan'el followed, praying fervent silent prayers.

The inside courtyard was nothing like he'd expected. It was awash with filthy rainwater mixed with old feathers, pieces of shredded canvas, and ash. The canvas, he saw, came from crude and ratty shelters set up along the wall. Beneath the shelters, creatures—mostly Wraith Mice, from what he could tell—labored at polishing or repairing weapons. They must have been lower-class Wraith Mice because their clothes were filthy and couldn't have been that warm.

The inside of Arashna was effectively a maze of buildings, spacious courtyards, and corridors. Dikiner hurried them to a walkway covered by a stone overhang; from there, he found an empty doorway into a building built right into the wall.

"His Majesty will be at the palace at this time of day, Princess," he said quietly. "It isn't much farther."

"Of course," Nurida murmured, showing neither displeasure nor approval.

The passageways inside Arashna were lit with oil lamps hanging from the ceiling that gave off no smoke. In fact, they exuded a smell that was almost pleasant, and Nathan'el figured either this was where the wealthiest Wraith Mice lived or this was the hall that the king most commonly used to travel from his throne room to the outside.

When he'd last been in Harboday, there had been rumors that Queen Demeda had died, but no announcement. Nathan'el didn't know the day she died with any certainty. He only knew that she was dead. The whole of Arashna, it seemed, had been made to know it, too, because when Dikiner opened a door, it led into a room that Nathan'el would not have expected to exist in Arashna under Queen Demeda's rule.

Demeda had many honorable qualities; one of them was thriftiness. This room displayed none of that. The candle holders were artfully designed of gold and stood on stands of teak wood. Lamps of silver and precious stones let off smoke accented with exotic herbal aromas. The floor was covered in rugs made of silk and trimmed with fish scales. They caught the light of the lamps and candles and sent patterns dancing off the walls.

Nathan'el was sure that each rug was worth more than he and his father together made in a year.

Demeda had never been ascetic, to be sure, but nor would she ever use gold and fish scales to adorn a waiting room. And that was all the room was—a waiting room.

"Wait here, if you please," Dikiner said brusquely, "while I speak to His Majesty."

Nurida nodded obligingly and sat down on a cushioned bench. Nathan'el remained standing. Dikiner spared a glance for him and then said to Nurida, "I'll come for you and your servant when His Majesty is ready to speak to you."

The princess nodded. "Please inform His Majesty that this is a matter of utmost urgency."

Dikiner nodded and then stalked out, closing the door behind him.

"He'll be setting spies after us in a minute," Nurida murmured. "Nathan'el—keep following my lead."

"I'm impressed," Nathan'el murmured. "You improvise very well."

Nurida gave him another smile. "I was raised like this. Don't say another word."

Nathan'el found himself short of breath again, and he admitted—he was afraid.

In less than five minutes, Dikiner returned for them. He held open the door and said, "Princess."

Nurida stood and slipped out the door, Nathan'el hard on her heels. She paused long enough for Dikiner to take the lead again; he then led them down the rest of the corridor to a door at the far end.

Nathan'el had been expecting a throne room; instead, it looked like more of a sitting room. There was an elevated dais, upon which were two functional chairs, and opposite them was a cushionless bench, flanked by two tables laden with food of one kind or another. Mostly light refreshments, Nathan'el figured.

Only one of the chairs on the dais was occupied, and Nathan'el didn't need to be told the name of the mouse sitting there.

He seemed to carry a cloud of superiority around him without needing any kingly trappings. His eyes were shrewd, and he was poised like a coiled spring, like any skilled swordsmouse. When Nurida stopped in front of the dais—Nathan'el had stayed back behind the bench—King Mokimshim tipped his head one way and observed, "Not the Miamuran princess I was expecting to see."

"Which is why I am here, Your Majesty," Nurida replied. With that, she dropped into a shallow but graceful curtsey.

Mokimshim watched her calculatingly. "Princess Nurida. Please sit."

Nurida took her seat on the bench, sitting perfectly upright. Nathan'el lowered his eyes, but not so much that he couldn't see the princess.

"I had heard, Princess," Mokimshim began, "that you were a singularly removed character. That your primary interests lay in scholarly pursuits. I must confess that you are one of the last creatures I expected my patrols to come across in the woods of Dobar."

"Desperate times often call for desperate measures," Nurida replied smoothly, but with an undercurrent of anxiety.

"I think even you, Princess, are aware that the situation between myself and your oldest brother is not cordial," Mokimshim said, a little sharply. "So I cannot understand why you should be anywhere near my kingdom."

Nurida made a delicate noise of scorn. "The situation between *my*self and my oldest brother is not cordial, either," she replied. "I am here for another sibling. A sister."

There was a pause before Mokimshim murmured, "Kiarna?"

Nurida shook her head. "No. I know her no better than Galledor. I meant the only sister younger than I. The only one who deigns to speak with me. Lochuran."

There was another puzzled silence; then Mokimshim said, "I don't understand."

Nurida sighed and rested her forehead in her paw. When she spoke, her words were directed at the floor.

"I'll be completely open with you, Your Majesty," she said, "since it seems to be my only option. Your Majesty was informed correctly about me—that my interests are largely confined to the realm of scholarly achievements. There is but one exception, and that is—" her voice caught—"my little sister."

She took a deep breath, as if steadying herself; then she continued, "Some weeks ago, she went missing. No one's found her. I was the first one into her chambers after she was declared missing. I found, in her dresser, the draft of a letter. It was addressed to you, Your Majesty."

"And what did the letter say?" Mokimshim asked warily.

Nurida shook her head miserably. "In truth, Your Majesty, I did not read it. I burned it. But I know Lochuran—so I know the letter would have gotten her into trouble with Galledor."

"And so you committed high treason against your brother to protect your sister?" Mokimshim demanded, sounding incredulous.

Nurida's shoulders steeled, and she straightened. "Forgive me, Your Majesty, but I do not believe you know what it is to be someone like me. Your family was small, and you were the eldest. I was the little one, the quiet one, the one unworthy of any interest except scorn. All my family never gave me any attention except to disdain me. All except Lochuran. She was the only bit of kindness in my life. I would commit *high treason* for her a thousand times!"

There was a ponderous silence. Then Mokimshim murmured, "But why are you here?"

"To reassure myself," Nurida replied bitterly. "If she were communicating with you, Your Majesty, I cannot help but think she might come here. Once I knew she was safe ..." Tears intruded on her words. "That is all I ask. I only ask to be reassured that my dearest sister is well."

Nathan'el found himself believing it. All of it. Then he reminded himself that she knew exactly what had become of Lochuran.

"I don't suppose it's occurred to you that, as you know of your sister's treachery, you may be quite dangerous to let go from here?" Mokimshim pointed out sharply.

Nurida laughed tiredly. "Your Majesty, the knowledge that my sister is alive and well is the greatest gift you could possibly give me. Show her to me, and let me see that she is content, and I will be in your debt. It will be no trouble to remain silent. I will say nothing."

Mokimshim was silent for a bit. Then he said, "Perhaps you would be willing to do more if your sister asked you."

Nurida laughed bitterly, but her laughter mixed with sobs. "Show me my sister. Let me speak to her. Then ask again."

There was a bit more silence. Then Mokimshim asked, "How long have you been in the wild?"

Nurida shrugged and gave no better response.

"Won't you be missed at Miamur by now?" Mokimshim asked in surprise.

Another bitter laugh. "I highly doubt it. Not with Lochuran gone."

More silence. Then—

"Your sister is not here," Mokimshim said quietly. "Not yet. But she should be here in two or three days."

Nurida closed her eyes in relief. "Thank the Bear King."

"If you are willing to wait for a few days, I will make sure you are comfortably lodged," Mokimshim finished. "You and your servant."

"I don't care about him," Nurida said dismissively. Then her head shot up. "Except for one thing. I have instructed him not to tell anyone that he is in my employ. Would you be so kind as to conceal my being here as well?"

Mokimshim must have nodded. "As you like, Princess. I will have your servant housed in the servant's quarters. You yourself shall be given fine quarters, and I will send someone for you the moment Lochuran arrives."

Nurida sagged with relief. "Thank you, Majesty."

"My servants will show you to your rooms," Mokimshim decided, "and serve you a hot meal. You look as though you could use it. My guards will escort your servant to the servants' halls."

34

IN THE DARK HALLS

The last time Nurida had stood in such a comfortable chamber, it had been her own back at Miamur. The rooms Mokimshim had lent her included a bedchamber, which was twice the size of her own, but then, here in Arashna, the bedchamber and sitting room were combined. The furniture was elegant: couches, chairs, bookshelves all in a semi-circle around the door, and two steps up was a four-poster bed, a wardrobe, and a basin and pitcher on a nightstand. Silver curtains hung from the bed's four posts, to keep away the nightly chill. On the same level as the bed was a door that led to a washroom and another one that led to a balcony overlooking the sea.

Nurida pulled aside one of the silver, silky bed hangings and looked at a bed covered in thick blue blankets and no doubt softened by a mattress filled with feather down. It was a pity she wouldn't be here long enough to enjoy it.

Some of Queen Karena's maidservants had hastily put a few fresh dresses in the wardrobe and plates of steaming food on the table. Nurida slipped into the washroom, shed her much-worn tunic, and allowed two of the female servants—Wraith Mice that didn't say a word as they attended the princess—to pour warm water over her and rinse away all the filth she'd accumulated in the woods. Then she pulled a dress of dark green and amber thread over her head.

Being clean again gave her new strength.

She sent away the serving maids, saying she'd ring the bell if she needed anything, and then sat down to devour her supper.

Being full again strengthened her, too.

Once she was finished with her meal, she stood up and slipped to the balcony.

By this point, the clouds had gathered, but instead of the silence of falling snow, there was the soft and soul-soaking sound of rain falling on the water to the north. It was still dry, for now, on Nurida's balcony, but the wind blew gently from the north, so it could be only a matter of time before the rain reached Arashna.

Not far north, the land rose up. It wasn't quite a cliff so much as a pair of very steep hills. They were heavily wooded, but in-between the trees, Nurida thought she saw lights that must have come from cottage windows. At the water's edge was a haphazard collection of wooden buildings, windows all ablaze with firelight. Jutting out from these buildings were long piers lined with ship. This, Nurida supposed, was Myanka.

Interesting, Nurida thought. Arashna might be on an island, but it could never be completely separated from the mainland.

The Miamuran princess stood at the balcony a while longer, inhaling the combined smells of salt and rain. Then she turned and went back inside.

Surely the patrol was back by now, she thought. It must have been hours. They had all heard her announce herself as a Miamuran princess. They would gossip—hopefully their gossip wouldn't reach the servants where Nathan'el was—but it would have to reach the pirates.

Particularly one that Nurida hoped would be helpful.

Nathan'el was shown to a long, low sleeping hall that, he was told, was almost directly three floors down from where "his lady" was lodged. He silently marveled at Nurida's cleverness. By requesting that she not be announced as a Miamuran princess, she had ensured that he could ask questions and no one would think twice that he had a Cliff Mouse accent.

Not bad, for a princess.

He knew what he had to do.

He didn't look at anyone in the hall. Slipping along the long row of double-layered beds, mumbling apologies to anyone he came close to, he made his way to the other end. Sure enough, there was a second door. He slipped through it and filtered back into the nearly silent halls of Arashna.

First, he had to get his sword back. His weapon had cost two seasons' of his savings—he had been forced to leave it with Dikiner, and it could be anywhere. No, first he had to find his mother. Maybe if he got out alive, Nurida could give him that reward she'd mentioned.

He was puzzling over his options when he rounded a corner and ran into someone.

"Watch where you're going, fool!" the mouse snapped.

Nathan'el recoiled. "Sorry," he mumbled.

But unlike the mice in the sleeping hall, the newcomer didn't dismiss him so easily. Nathan'el at first thought she was a Wraith Mouse, but she didn't have the characteristic white face, and her fur was brown instead of black.

"Where're you going?" she demanded. Her words carried a northern Cliff Mouse accent, similar to his own.

"Um—the prisons," he improvised. "I'm supposed to—well, actually I'm not sure what I'm supposed to do. Just go there and meet someone, I guess."

"You new?" the stranger asked, her voice annoyed but less furious.

"Just got here yesterday."

The Cliff Mouse made a disgusted noise and shook her head. "C'mon. I'll show you the way."

"Thank you—uh–"

"Never you mind," she said brusquely, turning away and striding into the dark corridors.

Nathan'el followed her, rejoicing. He'd have to find a way to get back to Nurida, of course, but he could deal with that later.

The pathway was winding and confusing—and completely unlit, to boot—but Nathan'el almost didn't care. Especially not when the guard stopped at an intersecting corridor.

"Go left," she said dispassionately. "It goes down some stairs. Prisons are at the far end."

"Thank you," Nathan'el replied.

"This is the only way down there, of course," the guard continued in the same bored voice. "At least, the only one that's supposed to be here. The cell on the farthest end has a crack in the upper left corner. It's wide enough for a creature to squeeze through—if you were brave enough to face the sea, anyway."

"Um …," Nathan'el replied carefully.

"You'll hear about it soon enough from the other servants," she rambled on. "So I'm not committing any crime by telling you."

"Oh."

"If I were you," she continued, still sounding bored, "I'd use that tonight. There are more dangerous things than the sea in this place."

Nathan'el frowned. "Um—I understand, but if I wanted to leave, what's to stop me from just using the bridge?"

The guard sighed and shook her head. "You *are* new. The simple fact is leaving Mokimshim's service is hard. He's got all kinds of creatures under his paw, one way or another. I can think of a lot of river otters that are about to discover that—once the prizes Mokimshim dangles in front of their noses no longer hold their sparkle, there'll be other things tying them to the king of Arashna. Eeriedens, too, and lots of pirates—they'll discover what Mokimshim's got up his sleeves. Coercion, I think it's called. The longer you stay, the harder it becomes to leave. You should go while you can still be free."

Nathan'el stared at her. *Never* had a Wraith Mouse monarch resorted to coercion to keep up his or her forces. River otters allied themselves to the monarchs out of good faith. Cliff Mice joined the armies in honest trust. *Coercion.*

"Besides," she continued, her eyes still dull, "Mokimshim is terrified that his sister is sending her spies into the castle."

Nathan'el felt cold all over. "Is that—is it true?"

The guard shrugged, a crafty gleam entering her eyes. "I have no idea, and I really don't care. But as long as Mokimshim thinks that, he pays the mercenaries a little extra. So I'm not going to *interfere* with any spies, if there are any. More's the pay for me."

She gave a shake of her head. "Anyway—I need sleep, and you need to meet whomever. Good luck to you."

"And you," Nathan'el called to her retreating back.

Nurida didn't have to wait long. She had barely returned to her seat from the balcony when there was a soft but insistent rap on her door.

"It's open," she called.

The creature who stepped in was undeniably a pirate. Nurida had never seen a pirate before, but the weather-beaten coat and the compass hanging on a strap around his waist were something of a giveaway.

He closed the door and swiftly crossed the room until he stood before the table. Nurida stood up as he approached but did not speak first.

"I heard," the ferret said in a level voice, "that a Miamuran princess wanted a word with Mokimshim."

Nurida tilted her head to one side. "You are Captain Eneng, I take it?"

The ferret blinked. Then he lowered his voice. "Kiarna's safe, then?"

Nurida nodded. "She is."

The pirate gave her a look that silently paid no compliments to her intelligence, but his only words were, "Then why in Cerecinthia are you here ... uh ..."

"Nurida," the princess supplied. "And I am here to repay a debt. I am here for the sake of Prince Johajar."

Eneng frowned at her. But instead of asking questions, he just said, "Start at the beginnin'. But make it fast."

Nurida quickly recounted her story—whom she had been looking for, how she wound up in Nathan'el's company, and how his quest to free her mother gave her an opening to help her friend. Eneng didn't interrupt even once; but clearly he had a good memory because everything that had confused her, he was able to clarify once she had finished speaking.

"Winterblade is my sister," he murmured. "She, Arasam, and I were sent to look fer Princess Zuryzel. We all knew her—but that don't matter now. What *does* matter, Nurida, is that you cannot be 'ere when yer sister is finally brought. I know the sailors who are escortin' her back, an' they love t' take their own sweet time." He let out a barking laugh. "Y're really bent on springin' Johajar?"

Nurida did not miss the fact that Princess Zuryzel was the only one to whom Eneng ascribed a title. Whether that was a sign of special respect or an attempt to hide any close familiarity, Nurida wasn't sure. She just answered, "You helped my sister. Can you not help me?"

Eneng laughed bitterly. "No. I can't."

Nurida felt as if she'd been doused in cold water. "Why not?"

Eneng sat on the chair, and the princess mirrored him by sinking onto the sofa. "Because, Nurida, yer sister knew the hallways of Arashna. If you were hopin' I could serve as a guide, an' show you t' where Johajar's bein' kept, I'm sorry t' say I can't."

Nurida's heart nearly stopped.

But the pirate was not finished.

"I *do*," he said quietly, "know someone who may. Someone who'll help. Possibly. But it won't be easy, an' I doubt it'll be free."

"I can get money," Nurida insisted.

Eneng sighed and nodded slowly. "Then get ready t' go—quiet-like. I'll be back in a few minutes. As fer yer friend—well, y'll have t' hammer that out later."

"Thank you," Nurida whispered gratefully.

Eneng sighed. "Don't thank me. Johajar's my friend, too, same as Kiarna. Any loved one o' Princess Zuryzel's is."

With that, he was gone.

Nurida found, among the dresses that Queen Karena had loaned her, something that must have been designed for exploring the beach and tide pools. She pulled that on and then strapped her knife around her waist. Then she found a hood—something dark that covered her shoulders and ears and tied in the front beneath her chin—and sat waiting for Eneng.

He was back quickly with another ferret, this one a female. She had stone-hard eyes as black as the walls around them, and Nurida found herself struggling not to flinch.

Eneng shut the door behind him and the other ferret. Then he turned to face the two waiting creatures and said, "Well—interductions. Snowhawk, meet Princess Nurida of Miamur. Nurida, meet Cap'n Snowhawk of the *Nygoan*."

Nurida nodded politely. "Captain."

Snowhawk's only response was to murmur, "Princess."

After a moment, she turned to Eneng. "Somethin' in mind, Eneng?"

The captain gestured at Nurida, and Snowhawk turned back to face her. Steeling her nerves, the princess replied calmly, "Prince Johajar is my friend. I found myself in a position to help him, and I intend to."

"Help 'im how?" Snowhawk inquired coolly.

Nurida smiled faintly. "Spring him."

"How?" Snowhawk repeated, her tone laden with disbelief rather than curiosity.

"He's already escaped once," Nurida replied, her confidence growing. "When I find him, he'll know more. I just have to find him, which is what I need your help with."

"If you're caught, y'll give me up sooner or later," Snowhawk observed coldly. "Then it's my *life*."

"I won't give you up," Nurida replied firmly. "They can't torture a princess."

Snowhawk snorted derisively. "They can't lay a *paw* on a princess. There're other ways o' torture."

Nurida called her bluff. "If you don't intend to help me, then why are you still here?"

Snowhawk didn't move a muscle in reply.

"Snowhawk," Eneng murmured, "what happened t' Winterblade an' me c'd just as easily 'appen t' you."

"Yes," Snowhawk agreed softly.

And then Nurida realized she was angry, not cautious. For some reason, she was furious with the King of Arashna. "You have no love for Mokimshim," she observed.

A dreadful sneer spread across Snowhawk's face; it was almost a snarl. "I 'ave no love for anyone who thinks I am his to do with whatever he *pleases*."

With that, the pirate turned to face her fellow captain. "You sh'd go, Eneng," she said, just as angry but now full of purpose. "Keep the attention o' Mokimshim's eyes 'n' ears."

Eneng nodded. "Bear King stay with y' both," he murmured. He still looked as if he thought Nurida insane, but as he left, the princess noticed that Snowhawk was wearing an anticipatory, mirthless smile.

"We should wait a few minutes," the pirate captain said. "Then any spies will be focused on Eneng. We c'n slip out."

Nurida nodded and sat down to wait. Snowhawk did the same.

"Tell me," the pirate murmured, "are you friend to Zuryzel?"

"I've never met her," Nurida replied quietly. "I know little of Mokimshim, but I do know that he sent some of his mercenaries to kill my sister. I cannot do anything *except* stand against him. Especially when someone's life may be at stake."

"I doubt Johajar's life is *at stake*," Snowhawk replied dryly. "Fer the time bein', anyway, the prince is too valuable t' throw away."

"How so?" Nurida asked.

Snowhawk laughed, and she actually sounded amused. "Ha— he's precious t' his sister. So long as Zuryzel knows Johajar is held captive, she'll prowl the line lookin' fer a way t' set him free. Aye, it's a sure thing she will. I know the princess well. Used t' be friends with her."

"Then why do you stay with her enemy?" Nurida murmured.

Snowhawk smirked. "I'm a mercenary. 'Tis my trade." With that, she gave a little toss of her shoulders. "C'mon. Now or never."

Nurida followed hard on her heels as the ferret cracked open the door and eased into the hallway.

Snowhawk *did* know the halls of Arashna. She knew where there were spies waiting behind the walls, where the night guards inspected on their rounds, and even where a few passages were concealed by clever stonework. There were no tapestries or statues in this palace, so compared to Miamur it seemed stark and barren, but here and there, fine silver designs were attached to the walls. One hallway gave Nurida the feeling of being in a silver forest.

The stairs were interesting, too. There were only four flights they had to descend, and they spiraled gradually to Nurida's left.

"Why do the stairs turn to the left?" she whispered to Snowhawk.

"So that a defender c'n rest 'is shield-paw on the wall an' swing with 'is sword-paw free, while an attacker finds 'is sword-paw against it," the pirate replied quietly. "Don't speak now."

At the fifth flight of stairs, Snowhawk stopped. She beckoned Nurida close and murmured in her ear, "At the end o' the stairs, go straight. Prisons are right there. I can't go with you—the prisoners'll blab that I was down there if they thought it'd help them any. But I'll wait 'ere fer twenty minutes. If Johajar's guarded, come back, an' I'll get y' out another way."

Nurida nodded. "Thank you."

Then she hurried down the dark stairs as quietly as she could.

When Nathan'el first slipped into the prisons, he was all but holding his breath. The prisons were a strange affair; the ceiling was low, but it was supported by massive columns at least as wide as Nathan'el was tall. It was around these columns that the prison cells were. There were some along the walls, too, but most of them were around the columns, which made something of a maze, the edges of which were impossible to see. It was pitch black beyond the first few columns. Nathan'el heard the echoing of three different sets of pawsteps—guards, no doubt.

The cell nearest him was empty; he crept up to it and crouched in its shadow. After a few minutes, the guard walked by. He was paying no attention and didn't notice when Nathan'el jumped up and smashed his paw into the guard's face. He fell without a sound, stunned.

And he was carrying a *sword.* Good.

Nathan'el took both the sword and a dagger from the guard without making any noise. Keeping the sword unsheathed, he sat down to wait for the other guards.

But before another came along, a paw wrapped around his mouth.

He jumped, startled, and started to swing his sword back; then a voice hissed in his ear, "Revenge is sweet."

Angrily, Nathan'el yanked Nurida's paw from his mouth. "What?"

"I wanted to make sure you didn't shout," Nurida replied dryly.

It was a moment before Nathan'el remembered that he had done the exact same thing to Nurida when he'd found her in the woods. He rolled his eyes in annoyance and then muttered, "One guard's down. Two more."

Nurida nodded in silent understanding. Then she backed away a little further and hid in the shadow.

The first guard—a Cliff Mouse—had been paying scant attention to his duties. The second and third didn't come near the entrance to the prisons, and so Nathan'el decided he had to go after them. He motioned Nurida to stay hidden and slipped into the shadows.

Were the prison brightly lit, it would have been straightforward enough, but the shadows made it seem endless and labyrinthine. Nathan'el stayed as close to the walls as he could, determined to be seen by neither the guards nor the prisoners.

Nurida stayed crouched in the shadows, heart pounding. All her confidence had evaporated, and all she could think was, *Bear King, I want out. I'm scared.*

Was this how Kiarna had felt on that night she had escaped from Arashna? How had she kept up her courage? And how had she gotten off the island, if the only way was across the bridge? What else had she said about what she found in Arashna?

And his brother, Johajar … No, do not ask me about Johajar.

Oh, so even Johajar had lied!

Nathan'el's luck didn't hold.

Of the two other guards, the first one he came across was an idiot. It took no skill for Nathan'el to wait for him between a pillar and the wall and smash the hilt of his scrounged sword against the Cliff Mouse's skull. But the next guard was a fox.

While he crouched in a corner between two empty cells, Nathan'el caught the sound of the fox's breathing and froze, meanwhile thinking, *He can smell me!*

The fox had stopped, possibly listening. Nathan'el didn't move, and after several tense minutes, the fox took a few steps forward. The movement allowed Nathan'el to pinpoint where he stood, and if the fox went just a little to his right, then maybe the Cliff Mouse could sneak up behind and knock him out.

Cautiously, Nathan'el felt the ground beside him and found a loose pebble; with a smooth underhand toss, he sent it crackling against the wall. But instead of following the pebble's sound, the fox whipped his head around and looked straight at Nathan'el.

Oh, no!

Before the fox could yell, Nathan'el launched himself forward, and there was a *clang!* as their swords met. Nathan'el tried to dart away and attack from another angle, but the fox attacked again too quickly. He swung at Nathan'el's head. Nathan'el ducked, but an instant later the air was knocked out of him as the fox side-kicked him in the stomach.

He fell against the damp stone and rolled backward, springing to his paws, but already the fox was upon him. Nathan'el barely managed to block the strike, but he found himself dodging a rapid succession of kicks and swipes.

It was just a matter of time.

And then a high-pitched but determined voice rang across the dungeon: "*Behind you!*"

It didn't matter what she said; the minute they heard Nurida, both fox and mouse looked in the direction of her voice. The fox hadn't raised the alarm because the intense speed of the fight required complete attention. Now the fox's attention was snatched by a new voice, one that he hadn't expected or sensed. Nathan'el realized what happened a moment before the fox did, and that moment was just enough for him to plunge his sword into the fox's heart.

There was no mercy in such a swift fight. Mercy required time.

Nathan'el pushed the fox's carcass off his sword and then started forward, only to angrily careen into Nurida. He grabbed her arm in a tight grip. "*Idiot!* He might have come for you!"

Nurida's green eyes were the only thing he could make out clearly in the dark, and they were round with fear. "I-I heard the fighting—did you kill him?"

Nathan'el pulled her away from the scene of the fight. "I had to. It's too dangerous in a fight to leave your opponent—"

"I know!" Nurida shakily interrupted him; she sounded sick. "Then—are you *sure* he's dead? He's not going to raise the alarm?"

Nathan'el stared at her a minute. Then he relaxed. "If he's not dead, he at least won't be able to move for a few hours. Maybe his friends will help him. We have our own friends to find—*stay with me!*"

Nurida's green eyes bobbed. She must have nodded.

Once they were no longer sticking to the shadows, they discovered there were plenty of places adequately lit by feeble white moonlight drifting in through a few windows high in the wall. Nathan'el expected the prisoners to have been woken up by the clanging of swords and the loud scuffles, but to his surprise, most of the ones they passed were on their sides, breathing deeply and apparently unconscious.

"Palace guards fight a lot," Nurida murmured. "I'd bet there's a scuffle here every night."

There were a few exceptions, though. In one cell they saw two Cliff Mice asleep and one river otter sitting bolt upright and staring with all her might at nothing at all. Nathan'el flinched when he first saw the otter's wide-open eyes, but then he realized that the otter didn't register him. She was also quite young.

"I think she's been there a long time," Nurida murmured. "Probably held so that her family would cooperate with Mokimshim."

Nathan'el wrenched his eyes away from the wretched creature.

It was three cells down from the otter that Nathan'el spotted a familiar mound of creamy brown fur.

Mother?

Forgetting all about Nurida, he rushed forward and fell to his knees beside the cell. It was her—it had to be. She was still wearing the deep crimson cloak Nathan'el and Fal'ne had given to her for her last birthday. It was ragged now, and the clasp tarnished and grimy, but Nathan'el recognized it. She was huddled up, shivering, and so woefully thin.

Cautiously, Nathan'el reached through the bars and touched her shoulder. At first she didn't stir, but when he gently prodded her, she jumped awake. Then she held perfectly still, not even breathing.

"Mother?" Nathan'el whispered quietly.

A shiver shot through her, but beyond that, she didn't move.

"*Mother?*" Nathan'el whispered, more urgently.

Ran'ta sat up slowly and turned to face him. And for a moment, Nathan'el was too relieved to do anything besides drink in the fact that his mother was alive.

It was Ran'ta who broke the silence—she stared at Nathan'el as if her life depended on it, and whispered, "How did you find me?"

"Long story," Nathan'el replied.

But those two bare words were enough to jolt him back to the gravity of their situation. "We have to get you out," he whispered urgently, and then realized he had no way to open the locked bars. "Do you know where the keys are?"

Before Ran'ta responded, there was a jangling behind Nathan'el, and he turned to see Nurida extending a ring of keys.

"The first guard had them," she explained, her voice still shaky. "That's why I came looking for you—I mean before you started fighting that fox."

Nathan'el smiled his thanks. Supposedly he was the one keeping her safe, but she'd rescued him twice now. Maybe *he* was in *her* debt, not the other way around.

But if that were the case, how would he ever replace his sword?

He fumbled with the keys for several minutes before finding one that opened his mother's cell. The door opened quietly enough—it must have been opened often—and his mother scrambled shakily to her paws and staggered out.

"What happens now?" she whispered.

Nathan'el was tempted to open all the prison cells, but there was no time, and besides, the prisoners might be punished if the cells were found open and the guards had been attacked. Regretfully, he locked the cell again and then turned to give Nurida the keys. "Now we just have to find your friend."

Nurida nodded with trembling confidence. She took the keys and said, "The key to Johajar's cell won't be on this ring. It'll be stored somewhere, probably in a casket near his cell."

With that, she turned and began searching for her friend in the shadows.

Nathan'el paused just long enough to glance back at the prison cells they'd left behind. He had no idea what crime these creatures were accused of, but he was willing to bet they were all like his mother—innocent. Anger burned in his heart, anger for those like his mother. He couldn't free them now.

But ... maybe ... one day.

35.

Forests of the Moon

Nurida wasn't sure if fear or excitement dominated her heart, but her veins thrilled with one or the other. She knew the basic layout of every royal prison and knew the high-security prisoners would be kept separate from the others. Probably in the darker areas, too.

She turned a corner around a pillar, and yelped.

"Nurida?" called Nathan'el's voice.

"I'm fine," Nurida called back. "Come look at this!"

She stood on the edge of a wide staircase, descending into darkness. From below, she heard a faint whispering that grew steadily louder and quieter, a sound unlike any she could place. On the wall to her right was a tiny set of locked doors about eye-level, almost the kind that belonged to cupboards.

Nurida was fumbling with the keys as Nathan'el and his mother caught up to her. Nathan'el's voice echoed unnervingly as he murmured, "Your friend's probably down there."

Nurida finally located a single silver key too small to go to a cell door. She inserted it into the locked cupboard and replied, "And I think his key's in here."

The tiny doors opened and revealed a thick steel key hanging by a leather strap around a peg driven into the wall. Nurida took it without missing a beat, inhaled nervously, and then started down the stairs.

She lost most of the light about five stairs down, and she rested her paw on the wall for guidance. Coming from behind her was Nathan'el's soothing voice murmuring encouragement as he tried to help his mother navigate the stairs. About seven stairs down, Nurida was swept by a powerful sensation of déjà-vu that she couldn't place. Thirteen stairs down, she remembered—this was just like that old dwelling in the wild where the stairs had led to the forge.

Fourteen stairs down, light reached her eyes again. But not firelight, like from the forge. No, this was cold blue light, barely bright enough to do more than tease the eyes.

The staircase only had twenty stairs. The room they led to was barely any bigger than the bedchamber Nurida had left. The ground was uneven and pools of water dotted the floor here and there. When Nurida's paw touched the last stair, the light was a little brighter. It was enough for her to see the outlines of three cage-like cells. There were no elegant pillars down here—just very typical crevices with bars across the door.

In the far one, a familiar Wraith Mouse sat back against the far wall, looking almost relaxed. Certainly he looked indifferent to the fact that he was imprisoned. Nurida's fear melted away when she saw him and she ran forward, splashing through two puddles as she did.

"Johajar!" she gasped.

The Wraith Mouse prince had not been asleep. He jumped when he heard her voice, and when he saw her he crawled forward and grasped the bars of his prison.

"*Nurida!* Princess, *what are you doing here?*"

She stopped just shy of his prison, taken aback by his stern voice. "Long story short, I found myself in Arashna anyway."

"And you decided you should come for me?" Johajar spluttered. "I told you to be careful!"

Nurida angrily held up the key she'd taken from the cupboard. "I have the key. Do you want me to use it or not?"

Johajar nodded quickly. "Yes—yes, sorry."

Nurida's paws shook as she inserted the key, and she twisted it as hard as she could. The lock creaked, and when it clicked, Nurida pulled back on the door with all her might. It barely budged.

Johajar shoved against it with his shoulder. It inched open a little more, just enough for him to slip out.

No sooner had he gotten out than Nathan'el and his mother reached the floor. Johajar cast them a confused look, but instead of asking questions, he said, "We need to get out quickly."

Nathan'el began, "A guard told me something about a crack—"

"It's this way," Johajar interrupted. He hurried over to the cell on the farthest end and wrenched open the unlocked door.

"Wait!" Nathan'el called. "It was high tide when we crossed the bridge, and that can't have been three hours ago!"

Nurida stared at him in confusion. "What does that mean?"

"It means your paws will be getting wet, Princess," Johajar called back. "We can't wait for low tide. Hurry!"

"Where are we hurrying to, exactly?" Nurida asked as she followed Johajar into the last cell, Nathan'el and his mother right behind her.

"Arashna wasn't built just on the island," Johajar explained, his voice very focused. "Some parts were built *into* the island. Sometimes it's hard to tell where the island ends and the castle begins. The room we're in right now is a cave, and caves are always changing. At some point, the rock up above wore away and left a hole that opens near the tidal flats."

"*Up above?*" Nathan'el echoed.

Nurida glanced over her shoulder and saw his mother's thin form. She must have been in that prison for months—could she make the climb?

"Not *very* high," Johajar replied. He was examining the rock, even though it was too dark for Nurida to make out any details. "Where is …"

Nurida looked up at the ceiling above her; then she stretched up. She couldn't *quite* touch the ceiling, but she was sure Johajar and Nathan'el could. "Um … are you sure this is the right cell?"

Johajar must have seen her measuring the ceiling, because he said, "Come over here, Nurida."

She crossed the cell to stand in front of him.

"Stand here," he said, repositioning her. "With your shoulder against the wall. Now look up."

Nurida craned her neck looking up; a moment later, a drop of stinging water landed in her eye. "Ow!" she cried out in surprise.

"Saltwater," Johajar explained. "Better get used to it."

Nurida forcefully reopened her eyes, embarrassed by how much she had just sounded like a primrose. Holding one paw slightly above her eyes, she looked back up and saw a narrow fissure between the ceiling and the wall. The top was lost in darkness, but the odd rushing sound she'd heard earlier was distinct from here.

"We just have to find the right pawhold," Johajar explained, gently nudging her away from the wall. "And then straight up from there. It isn't far."

Nurida glanced back at Nathan'el. He was supporting his mother, still looking anxious. They were paying no heed to her and Johajar.

The princess murmured very quietly, "It wasn't Karena who released you. Was it?"

Johajar's searching grew still.

"*That's* why Kiarna was pursued," Nurida added. "The timing's exactly right. She mentioned something about unused passages, but those would be useless if the only way out of Arashna is to cross that bridge. Kiarna must have come down here to get out."

It was hard to tell, but it looked as if Johajar nodded.

"What happened?" Nurida asked, still keeping her voice low.

Johajar returned to searching the wall, anger and pain evident in every gesture. "River otters—Doomspear, I think. They attacked only a week into the wild. It was night, and somehow, I got separated."

"That's why you were still in the wild," Nurida realized. "Listening for Kiarna."

But the Wraith Mouse prince wasn't listening to her anymore. "Found it!" he exclaimed triumphantly. "Right here! I'll go up first—follow me closely!"

He rested his paw on a piece of rock and then hoisted himself up, disappearing from their view in seconds.

Nurida looked to Nathan'el and his mother. The Cliff Mouse nodded at the wall. "Nurida—you go next."

Swallowing, the Miamuran princess stepped carefully onto the rock protrusion and began to climb.

Nathan'el was profoundly grateful that the princess he'd come across was so quick-thinking, even under duress. He'd never have gotten his mother away alive without her. Several times, Nurida paused in her climbing to give Ran'ta a helping paw. The crack they climbed through was barely wide enough to fit a mouse's frame.

It wasn't far to the hole Johajar spoke of. When first Nurida and then Ran'ta disappeared—presumably through the crack—Nathan'el still hadn't cleared the cell. The space between the ceiling and the hole was less than his height.

When he reached the rock that Nurida and Ran'ta had disappeared behind, the first thing he noticed was an immediate rush of fresh sea wind. He looked to his right and saw a faint outline of sky and night sea.

This was the hole? It was barely big enough for a mouse!

Nurida's face appeared in the hole, outlined by stars and sea, and she wordlessly extended her paw. Nathan'el managed to grasp it and, without getting stuck, struggle through the opening.

He found himself on the rocky island shore, staring straight south. Ran'ta had wrapped her paws around herself and was shivering violently between two tall, nearly black rocks. Johajar was scrambling carefully down the rocks, calling over his shoulder, "This is the easiest way down."

Ran'ta held out her paw to Nathan'el. "Son—go on without me. I can't—I can't stand against the sea."

Before Nathan'el could retort that he wasn't leaving her *anywhere,* Nurida laid her paw on Ran'ta's shoulder. "Begging your pardon, ma'am, but an armed patrol and two fortresses full of guards weren't enough to keep your son from getting you out. I don't think you could change his mind right now."

Burning heat seared up Nathan'el's face, and he ducked his head, embarrassed. But Nurida didn't wait for a response from Ran'ta before hopping down to a lower rock and extending her paws to the older mouse.

"This is an easy step," she said encouragingly.

Nathan'el watched in amazement as Nurida guided his mother down to the tidal flats, expertly finding the easiest changes and kicking loose stones out of the way. The Cliff Mouse was close behind, ready to grab his mother if she should fall, but Nurida took such good care of Ran'ta that he needn't have worried. When all four of them had made it to the tidal flats, pressed against the rocks of the island to keep from being seen by sentries, Nathan'el murmured to the princess, "I didn't know princesses were also guides."

Nurida shrugged. "I've been guiding my blind older sister around since I could walk."

"Wouldn't servants do that?" Nathan'el asked, puzzled.

Nurida gave him a thoroughly offended look. "Why would I let servants do that? She's my sister!"

"So was Lochuran."

"That's different," she said acidly.

"We have to get back to the shore and go straight south," Johajar said quietly. "If we stay in the waves, there's a chance we won't be seen." He pointed south. "Do you see that outcrop of rock?"

He pointed to a place where the trees came almost completely to the water and only a thin band of large rocks separated them from the waves. "Once we get there," he murmured, "we should be safe." He turned away, but Nathan'el still distinctly heard him mutter, "I hope."

"What's beyond that?" Nurida asked nervously.

"Woods," Johajar replied. "Patrols. Most likely some sentries in the trees. But it's out of sight of—"

"What about a river otter tribe?" Nathan'el burst out.

Johajar shifted uncomfortably. "There is a tribe a little south of here that's ruled by an otter called Shinar, but they were in service to my father. I have no idea whose side she's on now, my brother's or my sister's."

"I recognize the name Shinar," Nurida murmured softly. "Kiarna mentioned her. As a friend."

Johajar glanced back at the princess; his eyes had flickered at the mention of her older sister. "In that case," he murmured, "we'll go south until we find her caves."

Gripping the rocks, he began wading out into the waves.

Nurida glanced back at Nathan'el once, green eyes calm, and then followed Johajar. A minute later, a wave crashed into her and nearly knocked her off her paws.

"I'm all right!" she gasped, floundering.

"You'll get used to it," Johajar offered.

The Wraith Mouse must have had a great deal of character. It was the dead of night; he could just turn invisible and melt into the trees. Instead, he was staying behind to help the others.

Nathan'el gripped his mother's paw as they both stepped carefully into the waves. The familiar tug and pull of the water sent his heart to thrumming. There was a sense of freedom in their power, but also a frenzied fear. The fact that it was barely above freezing didn't help.

Nurida and Johajar had begun struggling further inshore, pressing tight against the bridge. Soon the rocks beneath their paws turned to sand, which made it nearly impossible to get a firm purchase against the buffeting of the waves. Johajar glanced over his shoulder frequently, watching Nurida, but when he saw Ran'ta stumble and sink beneath the waves, he started back toward them.

Nathan'el quickly pulled his mother back above the water, and she emerged gasping. Johajar grasped her other paw and urged, "Nurida, go on carefully!"

Nurida obeyed him without question, forging onward bravely. The others followed her, some distance behind.

The clouds parted, and the full moon shone in the sky. In its light, the bridge threw a shadow over them. Not long after, Nathan'el noticed the water came up only to Nurida's waist instead of her shoulders.

"Almost there," he murmured encouragingly to his mother.

Nurida was still quite a ways ahead of them, but by now, she had stopped to wait for them. Nathan'el could actually see her shiver in the cold night air as they drew closer.

"Why did you stop?" Johajar whispered.

For answer, Nurida pointed upward.

They were less than a hundred steps from Dobar by now, and there was a sentry standing on the platform overlooking the bridge. Johajar murmured quietly, "Good eyes. This is where things get interesting."

Nurida winced.

Johajar pointed south and east; Nathan'el saw the path he and Nurida had followed earlier. Just south of that, the trees came all the way to the water. "Go for those trees," Johajar whispered. "Stay *low*. The way the waves are playing with the moonlight, the best chance is to be lost amid all the light tricks. Go on—I'll be right behind."

"What are you doing?" Nurida whispered.

Johajar smiled faintly. "Causing a distraction. When you hear the yelling, start for the trees."

With that, the air around him turned frigid, and he completely vanished.

"I've never seen *that* before," Nurida murmured.

Ran'ta glanced curiously at her. "While we're waiting—I don't believe I caught your name."

The princess smiled. "Nurida, ma'am. Your son saved my life when I was lost out in the woods."

"And she saved mine when we were almost caught by some patrols," Nathan'el added.

Ran'ta smiled joyfully at her son and then addressed the princess again. "And how did you ... wind up in the woods?"

Nurida shrugged. "Truthfully, I'm not really sure." Her green eyes danced like the moonlight on the waves.

A moment later, there was a startled shout, and the moonlight was interrupted by a burst of orange glow. Nathan'el looked over at Dobar and saw, to his alarm, that massive tongues of flame curled out of the door leading onto the bridge.

Nurida saw them, too; a moment later, the sentry abandoned his post and hurried to help with the flames.

"That's our cue," Nathan'el whispered.

Nurida promptly took Ran'ta's other paw, and bending at their knees, they crept through the water for the trees, the blaze of orange flames and shouts from the fortress echoing behind them.

Away from the bridge, the waves were smaller, but the undertow pull was far stronger. One particularly strong tug dragged Nurida under, but she emerged in the next second, shaking water off her face. "I could get used to this!" she declared bravely.

The ground beneath their paws turned from sandy to pebbly before they reached the trees. The water didn't get any shallower by the time branches were tickling their heads. The first tree they found was a stately cedar with branches spreading over the waves. Nurida ducked under the boughs and then called out to the other two, "Come here!"

Nathan'el pushed the draping boughs aside and saw Nurida perched on a fallen log that had gotten tangled up in branches and ivy vines. Ran'ta struggled up onto the log, assisted by both younger mice, and Nathan'el promptly followed her.

Beneath the curtains of cedar, Nathan'el felt oddly safe. He looked to the two female mice, shivering from a combination of chilly saltwater drying in their fur and a brisk sea breeze dancing between the trees. "You two all right?"

"Sh-sh-should we w-w-wait for Joh-ha-hajar?" Nurida shivered.

She reminded Nathan'el of Mar'e when she stammered, but the glimmering determination in Nurida's eyes was very different. "For as long as we can," he replied firmly. "He said he'd join us."

Nathan'el peeked through the branches back at Dobar; the orange glow had faded. "I think the fire's gone out."

"He must have knocked a phosphorescent lamp into some oil," Ran'ta murmured. "That would make giant flames, but they don't spread much. Not as long as the oil's in one place. That happened at Harboday once—do you remember, Nathan'el? When you were very little?"

Nathan'el smiled at his mother. "I remember Fal'ne pointing at it."

There was a sudden rattling sound through the trees, and all three of them grew sharply silent, listening. There came a rasping sound of metal on metal, like a sword being drawn, and then the woods grew quiet.

Nathan'el was scared again. He clutched the sword he'd taken from the guard, wary of making any noise. But he forced himself to appear relaxed. If he looked scared, Nurida would be even more frightened.

Suddenly the air grew colder; the cedar branches rustled, and Johajar became visible, still standing in the water, eyes alert. He tapped his ear, looking inquisitively at Nurida, who wordlessly pointed in the direction of the metallic rasping. She then made the gesture of drawing a sword.

Johajar seemed to understand. He pointed along the log they were crouched on, and Nurida stood and began tippawing along it. The cedar branches shook a disturbing amount as she slid between them, making Nathan'el cringe. He rose to his paws and slipped between the branches after her in one fluid motion. If there was something on the other side of those branches, she wouldn't be the first to confront it.

To his surprise, the fallen log they'd been sitting on was an entire tree, and it was only one of many beyond the cedar branches. It seemed as though the waves washed all floating debris against the coast where they caught on the rocks because they were looking at a cluster of driftwood, with patches of dark water showing between the logs.

Nathan'el put a paw on Nurida's shoulder. She stopped and looked back at him. He jumped nimbly onto an adjacent log, feeling it sway, and then back onto the log in front of her. He then began edging forward, beckoning for her to follow. Overhanging trees screened them from Dobar's sight, and not far in front was the jutting cliff Johajar had pointed out when they were still on Arashna.

The Cliff Mouse stepped carefully from log to log, keeping as near to the trees as he could. He heard Nurida close behind him; she gasped quietly every time she stepped onto a different piece of driftwood. When Nathan'el glanced over his shoulder, he saw her balancing precariously on the same log he'd just vacated and his mother and Johajar following them with practiced ease. Everyone who grew up on the coast spent days climbing all over driftwood as a game.

Nathan'el ducked under the branches of a Douglas fir onto one large gray rock that jutted up past the water. A moment later, he heard a loud shaking and a startled shout. He turned quickly and saw Nurida lose her balance on the log and fall into the water with a *splash!*

Nathan'el dropped quickly to his knees, praying no one had heard that, praying she hadn't hit her head. The second prayer was answered quickly, as her head poked above the water, eyes wide with horror. A moment later, they heard a clear ringing of steel on steel, and Nathan'el's heart plummeted.

He gripped his sword, ready to fight, and stared hard at the trees. Nurida's knife was in her paw, shaking violently.

"Who's there?" called a menacing voice from the trees.

And then, Johajar cried in a burst of relief, "Shinar, it's *me!* Johajar!"

Nurida sagged with relief, dropping her knife onto the wood in front of her. A moment later, the air turned frigid again and another Wraith Mouse appeared, sword still drawn, leaping lightly onto the wood and throwing her paws around the Wraith Mouse prince.

EPILOGUE

Zuryzel did not at all envy Princess Nurida.

They were sitting in what Shinar fondly called the Domain, a network of caves and tunnels in the cliffs south of Dobar. Two cliffs met together, forming a deep *V*-shape, and in the point of the *V* was a series of rapids spilling and splashing into the ocean. Between the two cliffs was an area of relatively calm water at high tide and a sandy open space at low tide. In the cliffs themselves, hidden by towering trees and the rapids, were the entrances to the caves. Shinar's tribe inhabited these caves, which looked nothing like caves on the inside.

Nurida, Johajar, and the Cliff Mouse Nathan'el had been brought to one of the armories, while Ran'ta was given to the charge of Shinar's healers. In the armory, Nurida did most of the talking—to her oldest sister, who was, to say the least, furious.

"What was I supposed to do?" Nurida exclaimed after recounting her tale for the third time.

Zuryzel had drawn Johajar off to one side to listen, and both of them were trying not to laugh at Nurida's indignation. When Zuryzel had met Kiarna in Lunep and when Shinar had announced that she had to return to her tribe, Kiarna had politely but firmly requested to go with her. "I want to confront Doomspear," she'd said, a steely glint in her blue eyes. Kiarna was no warrior princess, but she was also not one to be taken lightly. So Zuryzel had gone as well to keep an eye on her oldest friend.

Of course, Kiarna hadn't at *all* expected to find her second-youngest sister near Dobar and Arashna.

"You should have gone back east instead of going—what was it? Northwest?" Kiarna retorted angrily.

"But I hadn't found Ressora," Nurida protested.

"You might have been *killed!*" Kiarna exclaimed.

"So might you have been," Nurida replied quietly.

Johajar spoke up calmly. "She's right, Kiarna," he pointed out. "It's no different from what you did."

Kiarna's blue eyes flickered to Johajar, and they were troubled. When she'd heard Mokimshim had imprisoned Johajar for a slip of the tongue, Kiarna did exactly what she believed to be right. She'd clung to the chance that Mokimshim had only acted in haste, in anger, and she'd gone back to Arashna to try to reconcile them. Just like she had reconciled their quarrels when they were younger and Kiarna lived with them and Zuryzel in Arashna.

But those days were gone. Zuryzel realized she was playing with her necklace again and dropped her paw. She really had to quit doing that.

Kiarna finally shook her head and embraced her little sister. In spite of Kiarna's anger, which was still clearly evident on her face, Nurida burrowed into her sister's embrace like a little child.

"They're so *much* alike, aren't they?" Johajar murmured in Zuryzel's ear.

She nodded, having noticed that, too. "And lucky for you they are," she teased her twin.

Kiarna finally turned her attention to Nathan'el without taking her paw from Nurida's shoulder. "Thank you," she said, "for protecting my sister."

Nathan'el ducked his head, clearly embarrassed. "I only did what I thought was right," he mumbled.

Nurida chuckled, and Zuryzel suddenly thought she *looked* like Kiarna, too, not just acted like her. They had a very similar smile.

"Thank you, nonetheless," Kiarna answered. She looked to Shinar, who had been silent throughout the interview, lounging against a row of spears. "Could your healers perhaps ascertain my sister is unhurt as well?"

"Naturally," Shinar replied calmly. "And I imagine Nathan'el will want to see his mother. Follow me, I'll show you both the way."

Kiarna let Nurida go with some reluctance, it seemed.

Outside in the passageway, Nurida was still chuckling at Nathan'el. He gave her a slightly offended look and asked, "What?"

"I could almost hear you thinking *this is ridiculous,*" Nurida smirked.

Nathan'el shrugged but offered no reply. They didn't speak another word until they reached the infirmary, a white-washed cavern lit with a combination of bright candles and polished mirrors. Ran'ta had fallen asleep on the low mattress she'd been taken to, and Nathan'el immediately sat down beside her.

After the healers finished inspecting Nurida, she joined him by his mother's bedside. He was somewhat surprised by this and gave her a quizzical look. She cast around for words for a while, and then asked, "Were you thinking about those creatures in the prisons?"

Nathan'el nodded. "It would have been impossible to get them all out."

"But you're thinking you want to try," Nurida murmured.

Nathan'el nodded again. "Yes. One of the soldiers I saw in the castle—I think she knew I wasn't who I said I was, but she let me go anyway. I think … maybe …"

"Maybe some of the guards would help?" Nurida finished.

Nathan'el nodded.

"It's a possibility," Nurida agreed. "So—where do we start?"

Nathan'el smiled at the princess. "Before I do anything else, I'm going to take my mother home and make sure my sister is really safe."

When Johajar was consigned to the healers as well, Zuryzel slipped outside. She knew she was safe; Mokimshim's patrols never came this close to Shinar's caves. The rain clouds had rolled south, and now rain fell lightly on the sea around Zuryzel.

She could still see Arashna—even in the dead of night, even in the rain. Her *home*. So close, but impossibly far away.

Mokimshim had ordered her taken prisoner because he believed she threatened his reign. Zuryzel was at first convinced that, if she just showed her brother that she meant to support him, not undermine him, everything would be smoothed over. But when the first reports of what was happening in Arashna reached her ears, Zuryzel realized Mokimshim had been right. She *was* a threat to his rule because he had no intention of ruling according to the laws of the Wraith Mice. Even the king was bound by those laws.

Mokimshim had broken them unforgivably, and Zuryzel meant to hold her older brother accountable. Nothing—*nothing*—would stop her.

She pawed her sword hilt coldly, staring at Arashna, her heart blazing with the determination to face her brother and take the crown that had become hers.

Also by Marta Stahlfeld

Darkwoods
Book 1
A Fight for Freedom that Draws All Warriors!

The death of the foxes' ruling oracle, Scythe, bodes ill for the Wraith Mice around Darkwoods and their allies near and far. With the change in leadership, all sides know their uncertain relationship with the foxes will, too soon, erupt into a vicious war. Possessing the ability to melt into the darkness and renowned in warfare, the Wraith Mice rally the squirrel tribes, Ranger Mice, and others to defend their territory—and their very lives.

A young one among them, Princess Zuryzel understands the gravity of the situation and rises fearlessly to the challenges of the ruthless invaders. Possessing the traits of a natural leader and wise beyond her years, Zuryzel knows she must follow the difficult path before her. But can she overcome the challenges in time to defeat the hated foxes?

Stahlfeld skillfully weaves romance, intrigue, and intense action into this epic tale of the creatures of Darkwoods and beyond. With a nod to life as it truly is, Stahlfeld presents characters of complexity—each with weaknesses as well as strengths—and a story of constantly shifting "certainties." More than a battle of good against evil, *Darkwoods* challenges the reader to discover the truth. Who can be trusted? Are all foxes, indeed, dastardly creatures? Who is the spy within the Wraith Mice's midst? And, ultimately, can good ever win?

Available on Amazon.com in hardcopy or Kindle
Or get your signed copy directly from Marta at
www.DarkwoodsBooks.com

Darkwoods Reviews

"*Darkwoods* was an interesting, fun read in the tradition of J.R.R. Tolkien's *Lord of the Rings* Trilogy and the *Chronicles of Narnia* series by C.S. Lewis. Within reading the first chapter, you will realize that the author has a creative and unique imagination. I was hooked into the book . . . I recommend the book to everyone."
Billy Burgess, *Jacketflap* (2011)

Darkwoods "is a book unlike anything else I have ever read, and I have read a lot of books....I became fascinated by the entire world that Marta Stahlfeld has created.... Everything is so thought out, the personalities and traits of all the creatures, the names of the places, everything. I became so wrapped up in the world that that fact that the characters were all animals slipped to the back of my mind... This world is truly magical and I love becoming immersed in the fantasy of it all."
Joni Thomas, Lost in YA Wonderland (2012)

[*Darkwoods*] "is impressive because it's very elaborate and well written.... As an author, [Stahlfeld] has a great passion for her work and can keep her audience captivated by imagination without having to rely on shock value, sex or violence."
Allison Lee-Moore, owner of Burien Books (Highline Times 8/24/2011)

What Readers Are Saying about *Darkwoods*

Darkwoods is an action filled adventure. It really pulled me in when reading it and I didn't want to put it down. It was so exciting! All the different characters and their abilities, the plot, everything was amazing! This is a great book for teenagers. I can't wait till the next book comes out!
Emily, age 15

"Awesome book! This is THE best book ever! Feldspar is my favorite character. Best. Book. Ever."
Jake age 12

"*Darkwoods* is an amazing book for people of all ages and keeps readers on the edge of their seats. The book tells the stories of many different characters and how their lives clash when the foxes declare war on the mice. The story starts out with all characters being either good or bad but as the story progresses the characters become more defined and they aren't always so black and white. This is an amazing book and it was written by an amazing person. I love this book and you will to!
Courtnee age 13

Your books are so good! I can picture every event that is going on! And I love how you show everybody's different sides of the war and not just one person's side. My favorite foxes are Fawn and Poison.
Erin, age 9

Pasadagavra
Book 2
A Fight to Defeat Evil Continues!

Leaving behind a desperate war, Princess Zuryzel races to the coast, intent on bringing aid to her struggling army. On her journey to the sea and to adulthood, she will encounter friendship, betrayal, pain, and a secret she would much rather stay hidden. Through it all, Zuryzel knows that at the end of her journey she must face and destroy the might of Darkwoods that has laid siege to the great Stone Tribe city of Pasadagavra.

A myriad of questions await the Wraith Mouse along her quest. She soon learns that someone is pulling strings behind the war, and no longer are things as simple as they seem. One who knows the identity of the mysterious puppet master is a self-deprecating pirate captain with uncanny sword skills and a mind too shrewd to be trusted. Zuryzel is determined to figure out the bewildering puzzle--but finding the answer may cost her someone she holds very dear.

As Zuryzel feverishly works to bring them support, the squirrels and mice defending Pasadagavra fear they cannot hold out against the onslaught of the Darkwoods Foxes. But as the battles rage, they learn the depths of their own strength and bravery. The struggle to defeat the loathsome and greedy evil that has crept across the world may cost their very lives, but they are determined to prevail.

In this exciting second installment of the Darkwoods series, Stahlfeld combines wild action and fierce loyalty in an epic tale of a fight to preserve everything precious in the world. The intense story of good versus evil presents characters of honor and of depravity, all caught up in a vicious struggle. At the center is a princess learning to be a queen.

Available on Amazon.com in hardcopy or Kindle
Or get your signed copy directly from Marta at
www.DarkwoodsBooks.com

Pasadagavra Reviews

"*Pasadagavra* is the second book in the *Darkwoods* series by teenage writer Marta Stahlfeld as she presents a fantasy very much geared towards her age group as Zuryzel comes of age and finds the weight of the world thrust upon her to bring the support needed to save the Stone Tribe City. Pasadagavra is a read well worth considering for young adult fantasy and fiction collections, recommended.
Free Library The Fantasy/SciFi Shelf (2012)

"What a wonderfully vivid world created by author Marta Stahlfeld. . . . This is a great series for middle grade age kids especially or even for those of us that enjoyed *Narnia*. With promises at the end that there is more to continue, I look forward to continuing this series."
Flora Bateman, From the Bootheel Cotton Patch (2012)

"There is a very detailed mythology of the Darkwoods which gives depth to the plot and characters. The Princess Zuryzel is a strong willed character that female readers will enjoy reading about, whereas male readers will enjoy the war scenes. Adults will like the imaginative narration from the eighteen-year-old author and the fantasy aspects of the story. *Pasadagavra* is a fast-paced sequel that is just as good as the first book, *Darkwoods*. I recommend all readers to give the series a try.
Billy Burgess, Goodreads (2012).

What Readers Are Saying about *Pasadagavra*

I just loved *Pasadagavra*! *Darkwoods* was exciting, and *Pasadagavra* continues the story with lots of action and adventure. It has a great story with lots of real-life hard choices which the characters have to make - something teenagers understand. Way to go Ms. Stahlfeld! Keep it up. I can hardly wait for book three!
Jennifer, age 14

Pasadagavra is a fantastic read! The characters have individual personalities that strengthen the story and keep the exciting plot intact from *Darkwoods*. *Pasadagavra* was a fun read and went by too fast! I could hardly put the book down!
Andrew, age 13

Even if you haven't read *Darkwoods*, you will enjoy *Pasadagavra*. It is a great story for the family and animal lovers! The characters seem to come alive and jump right off the page. Don't miss this read!
Sydney, age 15

Pasadagavra is a great sequel to *Darkwoods*! The story continued with the same fabulous characters and more exciting action. Pasadagavra was a fun read and went by too fast!
Drew, age 14

About the Author

Twenty-year-old Marta Stahlfeld is a voracious reader, enjoying epic fantasy and historical novels, as well as books on history. The Seattle native has a particular interest in World War II, devouring both books and movies regarding that era. In fact, her Darkwoods' Ranger Mice characters were inspired by the U.S. Army Rangers who scaled Pointe du Hoc on D-Day.

Marta began writing Darkwoods at age twelve, rewrote it numerous times, and through it all has known that her future lies in a career in writing. *Darkwoods,* published in 2011, is the first in the new series by the same name for middle-grade and young adult readers. In 2012, Marta published the second book in the series, *Pasadagavra,* and Book 3, *Graystone,* was published in 2014.

Marta is a student at Wisconsin Lutheran College in Wauwatosa, Wisconsin. In addition to continuing with her writing, Marta is majoring in English Literature with the goal of becoming a teacher as well as a novelist. Whether through her writing or as a teacher, Marta encourages all kids and teens to read!

Email Marta at DarkwoodsBooks@aol.com
—she loves to hear from readers!
Follow Marta at any of the following:
Marta's Blog: http://martastahlfeld.blogspot.com/
Darkwoods on Facebook: https://www.facebook.com/DarkwoodsBooks
Darkwoods on Twitter: https://twitter.com/DarkwoodsBooks